TIME KINGS OF LAS VEGAS

By Drew Karpyshyn

A Minor Malevolent Spirit and Other Tales

The Chaos Born Trilogy
Children of Fire
The Scorched Earth
Chaos Unleashed

Star Wars: Annihilation

Star Wars: Revan

The Mass Effect Trilogy
Revelation
Ascension
Retribution

The Darth Bane Trilogy
Star Wars: Path of Destruction
Star Wars: Rule of Two
Star Wars: Dynasty of Evil

Baldur's Gate II: Throne of Bhaal

Temple Hill

TIME KINGS OF LAS VEGAS

DREW KARPYSHYN

Drew Karpyshyn Creating Writing LLC

Published in the US by Drew Karpyshyn
www.drewkarpyshyn.com

ISBN 979-8-9865396-0-7
ebook ISBN 979-8-9865396-1-4

Cover Design by Lieu Pham
www.covertopia.com

Printed in the United States through Ingram Spark

ACKNOWLEDEGMENTS

This book would not have been possible without the amazing support and contributions of all the fans who supported my Kickstarter project to create this novel.

To each and every one of you, I want to say, "Thank you for taking a gamble on Time Kings of Las Vegas."

Prologue

January 30, 1994 – Buffalo, NY

"Goddammit! It's like we're fuckin' cursed."

Super Bowl XXVIII had ended almost two hours ago, in an all too familiar fashion: with Buffalo losing to the Dallas Cowboys 30-13. Most of the customers who'd gathered in Shorty's Bar and Grill to cheer on their hometown Bills had left long ago, despondent and defeated. Only a dozen diehards remained, drinking away their sorrows in clusters of twos and threes scattered about the room.

William was sitting on a stool up at the bar, nursing a beer while his friend Mike ranted about the loss.

"Un-fucking-believable!" Mike spat, pounding his mug on the bar top hard enough to send beer sloshing over the side. "Four Super Bowl losses in a row? Four? Bullshit, man. Total bullshit!"

Mike had claimed his seat at the bar an hour before kickoff, right in front of the 40-inch Sony Trinitron mounted on the wall above the shelves of booze. In the seven hours since then he hadn't moved - not even to use the restroom - despite downing what William estimated to be somewhere in the region of twenty pints of beer.

William had been here just as long, occupying the stool beside Mike. But he'd only had four beers, and he'd gotten up to pee several times during the game. Of course, he was also pushing fifty; almost two decades older than Mike.

"At least they made it to the Super Bowl again," William offered as consolation. "Nobody else has ever gone four times in a row."

"Nah," Mike objected, shaking his head. "You don't get it 'cause you didn't grow up here. This is like a kick in the nuts. Losing is worse than not going."

"He's right," Tom chimed in from behind the bar. "The whole country's watching. All of America saw us choke. Again."

"It's like we're stuck in a time loop or something," Mike muttered.

"Time doesn't loop," William said, with a rueful smile. "It is fluid, though."

"Fluid?" Mike parroted, blinking his eyes in confusion.

"Relative is more accurate," William amended. "Time can speed up or slow down, based on the velocity of an object. The faster you go, the slower time moves."

"Bullshit," Tom snorted, wiping down a glass and crouching down to set it on the shelf beneath the bar.

"Hey, now," Mike said, holding up a hand in his friend's defense, "Billy's a smart guy. He knows what he's talking about. Einstein and shit, right?"

"More or less," William acknowledged.

"Bullshit," Tom said again as he stood up. "Time is time. It doesn't change."

"They proved it," William assured him. "Verified with an atomic clock."

"Atomic?" Tom said. "Like a bomb?"

"Shit, you're stupid," Mike laughed. "It's not a bomb. Just real accurate."

"Precisely," William concurred. "An atomic clock is very, very accurate. In 1971 two men named Hafele and Keating conducted an experiment. They synced two atomic clocks and put one on a commercial jet. The other stayed on the ground.

"After the flight, they compared them and found the clocks were out of sync. The one on the plane had fallen behind by a few nanoseconds due to kinetic dilation."

Seeing the blank stares of the other two, William clarified. "Because of how fast it was flying, time had moved more slowly on the plane."

"Fuck me," Mike muttered, though William suspected his amazement was more due to alcohol than the wonders of science.

"As I said, time is relative. Fluid. Malleable."

"I still say bullshit," Tom grumbled, tossing his dishtowel over his shoulder and disappearing into the bar's back room.

"Level with me," Mike asked after Tom had left. "Is that story true?"

"A bit over-simplified," someone answered from over William's shoulder, "but essentially accurate."

William didn't need to turn around to recognize the speaker. He'd been dreading hearing that voice for years.

"Who the hell are you?" Mike asked the newcomer, eyeing him suspiciously.

"William and I go way back."

"That true?" Mike asked, as William stared pointedly down at his beer. "This guy a friend of yours?"

"Mike," William said without raising his head. "Can you give us a minute, please?"

Mike hesitated, sensing something was wrong. Then he pushed his seat back from the bar and stood up. "Gotta take a piss anyway."

The newcomer took the seat on William's opposite side as Mike staggered off.

"It took us a long time to find you," he said, his voice calm and relaxed, speaking softly enough so no one else in the bar could overhear. "I'm impressed."

William didn't answer.

"Where's Dr. Schuller?" the man asked.

The question had no urgency. There was no malice or threat in the tone. But it was there, nonetheless.

"Lisa and I went our separate ways when we left the project," Willaim replied, keeping his gaze fixed firmly on his beer. *Thank God you haven't found her, too.*

"What about the girl?"

"Her name was Beth."

"Was?"

"She died last year. Ovarian cancer."

"So young," the other man remarked, without any real emotion. "Her cancer... was it caused by the project?"

William shrugged, still staring at his mug. "Probably. No way to know for sure."

"And her offspring?"

Offspring. So cold. So clinical.

"I don't know. Made sure I didn't know. In case you found me."

"I believe you, William," the voice said. "You're a smart man; you know ignorance is the only way to protect them. But you'll still have to come with us so we can be sure."

He speaks with the ease of a man asking about the weather. What kind of person can be so casual while threatening another human being with torture?

William finally turned his head to look at the man seated next to him. Dr. Arvihd Singh had changed little over the last few years - short, thin, balding. He wore the same wire-rim glasses, perched on the bridge of his long, narrow nose. His black beard was still trimmed to a sharp point, though William noticed a few strands of gray in it now. And his brown skin had a few more lines around the eyes. But otherwise he looked as he always had: academic and professional in his manner and appearance; completely unassuming.

But William knew the things he'd done. And he could imagine the things Dr. Singh was going to do to him once they left the bar. The man was a monster.

He hadn't come alone, of course. Two men in black overcoats hovered near the door, their features hard and chiseled, their eyes hidden behind mirrored sunglasses even though they were inside a dingy bar.

"What if I refuse to go with you?" William asked.

"You must decide," Singh explained. "Do you come quietly, without making a fuss? Or do you resist and force us to kill everyone in here before dragging you out that door? Either way, it ends the same for you."

His tone never changed. In all their years working together, William had never heard him yell. Or shout. Or even raise his voice. It was as if he knew his words - his orders - were inevitable.

William pulled a folded wad of bills from his pocket. He always paid cash for everything. He placed the entire stack on the bar - all the money he had on him - then slowly pushed his stool away and stood up.

"Let's go," he whispered. "Before Mike comes back."

A minute later the younger man returned from the restroom to find only an empty seat and a pile of twenties where his friend had been. He never saw William again.

CHAPTER 1

Part One: Carson

March 15, 2019 - Las Vegas
One month before the D Street Massacre

My name's Carson. Carson Gaines. There are three things you need to know about me. The first is that I'm a professional gambler. I'm not an addict. Not quite. But it's probably safe to call me a degenerate.

Carson shifted in his seat, trying to get comfortable. For the past four hours, he'd been hunched over a blackjack table in the Siegel Suites Casino, grinding away hand after hand, and the chairs weren't built with someone six-three in mind. As the dealer flipped out another round of cards, Carson rolled his head from side-to-side, listening to the snap-crackle-pop of the joints in his neck.

Such is the glamorous life of the professional card counter.

The Siegel wasn't one of the fancy mega-casinos that line the Strip. It wasn't even one of the kitschy "old Vegas" joints down on Freemont Street, refurbished and cleaned up to draw in the tourists and suck the dollars from their wallets while giving them free drinks to numb the pain of losing. Conveniently located close enough to skid row to smell the piss, the Siegel Suites could be charitably called a "locals-only" casino.

Carson just called it a shithole.

Despite being a Friday night, the place was almost empty; the March Madness crowd wouldn't hit the city until next week. At most there were two dozen people in the whole place, not counting the staff. The majority of the patrons were playing nickel slot machines, their eyes glazed over as they slapped the SPIN button in a repetitive, robotic trance.

Vegas had been built on the one-armed bandits, but the slots didn't even have handles anymore. It was all digital video bullshit now - cheaper to make, and cheaper to maintain.

Carson never touched the slots; the house edge was too high. He was a stats guy. He knew the odds of every game in every casino in Vegas.

The slots will bleed you dry in no time.

Blackjack, on the other hand, was a game smart players could control. Counting cards and adjusting your bets when the deck was running hot shifted the odds in the player's favor. It wasn't much, but it was just enough to turn a steady, reliable profit over the long haul.

Carson had been counting cards in Vegas for almost two years. All the good spots - places that didn't reek of stale cigarette smoke and weren't crawling with hookers and junkies - knew him by now. If he sat down at a blackjack table in any respectable casino, it wouldn't take long for security to swoop in and shut his action down. So, he had to set his sights lower.

And the Siegel is as low as it gets.

Besides the mindless slot jockeys, the rest of the crowd was a mix of hookers hunting tricks, junkies looking to score and stubborn players like Carson huddled around the four tables in the middle of the room that made up the tiny blackjack pit. Only two of the tables even had dealers; the others stood empty and abandoned. In any other casino, someone would have at least shooed the hookers and junkies away. In the Siegel, nobody could be bothered.

Fortunately, the apathy of the staff worked in Carson's favor. Counting cards in real life wasn't like it was portrayed in films. It wasn't possible to just grab a chair and win right away. It took focus and patience; it was a marathon, not a sprint. Every hand Carson would squeeze out tiny mathematical advantages that would gradually add up over time... as long as he didn't get caught.

That's the real trick to counting cards. The math is simple. But staying off the casino's radar takes work.

He was dressed to avoid attracting attention: faded jeans and a long-sleeved, black t-shirt. More importantly, he was keeping his bets small. Even a dump like the Siegel had security cameras everywhere. Lower bets cut into his profits per hour, but it was a necessary sacrifice. Winning too much too fast would draw unwanted scrutiny from the eyes in the sky.

Carson looked over at the king sitting in front of the dealer, then glanced down at his cards: a pair of 4's.

Don't like those odds.

He tapped the table for a hit. The dealer flipped over a ten, giving him 18. Now he was stuck. He couldn't take another card without busting, but 18 probably wasn't going to win.

He waved off, and his fears were realized a few seconds later as the dealer flipped up another king, giving herself 20.

Sometimes you can see the train coming but you can't get off the tracks.

"New shoe," the dealer announced, snatching away his bet before shuffling up the cards.

Even with losing the last hand, a quick count of his chips confirmed Carson was up a little over $500.

Not bad for three hours work. Enough to buy Ella something nice. That's the second thing you need to know about me: I have a daughter. Ella's four. She lives with her mother in LA. We got divorced two years ago, and I moved to Vegas right after. My gambling wasn't the reason we split up. But it sure as hell didn't help.

Knowing he had a few minutes before play would resume, Carson scooped up his chips and stuffed them into his pocket before heading for the restroom. Unlike the higher end casinos, the Siegel wasn't the kind of place where it was safe to just leave your money sitting on the table.

He took a quick piss, hurrying so he could get back before the next hand was dealt. He washed and dried his hands, then stepped back out onto the casino floor... only to find two men in dark suits waiting for him.

One looked to be about forty; the other was probably ten years younger. Square heads, thick jaws, identical grim expressions. Both men were very large and didn't try to hide it; their suits were cut to accentuate their thick, muscular frames rather than concealing them.

If you looked up "casino security" in an illustrated dictionary you'd find a picture of these two gorillas.

"Can I help you boys with something?" Carson asked, putting on a thick Southern drawl.

"You need to come with us, Mr. Gaines," the older one replied.

"Think y'all are a bit confused," Carson said, staying in character. "Name's Stevens, not Gaines."

"There's no mistake, Mr. Gaines."

Busted.

Carson didn't know what had tipped them off to his real identity. He wasn't betting heavy, but maybe someone watching from upstairs had gotten suspicious about the new player hanging around the tables the past few nights. It wouldn't have been hard to grab an image of his face from the cameras and pass it around to the surveillance crews at a few other joints. The casinos watched out for each other like that. Someone probably recognized him and was only too happy to tell the Siegel all about Carson Gaines, notorious card counter.

I just can't catch a fucking break!

"Let's go to the security office in the back and have a little chat, Mr. Gaines."

Right. Chat.

The bigger casinos, like the ones on the Strip that target tourists coming to Vegas to blow their wad, wouldn't actually do much if they caught someone counting cards. They might ban a counter from the blackjack tables; maybe charge a player with trespassing if they tried to sneak back into the game after being warned. But they were too worried about their reputations to do anything drastic.

The Siegel was different. The people running it cared a lot more about a few hundred dollars in chips than their already worthless reputation. And the goons in front of him clearly weren't going to shy away from the rough stuff.

"I'd love to stay," Carson said, "but it's getting late."

"This won't take long," the older man said, stepping forward and reaching out with a meaty paw.

**** FREEZE! ****

The man halted mid-stride, instantly paralyzed. His clutching hand hung motionless in the air, only a few inches away from the collar of Carson's shirt. Over his shoulder, Carson could see the other security guard's lips had curled up in a cruel grin, and his eyes were wide with the eager anticipation of impending violence. But like his partner, he was completely frozen in place.

That's the third thing you need to know about me. I can stop time.

It wasn't just the security guards who were affected. Every person in the entire casino was completely immobilized. Some were fixed in place with their hands hovering over the SPIN buttons of the slots; others were held fast as they fed more bills into the insatiable money-eaters. A $5 chip tossed towards a blackjack dealer as a tip was suspended in mid-air.

Even the slot machines were frozen, the whirling images of their virtual reels stuck in mid-spin. There was no sound - the omnipresent cacophony of the chiming slots and the disgruntled mutterings of frustrated players had been swallowed up in an eerie, oppressive silence. The entire scene was motionless and still as a painting, or a video after someone hits pause.

That's my power. My gift. With a single thought, I can stop the entire world. But here's the kicker – whenever I do, I'm just as helpless as everyone else. While the world is in stasis, I can't actually do anything. Not even move my eyeballs to change what I'm looking at. I'm just... stuck. Trapped until I start everything up again.

When that happened – when Carson let the world snap back to normal and time began moving again - nobody would have any idea that they'd been temporarily frozen. Nobody would have any awareness of what he'd done, or that anything strange had happened.

Nobody but me.

But even though Carson couldn't move when the world was frozen, stopping time still had its uses. It gave him time to think. Analyze the situation. Formulate a plan whenever things took an unexpected turn... like running into a pair of security goons on the way back from taking a piss.

He surveyed the situation carefully, evaluating his options. He was taller than either of the guards, but they each outweighed him by at least thirty pounds. He wouldn't stand a chance against them, especially not two-on-one.

Not a problem. I usually prefer flight to fight anyway.

The guard reaching out to grab him was leaning forward. Anticipating Carson might try to scramble backwards, he'd shifted all his weight onto his front foot in a quick lunge. He was motionless now, of course, but from his position Carson could tell his center of mass was over-extended. Easy to knock off balance.

That's my angle.

He'd use his eagerness against him. Catch him off guard by doing the unexpected: attack instead of retreat. And then hope his partner couldn't react in time.

At least, that was the plan.

**** GO! ****

The world exploded back into life with a burst of motion and sound. The slot machines whirred and chimed as players resumed their robotic pawing at the buttons, completely unaware they had all just been released from a temporal prison.

The security guard's clutching hand snapped forward, but Carson was ready for it now. Stepping nimbly to the one side, he grabbed the sleeve of the guard's jacket and pulled down, hard.

The sudden ploy caused his surprised opponent to stagger forward and fall to the floor. Behind him, his less experienced partner looked on with an expression of shock and confusion.

Carson seized on his bewilderment by stepping forward to deliver a swift kick to the younger man's crotch, causing him to double over with a loud groan.

Dirty move, but I don't have a lot of options.

As the younger guard clutched his balls and sank to the ground, Carson hurdled over him and started running. Weaving his way between the tables and slots, he made a beeline for the doors leading to the street outside. Behind him, one of the guards shouted out for someone to stop him.

Curious about the ruckus, a frail old woman stood up from her slot machine and turned to see what was going on, stepping right into Carson's path. He swerved to the side, narrowly avoiding barreling her over. But his left knee clipped the corner of one of the slot machines and the impact sent him crashing to the floor.

He scrambled back to his feet, trying to ignore the throbbing pain in his bruised knee as he limped towards the exit. As he burst from the casino the cloying curtain of stale smoke gave way to the crisp air of a mid-March night. But Carson didn't have time to stop and appreciate it.

Favoring his injured knee, he half-ran, half-hopped down the block. He only made it to the next corner before one of his pursuers crashed into him with a flying tackle from behind. They both slammed into the pavement, knocking the wind from Carson's lungs as the heavier man landed on top of him.

Momentarily stunned, Carson rolled onto his back, gasping for breath. Before he could recover, the second guard caught up with them and the two men yanked Carson to his feet. The younger man pinned his arms behind his back while the older man started unbuttoning his jacket.

"You stupid son of a bitch," he snarled, tossing the jacket to the ground and rolling up the cuffs of his shirt. "You think just because we're a small casino that we can't spot a fucking cheater?"

"Counting cards isn't cheating!" Carson protested, struggling vainly against the iron grip of the man holding his arms. "And it's not illegal!"

"Tell it to someone who cares, fucktard!" the man replied, crouching down and cocking his fist before launching it toward Carson's midsection in a vicious uppercut.

*** *FREEZE!* ***

His fist stopped mere inches from Carson's gut. Carson's head had already recoiled slightly in anticipation of the blow, making the muscles of his neck taut. Despite time being frozen, he could sense the man holding his arms had shifted his weight forward, bracing for the impact.

I don't know why I have this power. I've been doing my trick as far back as I can remember – even as a little kid. It's like walking or talking; just a natural thing I don't even remember learning to do.

But it's not all it's cracked up to be. Stopping time never really solved my problems. Not the ones that mattered. It couldn't make me popular with the cool kids in high school. It couldn't make the girls like me. It couldn't bring my parents back after they died in a car crash. It couldn't save my marriage.

And in this case, stopping time didn't change the fact that Carson was about to get his ass beat. He could hold his attackers at bay indefinitely. Just keep the world frozen, with that punch stopped a few inches from his gut. But to what end? Eventually he had to let the world start up again. And that swinging fist was going to land. Some things were inevitable.

Sometimes you can see the train coming, but you can't get out off the tracks.

*** *GO!* ***

The punch slammed home, just beneath his rib cage. Carson grunted in pain, gagging and coughing. The man pinning his arms chuckled, the sound echoing loudly in his ear. Two more blows caught him in the stomach; if he wasn't being held up, he would have doubled over on the ground.

With their victim gasping desperately for air, the first man scooped up his discarded jacket and wrapped it around his right hand. The he slammed his cushioned knuckles into Carson's jaw. The impact turned his world into a swirling mass of lights and colors; he barely even felt the next two blows.

The man behind let go and Carson crumpled to the curb. Still dazed, he felt something warm on his lips and chin, and there was a sticky taste in his mouth. It took him a second to realize it was blood gushing from his nose.

"Those chips are property of the Siegel Suites," one of the men growled, as they rolled him over and started rifling through his pockets.

Carson clutched and pawed at the men; an instinctive - yet futile - attempt to stop them from robbing him of his winnings for the night. All his efforts earned him was a swift kick to the midsection.

"Hey, you worthless bastards!" a woman's voice suddenly rang out. "Leave him alone!"

His assailants stood up and took a step back, wary of the unexpected interloper. Carson gingerly rolled onto one side to take a look at his savior as she came into view, materializing like a guardian angel from the darkness.

*** *FREEZE!* ***

The pain and disorientation clouding his thoughts vanished, but he knew from experience they'd return with a vengeance as soon as time started moving again. At least this gave him a clear-headed moment to take stock of the situation.

The woman was a stranger. White. Tall and thin. Older; sixty, maybe. Platinum-blonde hair cut a few inches above the shoulder; sensible yet stylish. Her expression was hard and determined - eyes narrowed, jaw clenched. She was wearing dark pants, black calf-high boots with a low heel, and a long white coat belted at the waist. Her right arm was extended straight out in front of her, clutching a small can of what looked like mace. Pointing it right at Carson's new best friends.

On the edge of his peripheral vision Carson could just make out the older of the two thugs. He looked worried.

It's one thing to beat the shit out of some punk card counter. But roughing up a random woman in the street isn't in his job description.

Carson had no idea who the woman was, or why she decided to step in and help him.

But right now, I'll take all the help I can get.

*** *GO!* ***

Carson's world was once again enveloped in a concussive fog, his head still woozy from his recent beating. No longer frozen by the stoppage of time, the woman came closer with quick, deliberate steps, the can of mace held before her like a talisman.

"Back off!" she snapped at the still hesitant security goons. "Get your steroid-stuffed asses out of here before I call the god-damned cops!"

The older one tilted his head back in the direction of the casino in a silent signal to his partner, and they slowly backed away.

"They stole my chips," Carson tried to say, but all that came out was a low groan.

"We better not see you around here again," the older thug called out to Carson as they retreated.

"Keep moving!" the woman hissed in response. "Get out of her before you really piss me off. Go!"

She stared them down, keeping her mace at the ready until they disappeared around the corner. Once they were out of sight, she pocketed the mace and dropped down on one knee to help Carson into a sitting position. By this time, his head was clearing enough for him to try and speak again.

"Thanks," was all he could muster.

"This will probably hurt like a son of a bitch," she whispered to him as she cautiously felt along his ribs. Carson moaned loudly as her fingers found a sore spot.

"Don't be such a baby. They're just cracked, not broken.

"Let me check the nose," she said, grabbing him firmly by the chin.

He flinched as she roughly wiggled the tip back and forth.

"Huh. That's not broken either. Guess it's your lucky night."

"Yeah, I won the fucking jackpot," Carson replied, gritting his teeth against her continued poking and prodding of his face.

"Jaw and orbital bones seem intact. Can you stand?"

"I think so."

He leaned on her more than he meant to as he struggled to his feet, but she bore his weight with surprising ease.

"Let's get you to a hospital," she declared.

"I'm fine," Carson said, with a shake of his head.

The movement made his world lurch and sway, and he would have stumbled if she hadn't grabbed him.

"Don't be a dumbass. You've got a concussion. It could be serious. You need to see a doctor."

Realizing he was in no shape to argue, Carson let her lead him away.

CHAPTER 2

Carson spent the rest of the night in the hospital for observation. When they released him the next morning, the platinum-haired woman who'd come to his rescue was gone.

He wasn't surprised she'd left; he hadn't expected her to stick around all night. But it would have been nice to thank her properly.

No chance of that now. Never even got her name before she disappeared.

He caught the bus back to where he'd parked his car near the Siegel. Sometimes he'd try to make some extra cash picking up fares on Uber or Lyft – being a professional gambler wasn't always the most stable stream of income. But sitting behind the wheel he knew that wasn't going to be an option today.

Really not a good idea to be driving people around the city when I'm feeling this woozy.

The goons had given him a concussion, and the doctor had warned him he'd experience unpleasant symptoms for the next few days. Rather than fight it, he decided to take it easy and rest up.

Somehow, he made it safely back to his apartment, but even that short drive left his head pounding. For the next two days, he barely got out of bed. He slept fitfully, plagued by hazy nightmares of his beating. In his dreams, the thugs who worked him over were faceless blobs, and the foul-mouthed woman who rescued him was a figure bathed in shining silver light.

Each time he woke, he'd kick off the covers and try to get up... only to crawl right back into bed when the room started spinning and his stomach tried to puke itself up. Even lying down he didn't feel great, though his symptoms seemed to come and go in waves. When things got really bad - when the vertigo and the nausea and the pounding in his skull became too much to bear - he'd stop the world.

*** *FREEZE!* ***

He didn't feel sick when he stopped time. No headaches. No nausea. His symptoms were paused along with the rest of the physical world. But it was only a stopgap solution. He knew it would all come back the instant he started time up again.

Still, it's nice to take a break from feeling like shit. Even if it's only temporary.

His parents had no idea he could stop time. He'd asked them about it once when he was five or six. But they didn't know what he was talking about, and he was too young to properly explain it. In the end, they just assumed he was talking about a fantasy children dream up, like an imaginary friend or a monster in a closet.

Growing up, Carson had to figure things out for himself. What he could and couldn't do. Testing the limits of his power. But even after all these years, he still had no idea how long he could actually keep things locked in stasis. Seconds, minutes, hours - all those markers cease to have meaning when time itself no longer existed.

When the world is stopped, everything just happens in the now.

All Carson knew was that the longer he kept time frozen, the harder he had to concentrate. Eventually something would slip, and the universe would snap back into motion, seemingly oblivious to his temporary interruptions.

*** *GO!* ***

By Monday morning he was starting to feel like himself again. He managed to shower and eat breakfast without the room spinning even once. Rested and re-energized, he sat down at the kitchen table, fired up his iPad, and got to work.

When it came to counting cards, Vegas was basically dead to him now. If the crew at the Siegel could spot him, he didn't have much chance of going unnoticed anywhere else. But there were other ways to make money in Sin City.

And I'm not talking about driving for Uber.

The Men's NCAA Basketball Championship was starting in two days: sixteen games on Thursday, sixteen games on Friday, and sixteen more on the weekend. By then every hotel room on the Strip would be booked. Every sports bar and pub in the city would be packed with rabid fans. Every casino would be so crowded you could barely walk from one side to the other. It was called March Madness for a reason.

For the casinos, it was a gold mine – their most profitable weekend of the year. And Carson had every intention of getting himself a piece of that action. All he had to do was capitalize on what Vegas called "dumb money".

And nobody's dumber than college basketball fans at the start of March Madness.

Most people bet with their heart, not their head. They backed teams they already had a vested interest in: their alma mater; the local college; big name universities with national profiles like Notre Dame and Duke. Some people latched onto a school because of the mascot, or the color of the jerseys. Or maybe they got swept up in a great tournament run by a Cinderella team a few years ago, and just kept betting long shots hoping to recapture the magic every year after that.

Whatever the reason, it all boiled down to the same thing. They'd throw their money down on the team they *hoped* would win, as if their blind loyalty could help bring victory. They followed their gut. And the way to beat people who bet with their gut was simple: look at the numbers. Study the stats. Trust the math.

In the modern age it was possible to get literally thousands of data points on every team and player. Injury reports. Strength of schedule. Net plus/minus. Over/unders. RPI. A lot of it was just white noise, but if you were willing to sort through the static, you could find the real signal.

He analyzed all thirty-two first round matchups in detail, cross-referencing and comparing the teams as he searched for the soft lines.

Hunting for those precious spots where dumb money had pushed the odds too far in one direction or the other. Looking for the tiny edges he could exploit.

When he finally shut his laptop down, five hours had slipped away. His eyes were blurry, and his headache had come back from staring at the screen for so long, but he had his picks.

Satisfied, he set his alarm for seven pm, crawled into bed and closed his eyes.

***

The shrill beeping woke him from a deep and dreamless sleep. Groggy and disoriented, he forced himself to get up and stumble to the kitchen. There he plopped himself down at the table and opened up his iPad.

Taking a second to compose himself, Carson tapped the FaceTime icon on the screen and called his ex-wife. A few seconds later, Sarah's face popped up into view.

"You'll have to make it a quick call tonight," she said by way of greeting, sounding tired and defeated. But her tone quickly changed to one of concern.

"Oh my God, Carson! What the fuck?"

For a second, he didn't know what she was talking about. Then his eyes flicked to the tiny image of himself in the corner of the screen, and he realized his face was an absolute mess.

He'd been cleaned up at the hospital, but there were still angry scrapes on his cheeks and a thick scab on his chin from being tackled on the pavement. His lip was split and swollen, and his eyes were a black and purple raccoon's mask.

"I ran into some trouble this weekend."

""Do I even want to know what?" Sarah asked, exasperated.

"A couple over-zealous casino security guards. No big deal."

Sarah pursed her lips, clearly wondering what he was holding back. But Carson didn't want to get into the details.

"Can I talk to Ella?"

"I can't let her see you like this!" Sarah protested.

From off-screen he heard Ella's voice call out, "Is it Daddy?"

"Come on, Sarah," Carson pleaded. "Let me see her."

Technically, she didn't have to say yes. Sarah had asked for full custody in the divorce, in exchange for not having to pay child support or alimony. Carson had agreed to her terms.

Not like I had much choice. If I fought her, she'd just play the "gambling addict" card. No judge in the world would take my side.

But Sarah wasn't a bad person. She was good about letting Carson be part of Ella's life. So after a few seconds, she rolled her eyes in resignation, then passed the iPad down into her daughter's waiting hands. The view on Carson's screen spun and flipped as Ella oriented the iPad on her end, and his stomach heaved.

Still a little woozy, I guess.

"Hi, Daddy!"

"Hello, Pumpkin!"

Ella's eyes went wide as she focused on Carson's image, though she seemed more fascinated than repulsed.

"What happened to your face?"

"I fell down," Carson said. "And I bumped my head. But I'm okay now, sweetie."

"I fell down, too!" Ella exclaimed, flashing an enormous, toothy grin. "Look!"

She tilted the iPad down to show a large bandage plastered over one knee.

"Oh, Ella - did you hurt yourself?"

"Uh-huh. It was bleeding and everything, but I didn't cry."

"Wow, what a brave girl you are. Did Mommy put that band-aid on?"

"No, other Daddy did. He kissed it better, too."

Other Daddy. Ouch.

"Well, I'm glad you're okay now honey."

"I didn't even cry."

Carson laughed. "I know. You told me. You know what, honey? Daddy cried a little when he fell down."

Ella laughed. "Daddies don't cry!" she insisted.

"I guess I'm not as brave as you are, sweetie."

They talked for another twenty minutes; Ella prattling on about play dates with friends Carson had never met and kids' shows he'd never seen. Carson relished every second of it. It gave him a connection to her life, even from hundreds of miles away. And then, all too soon, it was time to say goodbye.

"Okay, Ella," he heard Sarah chime in from off-screen. "We better let Daddy rest."

"Mommy's right, kiddo. I should go."

"Okay, Daddy. Bye!"

"Bye, kiddo. I love you."

"I love you too, Daddy!"

And with that, Ella vanished, handing the iPad to her mother as she rushed off on another adventure Carson couldn't be a part of.

"Thanks for letting me talk to her," he said to Sarah once she was gone. "Even looking like this."

"You have a right to be in her life," Sarah grudgingly acknowledged. "You're her father."

But I'm not her only father anymore, am I?

"So... I guess she's calling Greg 'Daddy' now?"

"She's been calling him Daddy for almost a year," Sarah said. "Ever since we got married. Is that a problem?"

"No, no," Carson hastily replied. "Greg's a good guy. It just caught me off guard, is all."

There was an awkward silence before Carson asked, "Her knee? When she fell? Was it another seizure?"

Sarah didn't say anything, but she nodded faintly.

"You didn't bother to tell me?"

Carson was surprised at how sharp and accusing his words sounded.

"What would be the point?" Sarah's shot back, mirroring her ex's tone. "You can't do anything about it when you're out there in Vegas."

FREEZE!

Carson had never told Sarah about his power; she had no idea he could stop time. But he'd used his ability plenty of times during their relationship.

Whenever they were on the verge of an argument, he'd freeze the world. Then he'd carefully collect his thoughts and present a rational and cogent counter argument in an effort to try and defuse the situation. Sometimes it worked. Usually it just made things worse.

Logic isn't always the best way to navigate a relationship.

In this case it was obvious why Sarah was so tense. But he wasn't ready to back down – she didn't have a monopoly on caring about their daughter.

****GO!****

"I know you're worried about her," he said, keeping his voice level but firm. "But so am I. I have a right to know what's going on."

Sarah sighed and reached up to rub her temples. When she finally answered, her anger had been replaced by weary resignation.

"It's been a bad week, Carson."

"I thought this new drug was helping."

"It's better. She went almost two weeks without a seizure before this last one. But it's not a cure."

"What about that specialist?"

"We have an appointment Friday."

Carson nodded. "Let me know how it goes."

"I will."

"I'll call again next week" Carson promised. "Same time if that works for you."

Sarah nodded but didn't speak. There was a long pause, as if she was working herself up to say something more.

Or maybe she's waiting for me to say something.

But whatever it was, whatever words she wanted to say or hear, never came. Instead, she simply said, "Goodbye, Carson." Then she abruptly ended the call.

Communication was never our strong suit.

He stared at the blank screen for a few more seconds before closing FaceTime and crawling back into bed.

CHAPTER 3

It was just past nine pm on Friday when Carson arrived at the Planet Hollywood Hotel and Casino on the Las Vegas strip. The first round of March Madness was in the books, and he'd already run up a 7-3 record on his bets, netting almost four thousand in profit.

About time my luck turned around.

Tomorrow he'd start looking for more soft lines to wager on in the second round, scoping out the Sunday games to parlay his winning streak. And on Monday, he'd visit the bank and wire a chunk of his profits to Sarah to help cover Ella's medical costs.

She'd never admit it, but I know that specialist they're taking her to won't be cheap.

But tonight, Carson wasn't focused on any of that. He was riding the high of his wins, and he had every intention of reveling in his triumph.

And there's no better place to celebrate a big payday than Planet Hollywood.

Carson felt a primal, Pavlovian response as he rode the escalator from the lower lobby up to the main floor. His body tingled with nervous energy as adrenaline surged through his veins and he felt the heady rush of anticipation.

The scene that greeted him at the top of the escalator was simultaneously chaotic yet comforting. The PH gaming floor was a demented mash-up of bordello, night club and casino. The garish decor of ruby red hearts on dark red walls above a crimson carpet was accentuated with an overabundance of pink and purple neon. Pounding hip-hop and pop remixes blasted over the speakers, drowning out the drunken laughter, triumphant cries and sorrowful lamentations of the players crowded around every table in the place. Cocktail waitresses wearing hot pants and barely buttoned tops weaved their way among the crowd, carrying trays of complimentary drinks. And in the center of it all stood the infamous Pleasure Pit, where the card tables were staffed by gorgeous women in lingerie corsets flanked by limber, scantily clad pole-dancers on conspicuously placed stages.

Carson paused for a moment to let it all wash over him, reveling in the overwhelming mish-mash of sights and sounds.

Every casino in Vegas had its own unique vibe. Venetian; New York, New York; Paris - unabashedly faux tourist traps. Caesar's Palace and the Wynn were old money; stuffy and too quiet for Carson's taste.

But the PH hits my sweet spot.

Young, upscale crowd; twenty and thirty-somethings with money to burn. Lots of bachelor and bachelorette parties; even the odd pro athlete or celeb kicking around. Everyone having fun, or at least pretending to. Including Carson. Tonight, he wouldn't be grinding at a blackjack table counting cards. He was here to cut loose and gamble.

He'd swapped out the non-descript clothes he'd worn at the Siegel for an outfit that screamed 'player': black blazer; gray slacks; cream shirt and a red pocket swatch for an eye-catching splash of color. His most prized possession - a 1993 stainless steel Rolex Submariner his parents had given him when he graduated high school - was prominently displayed on his wrist. Carson believed in math, stats and the science of probability... but he never gambled without his lucky watch.

Place is jumping tonight!

The first days of March Madness were the busiest weekend the casinos would see all year. Crazed college hoops fans had descended on the city like a plague of locusts: a swarm of obnoxious, drunken alumni proudly wearing their garish school colors, mindlessly handing their money over to the casino while keeping one eye on the TV screens mounted over every other table so they could watch the games and cheer on their teams.

As he made his way through the shoulder-to-shoulder crowd in the casino, he got a succession of friendly nods and waves from the staff. When he wasn't counting cards, the PH was his preferred haunt, and most of the dealers knew him by sight if not by name. He wasn't a high roller; just a semi-regular local. But it wasn't hard to get on good terms with the casino staff: just don't be an asshole and remember to tip. It sounded simple, but Carson was always amazed at how many people couldn't pull it off.

His first stop, as always, was the craps pit. With the March Madness crowd every table was busy, but as Carson drew near, he saw only one was really buzzing. There was an electricity around a hot craps table; a crackling energy in the air that made his skin actually tingle. It was a rush unlike anything else in Vegas - better than roulette or blackjack, and a damn sight better than the mind-numbing slots.

A tiny Asian girl in a sparkly LBD was rolling the dice at the far end of the table. A young black man wearing dark jeans, a hot pink shirt, a black jacket with rolled up sleeves and a grey fedora was pressed close against her side, one arm wrapped possessively around her hip, a drink clutched in his free hand and a ten-mile-wide grin plastered on his face. Flanking them were two more fashionable young couples; a posse of hipster kids taking a run at the casino before hitting the clubs.

A dozen other players were also packed in along the entire length of the craps table's rail, including four muscular brosephs in jeans and t-shirts, their skin bright red from too long out at the pool without suncreen; an older white man wearing a rumpled brown jacket; an overweight sugar-daddy with a cowboy hat and rhinestone suit and the much younger, bleached-blonde arm candy fawning all over him.

They were jammed in so tight that they couldn't help but rub up against each other, bumping shoulders and elbows as they tossed their chips on the table. But since they were all winning, nobody cared; every- one was laughing, yelling and high fiving. It was loud and crowded and chaotic and beautiful: the glorious cacophony of the dice.

Nothing brings people together like a hot streak at a craps table.

There was an unmistakable rhythm to the sound of craps; an almost hypnotic pattern. It started when the stickman passed the dice to the shooter. Players began calling out bets and throwing chips on the table, scrambling to make their plays: "Press up my inside!"; "Gimmie five on the hard six!"; "C and E! C and E!" The buzz built as the shooter picked up the dice, and players started shouting out encouragement - "Keep it going!"; "Hit that six!"; "Gimmie a yo!" "Thirty-three! Thirty-three!" - each cry louder and more urgent than the one before it.

"Bring it home, BABY!" the grinning boyfriend bellowed as the girl in the LBD awkwardly rattled the dice around in her palm. "You got this!"

"Come on six!" she squealed, snapping her arm forward in a clumsy underhand toss that launched the dice high in the air.

The sound dropped as the dice were released, every player involuntarily sucking in his or her breath in anticipation as the little plastic cubes soared across the felt, ricocheted off the back wall and bounced to a stop. There was a brief moment of heavy silence as eyes darted back and forth between the dice, alcohol-addled minds struggling to add up the pips showing on each face - the calm before the storm.

"Eight the hard way!" the stickman called out, and the table erupted with cheers. Another winner.

Carson moved in closer but didn't carve himself out a place on the rail right away. It was bad karma to just jump right in.

Craps 101: respect the roll, and never mess with the momentum of a hot table.

He lingered just behind the players as they tossed more chips onto the table to press up their bets. Giggling and laughing, the girl fumbled with the dice, struggling to pick them up. Clearly, she was a newbie.

The young woman cocked her entire arm back and launched the dice again, sending them on another high, looping arc. At the same time, someone behind Carson slapped him hard on the ass.

Still jumpy after his recent beating, his reaction was instant and instinctual.

****FREEZE!****

The noise and chaos of the casino stopped. Everyone - the staff, the servers, the players – had been transformed into statues sculpted by an artist with a penchant for ludicrous poses. Some had their arms raised in giddy anticipation, others were leaning forward or slapping their neighbor on the back. One man was suspended a half-foot above the ground, caught mid-air as he leaped with excitement.

In front of Carson, the dice hung motionless a few feet above the center of the table. The two little red cubes stared back at him like the wily eyes of an otherwise invisible monster.

On the very edge of his peripheral vision he could just make out a cocktail waitress at the next table extending a drink to an older gentleman. His gaze was firmly fixed on the ample cleavage exposed by her skimpy uniform.

Carson registered all this in an offhand, almost automatic way as he tried to figure out whose hand was still firmly planted on his left buttcheek. After a moment, he realized there could only be one answer.

Maya Belfour.

**** GO! ****

As the world lurched back into motion, Carson smiled and turned to face the woman who had snuck up behind him. Over his shoulder he heard the stick man call out, "Six!" and a round of cheers erupted from the table.

Another winner.

Maya Belfour always stood out in a crowd. She was tall: almost six feet in her heels. And she was gorgeous: flawless light-brown skin; long, lustrous black hair, and a sense of confidence and style that even the standard issue casino security uniform of a black jacket and pantsuit couldn't hide.

"Hey, Maya. You're looking good tonight. Is that a new jacket?"

Maya smirked at the joke – she'd been wearing the same outfit every night on the job for the past two years. She gave him a quick hug by way of greeting, then took a step back and raised one eyebrow.

"You look like shit, Carson. What the hell happened?"

She had the hint of an accent Carson had never been able to place. Cuban, maybe. Or Cajun. But he knew better than to bring it up. Every once in a while, some wannabe smooth talker would ask what her heritage was, and she always fired back with "American!".

"Security at the Siegel decided to have a chat with me," Carson explained, self-consciously rubbing his scabbed chin. "Guess those boys haven't learned to use their words yet."

"Fucking amateur hour over there," she hissed, shaking her head.

"That's why I'm back here," he agreed, giving her a playful wink.

"Just don't do anything foolish," she warned, placing a firm hand on his upper arm. "You know the rules. Stay away from my blackjack tables."

Maya was the one who had banned him from the PH blackjack pit nearly two years ago. Unlike the gorillas at the Siegel, she had handled it with class - a firm but polite warning was all it took.

"I'll stick to craps tonight. Scout's honor."

"Glad to hear it." She flashed a quick smile, and he caught a glimpse of her teeth, perfect and pearly white behind dark red lips.

Over the past couple years, Carson and Maya had gotten to know each other fairly well. Guest relations were part of her job, but he felt like it was more than that. There was a real spark between them.

*At least, I *think* there's a spark.*

They'd even gone for drinks a few times after her shift... though only as friends and never on an actual "date".

"You file a police report on those Siegel jag-offs?" Maya asked.

"Figured it would be a waste of time."

"True enough," she agreed, rolling her eyes.

Maya had been a cop before she got the casino gig, but she didn't have much use for the police now. She'd once told Carson every officer on patrol in Vegas was just building up experience for their resumes so they could apply for a job with casino security. Better pay, easier work.

"Anyone half decent gets scooped up within three years," she'd explained once. *"The cops still on the job longer than that are either corrupt or incompetent."*

"I'm glad you came in tonight," she said, her hand dropping from Carson's arm. "Something I want to tell you when you have a minute."

The dice were calling, but for Maya he was willing to wait.

"I've got some time now."

She took him by the elbow and half guided, half dragged him away from the craps pit to a less crowded spot near the slot machines. After a quick glance to make sure nobody was close enough to hear them over the music blasting from the speakers overhead, she leaned in and spoke in a low voice.

"I'm not going to be working here much longer."

"Another casino making a bid to scoop you up?" Carson managed to ask after a moment of hesitation.

"Better. I've applied to the Bureau."

"The Bureau?"

"The FBI," she said with a grin, barely able to contain her excitement. "Been thinking about applying for a while now. Finally decided to write the entrance exam. Just got my results a couple days ago."

Always knew she was too good for this place.

"Let me guess - you passed the test with flying colors." Carson made sure his voice hid the disappointment he felt at the news.

Won't be the same around here with her gone.

"Don't spoil my story!" she objected, playfully punching him in the shoulder. "It's rude!"

"Sorry," he replied, sheepish. "Congrats."

"Thanks. Don't say anything, though. Haven't told anyone around here yet."

"You having a goodbye party?"

"Eventually. But I'm not leaving for a few weeks. The next class of recruits doesn't start until May, so I figure I'll work through March Madness. Rack up some OT before I start at the Academy.

"And it's still not official until I pass the fitness test," she added.

"Better hit the gym, then," Carson teased. "You're looking a little flabby lately."

She gasped in mock horror, then raised her right arm and cocked her elbow in the classic biceps pose.

"Feel these guns," she ordered. "Nothing flabby here!"

Carson reached out and gave her arm a gentle squeeze. Even through the fabric of her coat he could feel her muscle, taut and firm.

"Pretty good, right?"

"Exceptional," he agreed. Then added, "Who the hell am I going to shoot the shit with around here after you ditch me?"

"Look on the bright side," she replied. "Once I'm gone you can take another run at these blackjack tables.

"Just not tonight," she added quickly.

"Got it."

She spun away from him, heading off to another part of the casino.

"Good luck," she called out as she left.

Carson watched until she disappeared into the crowd. For months he'd been trying to work up the courage to ask Maya out. To tell her how he really felt about her. But he was worried how she'd react. Scared he might lose her as a friend. So he kept putting it off. And now it was too late.

Fucking coward. You had your chance and you blew it.

"Seven - out!" the stick man back at the craps table called, snapping Carson out of his pity party.

Quit mooning over Maya and focus on making some money.

He hustled back over to the table, his heart speeding up as the adrenaline rush of anticipation kicked in. The girl in the black dress wasn't throwing anymore, but most of the same people were still crowded around the game, yelling and laughing - a good sign that the table was still hot.

"Coming out!" the stick man hollered, indicating a new roll was about to start.

Perfect timing.

Squeezing in along the rail, he tossed his money down. Forty minutes later he was up almost two grand. But anybody could win money in Vegas; the real trick was not giving it back.

Step one - control the alcohol intake.

Rum and coke was his drink of choice, and he nursed each one. All he wanted was a mellow buzz to enhance the experience; he rarely went beyond that.

Step two - know when to walk away.

Counting cards was one thing; it wasn't even really gambling. Just grinding hour after hour after hour. A marathon. But craps was a sprint; a quick hit, the glorious rush of victory, and get out. And after two bad shooters in a row, he could tell the table had gone cold.

"Color me up," Carson called out, piling his chips on the table before the next roll started. His towering stacks of reds and greens were transformed into four pink chips, two blacks, and some change - roughly $2200.

"For the dealers," he said, tossing fifty bucks in leftover reds onto the table.

"Much appreciated, Mr. Gaines," the stickman said, raking them in and dropping them into the tip box.

Carson left the table smiling. The shit that went down at the Siegel had him thinking he was cursed. But since then he'd killed it on both his basketball plays and the craps table.

Maybe getting my ass kicked was a good omen.

Hot streaks never lasted long in Vegas; Carson was smart enough to know that much. But he had every intention of enjoying this ride while it lasted.

CHAPTER 4

Carson took the chips from the craps table over to the cash cage and exchanged them for hundred-dollar bills, then slipped them into his money clip. He was still amped from the rush of the table, his confidence high.

Looking for a distraction, he headed over to the Heart Bar in the center of the casino. The drinks there were overpriced, but he'd rather pay for his booze than risk his winnings by going straight to another table. He knew enough about how casinos worked to pace himself - the "free" drinks could get expensive.

The Heart Bar was small, but unlike the clubs there was no cover charge and no line to get in. About two dozen people mingled around inside, taking a break from the action on the casino floor, shouting at each other to be heard above the pounding music from the DJ booth in the corner. Couples were squished together on the loveseats and over-stuffed chairs lining the circular walls, laughing and drinking. Three dude-bros with Gonzaga hats, wearing Gonzaga tank-tops over Gonzaga t-shirts, were chatting up a bachelorette party. A gaggle of soccer moms were whooping it up on the dance floor, gyrating and grinding along with the thumping music, each of them raising the roof with one hand while clutching a yard-long margarita in the other.

Carson worked his way through the crowd and ordered a vodka red bull at the bar. Now that he wasn't gambling, he wanted something with a little kick extra kick. The first one went down easy. So did the second.

By the time he was onto his third, he noticed a pair of ladies sitting by themselves in the shadows near the back. The pale-skinned brunette was wearing a very short, very tight black cocktail dress, and her tanned, blonde friend was wearing a slinky gold number that showed a little less skin. They were both sipping on twisted crazy straws plunged into coconut half-shells. The brunette caught his eye and smiled in his direction.

In the low light of the bar, it was hard to tell for sure, but he guessed they were in their late twenties. Carson had been in Vegas long enough to spot a hooker from the other side of the Strip, but these girls didn't have that vibe. They were more cute than sexy, and they didn't carry the in-your-face attitude of a pro. Just two girlfriends on vacation, looking for a little adventure.

What happens in Vegas stays in Vegas.

It was amazing how many people actually bought into that slogan. He saw it all the time: women looking for a quick hook-up; something to feed the illusion that they were being wild and dangerous without any real risk. And Carson fit the profile perfectly. He was tall and in reasonably good shape. Decent looking. Well dressed. Most important, he looked like he belonged. He was comfortable and confident in the glittering madness - part of the whole Vegas experience, without too much of the sleaze. He could probably get laid every weekend if he wanted to. But the thrill of endless one-night stands had worn thin for him long ago. It wasn't that he never did it anymore; he just had to be in the right mood. Tonight, he was.

"Another vodka red bull for me, and two more of whatever those ladies are having."

The bartender whipped up the drinks while Carson tried to play it cool. He smiled back at the brunette and tilted his head in her direction. She laughed nervously and grabbed her friend's knee. The blonde eyed him suspiciously at first, but her expression softened to indifference after she gave him the once over and didn't see anything to set off any warning bells.

The bartender dropped the drinks on the bar. Carson scooped them up and headed over to where the women were sitting. He had his own drink clutched in his left hand, while the fingers of his right were splayed wide enough to grasp the two coconut-shell concoctions. The women watched him coming the whole way; the blonde apathetic, the brunette intrigued.

"Looks like you ladies need a refill," he said by way of introduction, holding out his gifts.

"Perfect timing - we just ran out!" the brunette answered enthusiastically as she wrapped both hands around one of the shells. The blonde only shrugged, but she still accepted his offer.

"Mind if I sit down?"

The brunette scooched closer to her friend and patted the couch beside her. "Got a spot right here for you!"

His weight caused the overstuffed cushion to sink down slightly as he settled in, tipping the brunette so that she slid right up against him. She giggled at the awkwardness but didn't pull away.

"I'm Maddie," she said, holding out her hand like the queen welcoming a visiting dignitary. "From Michigan."

Carson reached out, enveloping her hand with both of his.

"Hello, Maddie from Michigan. I'm Carson from Las Vegas."

"Ooh... I like your watch, Carson," she noted.

"Thanks. It was a gift from my father."

"I'm Sarah," her friend said abruptly, interrupting the flow of their banter. She leaned forward to look past Maddie and give Carson a nod but didn't bother offering her hand.

Carson was smart enough not to mention that Sarah was his ex-wife's name. Instead, he asked, "What brings you girls to my town?

"It's somebody's birthday," Maddie said in a sing-song voice, tilting her head in Sarah's direction.

"Happy birthday, Sarah!" Carson said, raising his drink.

"Hooray for me," she replied, her voice dripping with boredom.

"You two following March Madness?" Carson asked, hoping to find something that might spark Sarah's interest and draw her into the conversation before she tried to shut Maddie down. "The Spartans look strong this year."

"Fuck Michigan State!" Maddie bellowed, tipping her head back to holler at the ceiling. "Wolverines forever! Whooo!"

"Wolverines forever!" Sarah echoed, raising her drink to toast the team with actual enthusiasm.

Aha!

"I hate to burst your bubble, ladies," Carson said, shaking his head with mock sadness, "but I'm afraid your team doesn't stand a chance."

"We've been ranked top five all year!" Sarah shot back.

"That was before Irving blew out his knee. Without him, your team's cooked."

"Don't count Irving out yet," Maddie countered with a sly grin. "He might be coming back."

"Maddie!" Sarah hissed. "You're not supposed to tell anyone!"

Interesting.

"You girls got a hot tip or something?" Carson teased.

Maddie didn't say anything, but her smile spoke volumes. Instead of pressing her, Carson let the pause in the conversation linger. People were uncomfortable with silence; he'd learned they'd tell you all their secrets if you just gave them a chance.

Sure enough, Maddie leaned forward after a few seconds to spill her bit of juicy gossip.

"Sarah's uncle is one of the Wolverine trainers. He's been rehabbing Irving."

Sarah threw up her hands in exasperation. But Maddie was oblivious as she plowed on.

"He told us if the Wolverines make it through this weekend, Irving is going to play in the Sweet Sixteen."

The revelation was a key piece of data for Carson to add into his models... assuming it was true.

"Your secret is safe with me, ladies," Carson swore, placing his hand over his heart. "Scout's honor."

"What happened to your face?" Sarah suddenly demanded, clearly eager to change the subject. "You fall down the stairs?"

"Sarah!" Maddie gasped, playfully slapping her friend's thigh.

"It's okay," Carson reassured her. "I'm a card counter. Ran into some trouble a few days ago. Hazard of the profession."

Maddie's eyes went wide with excitement. "Really? What happened?"

Carson paused, letting the tension build. Maddie was clearly hooked, and even Sarah seemed mildly interested in the answer.

He took a deep breath, then opened with, "You ladies ever been to a casino called the Siegel?"

And just like that, he was in. As he spun his story, he bought them another round of drinks. They talked some more. They laughed. They danced and drank. Eventually the three of them walked over to the Karaoke bar in the adjacent Miracle Mile strip mall and sang their hearts out.

Four hours after they first met, Carson had Sarah bent over the bed in her hotel room, the two of them going at it like rabbits.

"Fuck me like you mean it!" she shouted.

He'd pegged Maddie as the one looking for a Vegas fling, but life was full of surprises.

"Harder! Harder!"

Turned out, Maddie had a boyfriend back in Michigan. Sarah, not so much.

"Pull my hair!"

Carson didn't argue; he just obeyed while thrusting wildly into her from behind.

"Oh, God! Oh, Jesus Christ!" she wailed. "Oh, God! Oh... my... guhhh!"

Her words transformed into animalistic grunts and moans. One hand reached back to claw at Carson's naked thigh while the other braced her body against the mattress as she savagely ground into him. Her moans put him over the top; he was ready to explode.

*** *FREEZE!* ***

Carson always stopped the world right before he climaxed.

Is that weird? Maybe. But I can't help it. It just sort of happens.

He'd been doing it ever since he was a teenager rubbing one out into an old sock, and some habits were hard to break.

Doesn't make my orgasm any better. I can't feel anything when the world is frozen.

It was purely a mental exercise; a way to savor the moment. With the world in stasis, he could fully appreciate the curve of Sarah's hips and buttocks. Or the way her hair cascaded over her one shoulder with her head turned back to look at him.

But it wasn't just about appreciating the moment. Inevitably, he always fell into self-analysis, rating his performance while the world was stopped.

Tonight I'd give myself a solid B+.

It had only been fifteen minutes since they'd reached the room and started ripping off each other's clothes. But what they lacked in endurance they made up for with intensity.

Sarah seemed to enjoy it, at least.

The women usually did, but Carson knew that didn't have much to do with him. Most of the girls he hooked up with in Vegas were already halfway there. They'd built the whole encounter up in their mind as something wild, dangerous, and dirty. Carson understood he was just playing a part in their fantasy.

All I have to do is show up, shut up, and keep it up and they usually get off.

In the end, it wasn't a bad deal. A little harmless entertainment and everyone ended up satisfied. No regrets, no guilt.

**** GO! ****

As the world started up again the incoming wave of sexual ecstasy crashed over him.

Boom goes the dynamite.

Twenty minutes later they were still cuddling on the bed, but Carson could feel it was starting to get uncomfortable. They were both a little drunk, but still sober enough to be aware of the awkwardness between them now that the deed was done.

This was always the worst time for him. It wasn't likely they'd ever see each other again, but he didn't want to be rude.

No point ending her Vegas fantasy-fling on a sour note.

Problem was, he never knew which way to play it. If he made some lame excuse and left, he'd seem like an insensitive asshole. But if he stayed too long, he'd seem like some kind of clingy stalker.

While Carson was debating his next move, Sarah turned her head towards the clock by the bedside.

"Three-thirty," she muttered. "Didn't realize it was so late."

"That's okay," he answered, relieved as he rolled out from under the sheets. "I should probably be going anyway."

She watched him gather up his clothes without speaking. He dressed quickly, but not so fast that it seemed like he was trying to escape. She only broke her silence once he was heading towards the door.

"Hey... it was fun."

Carson smiled and nodded, then slipped out into the hall. The door to her room closed behind him with a sharp *click.*

He took the elevator back down to the casino floor. It was late enough that most of the crowd had thinned out. But Maya was still working.

Carson noticed her watching him from the far side of the mostly empty casino.

Shit. Did she see me go up to Sarah's room?

There was no reason for him to feel guilty; it wasn't like he and Maya were dating. But he still felt his cheeks flushing with embarrassment as he made his way over to her.

"Saw you escorting that little blonde up to her room earlier," she said by way of greeting.

Her voice was light and easy; clearly his liaison didn't bother her at all.

I kind of wish it did.

"You keeping tabs on me now?" Carson answered, matching her tone. "If I didn't know better, I'd say you were jealous."

"Of a casino bunny?" Maya snorted. "Please."

"Come on," Carson said, hoping she wouldn't notice how red-faced he was getting. "You telling me you've never had a one-night stand?"

Maya held up her hands defensively.

"Hey, I'm not judging. I'm just surprised you're back so soon. Figured you'd have a bit more stamina."

"Ouch!"

"Call 'em like I see 'em," she said with a shrug. "You out of here?"

Carson knew her shift was almost over, and for one brief moment he thought about asking her to grab a drink when she got off. But in the end he couldn't pull the trigger.

"Yeah, I'm heading home. Busy day tomorrow. But if you're up for it, maybe we can do drinks again sometime before you head off to join the FBI."

Non-committal. Safe. Cowardly.

"I'd like that," Maya said, smiling. "What about that place we went to a couple months ago. Wolf something."

"Sparrow and Wolf."

"Right!" Maya laughed. "I'm surprised you remember – you got so drunk I had to drive you home!"

*** *FREEZE!* ***

Carson remembered that night all too well: a small restaurant/bar; romantic atmosphere; amazing custom cocktails. A tiny, intimate table.

She looked incredible. She always looks amazing, but something about her was different that night. It was like she was glowing!

He had wanted to kiss her. He had wanted to tell her that they should be more than just friends. But, just like tonight, he didn't have the nerve. So he'd just kept drinking, hoping enough liquid courage would spur him into action.

Instead, I got so stumbling drunk Maya had to half-carry me out of there.

But that wasn't the worst of it. She drove him home, and during the ride he'd shared his deepest secret with her. He told her he could stop time – the first time he'd told anyone since he was a child.

In a slurred, rambling, barely coherent monologue he had tried to explain his power to her – what it was; how it worked. Of course, she didn't believe him.

She laughed. She thought it was some kind of weird joke. Not surprising, given how drunk I was.

Looking back the next day, he'd been so embarrassed he actually avoided coming to PH for a couple weeks. When he finally got up the guts to return, Maya never mentioned it. Neither did he. They just carried on like it never happened.

Probably for the best.

Now she wanted to go back to the scene of his humiliation. But why? Had Maya sensed what he was thinking that night? Did she know how he really felt about her?? Was suggesting they go back there again a signal that she was interested in him, too? Or was she just craving the octopus appetizer and another of their Famous Freddy Fender whiskey highballs?

Shit. Quit over-analyzing everything. For once, just say yes and take the win!

**** GO! ****

"Sparrow and Wolf sounds good," Carson told her, his heart pounding so fast he was feeling light-headed. "But this time I'll try to pace myself a little better with the alcohol."

"Good plan," she said with a coy wink.

She leaned in and gave him a goodbye hug. Then, as he turned to go, she gave him another hard slap on the ass.

"Don't go looking for trouble, Carson."

"Never do." *But sometimes trouble just has a way of finding me.*

CHAPTER 5

The Sunday games weren't as profitable as the first round, but Carson still managed to keep his lucky streak going. Between the basketball and his run at the craps table, he was up almost five grand on the weekend. When the time for his Monday night call with Ella arrived, Carson was riding high and feeling good. But his mood changed quickly when he saw his ex-wife's expression on the video chat.

"Sarah? What's wrong?"

Her face was drawn, and her eyes were puffy, as if she'd spent all night crying instead of sleeping.

"Ella's asleep. We were at the specialist all day running tests. She's exhausted."

From her tone, Carson knew it wasn't good news.

"What did they find?"

Sarah shook her head and shrugged. "Nothing yet. They want to run more tests later this week. Maybe try some new drugs. Greg and I... we're trying to figure it out."

"What's there to figure out?" Carson demanded. "Just run the damn tests. If they want to change her meds, change her meds. Keep trying until we get this right!"

Sarah was silent for a long moment. When she spoke, her voice was barely more than a whisper.

"Greg's insurance won't cover it."

"Wait. This is about *money?*"

"Of course it's about money!" Sarah snapped back at him, her voice cracked and raw. "Do you have any idea how much all this costs?"

Jesus Christ – she's our daughter!

"Run the tests. I'll pay for them."

Sarah snorted in contempt. "How the hell are you going to do that? You don't even have a job!"

"Bullshit! You know I'm a professional gambler."

"That's not a job. That's a hustle."

"It pays my bills!" Carson fired back, not bothering to mention he was supplementing his income as an Uber drive now.

"I'm tired, Carson," Sarah said. "I don't want to do this tonight."

"I'll transfer you some money tomorrow," Carson insisted. "Five grand. I've had a good run lately."

"You think that will cover Sarah's medical bills?" she said, barking out a harsh laugh. "You really think Greg and I couldn't come up with five fucking thousand dollars on our own?"

Carson was stung into shamed silence by her words.

After a few seconds, Sarah closed her eyes, tilted her head back and took a deep breath as she tried to calm herself down. It was a reaction Carson recognized all too well from the days of their marriage.

"I'm sorry," Carson said. "I just want to help. How much are we talking about?"

"I know you want to be the hero here," Sarah countered, "but it's not that simple. Don't worry - Greg and I will figure something out."

"How... much?" Carson asked again, speaking each word slowly and forcefully.

Sarah hesitated before admitting, "The estimate they gave us on Friday was just over eighty thousand dollars."

Jesus Christ!

"And the worst part is, they can't even promise it'll work," she continued. "Nobody really knows what's wrong with her. They're just guessing at this point."

"You weren't even going to tell me about this, were you?" Carson snapped, his words dripping with accusation and resentment despite his best intentions.

"Oh, I'm sorry. I didn't realize you had an extra eighty grand lying around!" his ex-wife snapped back at him. "Guess all I had to do was ask, right? Thank God! Problem fucking solved!"

*** *FREEZE!* ***

Carson stopped the world before he said something even more hurtful in response. He needed time to think. Time to compose himself.

Lashing out at Sarah isn't going to help Ella. It'll probably just make things worse.

It was always easy to take the high road when he didn't have the adrenaline rush of emotions clouding his thoughts.

But in this case, it's important to remember we're both on the same side.

*** *GO!* ***

"I'm sorry," Carson told her, lowering his voice. "I'm just worried about Ella. And I know you are too."

Sarah sighed in acknowledgment of the apology. When she spoke again, the anger was gone. Or at least carefully buried.

"Greg and I are trying to work something out. Maybe a second mortgage. Something."

From the slight tremble in her voice Carson could tell she was barely holding it together.

"I'll send you the five grand," Carson vowed. "I know it's not much, but it's better than nothing. And we'll figure this out somehow. I promise."

Sarah forced a smile and nodded, but in her eyes Carson saw how scared and desperate she was.

"I should let you go," he said, filling in the uncomfortable looming silence. "Tell Ella I love her. Maybe I can call in a few days when she's rested up."

Sarah nodded again, then abruptly ended the call.

It's like she was afraid if she tried to speak, she'd break down completely.

Carson stared at the disconnected screen for a few seconds, trying to wrap his head around the price tag of his daughter's health.

Eighty thousand dollars!

Carson was a realist. He understood numbers and data. He knew the math. Eighty thousand was a big number. Overwhelming. Logically, there wasn't anything more he could do. But logic didn't count for much when it came to the well-being of his daughter.

There has to be something I can do. Some angle I'm not seeing.

Unbidden, his mind flashed back to Friday night at the Heart Bar.

Maddie said Irving was going to play if the Wolverines got past the second round.

The Wolverines had won on Sunday, barely scraping by to advance in the tournament. But there hadn't been any rumblings about their star player returning. Not yet. If Irving really was on the verge of playing again, they'd managed to keep the news out of the media so far.

Normally, Carson would never make a wager based on a tip he'd picked up in a bar. He preferred stats and analysis to unsubstantiated rumors. And he knew the Wolverines were heavy underdogs going into their next game. But Irving was the kind of player who could single-handedly lead his team to a National Championship. If Maddie was right – if Irving actually played – it would completely flip the odds. And nobody else knew about it. At least, not yet.

It's a risk, but it's my best chance to help Ella. Gotta ride the hot streak as long as it lasts.

News like this was bound to leak before the game, and once it did the betting line would change. If he wanted to take advantage of his inside info, he had to act fast.

Time to go see Mama Pearl.

***

Ten minutes later he was driving across town. Staring through the windscreen, he couldn't help but notice how shitty the city looked in the early evening sun. Vegas was meant to be seen at night. The glittering lights and flashing neon signs on the Strip might be tacky, but there was something alluring about them. Tempting. Tantalizing. In the fading daylight, though, everything just looked tired and worn. Run down. It exposed the city for what it really was: a grimy, dusty mirage of cracking concrete and melting asphalt plopped down in the middle of the god-damned desert.

And yet I chose to come live here. Just one in a string of many questionable life decisions.

The traffic was light, and it didn't take long to reach his destination: Flannigan's on D Street - a small hole-in-the-wall bar in one of Vegas's most rough and rundown neighborhoods.

He pulled up and parked right in front, underneath a sign that said LOADING ZONE – 15 MIN ONLY!

Plenty of time... I hope.

The inside of Flannigan's was a stereotypical dingy Irish dive bar. Poor lighting, out of date decor, a couple crappy TVs mounted at either end of the bar. A few regulars sitting on stools at the bar, some empty booths. A couple dusty old pool tables in the back.

"Hey, Carson," the bartender greeted him. "I'll go grab your money from the back."

"Actually, Jimmy, I'm here to see Mama."

Jimmy hesitated a moment, then nodded.

"Grab a seat. I'll tell her you're here."

Carson found a spot at one of the booths in the corner as the bartender disappeared into the back. A few seconds later he returned, followed by a mature Chinese woman wearing a cream-colored pantsuit covered in bright yellow flowers.

Mama Pearl was tiny - five feet tall and ninety pounds soaking wet. Her black, bobbed hair was short but thick, forming a semi-circular frame around the noticeable wrinkles of her face. She wore too much makeup, and her silver necklace and oversized matching earrings were cheap and tacky looking. Her age was difficult to peg; she could have been anywhere from fifty to eighty.

Flanking her on either side were two very large Latino men in expensive suits. Carson noticed the butt of a pistol in a shoulder holster peeking out from beneath the coat of the man on the left.

"Carson!" Mama Pearl called out, extending her arms as she approached. Carson obliged and stood up to receive an overly enthusiastic hug. "So nice to see you!"

She spoke with a thick Chinese accent, but sometimes Carson noticed it slipped just a little. He had a sneaking suspicion that the whole "Mama Pearl" thing was an act. There were rumors she had connections to the Hong Kong Triads, but he wondered if she'd made those up herself.

If she really works for the Triads, why aren't her bodyguards Asian?

Mama broke off the hug, then she slid into the booth across from Carson. Her bodyguards stood a respectful distance away, hands clasped calmly at their waists.

"You did good last week," she noted. "Lots of winners for Mama to pay out."

She bubbled with energy, her words quick, clipped, and always verging on a shout.

"I did okay," Carson answered modestly. *My wins are her losses. No point in rubbing it in her face.* "Guess I'm on a lucky streak."

"Not that lucky, maybe," she said, leaning forward to gently tap the faded scrape on his chin.

"No big deal," he assured her, mildly surprised she could make out his mostly healed injuries under the crappy neon lights.

Don't underestimate her. She's sharp and she's dangerous.

"You drink?" she offered. "Rum and coke, yes?"

Carson shook his head. "A little early for me."

Plus, the drinks here taste like warm, watered-down piss.

Mama Pearl hadn't bought Flannigan's to make money serving booze. The bar was just a front; a way to launder cash from her real business: one of the biggest illegal books in Vegas.

It wasn't easy being a bookie in a town where anyone could walk into a casino and place a bet twenty-four/seven. To compete, Mama Pearl had to offer certain advantages.

It started with a lower vig. Instead of the standard ten percent bookie fee, Mama Pearl only charged eight. Two percent might not seem like much, but over the course of the year it added up. More importantly, though, she let players bet on credit. The casinos all demand cash up front. By leveraging his credit line with Mama Pearl, Carson could maximize the edge on his bets.

Only this time I need to push things to a whole new level.

"What you want, Carson?"

"I need to extend my line of credit."

Mama pursed her lips, studying him closely. Carson had proven himself to be a reliable customer: if he lost, he always paid his debts on time. But she knew he was on a hot streak. Asking for extra credit when he already had several thousand in his account was unusual.

"How much you want?"

Carson had given a lot of consideration to that exact question. Mama typically let him run about five grand through her operation; add in the five thousand he was already up and he had 10k to wager. Double that with a big win on the Michigan game, and it still wasn't enough to cover Sarah's medical bills.

And that's just the up-front costs. If the new therapies work, the final cost could be way over the initial estimate.

"I want to place a bet for fifty grand."

The only sign of surprise Mama showed was a slight arching of one eyebrow.

"That a lot of money, Carson."

It was. But if he won, he'd have plenty to cover Sarah's costs... and maybe even a little left over for himself. And if he lost, it didn't really matter whether he owed Mama fifty thousand, or a hundred thousand, or a million – there was no way he could ever pay it back. If the Wolverines lost, this ended only one of two ways: with Carson on the run, or in a shallow grave out in the Nevada desert.

Hopefully, she doesn't know that, though.

"Why you so desperate, Carson?"

"I'm not desperate. I've just got a hot tip. One I can't pass up."

Mama nodded slowly, sensing this much at least was true.

"How you pay me back if you lose?"

"My parents. They've got money."

"So ask them to front you."

"They don't approve of gambling," Carson lied, leaning into the backstory he'd prepared. "They won't give it to me just so I can make a bet. But they'll give it to me if I need to pay you back. They know what will happen if I don't. Parents will do anything to protect their kid."

A flat out lie wrapped around a single grain of universal truth. The question is, will she buy it?

After several long seconds of silence, Mama finally said, "I need collateral."

"Hold onto the money I won this week."

"Not enough," she countered, shaking her head.

Carson had suspected she might push back on him. He reached into his jacket pocket, pulled out a leather case, and set it on the table. Then he popped it open to reveal his Rolex Submariner.

"My father gave this to me when I graduated high school. Worth twenty grand."

More like ten, but at this point what's a little more embellishment?

Mama picked up the watch and hefted it in her hand, as if she could verify the authenticity simply by weight. Then she set the watch back in the case and closed the lid. Carson's heart was pounding, but he did his best to keep his breathing slow and his demeanor calm.

"Not enough. What kind car you drive?"

"Nissan maxima. A couple years old."

"You leave car here. And watch. Plus, Mama get ten percent if you win."

*** *FREEZE!* ***

It was an outrageous – almost offensive – proposition. Bookies never took a cut from the winnings; it simply wasn't done. Basically, she was offering to front him the money, lay off the bets with other bookies to minimize her exposure, and then charge him 10% for the service. If he won, she made a cool five grand, with no risk. And if he lost, he'd have to cover the entire bet... plus an extra few thousand for her normal vig.

My watch. My car. My pride. She's got me by the balls, and she knows it.

Statistically, there was no way to come out ahead with terms like this. Not in the long run. It was a total sucker's play. But Carson was out of options. And so was Ella.

**** GO! ****

Ignoring every instinct that told him to get up and walk away, Carson forced a smile.

"Mama," he said, handing over his keys, "you've got yourself a deal."

CHAPTER 6

The day before Michigan's Sweet Sixteen game, rumors started leaking out that Irving would suit up. Money poured in on the Wolverines as frantic gamblers tried to get a piece of the action. By tip-off, the Wolverines had gone from nearly double-digit underdogs to four-point favorites.

Thanks to his early tip, Carson had his bets down at the original number. Michigan didn't even have to win. They just had to keep it close. If they lost by 9 points or less, he would still cash in.

The first half couldn't have gone better. Irving poured in twenty-two points, and the Wolverines were up by six. And then just before halftime, it all came undone. Irving stole the ball and went in for a thunderous breakaway dunk. But as he rose up from the floor, he let out a scream. The ball flew from his hands as he clutched at his knee and came crashing back down to the ground.

In that instant, Carson knew it was over.

There was no way to say for sure whether Irving had come back too soon and pushed his still healing body beyond its limits, or whether it was just a fluke injury that would have happened even if he was healthy and rested. And ultimately, it didn't matter. Michigan's star player - Carson's secret weapon - was done for the season.

It only took five minutes in the second half for the Wolverines to give up their lead. After ten minutes, they were down by seven. The injury to Irving had completely demoralized his team: crushed their dreams and ripped out their hearts.

With four minutes to go, they were down by sixteen and Carson was already packing. By the time the final buzzer sounded, he was at the Las Vegas Greyhound terminal, trying to sneak out of town before Mama or her goons knew he was gone. Running was a foolish, desperate move. But it was the only move he had left.

Guess my hot streak is over.

Mama Pearl still had his car, so he'd grabbed an Uber and got a lift to the downtown Greyhound station. He knew he should be terrified about what Mama would do to him if she caught him trying to skip town, but as he bought his ticket it wasn't fear that he felt. It was just a crushing, hopeless sense of defeat.

Ella needed me. And I let her down.

He'd thought about heading to LA, but on the off-chance Mama tracked him down he didn't want to risk putting his daughter – or Sarah – in danger. So he was heading east. Phoenix to start. Then maybe on to New Orleans.

Gotta put some distance between me and Mama.

But that meant moving even farther away from Ella. And then trying to explain to Sarah why he moved in a way that wouldn't make her cut him out of Ella's life completely.

Couldn't blame her if she did. Ella might be better off without me. A broke, gambling addict on the run from his bookie... what kid needs that?

As he waited for his bus, the feeling of despair began to recede. And now the fear began to trickle in to fill the void. It started in the pit of his stomach - a sense of looming dread and impending doom.

You're being ridiculous. Mama won't be looking for you yet. You still have until tomorrow night to pay her back.

Despite his own reassurances, Carson couldn't stop his eyes from darting back and forth across the other patrons in the terminal. When he spotted a large, bearded white guy in a black leather jacket, he almost panicked. The man looked to be about thirty-five; six-three and 220 pounds of muscle and attitude. Based on his size and expression, he looked like the kind of guy who might break legs for a living... the kind of guy Mama would send to collect her money.

Except that he didn't seem to be looking for anyone. The bearded man wasn't scanning the crowd, trying to pick anyone out. He was just making his way along and minding his own business like everyone else.

You're being paranoid. Jumping at shadows.

Carson took a few deep breaths to calm his nerves.

You're good. Just stay calm, get on the bus, and you're home free.

But a few seconds later, when Carson saw the woman with the platinum hair and the long white jacket - the one who helped him outside the Siegel Suites - he panicked.

**** FREEZE! ****

Stopping time was instinctive; a gut reaction to the woman's unexpected appearance. By coincidence, he'd frozen the world with his own focus directly on the woman. Like everyone else in the crowd, they were both completely motionless.

Carson he studied her features intently, hoping to find some hint of why she was here in her expression.

Maybe she works for Mama.

That didn't make any sense. But seeing her at the bus station while he was about to skip town was too much of a coincidence for Carson to ignore.

Maybe she's been following me ever since that night at the Siegel. Or maybe she was following me even before that!

It would explain how she had showed up when the security goons worked him over. But that wouldn't explain why she had bothered to step in and save him, though. Or why she would have been following him in the first place.

None of this makes any sense.

There had to be some explanation, but Carson couldn't afford to figure it out right now. Not if he wanted to stay one step ahead of Mama's goons.

Just stick to the plan and get on that bus.

She wasn't looking in his direction. She'd been frozen with her head turned so that her gaze was focused on the other side of the station.

Maybe I can just slip away. Blend in with the crowd and disappear before she... what... the... fuck?

The rest of the world was still frozen. Every soul in the bus station - including Carson himself - was trapped in place, still as statues. Except for one person – the bearded man in the leather jacket was moving!

No. This isn't possible.

On an intellectual level, Carson was completely stunned. But the emotional numbness that enveloped him during stasis kept him from completely freaking out. Instead, he studied the unprecedented development with a pure, clinical detachment.

The man was making his way carefully through the crowd, moving slowly with heavy and deliberate steps. Methodical. Forced. Like he was wading through waist high water and fighting against the current; or slogging his way through a pit of mud.

He was heading in Carson's general direction, but it didn't seem like the bearded man was coming after him. His focus was on someone else - a young white woman in a red coat with a large brown handbag slung over her shoulder.

Fascinated, Carson watched as the man's plodding progress finally brought him to the young woman's side. Then he reached into her oversized purse and started rummaging around.

Holy shit – he's robbing her!

The realization did nothing to satisfy Carson's curiosity. There were still so many unanswered questions. Who was he? Was he connected to the woman with the platinum hair? How come he wasn't frozen like everyone else?

And does he know I'm the one who made time stop?

*** --- ***

The last thought was disturbing enough to break Carson's concentration, and the world snapped back into motion unbidden. As the scene reanimated, the bearded man quickly tried to snatch his hand out of the woman's bag... but not quite fast enough. She turned her head and she saw what he was doing.

"Help!" she screamed, clutching her bag to her chest as she stumbled away from him. "Thief!" Her high voice pierced the general din of the crowded station, drawing everyone's attention. "Thief! Help! Thief! Thief!"

The bearded man spun on his heel and took off in the opposite direction, shoving people left and right as he plowed through the crowd, heading towards the steps leading back up to the street.

Knowing he couldn't let the man simply disappear, Carson took off in chase, even though he had no idea what he'd do or say if he caught up to him.

A good Samaritan jumped out from the crowd and tried to tackle the thief as he ran by. He grabbed the bearded man's jacket by the collar, yanking him backwards. The thief spun and twisted, one arm slipping free of his coat sleeve as he wheeled on the interloper. The bearded man lashed out at the Samaritan, dropping him with a short, sharp punch to the throat. The would-be hero crumpled to the ground, choking and gasping for air.

The thief jammed his arm back into his jacket sleeve and took off towards the exit again. The crowd parted quickly before him, nobody eager to become his next victim.

"Wait!" Carson called out as he shoved his way through the throng of bodies between them. He waved his arm high above his head in a vain attempt to get the man's attention. "Hold on! Stop!"

His words had no effect. The man took the stairs three at a time, bounding towards the exit doors at the top. Carson's instincts kicked in and he did what he always did when he was desperate.

**** FREEZE! ****

The world stopped. Carson hovered in the air between strides, his arm raised like he was hailing a cab. But the bearded man didn't stop. He wasn't frozen with the rest of the world. He just continued his escape, though he was moving slower now. Like he was running through glue.

Carson's mind was going in a thousand different directions at once. He couldn't seem to process what was happening as his quarry reached the station's exit.

Where are you going? I need to talk to you!

Straining with the effort, the man yanked the door open. And all Carson could do was watch, helpless and paralyzed.

Shit – unfreeze the world, dumbass!

***** GO! *****

Time cranked up again and the bearded man continued his escape, vanishing through the door and out into the street. The woman he'd tried to rob was still screaming for help, and people in the crowd were still pushing and shoving each other - some trying to get out of the way, others trying to get closer so they'd have a better view of what was happening. A few were looking around, bewildered by the sudden disappearance of the bearded man who - from their perspective - had been right there only an instant earlier. But in the chaos and confusion of his escape, nobody seemed to grasp exactly what had happened.

Nobody but me.

Separated by the length of half a bus station and a crowd of a few dozen people, Carson was forced to accept that the bearded man was gone. He slowed his pursuit just as he reached the Samaritan who'd been punched in the throat. He dropped to one knee to join the small crowd tending to the failed vigilante. His face was red and sweaty, but he seemed to be breathing okay.

With their attention focused on the victim, none of the people gathered around had noticed the wallet laying on the floor.

The bearded man must have dropped it. Probably fell from his coat when the other guy grabbed him.

***** FREEZE! *****

Carson's mind was still spinning, trying to piece together everything that had just happened.

His entire life, he'd thought he was alone in the world. Unique. Blessed and cursed with an amazing power nobody else could ever understand.

But the bearded man hadn't seemed surprised when the world around him stopped. He didn't react with horror or confusion. It was almost like he was expecting it.

How is that possible?

There were so many questions rattling in Carson's head it was hard to think straight, even with the world stopped.

Why was the man here? Was it just a freak coincidence they'd crossed paths in a Vegas bus station?

And what about the platinum-haired woman?

Carson couldn't see her right now, but his attention was focused on the man on the floor.

Is she still here? Is she part of this?

**** GO! ****

Carson stood up, casually placing his foot over the wallet to hide it from view. At the same time, he scanned the crowd. But the platinum-haired woman, like the bearded man, had vanished.

Are they connected somehow? Working together? Is that why she took off?

He only had one clue to go on. He dropped back to his knee as if checking on the fallen Samaritan again, leaning forward so he could reach down and cover the fallen wallet with a wide-splayed palm.

"Is he okay?" he asked of no one in particular.

"I think so," a middle-aged woman tending to him replied.

The man nodded. He seemed to be doing better, though his face was still red and he was rubbing his injured windpipe.

"Everybody give him some air!" Carson called out, standing up and stepping back.

In a crisis, people wanted direction. When something unexpected happened - an accident, an incident - they wanted an authority figure to take charge. They didn't question orders, they just followed them.

"You two, help him to his feet."

As the people complied with his instructions, Carson slipped the wallet he'd scooped up into his pocket. Nobody noticed. Everyone in the bus station was either focused on the man being helped back to his feet; or trying to calm the distraught woman he'd tried to rob; or trying to figure out where the thief had suddenly disappeared to.

A few more people pressed in to check on the fallen would-be hero.

"Don't worry," someone assured him. "I called the police."

Out of the corner of his eye, Carson noticed a security guard coming towards them.

He didn't really want to answer any questions - *what could I even say?* - so he took a step back and allowed himself to blend into the crowd of onlookers. Moving calmly and casually, he worked his way towards the exit, scanning the station in case anyone else was watching him. Coming up empty, he climbed the steps and slipped out into the night.

He walked a few blocks away before stopping under a streetlight and pulling out the wallet to look for some type of ID. There was $180 cash in the bill fold. A fistful of credit cards. And four driver's licenses.

Each one was from a different state and bore a different name. Robert Wilson from New York. Charles Smith from Michigan. Frederick Greene from Texas. John Goldman from LA.

Carson took a closer look at the credit cards. Some had names that matched the driver's licenses, but others didn't: Paul Flemming; Christopher Barnes; Jason King.

He chewed his lips, uncertain of what to make of his discovery. All thoughts of skipping town were gone. His entire life he'd had questions about his unique - and mostly useless - talent. Now, for the first time, there might be someone who could give him answers.

Maybe there's a way to use this.

There were still things he had to figure out. A thousand implications and possibilities to piece together. But a plan was starting to form in Carson's mind. A way he could still help Ella and get out from under Mama Pearl's thumb. But it all relied on finding the bearded man.

And I just let him vanish out the bus station door.

CHAPTER 7

Name's Charlie. Not Chuck. Not fucking Charles. Charlie. Last name? It doesn't fucking matter.

Charlie had grown up in the system. Foster care and group homes when he was younger, then out on the streets at sixteen. He'd been living off the grid ever since. No parents. No family. No social security number. And, at least so far, no rap sheet.

Pretty impressive, considering I'm a fucking thief.

Charlie was huffing and puffing, arms and legs pumping furiously as he sprinted down the dimly lit streets outside the bus station. He took a left at the end of the block, then a right at the next corner before slowing his stride and checking for signs of pursuit.

Nothing. Got away clean.

He'd come to Vegas to get a fresh start. Walking through the crowded bus terminal, he hadn't been planning on stealing anything. But when the world around him stopped moving, his instincts had kicked in.

Didn't figure the timeout would end that fast.

Charlie had no clue why the entire world would sometimes suddenly stop moving all around him. He never knew when it would happen, or how long it would last. There was never any warning, and no pattern he'd ever figured out. But he'd learned to take advantage of it.

He could always tell the instant it happened, and not just because everyone else stopped moving. The world felt different in a timeout. The air got thick. Sticky. The simple act of breathing took conscious effort. Actually moving around took even more effort. Everything felt heavier than normal; grabbing a wallet felt like lifting a twenty-pound dumbbell. Every time the world stopped, he got a hell of a workout... and he had the muscles to show for it.

The incident at the bus station wasn't the first time he'd been caught with his hand in the cookie jar. It probably wouldn't be the last. On some level, knowing he might get caught only added to the thrill.

When Charlie was a kid, he'd done plenty of stupid things in time-outs, like yanking some random guy's pants down around his ankles, underwear and all.

Laugh my ass off when the world started moving again and he's caught with his dick flapping in the wind.

As a teenager, he'd lifted up girls' shirts or skirts to cop a feel.

Makes me sound like a pervert, but I was just a horny kid. Any guy who says he wouldn't have done the same at that age is a fucking liar.

But even with puberty running the show, that got old after a while.

Grabbing a girl's tits or ass in a timeout isn't sexy. The flesh has no give; it's like squeezing a piece of hard plastic. Fondling a mannequin. Not worth it.

Now whenever the world froze, he just took stuff.

Charlie liked to keep things simple. Picking pockets. Grabbing a purse off the back of a chair in a coffee shop when a woman ducked into the restroom. Scooping up a phone or a laptop or a wallet from a table or bar when someone wasn't paying attention. The old grab and go.

He didn't even feel bad about it. He'd learned early on that if you want something in life, you have to take it. That's how the world worked. And anyone too stupid, lazy or careless to protect their shit deserved to get it stolen.

Still feeling amped after his recent getaway, Charlie reached into his jacket for his cigarettes. It was only then that he realized his wallet was missing.

"MOTHER FUCKER!"

He knew right away what had happened.

Fell out when that prick grabbed my sleeve.

The karmic irony of losing a wallet full of fake IDs and forged credit cards because he tried to steal a woman's purse wasn't lost on him, but it didn't make him feel any better.

"Fuck! Fuck, fuck, fucking MOTHER FUCKER!"

He snapped his head from side to side, looking for anyone nearby who might have reacted to his outburst. Someone who might take offense and want to say something. Start something. Someone dumb enough to give him an excuse to go ballistic and beat the shit out of them. But the streets were deserted.

With nothing to focus his anger on, his rage faded quickly. As he cooled off, he considered his options. Going back to the bus station was out of the question; the wallet and everything in it was gone. But he still had two hundred dollars stuffed into his right sock - enough to get a meal and a room at some shitty flop-house motel for a couple nights.

Not the welcome I was hoping for, but I've been in tougher spots.

He lit a cigarette, took a few puffs, then tossed it to the ground.

"Fuck this city," he grumbled, stomping the butt out with his heel before marching off with long, purposeful strides towards a glowing VACANCY sign in the distance.

***

Later that night, Charlie made the twenty-minute walk from his shitty hotel to Freemont Street, the bustling downtown core of old Las Vegas. Charlie had spent his entire life drifting up and down the East Coast. He'd visited his share of casinos in Atlantic City, and he'd watched plenty of movies and tv shows set in Vegas. But none of that prepared him for what he was seeing now.

Freemont Street wasn't anywhere close to the Strip, so the hotels and casinos here needed a hook to bring customers in. Their answer: Viva Vision; a 1,500-foot long, 90-foot wide LED screen covering a five-block stretch like a flashing neon roof.

Beneath the pulsing, glowing lightshow of the makeshift ceiling was a massive pedestrian plaza, overflowing with thousands of tourists. Speakers pumped out non-stop rock music, choreographed with animated lightshow performances on the LED screen above.

Costumed street performers wandered among the crowd, doing dances, acrobatics, magic - anything that might earn them a few bucks from the milling masses. Tiny gift shops and food vendors lined either side of the street, wedged in between casinos like the Golden Nugget and the Four Queens. Outside of every casino entrance scantily clad showgirls beckoned passers-by to come in and try their luck, while screaming guests whizzed by twenty feet overhead, dangling from the zip-lines that ran up and down the street.

It's like the bastard child of Times Square and Disneyland.

Fortunately for Charlie, the chaos of the scene was exactly what he needed.

Time to get to work.

Elvis's classic homage to Sin City started up, blaring from the speakers. Smiling, Charlie slipped into the crowd, singing along softly under his breath.

"Bright light city gonna set my soul, set my soul on fire..."

In the ocean of bodies, it was impossible not to bump, push and shove against others every step of the way - the perfect distraction for an accomplished pickpocket like Charlie.

"Got a whole lot of money that's ready to burn, so set those stakes up higher..."

Stealing during a timeout was easier, of course. But Charlie didn't like to wait, and in the chaos and confusion of Freemont Street he wasn't worried about getting caught.

"There's a thousand pretty women waitin' out there, and they're all livin' the devil may care..."

He picked his targets mostly at random, though he focused primarily on men - it was a lot harder to convince a salesclerk a credit card was actually his if it had a name like Susan or Emily on it.

"I'm just the devil with love to spare, so Viva Las Vegas! Viva Las Vegas! Viva... Viva... Las Vegas!"

By the time he'd worked his way from one end of Freemont Street to the other, he had a dozen wallets stuffed inside his jacket pockets. He could have grabbed more, but he didn't see the need.

Thirteen's an unlucky number. No sense risking the bad karma.

He hung around for another twenty minutes, soaking in the glorious cacophony of sights and sounds until the playlist of kitschy classic rock songs started to repeat. Then he made his way back to his hotel.

Inside his room, he tossed the wallets onto his bed as he rifled through them. He'd scored almost three grand in cash - much higher than he expected. People didn't typically carry a lot of bills these days, but Vegas was clearly an exception. The real prize, however, was the plastic - ATM cards, credit cards and IDs.

Most of the credit cards would be cancelled before he got a chance to use them, but inevitably a few would still be valid. It was amazing how many people had a spare card or two they rarely used sitting in their wallet; and how often they forgot to cancel those back-ups when that wallet went missing.

The ATM cards were another matter; without the PIN code they were useless. But Charlie knew from experience that if he cross-referenced the names on the ATM cards with the IDs, at least a couple of them would be using their birthday - either backwards or forwards - as their code. Once he found them, he'd be able to take out their maximum daily withdrawal every day until they either ran out of money or noticed someone was draining their bank account.

Serves them right if they're stupid enough to use their birthday as a PIN.

The best score, though, was the actual ID cards. A date of birth, a social security number and an address was more than enough to start applying for things like new credit cards, bank loans and even IRS refunds. Charlie didn't do that kind of thing himself - it took too long and needed too much paperwork - but the people who did would pay big money for this score. All he had to do was find a way to make contact.

***

An hour later Charlie was sitting at a small table in the back of the Spearmint Rhino. A topless bleached blonde with gigantic fake tits and a tiny black thong was grinding on his lap.

He was already on his third drink: just enough of a buzz to fully appreciate her writhing pelvis while Flo Rida blasting over the club's speakers urged her to get *low, low, low, low.*

"Damn, Candy!" he barked out over the blaring music. "You know how to make me feel like a man!"

"It's Brandy!" she shouted, wrapping her legs around his waist and leaning back until her hair touched the floor.

"Sure. Brandy. Right."

And then the world stopped.

Shit. Sometimes the timeouts are a pain in the ass.

The gyrating dancers were still as statues carved into explicitly awkward and unnatural positions. The heavy, pulsing music was completely silent. Even the familiar scents of the club - sweat and perfume and booze and desperation - vanished.

Even though he was just sitting in his chair, he could feel the weight of frozen time pressing down on him. It was relentless; exhausting. And if it lasted too long, all Brandy's work so far would be for nothing.

Nothing kills a hard-on like a timeout. Bad enough in a strip club. Worse if it catches me when I'm plowing some chick. Hard to keep the wood when she turns into a cold piece of plastic underneath me. If it lasts longer than a minute, I'm limp as a noodle when the timeout ends. Fucking embarrassing.

Fortunately, the world started up again after only a few seconds. As his surroundings sprang back to life, an exhilarating wave washed over him. It was more than just the inevitable burst of sound and motion. He always felt a sudden release whenever the pressure of inertia - that oppressive weight crushing him from all sides - vanished. It was liberating. Exhilarating. A rush better than any drug or fuck he'd ever had.

And I'm the only one in the world who ever feels it.

Charlie's semi-stiff pecker jumped to full attention in response, and Brandy subtly shifted her position on his lap.

Girl's a real pro.

As far as he knew, nobody else experienced anything like his timeouts. The world only stopped for him, and when it started up again nobody else ever noticed. This incredible feeling of utter freedom when time started rolling again was his and his alone. He owned it, and nobody else ever would.

Ride the fucking wave, man!

Unfortunately, the post-timeout euphoria never lasted very long. By the time the last few beats of the song faded away, Charlie already felt himself coming down from the high. But below the belt he was still at full attention.

Brandy untangled herself and stood up, one hand resting lightly on Charlie's shoulder.

"You seemed to enjoy that."

It wasn't all you, honey.

"Nice work," Charlie said out loud, slipping her an extra $100 as a tip. "Maybe you can help me with a special request."

She pressed the bills back into his hand. "Sorry. Not that kind of club."

"Not what I meant," he assured her. "You keep the money. All I want is a name."

Suspicious, Brandy tilted her head to the side and bit her bottom lip. A second later, she snatched the bills back from his hand.

"Who you looking for?"

"Someone who deals in plastic. Credit cards. ID. That kind of stuff."

"Stolen?" she asked, caressing his cheek and leaning forward so her breasts hung mere inches in front of Charlie's hungry gaze.

"Nah. Just found them on the street. A whole pile of them"

"I don't know anyone like that," Brandy said with an exaggerated shrug. "But a few of the other girls might."

Charlie laughed and slipped her another handful of 20's, then gave her a playful - but firm - smack on the ass. "You be sure and send one of them my way, then."

An angry scowl flickered across her face, but she quickly crammed it down deep inside and buried it with an ingratiating smile. "Wait here."

Charlie watched her walk away appreciatively, then held up a finger to signal for the cocktail waitress. He'd been to enough strip clubs to know getting handsy was a risk: most of the time a move like that would end up with a pair of bouncers tossing him out the door. But with the kind of money he was throwing around tonight he figured he could get away with it.

Being a high-roller has its perks.

He'd never had a real job; stealing was all he knew. He got by, but it wasn't a great living. He rarely got to splurge on the finer things.

That Fremont Street haul was rich, though.

He was tempted to go back, but it almost seemed too easy. He preferred something with a little more challenge... even if it backfired sometimes.

Like at the bus station.

Whenever something went wrong – whenever he got caught in a compromising situation – Charlie's first move was to run. Sometimes people got stupid and chased him. Most of the time he could give them the slip, but if they caught him or someone got in his way, things could get rough.

Growing up in the foster system, he'd learned how to fight at a young age.

Real fucking fighting - not that pussy shit on YouTube when someone videos two drunk assholes in a parking lot throwing wild haymakers that never land.

Charlie fought to win. He'd grab a weapon if one was around - pool cue; bottle; even a heavy beer glass could do a ton of damage. Then he'd go for the weak spots: eyes, throat, balls. Elbow. Kick. Bite.

Hit hard, hit fast, hit last. Whatever it takes to make sure I'm the one who walks away. Shit, I'll even go after someone in a timeout if I get the chance.

He'd learned the hard way that taking a swing at someone frozen in time was a bad idea. During a timeout, frozen flesh became hard as rock. Delivering a slug to someone's gut could break his knuckles. But there were other ways to take advantage of a completely immobilized opponent.

Sometimes all it took was tipping a guy off balance so he'd fall down when the timeout ended. Or pushing aside a hand so he could get a free swing at an unguarded chin once things started up again. Sometimes he'd just step around his opponent, then sucker punch him from behind as soon as the timeout ended.

Fighting fair is for chumps. I just want to be the last man standing.

The waitress dropped off another beer and he tucked a twenty into the cleavage of her top. She wrinkled her nose in disgust as his fingers lingered a little too long but managed to mutter "thanks" as she turned away.

Charlie didn't notice. His attention was focused on a tall redhead wearing a silver choker, glittering silver bikini bottoms, thigh-high silver boots, and nothing else. She was walking quickly through the crowd, her long strides making a beeline straight for him.

"Brandy said you're looking for a name."

"Brandy's a smart girl."

"Two hundred."

Charlie held up the cash. Instead of taking the bills, the redhead wrapped her long fingers around Charlie's wrist, grabbing so tight the tips of her ruby nails dug into his skin.

"If you try to slap my ass, the deal's off," she warned him.

She released her grip when he nodded in agreement, then held out her hand, palm up.

"I *like* you," Charlie said, leering as he placed ten $20 bills one-by-one into her waiting grasp.

CHAPTER 8

The March Madness crowd were still out in full force at the PH that Saturday night. The casino was packed with wall-to-wall drunken idiots in college basketball jerseys and tank tops. Less than a quarter of the teams in the field were still alive, but that left plenty of raving fans still clinging to unrealistic hopes and dreams.

"What a shit-show," Carson muttered under his breath as he pushed and shoved his way through the throngs, looking for Maya.

He'd gone from the bus station to a nearby hotel, where he'd been hanging out the past two nights. He doubted Mama would send anyone looking for him until Monday, but he wasn't about to take a chance.

Even in the crowded casino, he kept glancing over his shoulder to see if he was being followed. Not that her boys would do anything to him inside the building – too many cameras. But if they followed him back to his hotel...

Can't worry about that now. Gotta stay focused.

It was almost midnight – just a few minutes before Maya's break. Hopefully, she'd be able to help him find the bearded man.

As he crossed the casino, he saw her near the Pleasure Pit blackjack tables just outside the high limit room. The lingerie-clad dealers working those tables called it the fishbowl, because they were right in the open where everyone could see them. Even on slow nights, the fishbowl always attracted a crowd. Tonight the gawkers - mostly young men - were lined up three rows deep watching the action.

Maya was in the middle of the scene, arguing with two tall white men sporting Duke jerseys. One of the guys was leaning on his buddy, so drunk he could barely stand.

Carson wasn't close enough to hear what was being said, but from the expression on her face he could make a good guess.

Drag your drunk-ass friend up to his room so he can sleep it off!

She'd probably use a more tactful choice of words, but the message would be clear.

The sober friend suddenly stood up straight - he had to be almost six five - and took a half-step towards Maya, jawing away. Carson recognized the not-so-subtle move.

Trying to use his height and size to intimidate her.

Maya was having none of it. She held her ground, barked something out and pointed an emphatic finger towards the elevators.

Go! Get out of here! Now!

The drunk guy reached out and tried to put a hand on her shoulder, but she swatted it away and held up three fingers. Then two. Then one. The sober friend finally got the message and hauled his buddy away. Maya followed their progress with a hard stare as they slowly worked their way through the crowd to make sure they didn't try to double back.

Throughout the unfolding drama, Carson had been slowly making his way over to the fishbowl. Once the Duke boys were gone, he waved and called out to get her attention.

"Maya!" he shouted, hoping she'd hear him above the music and general din of the crowd. "Hey!"

She turned towards him, then crossed the distance between them with a half-dozen long, quick strides.

"Perfect timing. I'm just about to go on break."

"Good. I'll buy you a coffee."

They headed over to the Starbucks in the corner of the casino. It was still loud – it was impossible to truly escape the pounding music and the general din of crowd. But at least here they could talk without actually shouting.

"So," Maya said after taking a long sip of her coffee. "That text you sent me was pretty cryptic. *Need to meet ASAP. It's important.*

"Please tell me you're not in some kind of serious trouble."

He couldn't tell if she was just joking with him, or if she could actually sense something was wrong. But he didn't want to get into his situation with Mama Pearl; there was no sense making her worry.

And if this works out the way I hope, all my problems will be solved.

"I need to find someone," he told her. "Fast. I'm hoping you might know somebody who could help me out."

Maya's brow furrowed; clearly, she wasn't expecting this.

"I know a couple cops who left the job to become PIs. One of them's even pretty good at it. But he doesn't work cheap."

"How much?"

"I'd imagine it depends on the job. Who are you looking for, exactly?"

Carson dumped the fake IDs from the bearded man's wallet on the table.

"This guy."

Maya picked up one of the driver's licenses and gave it a closer look.

"Impressive craftsmanship. Almost looks real. Any idea where he got it?"

"No. I think he's from out of town. Ran into him at the bus station, and he dropped a wallet full of these."

"Any idea what his real name is?"

Carson shook his head.

Maya frowned and bit her lip, mulling the problem over in her head.

"If he's looking to stock up again, there's only a couple places he can go to get something this quality."

"So your PI friend could ask around at these places? See if this guy's shown up? Maybe tail him and find out where he's staying?"

She set the fake ID back on the table, then took a deep breath.

"Carson – what the hell are you mixed up in?"

"It's not... it's nothing. I just need to find this guy. Please."

For several seconds, she didn't reply. Her eyes were fixed on him, intense and focused – like she was trying to see into his soul to figure out what was really going on. Carson felt himself withering under her gaze, but just as he was on the verge of blurting out everything – every insane detail of his unbelievable story – her silent interrogation relented.

"Something like this could easily run you two or three thousand," she warned. "I might be able to convince him to give you a deal, but he's still going to want at least a grand up front."

Carson pulled out his dwindling emergency fund and peeled off a dozen $100 bills.

"A grand for him, and another two hundred for you. Finder's fee for hooking me up."

"Don't be insulting," she chided, pushing the extra $200 back across the table. "Just remember this when I come ask you for a favor someday."

"I will. I promise."

"My break's almost over," she said, pocketing the PI fee and abruptly standing up.

Carson reached out and grabbed her wrist – desperate and sudden. She looked down at him, but she seemed more surprised than offended.

"Thank you for this, Maya. I mean it. You have no idea what this means to me."

He let his hand fall away, embarrassed by his impulsive gesture. Maya leaned over and wrapped her arms around him in a fierce hug.

"Please be careful, Carson," she whispered in his ear before letting go and heading back to the casino floor.

***

There were plenty of second-rate hotels in downtown Vegas, and they all shared similar features: out of date décor, worn carpets, a few slot machines and video poker machines on the wall... and a mildly unpleasant smell Carson could never quite place.

Sitting in the lobby, Carson pretended to surf his phone while keeping one eye on the elevator leading up to the rooms. He'd been here for the past two hours, wedging his gangly frame into a rickety old wicker armchair. The worn-out cushions on the seat and back offered little in the way of either comfort or support, but the only other option was an old couch covered in too many unidentifiable stains to make it worth the risk.

It had taken four days, but the PI Maya recommended had come through with an address for the bearded man from the bus stop. He'd offered to tail the target for Carson to learn more about him - who he was and what he was doing in Vegas. But the last of Carson's bankroll was running low, and at $300 per day he decided he could follow the guy himself.

As he shifted position in his seat for the umpteenth time, trying in vain to get comfortable, he couldn't help but wonder if he'd made a mistake. His back was already sore from the shitty motel mattress he'd been crashing on the past few nights.

What do you expect for thirty bucks a night? Those rooms are usually rented by the hour.

Given his dire financial straits, he couldn't afford anything better. And sleeping in his own apartment wasn't an option anymore; he was already two days past the deadline to pay Mama Pearl back.

Probably got her goons staking out my apartment. Maybe even has her people searching the city for me.

Staying in Vegas was a gamble; the kind of risk Carson usually tried to avoid. But finding the bearded man had become an overwhelming obsession.

What if he knows something about my power? How I got it, or why? What if he can explain this?

Over the years Carson had learned how to use his special talent for his own benefit. He'd accepted it was a part of him. But he still didn't understand it. Not really. If there was any chance of finally getting some answers, he couldn't walk away. Not even with all his other problems.

And if I find this guy, maybe those other problems can all go away, too. The debt I owe to Mama. The money for Ella's treatments. If I stop time in a casino with a partner who can move while the world is frozen...

Carson pushed the thought aside. The first step to all of this was finding out more about the bearded man. He couldn't allow himself to get distracted by thinking about future possibilities. Not yet.

But time is running out. Maya's PI found my guy in only four days. What if Mama has someone like that on her payroll looking for me?

He heard the ding of the elevator, and he casually glanced up as the doors opened. He'd already been through this routine dozens of times, so he wasn't expecting anything. But for once, Lady Luck smiled on him, and the bearded man stepped into view.

Bingo!

Carson's mind was racing. He could feel his heart pounding, and his breath was coming in short, ragged bursts. It took all his willpower not to stop the world. His entire life, his instinctive reaction to stress had been to freeze time. But doing so now might tip his target off.

Instead, he took a long slow breath to calm himself. Then he held his phone up closer to his face and hunched forward as if examining something interesting on the screen, while his gaze peered over the top to track his target as the bearded man walked across the lobby towards the front door.

Carson waited a second or two after he exited the building before standing up himself. Despite the near overwhelming sense of urgency, he tried to move with a casual calm. Taking long, quick steps - not quite a run, but definitely more than a walk - he headed out the door in pursuit.

Glancing left, then right, he caught sight of the bearded man a half-block away, walking briskly. Taking a half-dozen quick jog steps to close the gap slightly, Carson followed.

His quarry turned down a small side street. But when Carson rounded the corner, he was nowhere in sight.

****FRE--no!*

At the last instant he pulled back from stopping the world.

Old habits die hard.

Halfway down the side street a back alley branched off - barely more than a narrow corridor running between the brick walls of two neighboring buildings. Carson couldn't think of a reason for his quarry to go down the cramped alley, but there wasn't any other place he could have disappeared to.

Normally, Carson would have frozen time and methodically analyzed the situation, carefully pondering the pros and cons before forming a plan of action. But if he did that now, it would only give the bearded man more time to slip away.

For several seconds he stood, paralyzed by indecision. Quick thinking didn't come easy when you were used to stopping time whenever you wanted.

Fucking do something, you dumb shit!

He turned and ventured down the alley. Several dumpsters lined one side and he wrinkled his nose at sour stink. He took a few quick steps forward, then stopped when he saw it led to a dead end fifty feet ahead.

Something's not right. Where is he?

The bearded man charged out from behind one of the dumpsters, blindsiding him like a Mack truck.

The impact slammed Carson into the brick wall, knocking the wind out of him. Dazed, he crumpled to the street, only to be yanked back onto his feet a second later by the bearded man. He slammed Carson against the wall, pinning him there with his feet dangling a few inches above the ground.

"Who the hell are you," he snarled, "and why are you following me?"

Carson was too busy gasping for breath to explain.

"Let him go."

The unfamiliar voice was male; calm but full of menace.

Turning his head, Carson saw two very large figures blocking the alley's entrance.

Mama Pearl's boys.

"Who the fuck are you?" the bearded man spat, still keeping Carson pinned against the wall.

"He's coming with us," one of the goons replied. "Walk away while you still can."

The bearded man turned back to Carson, the confusion clear on his face.

"Friends of yours?"

Carson shook his head emphatically. The bearded man let him drop back to the ground and turned to face the two newcomers. Carson stumbled but kept his feet, pressing himself back against the wall to get as far away from everyone else as he could.

"Last chance," one of the goons warned. "Piss off."

"I don't take orders from shit-heels like you!"

The bearded man was grinning. As he dropped into a boxer's stance and raised his fists, Carson caught an eager gleam in his eye.

The goons each pulled out a gun.

"We're not fucking around."

The bearded man let his fists drop and took a step back.

"Jesus Christ, relax. You made your point. I'll go."

"No. You had your fucking chance. Now you're coming with us. We'll let Mama decide what happens to you."

"Fucking cowards," he growled, spitting on the street. "Two against one and you still need your god-damned pistols?"

"Come on. Both of you. Let's move."

Carson wasn't exactly sure what would happen to them once they reached Mama Pearl's bar, but he knew he didn't want to find out.

"I can get us out of this," he whispered, hoping only the bearded man would hear.

"What?"

"I can get us out of this," he repeated, louder this time.

"Shut up, Carson," one of the goons said, waving the barrel of his gun in his direction. "Let's go."

Carson ignored him.

He's not going to shoot me just for talking. I hope.

"If I help you, you help me," he said to the bearded man, though his eyes were on the pistols pointed in his direction. "When it happens, don't ditch me. You've got to get us both out of this."

"What the fuck are you talking about?" the bearded man replied. "When what happens?"

"You'll know. Just remember, it's not an accident. It's not a co-incidence."

"Carson, shut the fuck up!"

One of the goons was moving forward, raising his gun to pistol whip Carson into silence.

*** *FREEZE!* ***

The thug advancing on him stopped short, frozen in place along with his partner. And Carson. And the rest of the entire world.

But not the bearded man!

From his locked-in-place vantage point, Carson could see the bearded man turn his head from side to side, perplexed. Then his eyes went wide as the realization of what just happened sank in. He smiled at Carson... but of course he couldn't smile back.

Carson's lack of reaction gave him pause. But then he seemed to understand that Carson was just as frozen as everyone else. Fully grasping the situation, he nodded, then got to work.

He started with the nearest opponent - the one who was moving in to cold-cock Carson with his gun. He pried the goon's fingers off the butt of the pistol one-by-one, visibly straining from the effort. Once he had the gun in his possession, the bearded man placed his foot against the back of the other man's lead leg and pushed hard just behind the knee, causing it to bend forward a few degrees.

It didn't seem like he'd done much at all yet, but Carson could already feel the world trying to break free from stasis. He could hold on for a while longer, but he needed his new partner to hurry.

Only there's no way to let him know.

Clutching the gun he'd taken off the first goon, the bearded man strode over to the second. His steps were slow and awkward, just as they'd been at the bus station. He lifted the gun up and - still moving in a slow-motion pantomime - tapped it on the bridge of the second man's nose.

Then he stepped back and turned towards Carson, an expectant expression on his face.

Carson wasn't sure what he'd been hoping the man would do, exactly. But somehow, he thought there'd be more.

Mama's goons aren't fucking around.

Carson was really struggling to keep the world frozen now. He knew as soon as time started up again, they were going to come at them hard.

But the man didn't seem concerned at all. He was just staring at Carson. With obvious effort, he tilted his head to the side and shrugged, as if to say, "Well?"

What the fuck is he waiting for? He needs to take these guys down before—

_____

Carson's grip on time slipped, the world sprang back into motion, and all hell broke loose.

The goon coming towards him collapsed face first on the ground, his leg buckling beneath him as he screamed in pain. The second man's nose exploded like it had been slammed with a hammer - the slight tap from the pistol during stasis unleashing a geyser of blood now that time was moving again. The gun in his hand slipped from his grasp and he dropped like he'd been shot.

The bearded man swooped in and scooped up the fallen pistol, tucking it in his belt.

Carson looked down at the first man. He was crumpled at Carson's feet, clutching his right hand tightly to his stomach. He caught a glimpse of the fingers that had been pried from the gun: the digits jutted out at bizarre angles, dislocated and broken. He was blubbering softly.

Carson's attention snapped back to the bearded man as he raised the pistol and pointed it at the second thug from point blank range.

"No!" Carson shouted. "Don't!"

The bearded man turned to him, annoyed by the interruption. His victim was curled up in a ball on the ground, rocking from side to side and whimpering softly, his hands vainly trying to staunch the flow of blood from his nose.

"Someone pulls a fucking gun on me, I'm going to shoot their ass if I get the chance."

"Please," the cowering man begged. "Please, don't."

"They weren't going to kill us," Carson insisted. "Just... just let them go. Trust me on this."

Reluctantly, the bearded man lowered the gun. Then he loudly cleared his throat and spit on the helpless goon at his feet.

"You and I need to talk," he said, addressing Carson.

"I'll tell you everything. I promise. But only if you let these guys live."

"You heard him, shit-birds. Get the fuck out of here!"

The two injured men managed to stand up and limp away, leaving Carson and the bearded man alone in the alley.

"My name's Carson."

"Charlie." The name was barely a word – more a grunt of irritation.

"Pleased to meet you, Charlie."

Charlie snorted. "What is this? A date?"

"More like a business meeting. A potential partnership. I think we have complimentary skills."

"You really made everything stop just now, didn't you?"

"I did. Here, and at the bus station. Probably quite a few other times, too, I'm guessing. There are still some details I'm trying to figure out."

"You can do this anytime you want? Freeze time like that?"

"Basically."

A gleefully savage, ear-to-ear grin lit up Charlie's entire face as the potential implications dawned on him.

"Brother, you and I are going to own this fucking town!"

CHAPTER 9

Part Two: CJ

April 16, 2014 – Maryland
Five years before the D Street Massacre

CJ pulled out his ID badge and slowed his car as he approached the checkpoint outside the main gates of Fort Meade. He didn't recognize the guard in the security booth as he handed over his credentials.

Must be new here.

The young sentry carefully studied the picture and name on the ID badge - JAMES, CHAIRMAN RUSSEL - then gave him a long, probing stare. CJ endured his scrutiny with a patience born from a lifetime of being viewed with suspicion and mistrust.

The universal Black American experience.

"Chairman of what?" the guard finally asked.

"It's not a title, it's my name," CJ said, making no effort to keep the exasperation out of his voice.

CJ wasn't military; like most of the cryptographers working for the NSA he was a civilian. But even though he had no official rank, in the unofficial hierarchy of the base he was way above a lowly gate guard.

His tone made the sentry realize he had overstepped, and he quickly handed the ID back and briskly motioned him through. CJ didn't bother to say anything as he pulled away.

He let his mind wander as he cruised down Reese Road. Though technically on the base grounds after passing the checkpoint, he still had a good ten-minute drive before he reached his office. Fort Meade was a massive complex; a virtual city. Six thousand military families lived on the base, and more than fifty thousand people worked there.

In addition to the National Security Agency - where CJ had been employed for the past three years - there were also offices for countless other departments, including the United States Cyber Command, the Defense Intelligence Systems Agency, the United States Army Field Band and all five branches of the US Military: Army, Navy, Air Force, Marines and Coast Guard.

Of the literally thousands of structures on the base, the headquarters of the NSA was by far the largest: an imposing, boxy office building surrounded by a massive parking lot that stretched for acres in every direction. CJ's parking spot was on the far edge of the property. On most days, he'd head over to one of the shuttle stops and catch a ride to the main doors rather than make the fifteen-minute hike to the entrance, but he was early today and the morning was cool and clear.

The walk was soothing; a few more minutes of calm before the next eight hours grinding away at his desk. CJ knew he shouldn't complain; the NSA paid very well. But the flood of incoming data he had to analyze and decode every day was incessant and overwhelming. The advent of cell phones and e-mail had caused an exponential explosion in the amount of information the NSA was responsible for, and even with nearly fifty thousand employees across the country, they were always behind.

He showed his ID at the building's main entrance, then scanned it again as he stepped into the elevator and pressed his floor. When the elevator opened, he showed his badge one more time to the woman at the reception desk, who buzzed him into what CJ simply called "the box farm".

He had no idea what the other floors looked like, but where he worked there was nothing but cubicles - row after row of chest high fabric walls separating each person's desk and computer from their neighbors'.

The monotony of the layout matched the monotony of the job. Ninety-nine percent of the data the NSA processed was completely insignificant and mundane. And even the one percent that was interesting was typically fragmented and sent off piece-meal to several operatives to work on at the same time, so that no single individual could actually know more than a few scant details of what he or she was decrypting.

When CJ reached his cubicle, he was surprised to find his supervisor, Julia, waiting there for him. CJ wasn't late: a quick check of his watch verified he still had a few minutes before he needed to log in.

"CJ, you need to come with me," she said.

Her tone was calm, but he could tell something was bothering her.

"Am I in trouble?"

"I can't talk about it here," Julia explained. "Just come with me, please."

Why's she being so formal? So proper? This must be serious.

CJ was a model employee. He mostly kept to himself, but he was good at his job, and he got along well enough with both co-workers and supervisors. But was it possible he'd fucked something up? Something with major consequences?

Heart racing, he thought back over the past few weeks, trying to recall anything out of the ordinary that might give him some clue as to what this was about. His last performance review - given just last month - had been exemplary. All his reviews were exemplary. It was something he was used to.

He'd been smarter than everyone else around him his entire life. Going through the public-school system in Atlanta, he'd done well enough to earn a full scholarship to MIT. His grades at college were excellent, and he'd graduated near the top of his class. MIT didn't give out awards and distinctions like magna cum laude or First Honors - you practically had to be a genius just to get in, and they wanted students to work together and cooperate rather than compete. But even there CJ could tell he was one of the smartest students on campus.

Things came to him quickly and easily. He breezed through problems that stumped his classmates, aced his exams and was snapped up by the NSA right after graduation. There his pattern of success had continued: in just three years, he'd already been promoted twice.

That's it!

The hint of smile crept across his lips as the pieces fell into place.

That's why Julia's pissed. She doesn't want to lose me. They're moving me out of her department. Kicking me up the ladder again.

Julia led him to the elevator, swiped her access card, and pressed the button for the top floor. CJ's heart was still racing, but now it was from excitement and anticipation.

The elevator doors opened to reveal a security desk and small waiting room with a pair of bullet-proof glass security doors on the far wall, much like his own floor.

"Check in with reception," Julia told him, motioning him out of the elevator.

"You're not coming?" he asked her.

She shook her head. Then she smiled and added, "Good luck, CJ."

"Thanks."

He stepped out of the elevator and approached the young man sitting behind the reception desk.

"Name?"

The kid was all military - buzz cut, full uniform. Couldn't have been more than twenty.

"CJ James." Sometimes it was just easier to go by his initials.

"I'll tell them you're here, Mr. James."

CJ took a seat in one of the waiting room chairs, but he wasn't there long. In less than a minute the glass doors opened, and two armed guards entered.

"Mr. James? Come with us."

Hopping up from his seat, he fell into step behind the guards. They whisked him through the halls, passing several closed doors on either side of the corridor before stopping in front of the entrance to a small office. Two ergonomic chairs and a long, glass coffee table stood in the center. Otherwise, the room was empty; whoever he was supposed to meet had yet to arrive.

"Wait inside."

He stepped through the door, and the guards closed it behind him. He briefly wondered if they were still standing watch on the other side, or if they'd just lock him in. His confidence was beginning to waver - this all seemed a little much for a simple promotion.

Realizing there wasn't anything else to do but wait, he settled into the chair facing the door. Less than a minute later it opened, and an older Indian man entered. He closed and locked the door behind him, then turned back to CJ.

"Hello, Mr. James. My name is Dr. Arvihd Singh."

He didn't speak with any kind of noticeable accent, but there was a stiffness to his words that made CJ think he'd attended school some-where in Britain - Oxford or Cambridge, maybe.

Dr. Singh was a small man, thin and bald. He had a short, graying beard, trimmed to a nearly perfect point and small, wire rim glasses. He wore a black suit but didn't seem comfortable in it. He carried a folder with a typed label reading "James, C. R." on it.

CJ stood up and extended his hand as the doctor approached.

"Pleased to meet you, sir. Call me CJ."

Dr. Singh smiled as they shook.

"You seem quite relaxed," he noted as they both sat down.

CJ shrugged. "I haven't done anything wrong, so I figure I've got nothing to be worried about."

"I like your confidence."

Dr. Singh opened the folder and scanned what CJ guessed was his personnel file.

"Father, absent. Mother worked as a hotel maid," he muttered, flip-ping through the pages. "Grew up in the projects. Public schools. Excel-lent academic record. Graduated MIT in 2012. Started here soon after.

Model employee over these past three years. Promoted last October to the quantum cryptography division."

He closed the folder and set it on the table, then crossed one leg over the other. Leaning forward, he rested his forearm on his knee.

"Chairman. That's an interesting name."

"My mother named me after Chairman Fred Hampton," CJ explained.

"Of course. The Black Panther leader from Chicago."

CJ was mildly surprised. "Most people don't know the reference."

"He was quite the revolutionary," Dr. Singh noted. "Are you a revolutionary, CJ?"

"I'm not looking to change the world."

"Ah... but what if you could?"

"I'm not sure I follow, sir."

"You remind me of myself, CJ," Dr. Singh said, seemingly changing topics. "We both grew up poor. My parents were immigrants. My mother worked in a textile factory in Queens, my father was a school janitor.

"Nothing was handed to me. I earned my place in the world. As did you."

CJ shifted in his seat, uncertain how to respond. Poor black kid gets an education and makes good was an accurate - if overly simplistic - summary of his life. But it wasn't how he defined himself.

"Do you know why you're here, CJ?"

"If I had to guess, I'd say I'm being considered for a promotion."

"Precisely. For the past several months, most of what you've been working on has been connected to the project I oversee. I've been monitoring your performance quite closely during that time. And I've been very impressed."

"I do my best."

"Don't we all? But for so many, their best just isn't good enough. Not for me."

Dr. Singh leaned back in his chair and uncrossed his legs.

"It wasn't just your job performance that drew my attention, however. The specifics of your personal life also align with our needs."

"What do you mean?"

"Your mother passed away while you were in college. No father in the picture. No siblings. No significant romantic relationships."

"Wait... how do you know that?"

Instead of answering, the older man stood up and clasped his hands behind his back. Then he began to pace slowly about the room.

"Before we continue, I want to assure you that you are free to refuse my offer with no consequences whatsoever," Dr. Singh explained, not bothering to look at CJ as he spoke. "If you decide you are not interested, you can leave this meeting when we are done, and you will never see me again. You can continue with your career in the NSA, and I suspect your will continue to rise through the ranks.

"However, if you choose to join us, then everything will change."

Dr. Singh was circling slowly behind him, and CJ had to twist awkwardly in his chair to keep him in his sight.

"What I am involved in - the project I work on - is known only to a precious few. If you join us, you will become part of the inner circle. You will move to a new city. You will leave your old life behind."

"You're not with the NSA, are you?"

"My department is trans-organizational." He was standing just behind CJ's shoulder now, peering down at him.

"And what are you working on?"

"I'm afraid I can't reveal that. Not unless you accept my offer. The NSA has only given you confidential security clearance. My work goes much higher."

"Top Secret?"

"Beyond Top Secret."

"I didn't think there was anything beyond top secret," CJ remarked.

"This level of clearance doesn't have a name," the doctor admitted.

He reached down and clamped his fingers onto the younger man's shoulder. His grip was surprisingly strong, and CJ could feel the fingers digging into his flesh.

"If you join us, you can never, ever tell anyone about what you do. Not one single detail. Our security cannot be breached under any circumstances. If you tell anyone anything about your work, you will disappear. No arrest. No trial. You will simply vanish, never to be found again."

He spoke in a calm, even tone, his voice neither rising to a shout nor dropping to a whisper. Staring up at the man looming above him, CJ started to force a smile, then realized it wasn't a joke. He squirmed uncomfortably beneath Dr. Singh's vice-like grip, but the pressure didn't relent.

"Not only will you disappear," the doctor continued, "so will the person you spoke to. And anyone they may have spoken to. Old, young, man, woman or child... they will all suffer for your betrayal. Do you understand?"

CJ nodded, and Dr. Singh released his grip. He came slowly back around in front of CJ and sat down again in his chair.

"But if you keep our secrets, you will be very well compensated. Whatever number you imagine your salary might be, I guarantee you're too low."

Dr. Singh leaned forward and reached across the small table to gently pat CJ's knee.

"More importantly, CJ, if you join my team you will be part of the most amazing and important scientific advancement in human history."

The older man leaned back in his chair and crossed his arms and his legs, as if settling in to wait for the response.

CJ's head was spinning.

This can't be real. He's insane. Paranoid and delusional.

Yet somehow he'd arranged for a private meeting inside one of the most secure government facilities in the entire United States.

If what he says is true...

"This can't be legal," he finally managed to say.

"My work violates both US law and the Constitution on many levels," Dr. Singh freely admitted. "We operate in the shadows, with no oversight. But what we are doing is for the greater good. Not just for America, but for all of humanity."

"And if I say no, you'll really just let me walk away?"

"I swear you will never see me again... unless you are foolish enough to tell anyone about what has transpired in this meeting."

"I'm not a fool," CJ assured him.

"I'm well aware of that. Which is why I think you will ultimately accept my offer. But you must give me your answer before we leave this room."

CJ reached up and rubbed his chin, letting the words sink in. He had no family, no real friends. He was young. Ambitious. And he knew he'd never get another opportunity like this.

You don't even know what "this" is! What if they're plotting to overthrow the government? What if they're doing horrific medical experiments on children? How can you agree if you don't even know what you're signing up for?

"I'm interested," CJ finally admitted. "Very interested. But I can't say yes if you won't tell me more about what I'm agreeing to."

Dr. Singh uncrossed his arms and leaned forward again.

"Tell me why you joined the NSA."

"The money was good."

"You could have made more in the private sector."

"I wanted to serve my country."

"If you come work for me, you still will. But there was more to it than that, wasn't there?"

CJ hesitated, then slowly nodded.

"I wanted to be on the other side of the curtain."

Dr. Singh chuckled.

"Precisely. You wanted to be on the inside. To see the dark secrets we keep hidden from the masses. You wanted to learn the truths most people can't handle."

CJ nodded again.

"That is what I am offering you. What we are working on will astonish you. In time - once our work is done - it will change the world in ways you can't even imagine. This is bigger than the Wright Brothers. Bigger than Alexander Graham Bell. Bigger than anything Edison or Einstein worked on. Bigger than the atomic bomb. Bigger than the internet.

"So ask yourself: do you want to be part of the greatest single advancement in human history?"

Dr. Singh leaned back in his chair and re-crossed his arms, the hint of a smile on his lips.

"Take your time, CJ. But I think we both know what your answer will be."

***

As his plane began to descend for landing, CJ's head was still spinning. Things had moved fast after he'd accepted Dr. Singh's offer.

They'd given him one day to say goodbye to his coworkers at the NSA and pack up his apartment. The day after that, a black truck with no logos had had shown up at CJ's door, and an hour later the movers had everything he owned - his car; his furniture; his entire life - loaded up and on the road.

A black sedan had driven him to the airport, and he'd boarded a private jet. After a four-hour flight, they were now landing at a military airfield in the middle of the desert. The sun was just setting behind the distant mountains, casting a fiery orange glow over the miles upon miles of empty landscape stretching off in every direction.

Disembarking from the plane, he wasn't surprised to find Dr. Singh waiting for him on the runway. Two serious looking men in military fatigues and armed with machine guns stood at attention behind the scientist. Another man in a lab coat – tall, blonde, tanned, ruggedly handsome even though he was well past middle age – was standing beside Dr. Singh.

"CJ, this is Dr. Reed Belmont," Dr. Singh said by way of introduction. "He's my right hand here at Dreamland."

"Welcome to Edwards Air Force Base," Dr. Belmont said, coming forward to shake CJ's hand. "How was your flight?"

CJ didn't answer; he was still trying to process everything that had happened over the past 48 hours.

"We're in Nevada," he muttered, his mind pulling the location of the Edwards Base from some long-forgotten compartment deep inside his memory banks. "Area 51."

"We prefer the name Dreamland," Dr. Singh corrected him.

"Dreamland," CJ repeated softly.

"Your quarters are still being prepared," Dr. Belmont informed him. "I think you'll find them satisfactory. Certainly nicer than the apartment you were staying in before this, from what I've been told."

"Dr. Belmont wanted to greet you in person on your first day," Dr. Singh explained. "But he can't stay."

"That's right," Dr. Belmont agreed. "But I look forward to working with you."

The blonde man pumped CJ's hand twice, then hopped into one of several empty jeeps parked beside the runway and sped off. Bemused, CJ watched him go without saying a word.

"Would you like a tour of our facility?" Dr. Singh asked. "Or do you need some time to relax after your flight? Can we get you something to eat?"

"I'm good," CJ replied, the fog of confusion slowly lifting. "Let's do the tour."

They climbed into a second jeep - Dr. Singh behind the wheel and one of the soldiers in the seat beside him; CJ and the other soldier in the back.

It was too noisy to speak as they drove across the base, heading from the airfield past the residential buildings and towards several large hangars in the distance. CJ tried to take it all in, but the setting sun had almost vanished behind the peaks off to the west and it was hard to make anything out in the deepening dusk.

The jeep finally came to a stop just outside a small, man-sized door built into the side of one of the hangars. A single fluorescent bulb above it illuminated the words painted on the surface: KEEP OUT - AUTHORIZED PERSONNNEL ONLY!

Dr. Singh stepped out of the jeep and approached the door. After a moment, CJ followed, but the soldiers stayed in the vehicle.

"They're not coming?" CJ asked.

"They don't have clearance for what you're about to see," Dr. Singh explained.

On the wall beside the door was a security panel. Dr. Singh pressed his palm against its flat glass surface, then waited as it scanned his fingerprints. The panel beeped, and he bent forward and placed his eye into what CJ guessed was some kind of optical reader. Then he punched in a long code on the numeric keypad, his fingers moving so quickly CJ couldn't have followed them even if he wanted to.

"We'll set up your own code and biometric access tomorrow," Dr. Singh promised as the door beeped loudly three times, then slowly opened of its own accord.

The other side was a long, narrow corridor leading to a set of sealed elevator doors. Dr. Singh repeated the previous security procedures, and the doors opened with a soft "whoosh".

The two men stepped inside. CJ noticed there were only two buttons - an arrow pointing up and another pointing down. Dr. Singh pushed the latter, and CJ's stomach lurched as the elevator began a rapid descent.

"Are you ready for what I'm about to show you?" Dr. Singh asked him.

"I think so."

The older scientist laughed. "I promise you, you're not."

The elevator continued its downwards journey, going deeper and deeper beneath the surface.

"Mine shaft?" CJ asked.

"Very good," Dr. Singh replied. "Our lab is over a thousand feet below the surface."

"You still haven't actually told me what you're working on."

"What *we* are working on, CJ. You are part of the team now. Don't ever forget that."

"Right. So what are *we* working on?"

"It's easier if I show you. You won't believe it until you see it."

"Are you telling me all the rumors about Area 51 are true?"

"Dreamland."

"Dreamland, then. The name isn't the point. Are you saying I'm about to see a crashed spaceship? An alien corpse preserved in embalming fluid?"

"Is that what you're expecting?"

CJ thought about it for several seconds, the droning hum of the elevator the only sound breaking the silence.

"I think that's a very unlikely possibility," he admitted.

"Do you follow college basketball, CJ? Have you ever filled out one of those March Madness brackets?"

It was an odd question, but he saw no reason not to answer. "Sure."

"Have you ever gotten every game right? Or even heard of anyone getting every game right?"

"Of course not. The odds are over a trillion to one."

"More like one in 9.2 quintillion," Dr. Singh corrected. "Assuming you leave all the picks to random chance."

CJ stayed quiet, waiting for the doctor to make his point.

"But as low as the odds are, they are not zero. Which means that, if you believe in certain branches of quantum theory, there exists a reality in which someone has picked a perfect bracket."

The elevator slowed and came to a stop, but the doors didn't open right away.

"I'm sorry, Dr. Singh. I'm not sure I get the point you're making."

"No matter how unlikely an event is - no matter how much the odds are stacked against it - it can still happen. In fact, assuming infinite parallel realities, there exists a universe in which it *has already* happened. Why can't that particular universe be ours?"

Dr. Singh pushed the down button again, and the elevator doors slid open.

"Remember that, CJ, and it will be much easier for you to accept what you're about to witness."

CHAPTER 10

May 2, 2015
Four years before the D Street Massacre

They called it the Core. Buried deep beneath the earth at the Dreamland research facility, it was a small, self-contained metal bunker. The only access was via a long elevator ride down from the surface, followed by a brief walk down a short hallway to a heavy metal door protected by a six-digit pass code, a key card reader, a thumb print ID pad and a retinal scanner.

For his first six months at Dreamland, CJ had only been allowed to enter the Core when accompanied by Dr. Singh or Dr. Belmont. But a few weeks before this past Christmas, he'd finally been given full security clearance. Now he could visit on his own... within certain limitations. Since then, he'd spent more hours in the Core than any other member of the team. It wasn't a requirement of the job – most of his work could be done remotely in the data labs topside. But for CJ the Core had become something of an obsession.

He swiped his keycard, punched in the code, put his eye up against the tiny glass hole in the wall, then jammed his thumb against the scanner just below it. The metal security door slid open with an audible hiss to reveal a small observation chamber. The tiny room was crammed with a variety of machinery and electronics, ranging from microphones and video cameras to thermometers and Geiger counters – any and all manner of equipment to monitor and record everything that happened inside the bunker.

The monitoring equipment was linked to a pair of computer terminals in the middle of the room facing the large glass window overlooking the true miracle of the Core: a circular room thirty feet in diameter, partitioned off from the observation chamber by the twin doors of a small airlock.

Like the observation chamber, monitoring equipment had been strategically placed throughout the interior chamber. On the far side, away from the observation window and the air lock, stood a shiny metal tube - six feet tall and three feet across - with a long, transparent window running vertically for its entire length: the reactor. The softly pulsing heart of the core.

Inside the tube was a slowly shifting, translucent, blue fluid. Tiny flecks of glittering silver were suspended inside the fluid, floating in long, languid circles on invisible currents. A soft glow emanated from the reactor, bathing the entire room in an eerie green illumination like some kind of over-sized lava lamp.

The reactor was connected to a semi-circular control panel consisting of hundreds of colorful buttons, dials, knobs and switches - an exact replica of the cockpit controls recovered from the alien vessel that had crashed just outside Roswell in 1947.

CJ stood in front of the control panel, staring at it as his mind tried to make sense of the incredible complexity. His eyes scanned back and forth across the vast array of buttons and dials, his brain looking for patterns among the chaos... just as he'd done all the times before.

The control panel was overwhelming in its complexity and strangeness, but he was convinced if he studied it long enough, he'd stumble across some hint or clue - some magical key - that would help him unravel the puzzle of how the it could be used to control the reactor.

He wasn't the first to think that, of course. The scientists at Dreamland had built this panel decades ago, carefully modeling it after the original. And they'd been studying it ever since, with virtually no success.

During his first months at Dreamland, CJ had pored over the reports and notes from all those who had come before him – multiple generations of the country's most brilliant minds trying to solve the greatest scientific puzzle in human history. He'd studied the blueprints and layout of the control panel in detail; hundreds of hours over several months. But there was something different about seeing it in person. Something powerful and disturbing.

Standing before it was the only way to truly grasp the fundamentally alien nature of the Core. There was something off-putting about how everything had been arranged. It seemed to be a completely haphazard and random control scheme; a counter-intuitive design that was based on non-terrestrial biology, culture, and cognition.

CJ was convinced that studying the control panel in person, day after day, was critical to eventually understanding how it all worked. But there was also another reason he spent so much of his time down here.

The bursts.

When he first began at Dreamland, CJ had read the accounts of the men and women who'd experienced a burst first-hand. But it didn't take him long to realize that to truly understand the bursts, he would have to feel them for himself. And that could only be done from inside the Core.

He mentally settled in for the wait, knowing he could be standing alone in the tiny room for hours. Even then, there was no assurance he'd get what he came for. Like everything else about the alien technology, the bursts seemed completely unpredictable and random. Some days would see a half-dozen or more, other times they could go a full week without a single occurrence... though it was rare for more than a couple days to pass without at least one instance.

This was CJ's third consecutive day in the Core. Official protocols restricted each individual to two consecutive days of Core access, with a minimum 48-hour waiting period afterwards before coming back again. But his last two visits hadn't given him what he came for, so he was bending the rules to try one more time, waiting and hoping for the inevitable.

After three long hours, his patience was finally rewarded.

It began with the faint but unmistakable sensation of motion, as if he was being gently scooped up by an invisible hand. His mind had just enough time to register what was happening before the dim green glow from the reactor flared so brightly he had to shut his eyes, and an electric current raced from the roots of his hair to the tips of his toes. The air suddenly felt hot - thick and heavy.

Forcing his eyes open against the brightness, he blinked rapidly and waited for his sight to adjust. Everything was being recorded, of course - nothing happened in the Core that wasn't captured and cataloged by a dozen redundant systems. But he wanted to actually witness it for himself; to watch and process the incredible moment as it happened.

The electric current running through him intensified and spread, until it enveloped him in a cloud of shimmering energy, invisible yet somehow impossible not to see. His skin tingled and the hairs on his arms, neck and head all stood on end. He was burning up; the sweat running down from his brow to sting his eyes. There was a sudden pressure on his chest. Despite the heat, every breath stung his lungs like the sub-zero air of a frozen arctic night.

The reactor began to pulse in earnest, causing the illumination in the room to wax and wane.

He suddenly felt weightless, as if he was floating, though he could still clearly feel the floor beneath his feet. There was no sound - nothing any of their instruments could ever detect - yet he heard a faint, high-pitched hum as the charged particles in the air stimulated his ear drums.

CJ tried to absorb what was happening on a scientific, clinical level, but both his heart and mind were racing. His coherent thoughts crashed into each other, becoming a tangled vortex of raw emotion. He started laughing, giddy and euphoric. It was like his entire life he had been stumbling around numb and barely conscious, waiting for the burst to fully wake him. Under the pulsing glow of the core, he understood what it meant to be alive - truly, wholly and fully alive!

And then, as suddenly as it began, it was over. The reactor went dim and the pulsing glow receded. The electric charge coursing through him disappeared, and the heat and pressure enveloping him vanished.

CJ stumbled and dropped to one knee, head in his hands as he gasped for breath. The euphoria vanished, along with every other overwhelming sensation, leaving him empty and hollow inside. He felt a dark despair washing over him at what he had lost; in the notes other researchers referred to it as "the crash".

In his time at Dreamland, CJ had already experienced more than a dozen bursts... and the resultant crashes. He knew what was coming, and he fought against it with every fiber of his being, desperately trying to hold onto the memory of what he'd just experienced. But the details were already fading, slipping away like the remnants of some glorious, forgotten dream. Within seconds, he felt utterly lost and alone; an insignificant speck drowning in the vast void of existence.

Fortunately, the crash was as ephemeral as the burst itself. Within a minute the crushing despair lifted, freeing CJ from the rollercoaster of primal emotions.

Just like all the times before.

Instead of dwelling on the subjective elements of his experience, CJ shifted his focus to what he knew best - numbers and science. Getting unsteadily to his feet, he approached the air lock. He punched in his access code, stepped through the airlock's first door and then closed it behind him, sealing off the Core. He waited patiently while the automated systems scanned him for any irregularities: radiation; biological contaminants; chemical imbalances. When the green light came on giving the all-clear, he opened the airlock's second door that led back into the observation room and grabbed a seat at the nearest computer terminal.

Typing frantically at the keyboard, he called up all the data the various monitors and equipment had just recorded, then compared it to the established baselines from previous bursts.

By every measurable metric what he'd just been through had been a fairly standard incident. Nothing in particular jumped out when he compared it against the thousands of other bursts that had been recorded over the past two plus decades, including the 16 bursts he himself had experienced.

Inside the Core, both temperature and atmospheric pressure had spiked significantly. Every known type of radiation - alpha, gamma, beta, neutron and even x-rays - had increased to unnatural, though not immediately dangerous, levels. Electrical, magnetic, and even gravitational fields had shown massive fluctuations. Outside the Core, however, none of this had been recorded.

The numbers CJ was seeing - the scientific phenomena he had experienced first-hand - should have produced a significant ripple effect. Everything he knew about physics and the natural world told him that the amount of energy required to change the readings inside the Core so dramatically should have caused some kind of measurable reaction in the neighboring observation chamber as well, though to a lesser degree.

But the equipment outside the Core hadn't registered anything during the burst. In fact, it hadn't even registered the burst at all.

This matched the results of all the previous instances, yet it was so unbelievable - so improbable - that CJ had initially wondered if all the old research was somehow flawed. Even now, after experiencing the bursts and confirming the data each time himself, he couldn't help but wonder if there was something he was missing.

Deny it all you want, CJ. You know what happened.

There was one last reading to check.

The chronometers.

In addition to all the other equipment, Dreamland had equipped the underground bunker with a variety of atomic clocks. The oldest used rubidium gas trapped in glass cell chambers and were accurate to less than a nanosecond. A decade later, those had been supplemented by hydrogen beam clocks, which were reliable to the pico second. And in the last few years, cesium fountain clocks had been installed, a time piece so incredibly accurate it would lose less than 1 second every 300 million years.

Half of these clocks had been installed inside the Core, half in the adjacent observation chamber. Initially, every pair of new clocks had been synced with Universal Coordinated Time. Over the years, however, that had changed. With each burst, the clocks inside the Core had gained time, somehow racing ahead of the ones outside the Core.

CJ checked the chronometers in the observation chamber. As expected, they were all in perfect unison with each other. Then he checked the ones inside the Core. They were also still synchronized with each other, but the delta - the difference between the timing of the clocks inside the core and the ones outside - had increased by 87.04161454333523 seconds.

Incredible!

Somehow the clocks inside the core had gained almost ninety seconds during the burst, while outside the core time had moved less than a single thousandth of a second. The first time it happened, the researchers had checked and rechecked them, then rechecked them a few hundred more times. But it wasn't a malfunction or miscalculation. It wasn't that the clocks had simply sped up somehow: there were checks and counterchecks that verified that wasn't the case. For all intents and purposes, it was as if everything inside the core - including CJ himself - had experienced an extra minute and a half of existence.

Time outside the Core stopped. But somehow, we just kept going.

It was ridiculous. Impossible. And completely verifiable and expected. With every burst, a similar result had been observed. Over the past three decades - when the bursts first began - the oldest clocks inside the Core, the three rubidium chronometers, showed a difference of nearly 6,353,262 seconds between their corresponding twins outside the Core.

That's over 73 days.

Seventy-three days of temporal existence that were unaccounted for. With each burst, time inside the Core accelerated by a hundred thousand-fold, while time outside the Core kept moving along normally. And then, when the burst was over, time inside the Core reverted back to normal as if nothing at all had happened, falling instantly back into sync with the outside world.

Dreamland experts in a dozen specialized fields had been studying the Core for decades, trying to understand its mechanisms and purpose. The prevalent theory so far was that it was somehow linked to interstellar travel. Dr. Singh called it the Sojourner Hypothesis.

Time dilation - the idea that time was relative, and that it moved more slowly as an object approached the speed of light - was a well-known phenomenon in the field of relativity and quantum mechanics. Travelers on a spaceship approaching the speed of light would age more slowly than their friends and family left behind. Even if humanity ever found a way to travel at those speeds, astronauts returning from a decade-long round trip would find hundreds of years had passed back on Earth during their absence.

But the bursts seemed to invert that equation. If the Core was somehow able to alter the space time continuum in a way that made time outside a vessel pass more slowly than time inside the vessel, then crossing the vast distances of the cosmos became much more feasible. Inside the vessel, the journey might take a hundred years. But outside the vessel, only a few months would pass – a bizarre mirror image opposite of time dilation as it was currently understood.

Of course, this theory assumed that the crew of the vessel would have to be suspended in some type of cryogenic state in order to survive the century of time they would experience inside the vessel during the journey.

Which could explain why they weren't able to keep their ship from crashing in the New Mexico desert all those years ago. They were hibernating. Frozen in sleep, completely unaware that they had gone off course. And whatever automated system was supposed to wake them when they reached their destination was destroyed in the crash.

But even though CJ could buy the Sojourner Theory as an explanation for where the Core came from and what it was originally used for, it didn't explain the bursts. Why were they happening? What was causing them? Were they truly random events, or was there some pattern waiting to be discovered? Why did it take nearly forty years from when the Core was salvaged and rebuilt for them to start? Was there some outside catalyst triggering them?

If there was, nobody had found it yet.

That's why Dr. Singh brought me here. To figure this out.

CJ welcomed the challenge. He was used to being the smartest person in the room. He was used to being asked to solve the problems nobody else could.

Everything has a pattern.

Math, physics, chemistry, biology - they were all based on common, universal truths: the fundamental building blocks of life and nature. Everything was part of the same puzzle of existence. All CJ had to do was figure out the piece of the puzzle that was tied to the bursts. All he had to do was crack the code.

It's in there, somewhere. Buried in the data, just waiting to be found.

Three hours later, he was still seated at the computer in the observation room, studying the readings from the recent burst, when Dr. Belmont entered.

"We have a problem, CJ," he said.

CJ grudgingly looked up from his screen.

"Three days in a row is a violation of protocols," Dr. Belmont continued. "You know better than that."

"I'm on the verge of a breakthrough," CJ countered. "There's something here. Something hovering on the edge of my mind. The answer we've all been looking for. I just needed a little more time."

Dr. Belmont laughed.

"You really think you're the first person to feel like you're on the verge of some brilliant discovery?"

CJ didn't have an answer.

"It's a side effect of the bursts. The euphoria distorts your perspective. If you're not careful, it can make you manic. That's why we limit how often you can be here. It's for your own protection."

"I know my limits," CJ assured him.

"No, you don't. We've all been down this path, CJ. And if you don't follow the rules, it can end badly." Dr. Belmont sighed. "I'm sorry, but I have to report this to Dr. Singh."

"Really? You're going to tell on me? What is this, grade school?"

"He's going to find out when he reviews the Core's access logs anyway," Dr. Belmont explained. "Now come on – let's go back topside."

CJ hesitated for several seconds, then slowly stood up and followed the older man to the elevator. As they rode back to the surface, he couldn't help but feel a piercing pang of regret for what he was leaving behind.

***

CJ was going stir crazy. For the past 72 hours, he'd been confined to his quarters on base. All his internet and intranet access had been revoked, and a pair of armed guards were stationed outside his door around the clock. Meals were dropped off outside the door three times a day, but nobody would talk to or acknowledge him when they were delivered. All his notes and research, including his laptop, had been confiscated, leaving him alone in his room with nothing but his thoughts.

A little extreme just for spending one extra day inside the core.

He wasn't sure if it was Dr. Singh or Dr. Belmont who had actually ordered this punishment, and with all his communications cut off he had no way to find out.

The uncertainty of not knowing who was responsible, or how long it would last, was all part of the punishment. Whoever had given the order was trying to send a message he wouldn't soon forget.

When a knock finally came, he sprang out of his seat and bounded to the door, desperate for any interaction after three days of virtual solitary confinement. He wasn't surprised to find Dr. Singh waiting on the other side.

His superior entered without waiting for an invitation, stepping forward and closing the door behind him.

"We have rules for a reason," Dr. Singh said, jumping abruptly to the point.

"Rules help the ordinary," CJ noted. "But they only slow the extraordinary down."

"Everybody here is extraordinary," Dr. Singh countered.

Not like me, CJ thought. But he nodded in acquiescence.

"Dr. Belmont and I have been very impressed with your contributions to the project so far," Dr. Singh continued. "He even recommended I let you off with just a warning."

"Obviously, you disagreed."

"This is a military operation," Dr. Singh reminded him. "There is a chain of command. Orders must be followed without question. I can't have my scientists taking matters into their own hands... even someone as gifted as you."

So you admit I'm not just like everyone else here, CJ thought, though he was wise enough not to say anything out loud.

"Normally it takes years before I grant anyone clearance to visit the Core without supervision. In your case, I made an exception. But that privilege has a price. You must be held to a higher standard. Do you understand?"

"I do," CJ said. "It won't happen again."

"Good. Because a second infraction will result in termination of your contract. You will be exiled from the project. Do you fully appreciate what that means?"

It means you'll have government agents monitoring me for the rest of my life. Any hint that I may be sharing classified secrets will get me thrown into a deep, dark military prison... or worse.

If Dr. Singh revoked his clearance, CJ's career as a scientist or researcher was effectively finished. He'd never be able to work on anything innovative or cutting edge again without risking the wrath of Dreamland's extrajudicial punishments. The best he could hope for would be a low paying job at a small engineering firm, doing mundane, mind-numbing work for the rest of his life.

"I understand," CJ assured him.

"Good."

As Dr. Singh turned to go, CJ called out, "So have I served my time now?"

"Not yet," Dr. Singh said, not bothering to look back as he stepped out into the corridor. "One more week of confinement to quarters. Then a month with no access to the Core."

As the door clicked shut, sealing CJ into his room once more, he realized the true lesson he'd just been given - *Don't fuck with Dr. Singh.*

CHAPTER 11

July 7, 2017
Two years before the D Street Massacre

"Got a minute?" Dr. Belmont asked, popping his head into CJ's office.

"Sure, Reed," CJ answered, sliding his laptop aside to give his colleague his undivided attention.

Though Dr. Belmont was still technically CJ's superior, over the past two years they'd effectively become equals at Dreamland. Dr. Singh was as quick to reward achievement as he was to punish disobedience, and CJ's star was on the rise. He had entire teams reporting to him now, and everybody knew he had Dr. Singh's ear.

CJ didn't hesitate to take full advantage of the opportunities his position offered, but he was also careful never to overstep. He'd learned his lesson.

Be a good soldier. Obey orders. Follow protocols. Don't rock the boat. Never piss off Dr. Singh.

"You've been reviewing some of the older case files, right?" Dr. Belmont asked.

"I have."

Dreamland had been operating in one form or another for over seventy years now. Much of the research from the early days was still archived in paper folders and hand-written notes. Most of the scientists didn't bother with those older files: they preferred to focus on the most recent developments. But CJ had taken it upon himself to dig through the archaic records on the off chance there was some key piece of the puzzle that had been lost in the hazy mists of the past generations.

While he hadn't found anything specific yet, he was convinced studying the archives had given him a broader understanding of the project as a whole. And it was undoubtedly one of the reasons Dr. Singh continued to give CJ more and more responsibility.

I'm willing to do the dirty work that nobody else will.

"You ever come across anything written by Dr. Epstein? William Epstein?"

CJ took a second, running through a checklist of names from all the researchers he'd come across during his studies. CJ had an eidetic memory; while perfect total recall was a myth of Hollywood, he could typically remember details of documents he'd read with over ninety percent accuracy, even years after the fact. But the name didn't ring a bell.

"Doesn't sound familiar. Do you know when he worked here?

"I think it was in the 80's or 90's."

It was a time period CJ had studied in detail, but even with the dates to help him focus his recollections, he couldn't come up with anything.

"Sorry. Haven't seen anything from him."

"What about Dr. Schuller? Lisa Schuller? Same dates."

"No. I would have remembered that."

In all the decades Dreamland had been active, there had only been a handful of women on the project, and most had only joined in the past twenty years. If CJ had stumbled across any notes or files from a Lisa Schuller, the unexpectedness of her gender would have triggered a strong and persistent memory.

"Have you asked Dr. Singh about them?" CJ suggested. "He was here back then."

"Yeah. I know. I just didn't want to bother him with something trivial."

Something about Dr. Belmont's response set off alarm bells.

He seems nervous. He's trying to hide it, but he's scared!

"Hey, if you find something from either of them, let me know, okay? Epstein and Schuller."

"Got it. I will."

What are you up to?

Whatever it was, he clearly didn't want Dr. Singh to find out.

As Dr. Belmont left, CJ pulled his laptop over again. But he couldn't focus on the screen.

Should I tell Dr. Singh about this?

He liked Dr. Belmont – they worked well together, and he was a valuable contributor to the team. But CJ also didn't want to risk anything that might incur Dr. Singh's wrath.

I should file a report.

But really, what was there to report? Dr. Belmont was just asking about some former employees from thirty years ago. The fact that he seemed anxious to CJ wasn't evidence of anything sinister.

Would Reed report me if our situations were reversed?

CJ was pretty sure he knew the answer to that one.

He ratted me out when I was spending too much time in the Core.

But CJ wasn't looking for payback. And despite his loyalty to Dr. Singh and Dreamland, he didn't want to cause problems for Dr. Belmont. Not for something as small as this.

Instead, he turned his attention back to the reports on his laptop.

Two days later, Dr. Singh called CJ into his office.

"You wanted to see me, sir?"

"Dr. Belmont is no longer with the project."

The words were delivered with no emotion whatsoever, yet they sent a shiver down CJ's spine.

This can't be a coincidence!

"What happened?" CJ tried to keep his voice calm, but his head was spinning.

This has to be about Epstein and Schuller. Does Dr. Singh know Reed asked me about them? Is he mad I didn't report it? And why would that get him terminated?

"Reed was forced to resign due to health issues," Dr. Singh explained.

CJ had no way to tell if Dr. Singh was lying. He was as cool and composed as ever – if he was hiding something, he gave no hint of it.

"I'd like to send him a message. Let him know I'm thinking of him."

"Forward it to me and I'll pass it along," Dr. Singh said. "Since he's left the project, we've had to revoke his security clearances. He can't have any direct contact with anyone on the team ever again."

Convenient. But what about me? Am I still in trouble for this?

"I'll be assigning some of Dr. Belmont's duties and responsibilities to you," Dr. Singh continued. "And moving some of your current projects over to other members on the team."

Relief flooded through CJ.

Whatever happened to Reed, I'm still in Dr. Singh's good books.

"You don't have to do that," CJ insisted. "I can take on some extra work from Dr. Belmont without giving up any of my projects."

Dr. Singh gave a brisk nod. "Very well. If it all becomes too much to handle, delegate as you see fit.

"Congratulations, CJ. You're now the most senior researcher on this project."

Behind you, of course.

"Thank you, Dr. Singh."

As he left Dr. Singh's office, CJ's head was spinning. He'd just become Dr. Singh's right hand, but he was still troubled by how it had happened. The story of Dr. Belmont leaving for health reasons sounded reasonable but given their last conversation CJ just couldn't buy it.

He was digging into those researchers from the past. Epstein and Schuller. Dr. Singh found out, and he terminated him. But why?

CJ's naturally curious nature instinctively wanted to latch onto the mystery. But his rational mind knew better. Whatever Dr. Belmont had been investigating wasn't worth getting exiled from Dreamland. He wasn't willing to kill his career over this.

Or maybe worse – what if Reed is in prison right now? What if Dr. Singh is interrogating him to learn what he uncovered?

The thought came too easily into CJ's head. Dreamland had a dark history. Over the seven decades of its existence, there were multiple rumors of researchers who'd died or disappeared under suspicious circumstances for daring to violate the secrecy of the project. And Dr. Singh had been running Dreamland for almost forty years.

Does he have blood on his hands? Is that what this is about? Did he have Epstein and Schuller killed? Did he have Reed killed?

CJ *wanted* to believe that Dr. Belmont was somewhere in a hospital, getting treatment for his mysterious health issues.

It's a nice story. A happy story. Happier than the alternative, at least.

Dr. Singh had made it very clear to CJ what he was signing up for the day he'd been recruited. Dr. Belmont had probably been given the same speech.

Whatever happened to Reed, he brought it on himself.

At least, that's what CJ told himself.

CHAPTER 12

April 17, 2019
Two days after the D Street Massacre

CJ skimmed through the printouts piled on his desk, scouring through a daily summary of reports from various news outlets and government agencies. Ever since Dr. Belmont had left the project, this had become his new morning routine.

Over the past two years, he'd thrown himself ever deeper into his work: grinding through decades worth of compiled measurements and results, looking for clues and patterns others might have missed. Trying to answer seemingly impossible questions that had stumped the government's most brilliant minds for over seventy years.

During these studies, he'd come to fundamentally change his understanding of what the Core was and how it worked. He now believed that the bursts were a reaction to an outside stimulus; an effect triggered by an external agent located outside the Core itself.

The Catalyst Theory was just one of many proposed explanations for the bursts. But something in CJ's gut - an intuition built on experience and his natural genius for identifying codes and patterns - told him this was the right answer.

Logically, the idea that an unknown source in an undisclosed location could somehow influence the alien reactor buried hundreds of feet below the surface of the earth, without being measured or detected by all their sophisticated equipment, made absolutely no sense.

But that's the fundamental truth of quantum science. Logic has no place here.

The Catalyst Theory relied on the bizarre phenomenon of quantum entanglement: the observation that two distinct particles could be connected in a way that literally transcended time and space. Influencing one of these particles – such as by measuring it – instantaneously affected its twin, even if they were separated by thousands of miles.

The concept was so radical that Einstein originally dismissed it as "spooky action at a distance" when it was first observed. It violated all the known truths of his relativity theories, with the entangled particles seemingly sharing information in a correlated fashion that couldn't be measured or disrupted. The effect was instantaneous, with no regard to distance or location, meaning the transfer happened at speeds faster than light itself – something that was supposedly impossible.

Quantum entanglement was eventually proven to be fact, not fiction. It became one of the cornerstones of quantum theory, ripping unexplainable, unmeasurable holes in the neatly constructed space-time continuum Einstein and his cohorts had envisioned.

CJ wasn't the first to propose the Catalyst Theory. But after his access to the Core had been restricted, he had thrown himself into studying it in detail. He had built on the original hypothesis, expanding and developing the thought experiment until it could potentially have real-world implications.

If we can find the catalyst – identify and locate the source that triggers the bursts – then we can get one step closer to understanding the alien technology of the Core.

And finding the catalyst meant studying the data. Assembling patterns so complex and subtle they seemed completely random. Finding meaning in the chaos.

CJ couldn't accept that the bursts were random. On some instinctual, intuitive level he sensed there was a purpose behind them. Willful intent. Someone or something – maybe human, maybe alien - was intentionally causing the bursts.

Who's to say the bodies recovered from the crash at Roswell were the only visitors to our world?

Eventually he'd come to realize that if the Catalyst Theory was accurate, then it wasn't enough to study the data measured inside the Core. He needed to find evidence in the real world, outside the carefully controlled environment of the lab.

With Dr. Singh's approval, CJ had put together a team to create powerful AI algorithms looking for key words and phrases across news media and the internet. Dreamland also had the authority and clearance to gain access to any files or reports from other government agencies: CDC, NSA, CIA, FBI. Like the news coverage, these were fed into the algorithms for analysis. Overnight, anything relevant was summarized into the file that appeared on CJ's desk the next morning: millions of sources distilled down to a few dozen pages.

Each and every day, CJ reviewed the summary file in detail, hoping to find some small piece of evidence that would support the Catalyst Theory. Some small clue that would get them closer to solving the greatest scientific mystery humanity had ever faced.

Today, he hit the motherlode.

***

Dr. Singh flipped through the pages of the report in rapid succession, spending only a few seconds on each. But CJ knew he wasn't just skimming them. Dr. Singh was an accomplished speed reader, absorbing the information on the page at a rate that seemed nearly impossible. He also had an eidetic memory, meaning he would remember every word and image he looked at with perfect precision.

Dr. Singh set the report down on his desk.

"You're sure about this?"

CJ nodded.

"It caught my eye this morning when I was reviewing the daily summary. I had them pull the full FBI report, including the crime scene photos."

The FBI report was dated April 15, 2019 – only two days ago. It was the culmination of an investigation into a woman named Mama Pearl;

a racketeer operating out of Las Vegas. She had been under FBI surveillance for several months, with the Feds slowly building a case against her... only for their work to be cut short by a violent, bloody massacre in a bar she used as a front for her operations. There were eight dead, and several suspects were still missing and unaccounted for.

The savagery of the D Street Massacre, as it was being called, had made both local and national news. But that wasn't what triggered CJ's algorithms to flag the story. The FBI report contained several anomalies and inconsistencies. There were numerous elements that made no sense; evidence that seemed to defy explanation and believability; video and audio footage that the investigators had dismissed as malfunctioning equipment. But CJ suspected the real explanation was something else.

The images of the brutally butchered bodies in the crime scene photos from the file – slashed, stabbed and beaten – had burned themselves into CJ's brain; he feared they would haunt his dreams for years. But if the gruesome pictures had any emotional effect on his superior, Dr. Singh kept it carefully hidden.

"Does it strike you as odd that this happened in Las Vegas?" Dr. Singh asked.

Vegas was less than 100 miles from Area 51 and Dreamland. But for CJ, that only made things more intriguing.

"It could be part of the pattern. There may have been some attraction between the Core and the Catalyst. Something that was drawing the Catalyst here; a primal drive or homing instinct."

"Or it could just be coincidence," Dr. Singh countered. "Fifty million tourists visit Vegas every year."

"Maybe the Catalyst was just passing through," CJ conceded. "But I don't think this is a coincidence. The past few weeks have seen radical increases in activity: multiple bursts almost every night in unprecedented numbers. It's unlike anything we've ever seen before. Something big is happening."

"You think the increased activity is related to the Catalyst coming to Vegas?"

"It's possible such close proximity to the Core somehow intensified things. Pushed the Catalyst to another level. Maybe that's why this ended with so much bloodshed."

"Your Catalyst could be one of the victims."

CJ nodded. It would be frustratingly ironic to finally come across this lead, only to discover the proof he'd been searching for had been murdered by a small-time gangster and her crew.

"Even if the Catalyst is dead, I still think we should investigate."

"Of course," Dr. Singh agreed. "Grab your things and meet me at the helicopter pad. We'll leave for Vegas in an hour."

CHAPTER 13

Part Three: The D Street Massacre

April 5, 2019 - Las Vegas
Ten days before the D Street Massacre

Carson had felt like an outsider his entire life. His power – the strange, frustrating, impossible gift he'd been born with – made him different from other people. But he couldn't tell anyone about it. Not in any way that would make them believe him. He couldn't show them how he could stop time. Not in any way they could see. He couldn't prove it was real.

If he tried to tell anyone about it, they'd just think he was crazy. So it became a shameful secret. Something that he hid away and protected, careful not to let others see. Something that isolated him. Put a distance between him and everyone else in the world.

Maybe on some level Sarah knew I was never being completely honest with her. Maybe that's why our marriage never really worked.

When he first saw Charlie in the bus depot, moving while the rest of the world was frozen, he realized for the first time that he wasn't completely alone. He'd vowed to find Charlie, even if it meant sticking around town while Mama Pearl's goons were looking for him. Now that he'd tracked him down, however, it wasn't quite what Carson had been expecting.

He'd hoped Charlie would be a kindred spirit. Someone he could feel a connection with. Or at least someone who might be able to give him some answers.

Where did this power come from? Why was I born this way?

But Charlie didn't have any answers. Charlie barely even had any questions. He didn't seem to care about why Carson could stop time. Or why he could move when the rest of the world was frozen. Or what deeper connection the two of them might have.

"None of that shit matters," Charlie insisted. "We just need to figure out how to use this to our advantage."

Charlie threw back his tequila, slammed the shot glass on the table and motioned for the server to bring another round.

"Drink up!" he said, shouting to be heard above the blaring music in the bar. "We're celebrating!"

Carson dutifully raised the shot glass to his lips. Steeling himself, he swallowed it in a single gulp, grimacing at the taste.

Never been a tequila man.

They were sitting at a corner table in Cabo Wabo – Sammy Hagar's Tex-Mex themed Rock 'n Roll Bar located just outside the entrance of Planet Hollywood and the Miracle Mile. Guitars, gold albums, and posters of motorcycles, muscle cars, and scantily clad women with blown out hair and cartoonishly oversized breasts covered the walls in a haphazard fashion. The overall effect was as if a tornado had ripped through every 80's rock and roll cliché, swirled it all together, then dropped the wreckage here on the Vegas strip.

"Jesus Christ," Carson said, shaking his head and grinning. "Lighten up, my man. Do you know how fucking rich we're going to be?"

He's right. Try to look on the bright side, here.

This was a chance to pay Mama Pearl back. More importantly, it was a way to pay for Ella's treatments.

After years of being a fuck up as a father, I can finally make things right. Make her life better for once instead of worse.

The waitress dropped off the next round of shots. Carson raised his glass, forced a smile and said, "This could be the beginning of a beautiful friendship."

"Shit, yeah!" Charlie answered.

Carson couldn't tell if he'd caught the *Casablanca* reference. Not that it really mattered.

They downed the shots in unison.

"Fucking fantastic!" Charlie bellowed. "Now you're feeling me, brother!"

"I guess we need to figure out our plan?"

"Plan? We don't need a plan. Together, we're like fucking Gods! We can do literally anything! We walk into a bank, you do your little trick, and I walk out with a million dollars right under everyone's nose!"

Carson shook his head.

"That won't work. Banks don't have that kind of money just sitting around. It's locked in the vault, and without the combinations or codes we can't get in. Best we'd get is maybe twenty grand from the tills."

"Twenty grand from each bank!" Charlie countered. "Shit, hit a bank every other day and we're living like kings!"

"If money starts disappearing from banks, there's going to be an investigation," Carson warned. "I can't keep time frozen forever – we'd probably have to be inside the bank for you to grab any cash before the world snaps back into motion. We'd be on video surveillance.

"Even if they don't actually see us taking the money, they're going to get suspicious if the same two guys show up in every bank right before it gets robbed."

Charlie shrugged. "Okay, we hit the casino. They've got all those chips just sitting in the racks at the tables. You do your thing, I grab a handful and poof – we're gone."

"They track the chips. They'll notice if they're missing. And again, we have to worry about the cameras."

"Fuck, man," Charlie grumbled with a shake of his head. "You must be real fun at parties."

This isn't a party. It's a way to help my daughter.

"Look, we've got a golden goose here. I just want to be sure we can keep it laying eggs."

"Okay, genius – what's your bright idea?"

Carson reached up and absently stroked his chin.

"I'm still working out the details. We need a way to do this that won't attract too much attention. The best crime is one nobody even knows happened."

Charlie snapped his fingers. "I got it! Poker. High stakes. Every hand you freeze the table, and I can jump up and look at everyone's cards. We can't lose!"

"That could work," Carson admitted, "but I don't want to cheat the other players. That isn't right."

"Are you fucking kidding me?" Charlie demanded. "These people come to Vegas to lose money – they'll get over it."

"Why cheat the other players, when we can cheat the casino instead?"

Charlie's eyes lit up, and he grinned, showing off his uneven, yellow teeth.

"Ah, now we're getting somewhere! Blackjack? Swap the cards around?"

"They're always watching the blackjack tables," Carson warned. "Looking for card counters. If we win too much, too often they'll kick us out."

"How? They can't prove anything!"

"They don't have to. Casinos are private entertainment clubs. They can ban someone from their property for any reason they want. If we do this, we have to be subtle. The casino can't even suspect something's off."

Charlie sat back in his chair, his back stiff and straight. He reached both hands out and set them on the table, flat with the palms down. There was something undeniably menacing in the deliberate way he moved.

"I'm getting tired of this shit," he said, staring so intently at Carson it sent a shiver down his spine. "So quit dicking me around and just tell me the fucking plan."

"Roulette. But I haven't figured out all the details yet. I'll do some calculations, figure out how much we can win without drawing too much attention."

Charlie's posture suddenly relaxed, and he raised his hand to call the waiter over for another round.

"Good. You get right on that."

***

"Quite the set up you have here," Charlie said as he looked around the low-budget motel room where Carson had been holed up for the past week.

"Yeah, well… if I go back to my apartment, I've got a feeling Mama Pearl's goons will be waiting for me."

And they'll be even more pissed after what you did to them.

Carson had shoved all the room's furnishings – the nightstand, the bed and the cheap dresser with an ancient tube TV sitting on top – to one side of the room. On the other, he'd set up an old folding table, eight feet long and four feet wide.

The table was covered with a strip of green felt, with the numbers 1-36 laid out in three rows, along with a single and double zero at one end. Stacks of different colored chips were piled around the edges of the felt, two on each long side and another at the base. At the head of the table, just above the zeros, was a full-sized roulette wheel.

The casino-grade wheel had cost nearly twelve-hundred dollars, used. Carson could have found a cheaper home version for a tenth that price, but he wanted to practice on the real thing.

"This is what you've been up to for the past three days?" Charlie asked, raising a skeptical eyebrow.

"Not just this. I was also figuring out a betting pattern and limits that won't draw attention. Calculating how much we can win before it skews the casino returns enough that they start to get suspicious. Working out the all the details so we don't fuck this up."

"You worry too much."

Somebody has to, Carson thought, but he had enough sense not to voice his criticism out loud.

He gave the roulette wheel a clockwise spin, sending the painted numbers into a whirling blur. Then he put the ball just inside the edge of the wheel and flicked it with his finger, sending it flying in the counter-clockwise direction, rattling and bouncing across the tiny metal ridges that separated each spinning number.

"Let me guess," Charlie said with a grin, "you've been practicing your regulation spins."

Carson suspected he was being mocked, but he let it slide.

"I have. I've also been studying the way the ball bounces and jumps. Practicing my timing so I can stop the world just as it's losing the last of the momentum. That way, the ball will stay in place after you move it. In theory."

"You've really given this a lot of thought."

You don't know the half of it.

Carson had been so preoccupied with his plan that he hadn't even called Ella this week. Sarah had sent him a message to check up on him, but he'd kept his reply brief. *Working on something to help pay for Ella's treatments. Could be big.*

Sarah hadn't bothered to reply – she'd heard him talk about plans and schemes before.

But this time it's going to be different.

The spinning wheel had slowed down enough that it was possible to read the individual numbers as they went round and round. The ball was still bouncing erratically, but Cason could tell it wouldn't be long before it settled onto one of the numbers.

"Ready to give it a try?"

"I've been ready since the day we met."

"Let's try to hit lucky seven."

*** *FREEZE!* ***

Everything slammed to a halt: the roulette wheel was held fast, the bouncing ball hovering above it, stuck in mid-air. Everything was frozen. Except for Charlie. He looked around, turning his head slowly as he took in the motionless world around him. Then he stepped over to the wheel, reached out and plucked the ball from where it hung in mid-air, like he was picking a grape off the vine.

He studied the wheel for a bit, looking for his target. Then he placed the ball in the number seven slot, took a step back and winked at Carson.

**** GO! ****

The world sprang back into action. The wheel went round and round, slowing but not quite stopped. The ball jiggled and rattled... but it stayed in the number seven slot.

"Holy shit!" Charlie said, grinning from ear to ear. "It fucking worked!"

Carson didn't say anything; he was too stunned to speak. Even as he had been planning everything out – buying the roulette wheel, setting up the table, calculating how much they could bet without getting caught – he still wasn't fully convinced it would all come together.

It can't be this easy, can it?

Charlie stepped over and gave him a hard slap on the back.

"Let's go, brother! Time to hit the casino and make some fucking money!"

***

They started on Freemont Street. The limits were lower there, but even after the successful test run in the hotel room, Carson wasn't willing to try his luck at one of the marquee hotels on the strip yet.

"We can't win every spin," he reminded Charlie as they walked into the Four Queens Resort. "We lose enough that it doesn't look like we're cheating."

"Yeah, you already said that."

The casino was moderately busy, just as Carson had hoped. He'd picked a Thursday for their first run on purpose. They wouldn't have to deal with the chaos of the weekend crowd, but there were still enough people gambling that they wouldn't be the only ones at the table. He'd also told Charlie to dress casual so they wouldn't stick out; it was important their attire match the rest of the patrons.

"And you can't move the ball more than one slot in either direction. If you move it too far, the cameras might pick up something strange."

"Yeah, you already told me that, too."

"We follow the system. Stick to the plan. Try not to attract too much attention."

"Jesus Christ, you want me to go grab us some sunglasses and fake mustaches, too? Chill the fuck out, dude!"

Carson took a deep breath.

"Sorry. I'm nervous. I can't afford to fuck this up. I've got too much at stake."

"Yeah, I know. I already ran into your friends, remember?"

Mama Pearl's not my only problem. This might be my daughter's last hope.

"Relax," Charlie said, his eyes twinkling above a wide grin. "We can't lose, remember? So stop worrying and try to enjoy yourself. This is going to be a fucking blast!"

They made their way through the casino and over to the roulette table, where three other players were already standing. The dealer was a cute brunette, wearing the standard Four Queens outfit: black pants and a black, long-sleeved shirt with a small, bright orange stripe along the cuffs, collar and buttons down the middle.

She smiled at them as they each bought in for $500.

"Good luck," she said, as she pushed two stacks of colored chips across the table towards them.

"Thanks... Melody," Charlie said, leaning in a little too close to read her nametag.

Carson's heart was pounding as he organized his chips, hoping Charlie remembered the list of numbers he was supposed to bet. Carson had calculated a seemingly haphazard pattern of wagers for each of them that, combined, would give them maximum coverage on every section of the wheel.

He wasn't a fan of roulette. Like craps, it was a game where all the players were crowded around one table. But the experience of the two games couldn't be more different. In craps, most players were cheering for the same thing. You hit the point, the table wins. You crap out, everyone loses. There was a camaraderie; you shared your victories and your defeats with everyone around you.

In roulette, every player could theoretically bet on the same thing. But with 36 numbers – plus the 0 and 00 – it wasn't unusual for everyone to be cheering for different outcomes. If someone hits, there's a good chance several other players just lost. At the roulette table, it was every man and woman for themselves.

But that wasn't the main thing Carson hated.

"Get your bets down!" the dealer shouted, spinning the wheel and dropping the ball in.

Her call unleashed a frenzy of chaotic, scrambling action from the players. Wagering at the roulette table was basically a free-for-all. Every player had to personally place their chips on whatever number they wanted on the four by eight green felt grid covering the table, avoiding the glasses, beer bottles and ashtrays scattered around the edges.

And it wasn't just a single bet. In roulette, nobody only played one number. You'd put 5, 10 – even 15 or more – bets down on each spin. This required constantly maneuvering around the hands and chips of other players who were all doing the same thing. If someone already had chips on a number you wanted to bet, you just piled your chips right on top. If you wanted to bet a number on the far side of the table, you had to reach, stretch, or – if you had short arms – physically run over to where you were close enough to place the number. And you had to do all this before the bouncing ball stopped and the dealer called off the bets.

It was basically impossible not to be constantly bumped and jostled by the other players. Awkwardness, chaos, and confusion were unavoidable – as if whoever designed the layout of the game wanted to make the players suffer.

And yet it's one of the most popular games in the casino.

Fortunately, both Carson and Charlie were tall enough to reach all the numbers without too much difficulty. Each of them placed bets on seven individual numbers, along with three shared numbers that they both bet on – 5, 19, and 31.

"We're not going to switch up our numbers," Carson had explained on the way to the casino. "Most players stick with the same bets every spin, and we don't want to stand out. Anytime we hit a winner, double that number up for the next spin. That shouldn't draw too much attention - players like to press their bets when they're winning."

Every spin of the wheel, they were risking $100 between them. Every time they hit one of their numbers, they'd win $180... $360 if it was one of their shared numbers. And they'd win double those amounts if they hit a press.

"No more bets!" Melody called out, waving her hand over the table as the wheel began to slow down. "No more bets!"

Carson and the other players – including Charlie – stood up and leaned back from the felt, their eyes turning to the little ball bouncing and skipping across the numbered slots. After a few more seconds the momentum of the ball was spent, and it settled into the "6".

There was a mix of groans and cheers as the dealer placed the dolly – a small plastic marker, about three inches tall with a weighted bottom – on top of the 6 emblazoned on the felt. Then she reached out with her arm and scooped all the losing bets into a jumbled pile, sliding them across the table into a wide slot called the "gutter". The chips fell through the gutter into an automatic sorting machine underneath the table, where they were separated by color then pushed back up into little trays for the dealer to grab whenever she needed to pay someone out.

The only chips left on the table were the winners – ones touching the "6", or side bets like "even" or "black". Melody calculated the payouts with a practiced familiarity, then slid stacks of chips across the table to the winning players.

Both Carson and Charlie lost on the first spin, but that was part of the plan. Carson wasn't going to stop the world yet. He had to watch the wheel go around several times to get a feel for the timing and rhythm of the dealer. He knew when to stop the ball on his own spins, catching it just as the momentum was dying, but Melody would have her own idiosyncrasies he had to get used to.

With the winners paid out, the dealer scooped up the dolly and gave the wheel another spin.

"Place your bets! Get 'em down now!"

The chaos began again as everyone scrambled to make their wagers.

God, I hate this game, Carson thought, mumbling "Excuse me," as he reached around an overweight, middle-aged woman to get his bets down in time.

This time the ball stopped on 17. Charlie let out a whoop, clapped his hands.

"Fuck, yeah!"

"No F-bombs at the table, sir," Melody replied, her tone automatic.

"My bad, darling," Charlie apologized.

Carson's mind – used to counting cards at the blackjack table – instinctively started doing the math on their win.

$180 payout, less $100 on each spin, multiplied by two spins...

Even with the hit, they were still down $20.

That's how they get you.

Roulette, despite its popularity, had some of the worst odds in the casino. The house edge on craps or blackjack was less than 2%, even if you weren't counting cards. But on roulette, the casinos took in over 5% on every bet.

The only way to make money at this game is to cheat.

Luckily, that's exactly what he and Charlie were planning to do.

After a few more spins, Carson figured it was time. He didn't say anything to Charlie; there was no need to send him a signal. When the world stopped, he'd know what was going on.

Melody spun the wheel and dropped the ball in. Carson watched intently as it went round and round. And then, as the ball's last bit of momentum was fading away...

*** *FREEZE!* ***

The entire casino froze. Charlie smiled and gave Carson the finger guns. Carson was so used to everything being completely motionless when he stopped the world that watching Charlie move through the otherwise static scene was still a little unnerving.

He approached the wheel with slow, deliberate steps. Then he reached up over the protective glass surrounding the wheel and nudged the ball slightly, moving it into the "19". A winner for them both.

Once he was done, he methodically made his way back to his original spot and gave a thumbs up – the signal that he was ready for Carson to start the world up again.

*** *GO!* ***

The ball rattled and jiggled but stayed in its slot. Charlie let out a triumphant whoop and turned to give Carson a high-five that left his hand stinging.

At least he's selling it.

Charlie did a little shoulder-shimmying dance as Melody placed the dolly on the 19 then paid them out.

Holy shit. It worked. It actually fucking worked!

"Come to Daddy!" Charlie said, stacking his winnings. Then he flipped a $5 chip to Melody and gave her a wink. "That's for you, darling."

Melody accepted the tip with a nod, a smile, and a quick, "Thank you!"

"Plenty more where that came from," Charlie promised. "I'm feeling lucky tonight!"

An hour later it was time to move on. Between them, Charlie and Carson walked out of the Four Queens up nearly $1500.

"Remember – next time we play here we have to lose a little bit," Carson reminded his partner. "Keep them from getting suspicious."

"Yeah, I know," Charlie replied. "You've only explained your system to me a thousand times."

"Sorry."

Charlie clapped him on the back. "No worries, brother. Where to next?"

"I think it's time to pay the Golden Nugget a visit."

They spent the next five hours working their way up and down the Freemont Street casinos: the Golden Nugget; Golden Gate; Circa Resort; Main Street Station; The D. By the time they were done, they'd made almost six grand between them.

"Not bad for one night's work," Charlie said, hefting the wad of rolled up $100 bills in his hand.

"This is just the beginning," Carson reminded him.

Tomorrow they were going to hit the south end of the strip, where the limits were higher. The casinos on the north end would be the next night, and the ones in the middle of the strip would be the night after that. Then they'd go back to Fremont Street and repeat the entire pattern. By Carson's calculations, even if they lost at a few of the casinos the second time around to throw them off the scent, they'd still bank somewhere between five and ten thousand each night.

"So... where are we going to do to celebrate?" Charlie wanted to know.

"I'm going back to my hotel room to sleep," Carson said. "I'm exhausted."

Stopping the world had never felt physically strenuous before. But he'd never done it so many times in one night. By the end of the evening, it had taken all his focus and concentration to keep the world in stasis. Now his vision was blurring at the edges, and he could feel the beginnings of a migraine coming on.

"Come on, don't be a pussy! We should hit up one of the strip clubs!"

"I'm done, man. I need to rest up for tomorrow. But you go have fun."

"Without you and your sparkling personality? Shit, I don't know, brother. I guess I could try."

The insult was delivered with a good-natured grin. Carson responded with a weary smile of his own.

"Remember – 8pm tomorrow at Mandalay Bay. Dress a little nicer; it's more upscale."

"Got it."

"And do me one favor, Charlie... try not to get arrested."

Charlie laughed and slapped Carson on the shoulder hard enough to make him wince.

"No promises, brother. No promises!"

CHAPTER 14

By the next morning, Carson's headache had faded to a dull throbbing between his eyes. He'd probably frozen the world fifty times last night. Never for very long, but he'd never done so many stops so close together before.

Hopefully it'll get easier the more I practice. Like working out. No pain, no gain.

Even if it didn't, a lingering headache was a small price to pay for banking a guaranteed five grand in one night.

He pulled out his phone and called Sarah.

"Carson? Ella's not here right now. She's in daycare."

Good. She must be feeling better.

"I'm actually calling to talk to you. About those new treatments."

There was a long pause before Sarah replied. "We're working on it. I told you, we'll figure something out."

"Don't worry about. I've got it covered."

"Covered?" Her voice was a mixture of suspicion and hope.

"Covered. The whole amount. I'll send you five thousand today. Another twenty by the end of the week. That should be enough to get her started, right?"

"Yeah... I think so."

He could sense the hesitation in her voice, and he braced himself for a barrage of questions. *How is this possible? Where is the money coming from? Are you doing something dangerous? Illegal?*

But the questions never came. After a long pause, Sarah said, "Thank you, Carson. I've been praying for a miracle. Literally getting down on my knees and praying every night. But I never thought... I mean, I never expected you could... I'm sorry. Thank you. I just don't know what else to say."

"You don't have to say anything. She's our daughter."

Which is why you're not asking any of the hard questions.

He didn't blame her. He'd probably have done the same if she suddenly came up with the money under mysterious circumstances.

"Tell Ella I love her," Carson said. "I'll talk to her Sunday afternoon."

"I will. And Carson... thank you again. I mean it."

Sarah's tone triggered something inside him - a deep well of emotions: a sudden, fierce protectiveness for Ella; a deep, stabbing regret at losing Sarah; a glowing ember of hope for the future.

Overcome, he muttered a quick goodbye and hung up. Tears welled up, and he wiped them away. Then he started laughing.

Quit crying, you dumb goof! Ella's going to be okay. You saved her!

He took a few minutes to compose himself before making his next call.

"Flannigan's on D Street."

"Hey, Jimmy. It's Carson. I need to talk to Mama Pearl."

"Sorry, sir – nobody here by that name."

"Come on, Jimmy. Don't fuck around. I've got the money to pay her back. Or I will soon. I need to talk to her."

There was a long silence. When Jimmy spoke again his words were quick and angry.

"Listen, asshole. I don't know who or what you're talking about. Don't ever call here again!"

He slammed the phone down, disconnecting the call.

For a second, Carson was confused. Then the pieces fell into place and he realized how badly he'd just fucked up.

Shit. She's worried someone's bugged the phone!

Now Mama wouldn't just be after him for the money he owed her; she'd start wondering if he was an informant working for the cops.

Carson knew he could smooth things over if he could just talk to her, but he wasn't dumb enough to go down to the bar. At least, not until he had enough cash on hand to pay her back in full.

With a nice bonus to make her forget about all the trouble I've caused her.

The only way to get Mama Pearl off his back – and to help Ella – was to keep working the casinos with Charlie. Another couple weeks in the shitty motel room, and they'd have earned more than enough to pay off his bookie and get his daughter the best medical care in the world.

Just stick with the plan. What could possibly go wrong?

***

"I'm glad you texted me," Maya said as she sipped her coffee. "Haven't seen you around the past couple weeks. I was starting to get worried."

Carson and Maya were sitting across from each other at a small table in the Starbuck's located on the outer edge of the Planet Hollywood casino floor.

"Aw, gee... I didn't know you cared."

Maya gave a sarcastic smile at his meager attempt at humor, then shook her head.

"I'm serious, Carson. You ask me to help find some guy who's into fake IDs and God knows what else, and then you disappear for two weeks? What the hell am I supposed to think?"

Carson reached across the table and grasped her hand.

"Hey, I'm sorry. But everything's good now. Seriously."

Maya raised a skeptical eyebrow.

"So you found the guy?"

"I did."

"And everything's good?"

You could say that.

Carson and Charlie had been working the roulette wheels for three straight nights, cashing in big every time. So far, they were up over $25,000.

"Things are better than good. Great. Fantastic, even. I promise."

"Well... good, then. I'm glad to hear it."

He let go of her hand and they sipped at their drinks in silence. For a few seconds, it felt nice – comfortable, like they didn't need to speak to enjoy each other's company. But then the lack of conversation began to weigh on Carson, and he cracked.

"Everything still on track with your FBI plans?"

Maya nodded exuberantly, seemingly relieved to have something to talk about again.

"Ten more days and I'm out of here. Driving down to Virginia. Training begins at Quantico on May 1st."

Carson shook his head.

"You better be careful. Grabbing a coffee with a known card counter is a bad look for an FBI agent."

"I'm still in training," Maya said with a shrug. "Besides, every agent needs informants. I'll have to get used to socializing with low-lifes and reprobates."

"Reprobate? Really?"

"It's a fancy word for criminal."

"I know. I just prefer scallywag. Or rapscallion. Or roustabout."

"Let's just go with 'undesirable'," Maya suggested. "That works on so many levels."

"Ouch!"

They endured another awkward silence. Then Maya slurped down the last of her iced Frappuccino and stood up.

"Break's over. Back to the grind."

"Yeah," Carson said, standing up as well. "I should get going, too."

He was supposed to meet Charlie in twenty minutes at the Bellagio across the street.

"Am I going to see you again before I leave?" Maya asked as she gave him a quick hug. "You still owe me a goodbye dinner."

"I'll try to pencil you in," Carson teased. "You know how busy us undesirables can get here in Vegas. They don't call it Sin City for nothing."

***

The Bellagio was one of the more elegant casinos on the strip. The vibe was old world, European charm: marble floors, arched ceilings, sculpted columns. The casino floor was bright and spacious, and the limits at the tables were high. The dealers all wore blue, long-sleeved shirts with black slacks – understated and classy.

Carson wandered around in the casino, watching players make terrible decisions at the blackjack tables as he waited for Charlie to show up. Charlie was late, but Carson didn't mind. He was used to operating on "Vegas time" – whenever you made plans in this city, you had to understand that punctuality wasn't an option. Sometimes it was the traffic or the crowds of pedestrians jamming up the streets, slowing everyone down. Other times, someone couldn't resist the allure of a quick run at a slot machine or blackjack table as they walked by. Or maybe they were window shopping at the high-end stores – Gucci, Prada, Louis Vuitton – that lined the corridors of every pedestrian thoroughfare up and down the Strip. The entire city was designed to be one giant distraction, so it was easy for time to just slip away.

Forty minutes later, Charlie finally arrived... but he wasn't alone. A tall, stunning blond in a low-cut, tight red dress and four-inch heels was hanging from his arm. Charlie was wearing an expensive, cream-colored suit, the top two buttons of his shirt open to show off an ostentatious gold chain. The pair were leaning in close to each other as they sauntered leisurely through the casino, Charlie whispering to her as she laughed and giggled at every word.

"Really?" Carson exclaimed. "You brought along a hooker?"

"Fuck you," the blonde snapped. "I'm no hooker – I'm an escort!"

Charlie laughed. "She's got spirit, right? Carson, this is Misha. She's my good luck charm tonight."

"We don't need a good luck charm. And we're trying to avoid drawing attention, remember?"

Charlie looked around the casino, turning his head side to side in an exaggerated pantomime.

"Plenty of guys with gorgeous women on their arms here tonight. Misha will help us blend in."

He laughed again and gave Carson a chummy punch in the arm.

"Admit it, you're just pissed I didn't grab a girl for you. Or maybe you're into guys. Whatever floats your boat, brother. It's all good by me."

His words came in quick, staccato bursts – as if he was all amped up.

"Hey, how do you like my new threads? Pretty fly, right? Figured if we're going to act like high rollers, I need to start dressing for the part."

It was only then that Carson noticed how bloodshot Charlie's eyes were. And they kept shifting back and forth, as if they couldn't look at one place for too long.

Holy shit, he's high as balls!

"Are you coked up right now?"

"Relax, brother. I got it all under control."

"Uh-uh. No. No fucking way. I'm not doing this if you're high."

"What are you talking about? Just a little nose candy to keep me sharp. Relax. I got this. Now let's go make some money!"

Carson grabbed Charlie by the arm and pulled him away from Misha. Charlie shrugged and gave his paid companion a wink as he allowed the thinner man to drag him a few steps off to the side.

"We've got a good thing going here," Carson hissed in Charlie's ear. "And I've got too much riding on this to let you fuck it up."

Charlie's smile vanished as his brow furrowed and his jaw clenched. Carson let go of his arm and took a quick step back. They were about the same height, but Charlie had forty pounds of muscle on him; if things got physical, he wouldn't stand a chance.

Hopefully, he's smart enough to see I'm right.

After a couple seconds, Charlie's face relaxed and his exaggerated, coke-head smile came back.

"Okay, partner. We'll do it your way. I'll send Misha home."

Carson shook his head. But when he spoke, he was careful to make his tone one of pleading instead of command.

"Let's take a break tonight. Give us both a chance to blow off some steam. You go have fun with Misha. Come back tomorrow, alone and sober. Okay?"

Charlie gave a disdainful snort.

"Fine, you little pussy. Tomorrow."

He turned back to Misha and extended his arm.

"Come on, baby. Let's go hit the clubs!"

Misha slipped her arm into the crook of his elbow and purred, "Lead the way, Daddy," making Carson's skin crawl.

He watched them until they wandered out of sight. Then he made his way over to the craps tables.

Since I'm here, might as well play a bit.

Five minutes later he cashed in his chips and walked away from the table. He was up a small amount, but he just wasn't feeling the visceral gambler's rush. It was almost as if knowing he could win anytime he wanted at roulette had killed the thrill of craps.

He turned and started heading towards the exit, then stopped when he caught a glimpse of a familiar face in the corner of his eye. The woman with the silver hair and the long white coat was playing at one of the slot machines. She didn't seem to be paying any attention to Carson, but he knew her presence couldn't just be coincidence.

First outside the Seigel. Then at the bus stop. Now here. She has to be following me.

He started to make his way towards her, only to pull up short when a large man in a dark suit stepped directly in his path.

"Mama Pearl wants to talk with you."

FREEZE!

Everything in the casino stopped. It took Carson a moment before he recognized the man as muscle from Flannigan's. He was standing only a few inches away, his massive bulk blocking the rest of the casino from Carson's view.

Running wasn't an option; by the time Carson turned to take his first step, the goon would have his hands on him.

Not to mention he probably has back up nearby.

But as long as he stayed in the casino, Carson figured he'd be safe. The guy wasn't going to shoot him – not with all the security cameras around. And if he tried to forcibly drag Carson out of here, security would be all over him.

Mama knew all this, too. She wouldn't send someone just to rough Carson up. Not here, anyways.

The man said Mama wanted to talk. She knew Carson wasn't foolish enough to come down to her bar, so that must mean she was in the casino somewhere, too. Neutral ground.

*** *GO!* ***

"I guess Mama got my message?"

"She's in the lobby bar. Let's go. Don't do anything stupid."

Carson nodded. Together, they made their way through the casino to a small, upscale lounge just beside the hotel check-in. All thoughts of the silver-haired woman were pushed from his head as he tried to figure out what he'd say to Mama.

The bodyguard stopped at the lounge's entrance. With a nod, he indicated for Carson to go inside. Mama Pearl was sitting alone at a small table in the back.

She pointed at the chair across from her, and Carson dutifully took a seat.

"Why you phone my bar, Carson?" she asked.

"I wasn't thinking clearly. I'm scared. I made a mistake."

"You making a lot of mistakes lately. Mistake one – bad bet. Mistake two – late payment. Mistake three – fight with my boys who come to collect. This not like you, Carson."

"I know I fucked up. I'm sorry about that. But I'm going to make it right."

Mama raised an eyebrow.

"How? How you make all this right?"

"I'll pay you back next week. In full. With interest."

"Why should Mama believe you?"

For a second, Carson thought about trying to play on her sympathies. *I did it for my daughter. She's sick. I did it to cover her medical bills.*

But even if she believed him, she probably wouldn't care. Every gambler had a sob story. There was only one thing that mattered to someone like Mama Pearl.

"The money is coming. From my parents. I told you that when I placed the bet. It's just taking a little longer than I thought."

Stick with the original lie.

"You think Mama is stupid? I let you go, you leave town. Mama never gets paid."

Carson shook his head.

"If I was going to skip town, I'd already be long gone. I only stuck around because I meant to pay you back."

He paused to let the logic of his argument sink in before continuing.

"My parents are stubborn. They didn't want to give me the money at first. Wanted to teach me a lesson. But after I told them about your boys jumping me in the alley, they agreed to help.

"The money is coming," he insisted. "End of the week. I promise."

Mama gave a heavy sigh.

"It not just money anymore, Carson. Your friend hurt Mama's boys when they come to collect."

Shit.

"I'm sorry about that. Things just spun out of control. But I want to make this right. What if I throw in another twenty grand?"

Mama thought about it for a few seconds before countering with, "Make it forty."

Carson wanted to jump at her offer. The amount of money wasn't an issue; he and Charlie could pull in twenty grand a night if they had to. Winning that much was risky – it might get them banned from a couple of the casinos – but it was a lot less dangerous than pissing off Mama Pearl. But if he agreed to her terms too easily, she'd get suspicious.

"What if I give you an even eighty thousand. Forty this week, forty next. That covers the 50K in losses, the vig, the interest and any pain and suffering for your boys. And I get my father's Rolex back. You can keep my car."

A dangerous smile crept across Mama's face.

"You not really in a position to negotiate, Carson."

"Putting me in a shallow grave out in the desert doesn't get you paid," Carson reminded her. "Come on, Mama. This is a good deal for us both. You make a nice profit, and I get to keep breathing."

She stared at him long and hard, as if peering into his soul to see whether he was telling her the truth.

"Okay, Carson," she agreed. "Forty this week. Forty next."

Carson let out a breath he didn't even realize he'd been holding.

"Thank you, Mama. You won't regret this."

As he stood up to go, her hand snapped out and seized his wrist.

Christ – didn't know the old girl could move that fast!

"Don't fuck Mama again, Carson," she warned. "A shallow grave in the desert is how it ends. But there will be a lot of pain before that."

Carson nodded to show he understood.

He wandered back into the casino, glancing back to see if any of Mama's men were tailing him. After a few minutes, he figured the coast was clear. Only then did he remember that they weren't the only ones following him.

He went over to the slot machine where he'd spotted the silver-haired woman, but she wasn't there anymore. He continued to loiter in the casino, looking for her and watching for any signs of Mama's boys tailing him.

Just because she said we have a deal doesn't mean I'm in the clear. She still might bring me in for a beat down, just to make a point.

Until his debt was paid off, he needed to be careful. The casino was safe, but Mama probably wasn't above yanking him off the street. He knew he was being paranoid, but better safe than sorry.

After thirty minutes, he figured he was in the clear. He left out one of the back exits, looking over his shoulder the entire way back to his motel.

CHAPTER 15

Much to Carson's surprise, the next night Charlie arrived at the Bellagio on time and unaccompanied. He was wearing a different suit this time – canary yellow – but he still had on the same gold chain.

"I want to mix things up a little bit tonight," Carson said by way of greeting.

"Yeah?" Charlie answered, suspicious. "Mix it up how?"

"Let's play the high limit room. Really hit 'em hard."

"How hard?"

"Very fucking hard."

"Now we're talking, brother!" Charlie said with a big, toothy grin. "About time you saw the light!"

Two hours later they cashed out almost fifty thousand between them.

Can't come back here for a while. A win like this will raise all kinds of red flags.

"Holy shit, that was fucking AWESOME!" Charlie said, smacking Carson hard on the shoulder. "Dude – we have to fucking celebrate!"

When Carson hesitated, Charlie pressed his case.

"Come on, man. What good is all this cash if we can't enjoy ourselves?"

He's right. Plus, it'll keep up our image as high rollers. Make our heavy wagers look less suspicious.

"Okay," Carson agreed. "You want to experience the best meal you've ever had in your life?"

"Shit, yeah. I'm fucking famished!"

***

Le Cirque was one of the most expensive restaurants on the Strip – a Vegas transplant of the Michelin Star rated establishment in New York offering an unforgettable French dining experience.

"The menu's in French," Charlie complained once they were seated.

"Don't worry about it," Carson assured him. "Let me do the ordering."

"You don't know what I like."

"Trust me."

Charlie shrugged and shunted his menu aside. When the waiter came over, Carson said, "We'll have the Menu Prestige."

"Very good, sir. And the wine?"

"Whatever you think is best."

The waiter nodded his approval and slipped away.

"What's the 'Menu Prestige'?" Charlie asked. "It's not snails or horse meat or some disgusting shit like that?"

"It's a ten-course meal that will blow your mind," Carson promised. "Like you said, we're celebrating."

The sommelier brought over the wine and showed Carson the label. Carson stared at it for a few seconds, then nodded as if he actually had any clue what he was doing.

Could be the cheapest swill in the house for all I know.

The waiter poured him a small sample. Carson raised the glass to his nose, swirling the wine around and smelling the bouquet, like he'd seen on TV. Then he drained the glass, letting the wine linger on his tongue for a few seconds.

It's actually pretty good.

"Excellent choice," he said.

The sommelier filled both their glasses, then placed the bottle in an ice bucket beside the table. Once he was gone, Charlie picked up his glass to make a toast.

"To you, finally growing some balls and letting us make some real cash for once."

"I'll drink to that," Carson said with a smile.

Charlie took a sip, then made a face. "I'm more into bourbon."

"I'm sure the waiter can get you the best bourbon you've ever had in your life," Carson noted. "Everything here is top shelf."

"And five times more than it should be," Charlie grumbled.

"Didn't think you were the type to complain about spending money."

"I guess this just isn't my scene." He shifted in his seat, trying to get comfortable. "Too stuck up and stuffy."

"It's called 'atmosphere'. Give it a chance."

"Yeah, okay."

The waiter showed up with the first course.

"Hamachi drizzled with a vinaigrette reduction."

"Okay, I can handle sushi," Charlie said, picking up one of the paper-thin slivers of yellowtail with his fingers and popping it in his mouth.

"Well?"

"Pretty fucking tasty," Charlie admitted, grinning.

"See? Just follow my lead and I won't steer you wrong."

"Speaking of following your lead, why the sudden change in strategy? What happened to winning slow and trying not to attract too much attention?"

"Now you're complaining about how much we're winning?"

"Not complaining. Just curious. We're partners in this, remember? Something changed, and I think I've got a right to know what it was."

He has a point.

Carson took a deep breath, then let it out in a long, slow sigh.

"Remember those guys we ran into in the alley? They work for a bookie named Mama Pearl. She operates out of a bar called Flannigan's over on D Street."

"A bookie? No shit. How much you owe?"

"Now? Eighty grand."

Charlie let out a low whistle. "Damn, brother. Maybe you're not as much of a pussy as I thought."

"It's okay. I worked out a deal with her. I'll give her forty thousand this week, and forty more next week. And she won't break my legs."

"Wait a minute – you're actually going to pay this bitch?"

Carson was confused. "Of course I'm going to pay her. If I don't, they'll be finding pieces of me in dumpsters all over town!"

Charlie shook his head. "Seriously, man. Use your head. You don't have to give her one red cent."

"What the hell are you talking about?"

"Listen... we go down to this Flannigan's. You and me together. Tell her to back the fuck off if she knows what's good for her. Then you do your little trick. During the timeout I kick the crap out of her muscle. Send a message she can't fuck with us."

"Are you insane? You want to start a war with a mob boss?"

"Mob boss? Yeah, right. She's probably just some local two-bit hustler. We hit her operation hard, take out a couple of her guys – send them to the hospital – and she'll back off."

"Or she'll want revenge and come after us even harder!"

"How? She won't even know what happened. It'll be like magic. One second, we're standing in her bar, then – POOF – suddenly her guys are on the ground with broken bones. It'll scare the shit out of her. She'll think we're gods!"

Charlie grinned – a cruel, hungry, tooth-filled smile – before adding, "Fuck, brother – we *are* gods!"

"I don't think violence is the answer."

"Depends on the question. You didn't mind it when I saved your ass back in the alley."

"That was different. Besides, I've made a deal with her now."

"You had a deal with me," Charlie reminded him, falling into a mewling imitation of Carson's higher-pitched voice. "We can't win too much, can't risk killing the golden goose... blah, blah, fucking blah."

"You wanted to win because you're greedy," Carson reminded him. "I need to win to keep from getting my legs broken... or worse!"

"We're supposed to be partners in this," Charlie said. "But it feels like you think you're the fucking boss."

He stood up fast, his chair toppling over backward and crashing loudly to the floor. Everyone in the restaurant turned in shock, their luxurious meals interrupted by the sudden outburst.

"Calm down," Carson said in a forced whisper. "We can talk about this. Just sit down and lower your voice."

"Fuck you. I'm done taking orders."

Charlie spun around and stomped out of the restaurant, kicking the chair aside as he left. For a few seconds nobody moved, then one of the waiters scurried over and picked up the fallen furniture.

"Sorry, everyone," Carson said to the other diners. "I'm... I'm sorry."

Nobody verbally reacted to his apology, but after a few seconds they returned to their meals. Carson sat still as stone, flushing with embarrassment while simultaneously feeling his body quivering with a burst of adrenaline as his fight or flight response kicked in.

Only there's nobody left to fight.

That left only one option. He was just about to get up and go when an older woman – probably the manager – came over to his table.

"Sir, is there a problem?"

"I... I'm sorry. Do you want me to leave?"

She looked around at the other patrons, evaluating their mood.

"Is your friend coming back?"

"No. I don't think so."

She nodded. "Well, then. If you wish to stay, you're welcome to do so."

Fuck it. I came here for a good meal. Why should I leave just because Charlie's an asshole?

"I'd like to stay, please."

"Of course, sir."

As the rest of the courses were brought out, Carson realized he'd made the right decision. The meal was magnificent.

Expensive as hell, but worth every penny.

When they brought him the bill, he left a $500 dollar cash tip.

The least I can do after all the trouble I caused.

As he made his way out of the restaurant, his phone buzzed. He pulled it out of his pocket to see a text from Maya: *Get your ass down here NOW!*

***

Maya was doing her best to enjoy her shift. The crazy crowds of the Final Four were long gone, but the casino was still busy. She was hoping to get through her last Friday night of security at Planet Hollywood without having to deal with any raging assholes... a dream that died when she saw one of the floor managers coming her way with quick steps and a clenched jaw.

"Got a problem in the Fishbowl," he said.

Shit.

The Fishbowl was a small blackjack pit just outside the high limit room – six tables arranged in a tight circle. Staffed by gorgeous women wearing corsets and stockings, the Fishbowl was visible from all sides and angles, meaning it inevitably attracted more than its share of players, gawkers, and troublemakers.

Her long strides propelling her across the casino, Maya pulled out her walkie-talkie and called for backup.

Never hurts to be prepared.

As she approached the scene, she was already evaluating the situation. The major threat was obvious: a man in a bright yellow suit was standing up from his seat, yelling and gesturing angrily at one of the other players. He was tall – maybe six-three – and muscular, with dark hair and a short, thick beard.

"This asshole keeps taking the dealer's bust card!" he shouted to no one in particular as Maya approached. His words were slurred ever so slightly, and he seemed to be leaning to the side – sure signs his anger was at least partly fueled by alcohol.

"It doesn't matter," the pit boss replied, trying to calm the angry customer down. "You can't berate the other players. You can't swear at them. You can't insult them."

"I know what berate means, you arrogant fuck!"

The pit boss didn't answer. Instead, he turned to Maya.

"He's done," the pit boss told her. "Get him out of here!"

"I just bought in for five grand!" the man protested.

"Collect your chips and let's go to the cash cage," Maya told him. "You're done playing for tonight."

The man wheeled around to face Maya, momentarily losing his balance. He reached out to steady himself, grabbing the shoulder of the man sitting beside him.

"Get the fuck off me!" the man in the chair exclaimed, swatting his hand away.

"You fucker!" the bearded man shouted, spinning around and yanking him out of his chair and down to the floor just as two burly security guards arrived on the scene.

Security tackled the bearded man, pinning him to the ground. At the same time, Maya rushed to the side of the man on the ground, instinctively positioning herself between him and his assailant to prevent any possible retaliation.

"Are you okay?" she asked, offering her hand as the customer gingerly picked himself up off the floor.

"Yeah... I think so."

Glancing back over her shoulder, she saw security had restrained the bearded man, cuffing his hands behind his back with plastic zip-ties.

He looks familiar for some reason.

"Do you think you're up to filling out an incident report?" she said to the other man.

"What's that?"

"A witness statement we can show to the police when they get here. So we can press charges."

"With pleasure."

"Donnie will help you out with that," Maya said, nodding at one of the guards. "Thank you."

"Box up his chips," she told the pit boss. "Bring them down to holding."

"This is total bullshit," the man grumbled as Maya and the other security guard escorted him down to the holding room. "He hit me first. Check the cameras. You'll see."

"Oh, don't worry," the guard said, taunting his prisoner. "We'll check the cameras, all right."

Maya didn't say anything. Her mind was racing as she tried to figure out where she'd seen this guy before. And then it hit her – the fake IDs Carson had shown her last week!

Fuck.

"Take him down to the holding room for me," she told the guard. "Don't call the cops yet."

The guard gave her a quizzical look, then shrugged his shoulders.

"You're the boss."

She pulled out her phone and texted Carson: *Get your ass down here NOW!*

He replied a few seconds later with: *On my way!*

Maya went back up to the casino floor to wait for him to arrive, hoping some time cuffed and alone in a small room in the casino basement would calm the bearded man down.

Carson showed up ten minutes later.

"I got here as fast as I could," he said, slightly out of breath. "What's the problem?"

"Your friend was in here stirring up shit."

"My friend?"

"The guy you asked me to help you track down. Big, muscular, dark beard?"

Carson's shoulders slumped as he let out a big sigh.

"What did he do?"

"Got shitfaced. Had a temper tantrum at the blackjack table. Took a swing at another player."

"You call the cops?" Carson asked.

"Not yet. Figured I'd give you a chance to explain, first."

"Explain what?"

"Everything. Who is he? Are you working together? Was he here counting cards on my tables?"

"He's not a card counter," Carson said, holding up his hand. "Scout's honor."

Maya studied him for a few seconds, then nodded when she convinced herself he was telling the truth.

"So who is he? Are you guys related?"

"Related?"

"I didn't notice it at first because of the beard, but you two look a lot alike. I mean, you would if you ever bothered to hit the gym."

The little jab was her way of letting Carson know that even though she was mad, she didn't blame him for what happened. He smiled with relief, picking up on the signal.

"He's my cousin, Charlie," Carson lied. "He's kind of a fuck-up. He came here because he had nowhere else to go. I'm trying to help him get his life back on track."

It was a reasonable explanation, but something didn't quite track.

"He bought in for five thousand," Maya noted. "Where does a fuck-up get that kind of money?"

Carson shrugged. "I don't know. Maybe he hit a jackpot somewhere or something."

"Or maybe he's dealing drugs. Are you two mixed up in something dangerous?"

Carson didn't answer right away, setting off all sorts of warning bells in Maya's head.

"We're not doing anything illegal."

"That doesn't answer my question."

"I've got it under control."

"Clearly," Maya said with a snort. "That's why your partner's down in my holding room."

"I... I hate to even ask this," Carson said, clearly uncomfortable with what he was about to say, "but do you have to call the cops? What if I take him home and I promise he'll never set foot in here again?"

Maya took a deep breath, then nodded.

"Fine. Save me the paperwork. I've got less than a week left here anyway."

She took Carson down to the holding room, where Charlie was sitting on a small bench against the wall. His hands were still tied behind his back, forcing him to slump forward, his head hanging down. He looked up as Carson and Maya entered, swaying slightly in his seat. The alcohol in his system was really catching up with him now, leaving him bleary-eyed and woozy.

"What the fuck are you doing here?" he growled at Carson, slurring his words even worse than before.

"I've come to take you home. Unless you'd rather spend the night in jail?"

"Un-be-fucking-leviable," Charlie said, shaking his head. Then he looked up at Maya.

"You gonna cut me loose, then? These ties are cutting off my circulation. I can barely feel my fingers."

As Maya took a step forward, Carson pulled her up short by saying, "First, you're going to apologize to Maya."

"Fuck that," Charlie said. "I'd rather go to jail than apologize to this bitch."

"Fine by me," Carson said, turning away.

"Wait!" Charlie called out, realizing Carson wasn't bluffing. "Wait a second. Hold on."

Carson turned back expectantly. Charlie took a deep breath, then addressed Maya.

"Sorry. I... I think I had too much to drink."

"No shit," Maya replied.

"You can do better than that," Carson said, glaring at Charlie.

"I'm sorry I lost my temper," he growled. "I'm sorry I called you a bitch. It won't happen again."

Carson looked over at Maya.

"Good enough," she said, pulling out a small pocketknife and using it to cut the zip-ties.

"Ahhh," Charlie said, stretching his arms and flexing his fingers. "That feels better."

He looked at Maya, then at Carson, then back at Maya as a knowing grin crept across his face.

"So… how do you guys know each other?"

"Get him out of here," Maya said, ignoring the question. "And remember – he doesn't come back to this casino. Even after I'm gone. Got it?"

"We got it," Carson promised.

"Hey, what about my chips?" Charlie objected as Carson dragged the inebriated man to his feet.

"Over there," Maya said, nodding at a small, sealed box on the table. "Count them if you want."

"We don't have to count them," Carson answered before Charlie could speak.

Charlie gave him a dirty look but grabbed the box and tucked it away in the pocket of his jacket without saying anything.

"I really appreciate this, Maya," Carson said, glancing back over his shoulder as he led Charlie out the door. "I owe you one."

"Just one?" she called after them. "I figure you owe me at least five or six by now!"

CHAPTER 16

Carson led Charlie through the service halls of the Planet Hollywood basement with his drunken partner's arm draped over his shoulder. Charlie was staggering badly, and Carson strained to keep them both upright under his weight.

"Christ. It's only been a couple hours since I saw you. How much did you have to drink?"

"Relax," Charlie assured him. "Drinks are free in the casino, brother."

Brother. Maybe Maya's right. Maybe we really are related.

Carson didn't really see the facial resemblance Maya had mentioned, but they were similar heights.

Similar builds, too, if you discount the forty pounds of muscle he's got on me.

If they were related – if they had some kind of genetic connection; if they shared the same blood or DNA – it might help explain their complementary abilities.

"Did you ever tell your parents about how the world sometimes stopped around you?" Carson asked, hoping to learn something about his partner's upbringing.

"Parents?" Charlie said, giggling softly. "I don't got no parents. I'm a fucking orphan."

Odd.

They stepped through a door marked "EXIT" and into a back alley adjacent to the hotel parking lot.

"Hey, are we leaving?" Charlie asked. "I need to cash in my chips first."

Later," Carson said, as he lowered him down to sit on the curb. "I need to get you home before you fuck things up even worse."

Carson called up a Lyft, and five minutes later he was helping Charlie into the backseat.

The driver, a middle-aged woman, watched with an openly hostile expression.

"If he throws up in my car there's a $200 cleaning charge," she warned.

"I can hold my liquor," Charlie grumbled, slouching down into the seat.

"He's good," Carson assured her.

Charlie was silent for the first few minutes of the drive, and Carson thought he might have finally passed out. But then his eyes snapped open, and he started chuckling.

"What's so funny?" Carson wanted to know.

"That security chick. You banging her?" When Carson didn't answer, he added, "Hey, I don't blame you. She's a hot piece of ass."

Carson could see the driver's disapproving stare in the rearview mirror.

"We're just friends," Carson said, hoping it would shut Charlie up.

"Should've guessed," Charlie said, chuckling some more. "You're too much of a pussy to ever ask her out."

There might be some truth in that.

"Mind if I take a run at her?" Charlie asked.

"I don't think you're her type."

"Normally I don't like the yappy bitches," Charlie continued. "But she won't talk back if I give her something to keep her mouth full."

"Shut the fuck up," Carson snapped.

Charlie looked at him with sudden surprise, then started chuckling again.

"So, you do want to bang her!"

"We're here," the driver said, pulling up in front of Carson's motel. Her tone was clipped and cold.

Fuck. There goes my 5-star passenger rating.

"Come on," Carson said, grabbing Charlie by the shoulder. "Let's go."

It took almost a minute before he managed to drag Charlie's drunk ass out of the backseat. He barely had time to close the door before the driver peeled away.

"Bitch!" Charlie yelled after her as she disappeared into the night.

At least he didn't puke in her car.

"Let's go sleep it off," Carson said.

He dragged Charlie up to the room, fished his key out of his pocket and unlocked the door. Charlie stumbled forward, his legs suddenly unable to support his weight at all. It was all Carson could do to steer him so he fell face first across the bed.

"What the fuck, man?" Carson demanded. Charlie only replied with a deep snore.

There was only one bed in the room, and even if he was willing to share it with his partner, the way Charlie was lying – diagonally across it on top of the covers – made it impossible.

"Sleep tight, asshole," Carson muttered, grabbing a pillow and curling up on the couch.

He tossed and turned, trying to get comfortable as he scrunched and squeezed his lanky frame in between the arms of the couch.

Despite feeling exhausted, he couldn't stop his mind from racing. He kept thinking about Maya... and what Charlie had said about her.

You're too much of a pussy to ever ask her out.

Maya was leaving soon. They might keep in touch through social media, but she was effectively leaving his life. He was running out of time to tell her how he felt about her. He thought there was a spark between them – something more than the playful banter they exchanged on the casino floor. But what if he was wrong? What if Maya only thought of him as a friend, and nothing more? Did he really want to risk their friendship by asking her out on a date?

Christ, Charlie's right. I am a pussy.

Eventually he slipped into a fitful doze. The sound of drunken neighbors stumbling down the hall woke him up again, leaving him momentarily disoriented and confused. But when he saw Charlie sprawled across the bed everything came back to him.

Shit. What time is it?

He glanced over at the just slightly too bright digital clock on the nightstand beside the bed: 5:29 AM.

Sitting up, he rolled his head from side to side to work out the kinks in his neck and shoulders. He stood up and stretched his hands towards the ceiling, hearing every individual vertebra in his spine pop and crack as he did so.

Charlie was still passed out cold, but Carson knew he wouldn't be getting anymore sleep tonight.

I'm starving.

He grabbed the small box with the casino chips from Planet Hollywood.

Might as well go change them in for cash while I'm out.

Outside, the sky was gray with the first hints of the coming dawn. Carson pulled out his phone as he crossed the parking lot to call an uber for a ride. To his surprise he saw a missed call from Maya.

4:18 am. Just after her shift ended.

She hadn't left a message.

Probably just calling to make sure I got Charlie home okay.

He stared at her name and number on the screen, wrestling with himself over whether he should call her back.

It's been an hour. She's probably already back home and in bed.

Even if she was still up, what would he say to her?

Quit being such a fucking coward. Just ask her out to dinner. The worst she can do is say no!

He was so focused on his phone as he crossed the parking lot, he didn't notice the two menacing figures stepping out from the twilight shadows. He was oblivious as they closed in on him from either side, only becoming aware of their presence when the first delivered a brutal punch to his stomach.

In response, Carson's instincts kicked in.

**** FREEZE! ****

The sudden pain in his gut vanished as the world slammed to a halt. Carson was doubled over, staring down at his own shoes. His phone hung in the air, dropped from his fingers as he clutched for his stomach.

Because of his stooped angle, he couldn't see who'd hit him. But he damn well knew who sent them.

Mama Pearl had promised to give him another week to come up with the first fifty grand. Now Carson realized she'd only said that so he'd let his guard down. She must have had her goons watching him, and he hadn't bothered to check if he was being followed when he left the casino early tonight.

Led her goons right to my motel.

He should have expected this. Bookies didn't like it when you stiffed them. Now he was going to pay the price... unless Charlie woke up and came to his rescue. Even though he was passed out in the room, time was still moving for him.

Just gotta keep things frozen until he sleeps it off. Then hope he realizes I'm missing.

It was a longshot, but it was Carson's only option. That, or get his ass beat so bad he ended up in the hospital... or worse.

Working with Charlie, Carson had realized he could keep things in stasis for only a few minutes at a time. Long enough for his partner to move around a roulette table, fiddle with the ball and get back in position. But anything much longer than that, and the world would slip back into motion.

But I was getting stronger the more we did it. Building up whatever mental muscles I use to do this little trick.

He'd never pushed it to the absolute limit; he didn't want to risk Charlie getting caught in a compromising position. But if he really focused – put all his mental energy into keeping the world locked in place – maybe he could hold out long enough for--

Shit!

The world slipped and broke free. Pain shot up from Carson's gut through every nerve in his body. His phone clattered on the pavement, the screen shattering as he collapsed to his knees and vomited. Someone grabbed his hair and yanked his head back.

*** *FREEZE!* ***

This time he was looking up when he stopped the world. Right into the eyes of one of Mama's goons. Carson recognized him from the alley where he first met Charlie. His nose was bandaged; he recalled how Charlie had broken it during the timeout.

The man had his fist raised, wrapped around a small leather pouch filled with heavy metal shavings. One smack from that and it was lights out. But Carson couldn't see any way to avoid it now.

He just had to hold on. Hope Charlie would wake up. Hope he realized something was wrong and came looking for him.

Shit, how long will that take?

Charlie was still passed out. Could he sober up while Carson was stopping time? Could he even wake up when the world was frozen? Or did he need to be conscious when it happened to be immune to Carson's ability?

Doesn't matter. It's my only hope. Come on Charlie – I need you!

He had to hold on. At least give him a chance.

Come on... come on... come on...

Despite his desperate efforts, his grip on the world inevitably slipped. Time started moving, the leather pouch slammed into Carson's face, and everything went dark.

***

"Wake up, Sleeping Beauty."

Carson slowly came to, brought back to consciousness by a heavy hand slapping him swiftly and repeatedly on his cheek.

For the second time tonight, he was disoriented and confused as he came to. The first thing he noticed was that his arms and legs were restrained; tied to a chair. He snapped his head from side to side, frantically taking in his surroundings. After a few seconds, he realized he was in the back storeroom of Flannigan's. Two large men – including the one who'd knocked him cold - hovered over him.

"He's up," the other man said.

Mama Pearl stepped out from behind her body guards, shaking her head with exaggerated disappointment.

"Carson, Carson, Carson… what am I going to do with you now?"

She was dressed in her familiar matronly style – a cream-colored pantsuit and a silk, turquoise blouse. But all trace of her accent had vanished, confirming what Carson had long suspected: it was just an affectation to sell her image.

Can't be a good sign that she's giving up the act.

"I thought we had a deal," Carson said. "Forty grand by the end of the week, remember?"

"You broke our first deal when you went into hiding without paying me back," Mama noted. "So why should I honor the second deal?"

"For the money," Carson said. "Kill me now, and you don't get paid."

Mama shook her head.

"I'm not stupid, Carson. You were never going to pay me. I mean, how could you possibly come up with that kind of money that quickly?"

"I can get it!" Carson insisted. "I've got a plan."

"A plan?" Mama Pearl laughed. "I think Mike Tyson said it best: Everyone has a plan until they get hit in the mouth."

One of the bodyguards stepped forward and landed a hard right-cross on his jaw, punctuating her point. Carson's world exploded in pain.

*** *FREEZE!* ***

His head had snapped to the side, recoiling from the force of the blow. He couldn't see anything; his eyes had instinctively slammed shut on impact.

On the bright side, he couldn't feel any pain with the world stopped. But he could tell the inside of his bottom lip had been mashed against his teeth, slicking it open on the inside.

Is she softening me up so I'll agree to whatever new terms she wants to make? Or is she just torturing me as punishment for double-crossing her?

If he was lucky, it was both. At least then he could still negotiate with her. Maybe talk his way out of this. He just had to remain calm. Stay focused.

*** *GO!* ***

Carson grunted as his head recoiled so hard he felt like his skull was dislocating from his spine. He managed to open his eyes, but his vision was overwhelmed by a shimmering haze of slowly spinning stars. Blood welled up in his mouth from his split lip, choking off his air. He fought against the instinct to spit it out on the floor... the last thing he wanted to do was antagonize Mama further. Instead, he swallowed the warm liquid, gagging and coughing as he did so.

After a few seconds the stars faded away, just in time for him to see Mama Pearl stepping forward. She raised her hand, and he flinched away.

"I actually like you, Carson," she said, her hand gently caressing his check. "Even back when you were taking my money with your bets, I didn't mind. But then you got greedy. You went for the big score, and it backfired."

She sighed and let her hand fall away.

"I hate that it has to end like this."

"It doesn't!" Carson insisted, suddenly realizing he had one card left to play. "I can get your money. Check the pockets inside my jacket. You'll see!"

Mama nodded, and one of the goons roughly rifled through the pockets of his coat. He came out holding a small box – the Planet Hollywood chips Maya had set aside after Charlie was taken by security.

"Five grand in casino chips," Carson explained. "And I've got another ten grand in cash in my pants pocket."

Mama nodded again, and this time the goon jammed his hand into Carson's pants pocket, pulled out his money clip, and handed it to Mama Pearl.

"That's just from tonight," Carson told her. "Fifteen grand in a few hours. I can get that much every night. More even. Every night!"

Mama raised a curious eyebrow.

"You really think you can pay me back by counting cards?"

"Not counting cards," Carson countered. "This is something different. Foolproof."

"Tell me," Mama said, slipping the chips and the money clip into the pocket of her pantsuit.

"It's... it's hard to explain."

Mama nodded again, and her goon stepped forward, fist cocked back to deliver another right cross.

*** *FREEZE!* ***

Carson realized this game was going to get old in a hurry. He needed to convince her... but if he told her what was really going on, she'd never believe him.

Think, Carson. That's what you're good at. Figure out the angles. Look for an edge.

There had to be a way out – he just had to find it!

Carson held on as long as he could, trying to piece together some strategy that didn't end with a bullet in his brain. Trying to find some way to convince Mama Pearl that the impossible was real. Trying to keep the world in stasis so the fist hurtling towards his face didn't connect.

But eventually his hold slipped, and the world lurched back into motion.

The punch crashed home, crunching the bone in his nose. Carson screamed in pain, and blood poured from his nostrils, mingling with the blood still welling up from his cut lip.

"This isn't a negotiation," Mama Pearl explained as Carson let out a low, pitiful groan. "When I ask a question, you answer. Is that clear?"

Carson nodded. Even that slight motion sent a fresh jolt of pain through his fractured sinus cavity.

"Good. Now tell me what the scam is."

"Roulette," Carson croaked. "Two-man team."

"Your partner – he's the one who roughed up my men in the alley?"

"That's him."

"Where is he now?"

**** FREEZE! ****

Where is Charlie? Still passed out on the bed? Or is he up by now?

Carson had no idea how long he'd been out. They'd hit him pretty hard in the parking lot... he could have been unconscious for hours. If that was true, then maybe Charlie was already on his way.

No. That's a pipe dream.

Even if Charlie was awake and sober by now, he had no idea what happened. No idea where Carson had disappeared to. No idea he was even in trouble.

Fuck.

**** GO! ****

"I don't know where he is," Carson said. "Probably at some strip club, knowing him."

Thankfully, Mama seemed to believe him.

"How did you two meet?"

"I just... I just ran into him. We crossed paths at the bus station. Something clicked, and we partnered up."

Mama shook her head.

"You're holding something back, Carson. You can't do that any-more."

She nodded, and one of her goons stepped forward and grabbed Carson's pinkie finger.

"No, wait!" Carson cried out, struggling against his restraints as his finger was bent back until there was a loud SNAP!

****FREEZE!****

Carson realized he was going to die here: tied to a chair in the back room of a shitty dive bar.

There was nothing he could say that Mama would believe. Nothing he could tell her that wouldn't seem like made-up, utter fantasy, bull-shit. Without Charlie here, there was no way he could prove what he could do. No way to show her the truth.

So they were just going to keep torturing him. Snap his fingers one by one. Beat his face to a bloody pulp. Break his ribs, his knees, his elbows. And eventually – after hours of being brutally tortured – they'd put a bullet in his brain.

And there wasn't anything he could do to stop it.

*** *GO!* ***

As the world started up again, Carson began to cry. The realization that he was going to die – combined with the agony of his broken finger, his swelling jaw, his split lip, and his fractured nose – overwhelmed him, and he began bawling like a child.

Mama watched his outburst in cold, passionless silence. After a few minutes, Carson's wailing sobs subsided into pitiful whimpers.

"You can stop this, Carson," she told him. "Just tell me what I want to know. How are you and your partner scamming the casinos? All you have to do is tell me how it works."

"I can't," Carson croaked as fresh tears ran down his cheeks. "You'll never believe me."

Mama sighed, and Carson screamed as they snapped a second finger.

Everything after that became a blur. The interrogation continued for hours, with Carson blubbering and weeping uncontrollably, when he wasn't screaming in agony or begging for mercy. Sometimes he tried to tell the truth, even though he knew it wouldn't help.

I can stop time. I can freeze the whole world, except for Charlie. That's how we do it.

But his blubbering, rambling explanations only pissed Mama off. She thought he was fucking with her – giving her an absurd, bullshit story in an act of stubborn defiance. She responded with more beatings. More broken fingers. At some point they burned him with cigarettes: first on his arms, then his cheeks. The smell of his own cooking flesh made Carson throw up, but that didn't make the torture stop.

Carson kept freezing time over and over and over. At first it was a conscious effort; a way to grant himself a brief respite from his suffering and anguish. As the torture continued, it became an involuntary reflex. His rational mind slipped away, even when the world was frozen. Reason and logic had been beaten out of him, leaving only a primal, cowering psyche – an animal instinct that triggered a reflexive action in a vain attempt to make the pain stop, if only for a few precious moments.

He clung to those moments with a savage desperation. Dragging them out. Pushing himself to his limits and beyond. Holding the horrors of the world at bay for as long as possible. But ultimately, he would lose control. The world would start up again. And the torture would continue.

CHAPTER 17

Charlie groaned and rolled over as a sliver of light from the rising sun slipped through the blinds, striking with uncanny precision directly across his eyelids. Balanced on the precipice between sleep and wakefulness, his mind picked up subtle, subconscious details about his surroundings: unfamiliar smells lingering in the air; the unexpected hum of an air conditioner; a peculiar feel to the sheets and the pillow.

Where the fuck am I?

His eyes snapped open, taking in his surroundings as bits and pieces of the previous night came back to him in random, haphazard fashion – sitting in some fancy frou-frou restaurant; gambling at Planet Hollywood; stumbling from a cab while leaning on someone for support.

Fuck. I'm in Carson's shitty motel.

He sat up and looked over at the clock – 7:41 am.

Where the fuck is Carson?

He stumbled out of bed and headed to the bathroom. As he was pissing, the world suddenly stopped around him.

Jesus Christ – really?

There was little he could do but stand there waiting. He was caught mid-stream; if he moved now, he'd piss all over the floor – or himself – as soon as the timeout ended.

That'd teach the little fucker a lesson.

After a few moments, the world started up again. Charlie let out a long, satisfied sigh as his bladder emptied. When he was done, he wandered back out into the bedroom.

He was still trying to remember details from the previous night, but most of his recollections were hazy.

Shit. Must have really tied one on.

He opened the mini-fridge and grabbed a bottle of orange juice, then guzzled it down to rinse away the foul taste coating the inside of his mouth.

Carson and I got into it.

The reason for their fight still eluded him, but his memories were slowly starting to take recognizable shape.

That bitch at the PH had security drag me away from the tables. Then Carson came to pick me up.

Suddenly he remembered the little box Carson had pocketed as they'd left the casino.

Five grand in casino chips. That's my money, fucker!

He headed over to the room safe. It was unlocked, but there was nothing inside. Cursing under his breath, he turned his attention to the dresser, yanking open every drawer and rummaging through the socks, shirts and underwear Carson had carefully folded and tucked away.

Where'd you hide my money, you little shit?

He was just lowering himself to his knees to peek under the bed when the world froze around him again.

Fuck you, Carson.

There was nothing under the bed but a collection of dust bunnies and a few dead roaches. Charlie stood up again, struggling against the oppressive inertia of the timeout.

The timeout ended as suddenly as it had begun, freeing Charlie up to resume his frantic search at normal speed. He tossed the cushions from the couch, then dug his fingers into the folds where the back and arms met the seat. Finding nothing, he went into the bathroom, peeking behind – and then into – the toilet tank.

Shit. Bastard must have taken the chips with him.

Charlie had no idea where Carson had gone.

Probably went crawling back to that security bitch at PH to apologize.

He sat down on the edge of the bed, considering his options. He could wait for Carson to come back and force him to hand over the chips... but he had no idea how long that might take.

The world stopped around him again.

Jesus fucking Christ, what's wrong with you?

Then it hit him. Carson was fucking with him. Freezing the world to irritate and annoy him.

Cocksucker!

Charlie stood up and marched towards the door, moving as quickly as he could through the thick, heavy air of the frozen world.

Fuck this shit. I'm out of here!

The timeout ended just as he stepped out of the room, but Charlie didn't stop. He kept plowing forward, not even bothering to close the door behind him.

Hope someone steals all your shit.

It was at least an hour hike back to his own room near Freemont Street, but Charlie didn't care.

I'm not sticking around here to wait for that shithead.

As he stomped across the parking lot, he noticed a phone sitting on the pavement.

Huh. Kind of looks like Carson's.

He bent over and picked it up. The screen was cracked, but otherwise the phone was working. The screen was locked, but still showed a notification for a missed call: Maya, 4:18 am.

*It *is* Carson's phone. But what the fuck is it doing here?*

The world froze around him again.

Shit, something's wrong.

More memories bubbled up from the depths of Charlie's mind.

Carson was talking about owing money to that bookie. Mama Pearl.

Carson had said something about working out a deal, but Charlie didn't buy it.

After what I did to her boys in the alley, she'll want payback.

As the world started up again, everything finally clicked into place.

She took him.

Charlie's first thought was, *Fuck him.* This was Carson's problem, not his.

But he's my meal ticket. Without him, I'm back to being some two-bit grifter.

Plus, Charlie wasn't one to run from a fight.

But where did they take him? I think he mentioned something about this...

He closed his eyes, trying to recreate their argument from last night in his mind.

We were sitting in that restaurant. He was talking about Mama Pearl. And then he said...

"Flannigan's," Charlie blurted out loud. "He said she worked out of Flannigan's Bar on D Street."

The world stopped again, but now Charlie had some inkling of what it really meant. This time, he thought he could guess why Carson kept freezing time over and over. And it wasn't pretty.

With the world still frozen, Charlie zeroed in on an old, beaten-down pickup truck parked in the motel lot. By the time he slogged his way over to the door, the timeout was over.

He grabbed a nearby rock and smashed the window, then yanked open the door and slid into the driver seat. It had been years since he'd last hotwired a vehicle, but he'd always had a natural talent for it. In less than a minute, the engine roared to life and he peeled out of the parking lot.

Hang on, brother. Help is coming!

***

Carson's world had become a haze of unrelenting pain and hopeless despair. In a desperate attempt to escape the unrelenting torture, his mind had retreated in on itself. Even his efforts to stop the world had ceased; his will too broken to perform what had once been a simple, almost reflexive task.

"It's pointless, Mama. He's completely zoned out."

His ears heard the words being spoken, but he couldn't grasp their meaning.

"Let me try one last time."

He felt something against his cheek and flinched away. But instead of a strike or slap, he felt a soft, gentle caress.

"Carson, can you hear me?"

His eyes focused on the speaker. Mama Pearl was looking at him with a sorrowful expression, her head tilted to one side with concern.

"This is important, Carson. I need you to listen very carefully to what I'm about to tell you."

Her tone was soothing. Reassuring. Her gentle words reached down into the depths of his suffering, and he clung to them with the last threads of his sanity.

"Nod if you understand me."

He nodded.

"I thought you'd talk as soon as things got rough. Blurt out everything. But I underestimated you. You're tougher than you look. I'll give you credit for that."

Her hand fell away and she leaned in close.

"But we're coming to an end, Carson. There's no point in continuing if you won't tell me what I need to know. If that's the case, then we only have once choice. Do you understand?"

"You're going to kill me," Carson whispered, his throat raw and raspy after hours of screaming from the torture.

"Yes. But I don't want to do that. So, I'll give you one last chance. Tell me how you're scamming the casinos, and I'll let you live."

Carson knew she was lying. At this point, he didn't even care. He'd given up long ago. He reached the point where the specter of his own death wasn't something to be feared anymore. Now, he only saw it as sweet relief.

"I'm sorry Mama," he said, his swollen, bloody lips sliding up into the hint of a smile. "You'll just have to kill me."

"So be it," she said, shrugging and stepping back. She held out her hand, and one of her goons placed a small pistol into her waiting palm. Carson was actually impressed she was willing to do the deed herself.

But before she had a chance to raise her weapon, a thunderous crash erupted from the bar out front, causing everyone to instinctively turn in the direction of the sound.

"What the fuck was that?" Mama snapped.

Charlie!

Carson had no reason to believe the sudden, unexpected noise had anything to do with his partner. But in his gut, he knew it was true.

Charlie's coming to save me!

"Go see what the fuck just happened!" Mama barked.

As the two bodyguards who'd been torturing him rushed out to investigate, Carson felt a sudden surge of adrenaline that reenergized him.

*** FREEZE! ***

Go get them, you crazy son of a bitch!
***

For the first half of the frantic drive from the motel to the bar, the world kept slipping in and out of stasis around Charlie, making it nearly impossible to control the vehicle. The sporadic fits and starts threw him off, as his hands would instinctively clutch or turn the wheel each time the truck slammed to an instantaneous and unexpected halt. When the world started up again, he'd have to course correct quickly as the pick-up fishtailed and swerved, barely keeping it on track.

But then the timeouts stopped. Fearing what that meant, Charlie slammed the accelerator down, pushing the aging vehicle to the upper edge of its limited performance over the final few blocks.

As he rounded the final corner onto D street, the letters of *FLANNIGAN'S BAR* came into view, painted in oversized yellow print across the large plate glass window marking the front of the establishment. He still didn't have much of a plan, but planning had never been his strong suit. Charlie had gotten along well enough his entire life by following a few simple rules: *hit hard, hit fast, hit first, hit last.*

As the truck hurtled forward, Charlie never stepped on the brake. Never took his foot off the gas. Never turned the wheel. But he did briefly close his eyes as he plowed head-on through the plate glass window, almost perfectly centered between the twin *Ns* in the name.

The truck shattered the glass and went careening through the interior of the bar. The air bag deployed, smacking Charlie in the face like a heavy, padded, oversized fist. Tables and chairs were sent flying in all directions, barely slowing the momentum. Blinded and momentarily dazed by the impact of the airbag, Charlie instinctively slammed on the brakes. The pick-up bucked and thrashed, nearly rolling over before crashing into a quartet of half-ton billiard tables in the rear of the establishment that finally brought the vehicle to a jarring halt.

In the first few seconds after the crash, Charlie was too stunned to do anything. And then the world froze around him again.

Fuck yeah!

Charlie tried the handle on his door, but it was jammed – bent and twisted from the crash.

Everything's a fucking struggle in a timeout.

He threw his shoulder into it, straining with everything he had. It finally began to budge, but it was like trying to move a rhinoceros. He managed to wedge it open just enough to squeeze through.

Then the world started moving again.

"What the fuck!" a man shouted from the other side of the room as Charlie struggled to get his bearings.

There were two guys standing beside the bar, and another behind it.

Three on one. Don't like those odds.

The two men in front of the bar started moving towards him, reaching under their jackets to grab the guns Charlie assumed they were carrying. They stopped in their tracks as the world froze again.

Seizing the advantage, Charlie scooped up a pool cue lying beside one of the upended billiard tables and went on the attack. In stasis, the cue felt as heavy as an iron girder. He rushed towards his assailants, but every step in the soupy inertia of the timeout was a deliberate struggle. Still, he managed to close most of the gap before the world snapped back into motion.

Moving at normal speed again, he swung his makeshift weapon at his opponent's head. The man's eyes barely had time to widen in surprise – to him it seemed as if Charlie had teleported across the room, moving from the truck to the bar in a split second.

Charlie felt a satisfying *thud* as the heavy butt-end of the cue slammed into the man's skull. The cue snapped in two a few inches up from Charlie's grip. And then time froze again.

Flying splinters and a long, jagged chunk of spinning wood hung frozen in the air. The man's face was locked in a grimace of pain, the frozen flesh of his cheeks rippling and distorted from the force of the blow. But Charlie was already focused on his second opponent, who'd managed to draw his gun and point it in Charlie's general direction before the world had stopped.

The thin end of the shattered pool cue was still clutched in Charlie's hands. He stepped over to the man with the drawn pistol, then very deliberately drove the tip of the cue into his unblinking eye. The resistance reminded Charlie of wet sand, but he shoved with both hands, forcing it in as far as it would go.

He was still pushing when the timeout ended. The accumulated force of his actions during the stoppage was enough to send his victim flying backwards as time started up again. He launched several feet through the air before collapsing into a quivering lump of flesh on the floor, the nine-inch hunk of wood jammed into his brain still protruding from his eye socket.

Charlie turned to the third man, who had ducked down behind the counter. He popped up a second later with a sawed-off shotgun. Charlie leaped to the side as he pulled the trigger, narrowly avoiding the blast. Before the man could take aim to fire a second time, the world froze again.

Scrambling to his feet, Charlie slogged his way over to the bar. His heart was pounding and his muscles cried out in protest as he clambered over it – he'd never worked so hard during a timeout in his life.

Can't stop now. Not if you want to save Carson.

He noticed a heavy knife resting on a cutting board of sliced limes on the shelf behind the bar. Charlie scooped it up and dragged the edge across the bartender's throat. The world started up just as he finished. He was drenched in a spray of arterial blood as his victim dropped the shotgun and clutched at the mortal wound in his neck before collapsing on the floor.

Another gunshot rang out, and a bottle on the shelf behind Charlie exploded. He snapped his head around to see two more thugs had burst out of a door in the back of the bar with pistols drawn.

Charlie threw himself to the floor, taking cover behind the bar as the men fired several more shots. A shower of glass and booze from shattered bottles rained down on him as he crouched beside the blood-soaked, still-twitching, corpse of the bartender.

The world stopped again. Seizing the opportunity, Charlie forced himself back to his feet. The simple act of standing up was like trying to extract himself from a vat of wet cement. Struggling valiantly against the oppressive inertia of the timeout, he wrapped both hands around the hilt of the knife – which felt like it weighed a hundred pounds – and advanced on his helpless assailants.

Now it's my turn, fuckers!

Both men were frozen in classic action poses. The first had his right arm straight out, pistol clutched in his hand, with his left arm reaching back behind him to keep his balance as he fired. The other had crouched down on one knee, with both hands wrapped around the butt of his gun and his arms extended straight out in front of him.

Two bullets – one from each weapon – hung motionless in the air.

*No, not *quite* motionless.*

As he laboriously closed in on his targets, Charlie noticed the bullets were still moving. It was barely perceptible, but by the time he had crossed the length of the bar, the projectiles had each traveled about four inches along their trajectory.

So, time isn't actually stopped right now. It's just really, really slow.

Charlie didn't have the time – or the inclination – to consider the implications of this unexpected revelation. Instead, he focused on using the last vestiges of his waning energy reserves to carve up his paralyzed victims.

***

Carson kept stopping the world over and over. Each time he held on for as long as he could before his grasp slipped. When time started moving again, he would take a few seconds to gather his strength and recuperate, then freeze the world once more.

In between the stops and starts he heard shouts and gunshots from the other side of the door, though he wasn't able to piece together what was happening. And then – for the first time in his life – he reached the limits of his powers.

*** *FREEZE!* ***

But the world didn't stop.

*** *FREEZE!* ***

Carson tried again, but he had nothing left to give. His power was spent, and time refused to bend to his will. Mentally and physically drained, he let his eyes close and his head slump forward. It took him a few seconds to register that the gunshots had stopped. Everything beyond the door was suddenly quiet.

It's over. Either Charlie took out Mama's goons, or...

He wouldn't allow himself to consider the alternative. Charlie was his only hope.

Assuming he even knows where I am.

"Charlie!" he shouted. "I'm here! In the back!"

Mama Pearl's focus – like Carson's – had been fixed on the gunshots and screams from the other side of the door. But her attention snapped back to Carson as he called out.

She brought the butt end of her pistol down against his temple, and Carson's world went dark.

***

Charlie heard Carson calling out for help. But he hesitated before bursting through the storeroom door – he had no idea what might be waiting for him on the other side.

Come on, Carson. Give me another timeout, brother.

He waited a good thirty seconds, but the world didn't stop.

Guess we're doing this the hard way.

He scooped up the pistol from one of the men he'd just butchered, took a deep breath, then kicked open the door and charged through.

The room beyond was dimly lit; it took several seconds for Charlie's eyes to adjust to the gloom. And then he saw Carson – bloodied and beaten – tied to a chair. His head was slumped forward, his eyes were closed, and he wasn't moving.

Charlie rushed over to his side, never noticing the figure hiding in the shadows in the corner. He instinctively dropped his gun as he checked to see if Carson was still breathing.

He's alive!

His elation was short lived, however.

"Make one false move," a woman's voice said from behind him, "and I'll put a bullet in your spine."

Charlie froze, and slowly raised his empty hands above his head.

"Good. Now turn around. Nice and easy."

He did as instructed, only to find himself staring at a small Asian woman. She had a pistol trained on him, and from the way she held it he figured she knew how to use it.

"I'm guessing you're Mama Pearl," he said.

"And I'm guessing you're Carson's mysterious partner," she replied.

Charlie nodded.

"My men... are they dead?"

Charlie nodded again, and he saw her jaw clench with rage.

"Face down on the floor. Hands behind your head!"

He had no choice but to obey. Once he was in position – helpless and vulnerable – he heard her take two steps towards him. Charlie braced himself for the end. He flinched when the gunshot rang out... but he didn't feel the agony of a bullet ripping through his flesh.

Instead, Mama Pearl's body collapsed on the floor beside him with a heavy thump. Her dead eyes were frozen wide, giving her an expression of shock and surprise. Blood began to pool around her corpse, seeping out from the large hole between her shoulder blades.

Charlie turned onto his side to get a better view. A tall, silver-haired woman in a long white jacket was standing over him, still holding the gun she had just used to execute Mama Pearl.

"Cut Carson loose," she said, tossing the bloody knife from his killing spree in the bar onto the ground in front of him. "We've got about five minutes before the cops are crawling up our asses."

Charlie grabbed the knife and scrambled to his feet.

"Who *are* you?" he asked.

"Your guardian angel," she answered, turning away and heading to the back of the storeroom.

As Charlie sawed away at Carson's bindings, the woman began popping the lids off the large plastic pails lined up along the back wall.

"Jackpot!" she exclaimed, reaching into one and pulling out a thick bundle of cash.

The last of Carson's restraints fell away, and he toppled, still unconscious, into Charlie's waiting arms.

"Can you carry him?" the woman asked, dropping the money back into the pail and snapping the lid back into place.

"Yeah," Charlie said, hoisting Carson's limp body up over his shoulder.

"Then let's get the fuck out of here!"

CHAPTER 18

There was an unmistakable buzz in the air as CJ and Dr. Singh were led through the halls of the FBI's Las Vegas field office. Agents looked up from their desks as they passed, poking their heads over the walls of their cubicles to get a glimpse of the mysterious interlopers.

Their guide – Special Agent-in-Charge Daniel Krause, the senior ranking agent of the FBI's Las Vegas branch – brought them into a small room at the back of the building where two more agents were seated at a small table. The table was covered with several thick manila folders and a pair of laptop computers.

"Special Agents Briggs and Lopez," Krause said by way of introduction. "They're working the Mama Pearl case. This is Dr. Singh and Dr. James from... well, it doesn't really matter where they're from."

"Won't the FBI be angry about us swooping in on their jurisdiction like this?" CJ had asked on their flight over from Dreamland.

"They've been told to give us their full cooperation," Dr. Singh had assured him. "Not just by their boss, but by their boss's boss's boss. There won't be any trouble."

The two agents stood up and extended their hands. As CJ accepted the invitation, he noticed their grips were firm, bordering on aggressive. But beyond that, they projected an aura of model professional courtesy. If they were bitter about their case being taken over by Dr. Singh, they were working hard not to show it.

"Give the doctors a quick overview of what you've found so far," Krause said, taking a seat at the table. CJ and Dr. Singh did the same.

"You probably already know the basics," Agent Briggs began. "Six dead, including Mama Pearl herself. She was shot, but the others were beaten or stabbed. Based on the brutality of the murders, our initial theory is this was some kind gang-related payback."

"Your report mentioned video footage of the massacre," Dr. Singh noted.

"We've had a small surveillance operation on Mama Pearl for a few months now," Agent Lopez explained. "She was running numbers out of Flannigan's bar. Probably laundering money, too. We wanted to find out if she was working alone, or if some of those profits were being funneled up the chain to a bigger fish."

"We got a warrant and managed to install a small camera in the bar," Agent Briggs added. "We'd check the footage every few days, but the surveillance was mostly passive. Just gathering preliminary info. We had no idea anything like this was going to happen."

I guess not, CJ thought. "Could we see the footage?" he asked aloud.

"Got it right here," Agent Lopez said, spinning his laptop so they could see the screen. "Gotta warn you, though - there's some kind of tech malfunction."

"It sort of jumps and stutters," Briggs added. "You'll see what I mean."

The footage was black and white, with no sound, but the quality was surprisingly high. From the angle, it appeared the camera had been tucked away high in a corner of the bar - probably in an air vent. But the view gave coverage of virtually the entire room. There was a date and time code stamped in the corner of the feed.

It began with a simple enough scene: two men in suits were sitting at the bar, chatting while a bartender worked behind the counter. CJ watched, fascinated, as the three men leapt for cover as an old pick up smashed through the bar's front window and slammed into the billiard tables near the back of the room. Then, something very odd happened. One moment the driver was sitting inside the truck, seemingly recovering from the crash. The next, he was standing outside the vehicle, with the door open.

"There – see that?" Agent Lopez asked, pausing and rewinding the video. "That's one of the glitches. It's like he went from inside the truck to standing outside in a single frame of footage. Never see him opening the door. Never see him get out. All of a sudden, he's just here."

"The really strange thing is the time code doesn't jump when the glitch happens," Briggs added. "Had the techs look it over, but they couldn't find any explanation."

I've got one, CJ thought.

The strange video was what had originally triggered the warning flag in the search algorithm CJ had set up at Dreamland. The official report described it as an "unexplained temporal anomaly in the video footage".

"Very interesting," Dr. Singh mumbled as he watched the replay.

"You think that's weird, wait till you see what happens next," Lopez said.

As the video continued, the man from inside the truck suddenly seemed to teleport across the room. One second, he was standing beside his vehicle, brandishing a pool cue. The next, he was halfway across the bar, smashing the cue over the head of one of the other men.

CJ glanced down at the time code on the video. 9:54am, April 15th. In preparation for the trip, CJ had pulled up the logs from the Core. Beginning in the early morning of April 15th, there had been a prolonged series of bursts that lasted almost three hours. The frequency and duration of these bursts was unlike anything they'd ever seen before. And the timing coincided perfectly with the strange events of the D Street Massacre.

The rest of the video showed similar instances of the man seemingly teleporting around the bar, jumping from location to location instantaneously as he butchered his victims. Watching it only confirmed what CJ had already suspected.

Somehow, he's still active during the bursts. While the rest of the world is frozen, he's able to move around. Time isn't stopping for him. Just like inside the Core.

CJ's heart was pounding so fast he felt light-headed. Dreamland had been trying to understand the bursts ever since they'd recovered the wreckage from the Roswell crash. For decades, the researchers had been searching in vain for clues to help them unravel the greatest scientific mystery in human history. And now they'd stumbled onto the most significant piece of the puzzle in almost fifty years.

But what does it mean? Is the man from the truck the Catalyst we've been searching for? Is he actually causing the bursts? Or just reacting to them?

If Dr. Singh felt a similar excitement, he kept it well hidden. His expression and demeanor hadn't changed at all while watching the video. Taking his cue from his mentor, CJ struggled to keep his emotions in check.

As the video played on, two more men came bursting through a set of doors in the rear of the bar with pistols drawn.

"Do you have any footage of the back room?" Dr. Singh asked.

Agent Briggs shook his head.

"We were only able to set up that one camera."

"So there's no video of Mama Pearl's murder?" CJ asked, remembering from the report that her body was found in the storeroom.

"No such luck. And she was the only one of the victims who was shot."

"Is that significant?" Dr. Singh asked.

"Maybe," Briggs replied. "You'll see why in a moment."

After dispatching the two newcomers, the man disappeared into the back room. A few seconds later, a woman in a long jacket crawled into the bar through the smashed window. From the corner of his eye, CJ noticed Dr. Singh stiffen. The motion was subtle; none of the agents picked up on it. But this was the first time CJ had ever seen anything pierce the armor of Dr. Singh's unflappable composure.

He recognizes her!

The woman crossed the bar, heading for the rear doors. She pulled out a gun, cautiously pushed them open, then stepped through and disappeared from view.

"Our working theory is that the woman with the gun is the one who actually shot Mama Pearl," Briggs explained.

"Interesting," Dr. Singh muttered.

Who is she? How do you know her?

"Skip to the ending," Special Agent Krause instructed.

Briggs hit the fast forward button, skimming through the five minutes of footage that showed nothing but the aftermath of the attack in the empty bar. He stopped when the rear doors opened again. The woman emerged, carrying a large, bulky sac. The man from the pickup truck followed close behind her, a motionless body slung over his shoulders.

"Looks like this may have been a rescue operation," Agent Lopez explained, tapping a few buttons on the laptop to call up another video. "When we reviewed all our footage, we saw this from a few hours earlier."

The new video showed two men dragging an unconscious figure in from the street and taking him to the backroom.

"We think Mama brought this first guy in for questioning," Agent Briggs explained. "Then his friends came and busted him out. At least, that's our working theory."

"Have you identified any of the principles?" Dr. Singh wanted to know.

"All the victims were known to us already," Agent Lopez replied. "We've been following Mama Pearl for a while. The guys in the bar were all part of her regular crew.

"No idea on the woman in the coat, or the guy driving the pickup," Agent Briggs added. "But we managed to get a hit on the man they carried out.

"We cross matched our video with the casino facial recognition database. Carson Gaines. He's a known card counter. Been on their radar for a while."

"No criminal record, though," Lopez noted. "Nothing that would suggest he's mixed up in any gang activity. At least, not until this."

"Anything else?" Dr. Singh wanted to know.

"We pulled cell phone records on Gaines," Lopez said. "Found a bunch of texts to a woman named Maya Belfour. She's a security supervisor at the Planet Hollywood Casino.

"We were going to bring her in for questioning but held off when we got word you were taking over the case. Figured you'd want to interview her yourself."

"Do you think she's involved?" CJ asked.

"I hope not," Agent Krause replied. "She was recently accepted into the FBI training program at Quantico."

"That seems like an odd coincidence," Dr. Singh noted.

"Yeah. You might want to ask her about that."

There was a hint of sarcasm in the Special Agent's tone; another subtle sign that there might be some lingering resentment at having their case snatched away by some all-powerful, unnamed governmental agency. But Dr. Singh didn't bother to acknowledge it.

"We will need copies of all your footage and files," he said. "And I'd like to use one of your interview rooms when we bring Ms. Belfour in."

"Of course, Doctor," Agent Krause replied with a forced grin. "The FBI is happy to help with whatever you need."

***

"Thank you for coming down today, Ms. Belfour. My name is Dr. Singh. This is my colleague, Dr. James."

"Call me CJ," he said, extending his hand.

"Maya," she replied, shaking his hand before taking her seat at the small table in the center of the room across from the two men.

CJ would have rather conducted the interview in one of the agent's offices rather than an interrogation room. Even with only three of them, it felt cramped and oppressive. The lighting was cold and stark, accentuating the bleakness of the bare walls.

It's supposed to make suspects feel uncomfortable.

But Maya wasn't a suspect. At least, not yet.

She's our only link to Carson Gaines. And he's our only link to the man from the truck. The man who can move when time is frozen.

"Does this have something to do with my Bureau application?" she asked.

"Not exactly," Dr. Singh explained. "Though I hope your aspirations to join the Bureau will encourage you to be forthcoming with us."

"Am I in trouble?"

She delivered the question in a direct, no-nonsense tone. If she was intimidated by her surroundings, she was doing a good job of hiding it.

"No," CJ reassured her. "We're hoping you can help us with a case. The D Street Massacre."

Maya's eyes went wide with surprise, but her reaction wasn't unusual. The media had been flooded with lurid details of the violent crime over the past few days – it was on everyone's mind.

"I'm not sure how I can help you with that."

She still seems calm. If she was involved, I'd expect some signs of nervousness.

"What can you tell us about Carson Gaines?" Dr. Singh asked, jumping straight to the point.

"Oh, God... was Carson one of the victims?"

Her expression was one of genuine concern.

"No," CJ said. "But we think he may be involved."

"Carson? Involved how?"

"You're not working for the FBI yet, Ms. Belfour," Dr. Singh reminded her. "You're here to answer our questions, not the other way around."

Maya nodded her head in a silent apology.

"What do you want to know?"

"How well do you know Mr. Gaines?"

"I caught him counting cards at the casino about a year ago. Told him he couldn't play at our blackjack tables anymore. That's how we met."

"But he kept coming to the casino anyway?"

"Only to play craps. He wasn't banned. We just didn't want him playing blackjack."

"Was he there often?" CJ asked.

"He was a regular. Came by every week or two."

"Were you friends?" Dr. Singh asked.

Does she know we've seen their text messages? CJ wondered.

"I got to know him pretty well," Maya admitted. "He's a good guy. Yes, I consider him a friend."

"Just friends?"

Maya's eyes narrowed at Dr. Singh's implication.

"Just friends," she replied coldly.

"I'm sorry if this feels personal, Maya," CJ interjected. "But we're investigating a serious crime. Six people are dead."

"Of course," she replied, and CJ thought he saw some of the guarded tension slip from her posture. "I want to help. But I can't see how Carson would be involved with this. He's not a violent man."

"We have video footage that puts him at the scene," Dr. Singh informed her.

"Was he alone?" she asked.

"There was another man with him," CJ admitted, sensing she wanted to tell them something. "And a woman."

"Do you recognize them?" Dr. Singh asked, sliding a close-up photo of each suspect pulled from the video.

"I don't know her," Maya said, shaking her head. "But the man with the beard is Charlie. I don't know his last name."

"Where do you know Charlie from?" CJ asked.

"He's a friend of Carson's," she said. "Maybe a relative. I'm not quite sure how they know each other. But Carson looks out for Charlie."

"What does that mean?" Dr. Singh demanded. "Looks out for him?"

"Charlie came into my casino a few nights ago. Drunk. Belligerent. Got into a scuffle with one of the other players. Security had to drag him off. Carson came by later and smoothed things over. Took Charlie home so we didn't have to get the police involved."

"Charlie was violent?"

"I mean... yes. I guess. He shoved another customer. And it took two security guards to restrain him. He's a big guy."

There was a long pause. Neither Dr. Singh nor CJ spoke, letting the silence hang awkwardly in the air until Maya felt compelled to fill it.

"I don't know Charlie very well," she said. "But I think he's trouble. I know he had a bunch of fake IDs at one time. If Carson was involved in this in any way, it's only because Charlie dragged him into it."

"Do you know where Carson is now?" Dr. Singh asked. "Can you help us get in touch with him."

Maya hesitated, clearly uncomfortable at the idea of possibly ratting out a friend.

"I haven't heard form Carson since the night Charlie stirred things up at our casino. Sunday."

"So the night before the massacre?" Dr. Singh asked pointedly. "A few hours before six people were brutally murdered?"

"Yes... I guess so." Maya seemed taken aback by the realization.

She's definitely not involved. She's overwhelmed. Struggling to process this all on the fly.

"Maya, I know this is difficult, but would you be able to reach out to Carson for us?" CJ asked, trying to sound sympathetic and understanding. "We need to speak with him."

"I tried to text him a few times the past couple days, but he hasn't replied," she said.

"Is that normal?"

Maya shook her head, her brow furrowing.

She's worried about him.

"If he reaches out to you again, you have to let us know immediately," Dr. Singh told her.

"Yes, of course."

She's saying yes, but she's not really sure.

Dr. Singh must have sensed her reluctance as well.

"Ms. Belfour, please understand that we need to solve this case," he reminded her. "And if you help us, it could be very beneficial to your career in the Bureau."

The young woman's shoulders stiffened, and her jaw clenched. Clearly, she was interpreting Dr. Singh's words as an attempt to get her to sell out a friend for her own personal gain... and she was offended by the offer.

"If he contacts me, I'll let you know," she said, her words curt and sharp. "Is there anything else?"

"Not right now, Ms. Belfour."

She stood up and left, not bothering to say goodbye.

"You could have handled that better," CJ said once she was gone.

Dr. Singh shrugged. "If you really think so, feel free to talk to her again."

CJ hesitated a moment, then grabbed the file off the desk and went running after her.

"Maya!" he called out, catching up to her just as she was leaving the building. "Maya, wait! Please!"

She stopped and turned to face him, scowling.

"What?"

"I'm sorry about Dr. Singh. He can be a bit... abrupt. I apologize if he offended you."

"I'm not looking for an apology," she insisted. "I'm used to dealing with people like him. It doesn't bother me."

"Fair enough. But we really do need your help on this. And we need to find Carson. He could be in trouble. And not from us."

"I know," she admitted, her features relaxing a bit. "I'm worried about him."

"We don't think Carson is responsible for the killings," CJ said, taking a chance by revealing more details of the investigation. "But Charlie slaughtered five men with his bare hands. It's right there on the video. I've... I've never seen anything like it."

"Charlie wouldn't hurt Carson," she objected, though it sounded more like she was trying to convince herself. "They're partners."

"I think Charlie might be a sociopath," CJ countered. "The kind of brutality he unleashed... that's not something normal people are capable of. A person like that doesn't have any sense of loyalty or compassion. They wouldn't think twice about turning on someone they know."

Maya shifted from foot to foot, clearly uncomfortable, and CJ knew he'd hit a nerve.

"We have to find Charlie," he continued. "Get him off the streets before he hurts anyone else. And Carson is our only lead."

He handed Maya the file folder he'd grabbed from the interrogation room.

"I shouldn't do this, but I want you to take these. Photos from the crime scene. You need to see what kind of monster we're dealing with.

"I know you don't want to betray a friend. I get that. But even if Charlie isn't a direct threat to Carson, just being around someone like that is dangerous."

Maya took the folder but didn't open it.

"My personal contact number is inside," CJ told her. "If Carson reaches out to you – or if you think of anything else than can help us find him or Charlie – please call me."

"You're not really with the FBI, are you?" she asked.

"What makes you say that?"

"I don't know. Just something about the way you carry yourself."

"I'm not with the FBI," CJ admitted. "But Dr. Singh wasn't lying when he said it would be good for your career if you help us. He's a powerful man."

"Who do you really work for?"

"I'm sorry," CJ said, shaking his head. "I can't tell you that."

"Yet you want me to trust you?"

"I do. And you can. We need to solve this case. We need to find Charlie before he hurts anyone else. Carson's our only lead."

She considered his words carefully, then nodded.

"If I hear from him, I'll let you know," she promised.

Watching her go, CJ hoped she was telling the truth.

He went back into the interrogation room, where Dr. Singh was still sitting.

"Did your charms persuade Ms. Belfour to give us anything useful?" he asked.

"Not yet. But I think I got through to her. Made her understand how serious this is."

"I assume you didn't tell her anything she shouldn't know."

"I'm not a fool," CJ answered, harsher than he intended. "I know how to keep our secrets."

"Good."

"But I don't keep secrets from you," CJ added. "And I wish you wouldn't keep them from me."

Dr. Singh raised a quizzical eyebrow.

"The woman on the video," CJ pressed. "You know her, don't you?"

There was a brief pause before Dr. Singh let out a long sigh.

"I know her," he admitted. "Dr. Lisa Schuller. She worked for me a long time ago."

CJ recognized the name instantly. *Dr. Belmont asked me about her right before he "retired".*

"What's she doing here now?" CJ asked, hoping Dr. Singh hadn't picked up on the fact that the name was already familiar to him.

"It's a long story."

"I've got time," CJ said.

CHAPTER 19

Carson kept slipping in and out of consciousness. Even when awake, his world was shrouded in a thick fog – sights and sounds were muted and far away. But through the haze, he could still feel waves of pain rippling through his body, from the tips of his mangled fingers, through his busted ribs, and up through his pulverized face. He could also hear voices – one male, one female – but his mind was too lost to make sense of what they were saying.

Christ. We need to get him to a hospital.

No – too dangerous. They'll be looking for him. And you.

He's hurt bad. Those fuckers really did a number on him.

I know a place we can take him.

He was lying in the back seat of a moving vehicle. Every bump on the road sent a fresh bolt of agony through him. He slipped away into the merciful darkness, leaving his physical hell behind. A harsh, white light brought him back, shining down from above. He was lying on something cold and hard – a metal table.

Really? A fucking vet? He's not some dog we're looking to put down!

We're not putting him down. We're treating him. Stitches. Splints. Painkillers. Antibiotics. Human or animal, they're basically all the same.

A figure came into his peripheral vision. His swollen eyes couldn't make out any details of their features, but he saw they were holding something long and sharp. He began to whimper and twitch, instinctively recoiling from this new impending torture.

Hush. Hush. It's okay. This is going to help.

Someone was stroking his forehead with long, slender fingers. He felt a brief stab of pain in his shoulder, and then a warmth began to spread through him.

That should keep him under for a while. Give him another dose every twelve hours. But be careful. This is powerful stuff.

The inviting darkness swallowed him up again.

The next time he woke, he was lying in an unfamiliar bed in small room under a layer of covers. He carefully pushed the covers aside, noticing the fingers on both hands were wrapped in bandages and splints.

With the covers off, he felt a sudden chill. Someone had stripped him down to his underwear. Shivering, he sat up... and the world began to spin.

He lay back down with a groan, closing his eyes until some semblance of equilibrium returned. He tried to sit up again, moving more slowly this time.

Propped up on one elbow, he surveyed his surroundings. There was a bedpan on the floor beside him, but he wasn't in a hospital. There was a night table beside him and a dresser in the corner. In the corner was a half-open sliding door leading to a small ensuite.

I'm in somebody's bedroom.

The main door was closed, but he had no idea if it was locked. He debated getting up to check but doubted his body could handle the five steps to get from the bed to the door... assuming he was even able to stand on his own.

Just then the door opened, and a woman walked in. She wasn't wearing her long, white coat, but Carson recognized her platinum hair immediately.

The woman outside the Siegel Suites. And in the bus stop. And at the Bellagio.

"You're awake," she noted, sounding mildly relieved. "Are you hungry?"

Carson nodded but didn't speak.

"Good. You haven't eaten anything in almost three days."

"I've been out for three days?" he asked, his voice raspy and raw.

"Yes. How much do you remember?"

"Mama Pearl. Being tortured. That's it."

"You're safe here," the woman reassured him. "For now."

"Charlie?"

"He's here, too. Out grabbing some supplies right now. Said he was dying for a beer, so I let him go. He should be back soon."

"Who are you?" Carson asked.

"I'm a friend. Dr. Lisa Schuller. I've been taking care of you."

"You've been following me. I've seen you."

"I'm sure you have a million questions," she answered evasively. "But let's wait until you get your strength back, first."

Carson was too exhausted to argue, proving her point. He lowered himself back onto the pillow, the strain of propping himself up for thirty seconds already more than he could handle.

"I'll be right back with your soup," Dr. Schuller said.

When she returned, Carson had drifted back off to sleep.

***

Over the next couple days, Dr. Schuller and Charlie both came in to check on him several times a day. Dr. Schuller continued to avoid answering his questions, but Charlie gave him enough information to piece together most of what had happened. Stopping time over and over had tipped Charlie off, just as Carson had hoped.

"I'll never be able to pay you back," Carson told him. "You saved my life."

"Not just me," Charlie reminded him. "Dr. Schuller, too. If she hadn't shown up, we'd be under the dirt right now. She saved both our asses."

However, neither Charlie nor the doctor were forthcoming with many details about what happened.

They're worried about upsetting me. Think I'm not strong enough to handle it. Think I'm still traumatized by what happened.

Maybe they were right. Though he had no concrete memory of what had happened to him, there were jagged pieces lingering in his subconscious. He wasn't having nightmares – not that he could re-member – but whenever he woke up there was a brief moment of abject terror until he realized where he was. And even when he was awake, he would get sporadic, sudden bursts of anxiety - not quite panic attacks, but his heart would race and he'd feel an overwhelming sense of im-pending doom and despair. The incidents never lasted more than a few seconds, but they were intense and unsettling.

Carson's strength was coming back slowly. He was able to get up and use the bathroom without help, but the exertion left him so drained he usually fell back asleep immediately after. Eventually, though, he felt well enough to leave the bedroom and explore the rest of his surroundings.

His two caretakers were both there in a small living room when he emerged. Charlie was sprawled across a couch watching TV, while Dr. Schuller was sitting in one of two easy chairs staring at her iPad.

"It's alive!" Charlie said in his best Dr. Frankenstein voice, pausing the show he'd been watching.

"How are you feeling?" Dr. Schuller asked.

"Good," he said, taking small, unsteady steps over to the empty chair. He lowered himself gingerly into the seat. "I think I'm ready for some answers now," he added.

"About fucking time, brother," Charlie said with a grin. "You are never going to believe this shit!"

"Fair enough," Dr. Schuller agreed as Carson settled into the chair and got comfortable.

"Thirty years ago, I was part of a top-secret research project operat-ing out of Edwards Air Force Base."

"Area 51," Carson said, recalling a tourist brochure he'd seen in one of the casino lobbies.

"Yes, but we preferred the name Dreamland."

Does this have anything to do with my strange ability to stop time, Carson wondered, but he didn't ask the question aloud. Dr. Schuller had been following him, but he had no idea how much she knew about his powers... or how much Charlie may have already told her.

Instinctively, he glanced over at his partner, who was still grinning on the couch.

"It's okay, man. She fucking knows about us. She fucking knows *everything*."

"I have some theories," she corrected. "And what Charlie has told me supports them. But there's still a lot I'm trying to figure out."

"I'd be interested to hear those theories," Carson said. "After you tell us why you've been following me."

"It's a long story," she warned. "And it's hard to believe. You're going to have to keep an open mind."

"I can literally stop time," Carson said. "I doubt anything you say will shock me."

He was about to discover that wasn't true.

"As I said, I was part of a top-secret Dreamland project under Dr. Arvihd Singh. He was a genius. The most brilliant man I've ever met. And an absolute monster.

"We were studying the remains of an alien interstellar vessel that crashed outside Roswell New Mexico in 1947."

Carson had to hold back a scoffing guffaw. He'd heard the rumors about Area 51 before, but he usually dismissed them as the paranoid ravings of kooks and crackpots.

She doesn't seem like that type, though. And is an alien spaceship any crazier than being able to stop time with your mind?

"The military salvaged the debris after the crash and rebuilt the ship's cockpit in an underground facility. They called it the Core. And scientists have been studying it in secret ever since.

"But after more than thirty years, they'd still barely scratched the surface. Progress had hit a wall. When Dr. Singh joined the team, he pushed the project in bold – some might even say reckless – new directions.

"Is that when you joined?"

Dr. Schuller nodded.

"Dr. Singh understood that the physicists, chemists, and engineers had gone as far as they could. But there was more than just debris from the ship recovered from the crash site - they also found the remains of two alien pilots."

"Really? Now we're talking alien autopsies?"

"I warned you to keep an open mind," she reminded him. "I was a biologist working on my post-doctorate research with my partner, Dr. William Epstein. We were mapping the human genome back in the early 80's. Dr. Singh recruited us.

"He believed there was biological component to the Core. Some kind of alien genetic code that was integral to unlocking the extra-terrestrial technology of the Core."

She paused in her tale, her brow furrowing.

"You have to understand, when I started, I had no idea where things would end up. How fucked up things would get. I really thought our work would lead to incredible scientific advances that would change the world for the better.

"When you have those kinds of lofty goals, it's easy to delude your-self. Easy to justify things that would otherwise seem abhorrent. You rationalize your actions as being for the greater good. A way to help all humanity. You kind of get caught up in the moment and lose sight of what's right and wrong.

"Especially when you're working for someone as brilliant, charis-matic, and driven as Dr. Singh."

She was clearly upset about things she'd done, but if she was looking for absolution from Carson she wasn't going to find it. As strange as her tale was, he was still only focused on one thing.

"What does this have to do with me and Charlie?"

"Dr. Epstein and I studied the alien remains. We found the genetic sequencing wasn't that much different than ours... not in the grand scheme, anyway. They weren't as closely related to humans as primates, or even pigs, but they were much more similar to us than reptiles, for example.

"But we could only do so much with dead tissue. If we really wanted to learn about them, we needed living cells. We tried growing them in a test tube, but they couldn't survive. We didn't know enough about the alien biology to keep them from dying.

"It was actually Dr. Singh who suggested merging the samples with human cultures to stabilize them, though Dr. Epstein and I were the ones who actually had to figure out a way to do it."

"Jesus Christ," Carson muttered. "Alien human hybrids? Seriously?"

"I know it sounds unbelievable," she admitted. "And horrific. But at the time, we just saw it as a way to push the frontiers of science. Like I said, when you convince yourself you're doing something that can change the world, the lines between right and wrong start to blur."

Sounds like a convenient excuse, Carson thought.

"But even after we merged the samples with human DNA, we couldn't get a viable specimen to survive in the lab. And so we found women who volunteered to be impregnated with the hybrid eggs."

"Fuck me!" Carson blurted out. "I don't care how much you try to spin it, that's just…", he trailed off, unable to give words to his horror.

Over on the couch Charlie was laughing.

"I told you this shit was crazy, man!"

Dr. Schuller glared at him, and he stopped chuckling.

"We'd convinced ourselves we were helping these women," she explained. "Most were poor. Uneducated. Desperate. They were told they were taking part in fertility experiments, and we paid them very well. The money we offered gave them a chance at a better life."

"That actually makes it worse," Carson said.

"I know that now. But at the time we found ways to rationalize it. We were going to change the world."

Jesus Christ, this woman is insane. She's like the doctors that helped the Nazis!

"None of the pregnancies came to term. They all miscarried in the first trimester. We made dozens of attempts, tweaking and adjusting the cell cultures we used to hybridize the eggs before implanting them. None of it worked. Until Beth came along.

"All those women were heroes," Dr. Schuller said, her voice going soft. "Every single one of them. But there was something special about Beth.

"She was the youngest of the volunteers. Only twenty. She seemed so fragile, so vulnerable... but at the same time there was this quiet strength about her. A hidden spark that burned bright and fierce."

She loved her.

"Were you and Beth a couple?"

Dr. Schuller shook her head. "She didn't feel that way about women. But her and Dr. Epstein... I don't know. Maybe there was something between them. Maybe that's why Bill wanted to help her in the end."

She paused in her tale; clearly the memory of the young woman still affected her.

"Beth didn't miscarry. And we discovered she was carrying twins."

Carson's gaze snapped over to Charlie, who grinned and gave him a nonchalant shrug.

"Twins were never part of the plan. It was a fluke accident; her egg spontaneously split in two after it was impregnated. Maybe that's why her pregnancy was the only one that was viable. I don't know. There's so much we didn't understand. Still don't.

"But as her due date approached, Bill came to me. He asked me what would happen to the children after they were born. And I realized I didn't have an answer."

"What do you mean?"

"It wasn't something we'd ever discussed. Not in detail. We knew Dr. Singh wanted them for research and testing, but Bill and I were too focused on trying to get a pregnancy to come to term to think about what happened afterwards.

"The women had all been told their children would be adopted by loving couples. They understood as surrogates they'd never get to see them again, but they were promised their children would have a loving, caring environment to grow up in.

"But when Bill came to me, I realized that wouldn't be possible. Not really. We couldn't adopt the children out. Officially, they didn't even exist.

"Why did he suddenly start caring about this now?" Carson wanted to know.

"It was Beth," she explained. "As her pregnancy continued, she started to regret her decision to be a surrogate. She told Bill she wanted to keep her children, but he knew Dr. Singh would never allow that.

"And the more he thought about it, the more he realized what kind of future we'd be condemning her unborn children too. As far as we could tell, they were human in virtually every aspect - but that wouldn't stop them from being tested and experimented on.

"Best case, they'd be kept in a lab for study and observation for years before Dr. Singh lost interest. Worst case... well, I don't even want to think about what lengths he would have gone to. What kind of experiments he'd be willing to authorize."

The image of a baby being dissected popped into Carson's head - limbs pinned to a table like the frogs from high school biology while masked scientists poked and prodded the internal organs through its sliced open abdomen. Repulsed, he quickly shoved the image away as Dr. Schuller continued her tale.

"When Bill came to me, I finally realized what monsters we'd become. Dr. Singh had woven some kind of spell over us, but now it was broken. So we took Beth, and we ran."

"You ran?"

"We made a plan to sneak her out of the facility before she gave birth. We knew Dr. Singh would look for us; he had access to the full power of every governmental agency, and he'd never stop hunting. We knew we were condemning Beth – and ourselves – to a life on the run. But we didn't feel like we had any choice.

"She gave birth about a week after we escaped. Two healthy baby boys. That's when Bill decided we needed to split up to make it harder for them to find us. He took Beth and one of her sons and went east. I took the other and went west.

"We made plans to send each other updates, but we had to keep our communications limited to minimize the risk of being discovered. A few months after we split up, he sent me a message about Beth.

"She had ovarian cancer. Extremely aggressive. Untreatable. I later found out she wasn't the only one. The same thing happened to all the surrogates. Within two years, they were all dead."

"Jesus," Carson muttered.

"But her babies were healthy," Dr. Schuller continued. "I knew I could never raise a child – not while I was being hunted by Dr. Singh. So I found a young couple in LA that had been trying to adopt. Loving, caring... but unable to conceive. The waiting list for adoption was years, so I offered them an alternative."

Carson should have realized what she was getting at sooner; she'd been spelling everything out. But part of him refused to see what was right in front of him until he was forced to face the truth.

"I'm... adopted?"

As he said the words out loud, the room began to spin. His world had been rocked; the very foundation of identity and being had just been ripped out from under him. Everything went white, and he felt himself falling forward from his seat.

Dr. Schuller sprang up, catching him and gently lowering him to the floor.

"Take slow, deep breaths," she told him, cradling his head. "I know it's a lot to process."

As he lay there, memories from his childhood assailed him in a furious storm. He tried to sift through them, looking for clues that hinted at Dr. Schuller's stunning revelation, but the images came in fast and furious, crushing his rational thoughts beneath an avalanche of overwhelming emotions.

FREEZE!

Carson was staring up at the ceiling with Dr. Schuller cradling his head. Her words were still ricocheting around in his skull, but with the world stopped, he finally had a chance to make sense of it all.

It was possible she was lying, but too many things fit. Too many pieces supported her story. Maya had suspected Charlie and Carson were related; she saw the resemblance.

And it would explain why we have this bizarre connection.

In the corner of his peripheral vision he could see Charlie on the couch. Unlike the rest of the world, he could still move. He rolled his eyes and tilted his head back in exasperation at Carson's extreme reaction – he'd clearly already heard the story.

Fuck him; I still need a moment.

The thing that had rattled Carson the most wasn't her talk of secret labs and alien DNA. It was batshit crazy, but so was his ability to stop time. He could accept all that.

What had really thrown him for a loop was the idea that his parents weren't his real father and mother. That they never told him. That they had kept this incredible secret from him. That they had lied to him. That was what upset him the most. And now that they were gone, he'd never have a chance to ask them why they hadn't just told him the truth.

Fuck.

**** GO! ****

As the world started up again, Charlie grunted, "About time. I was just about to go over there and smack you."

Dr. Schuller's head snapped over towards him, then back to Carson. "You just did it? Stopped time?"

Carson nodded.

"My god," she muttered. "I never felt a thing."

Carson sat up, still on the floor but with his back leaning against the couch.

"I think I'm okay now," he said.

"I can only imagine how hard this must be for you," she said. "I'm sorry it had to be this way. But your parents could never tell you the truth. Not without putting you in danger."

"How much did they know?" Carson asked. "About the labs and Beth?"

"Nothing," she replied, shaking her head. "I told them you were my child. That I was on the run from an abusive relationship. That my husband worked for the FBI and was looking for me. That's all they knew."

"So you just left me with them?"

"Hey," Charlie snapped. "At least you got a fucking family. That dipshit Bill dumped me off in an orphanage!"

"He did the best he could," Dr. Schuller said, jumping to his defense. "He was caring for your mother as she fought a deadly cancer. Hiding out from federal agents. He didn't have a lot of options."

"Fuck that guy," Charlie snorted. "If I ever meet him, I'm going to kick his wrinkly, old ass."

"You don't have to worry about that," she bitterly assured him. "The messages stopped more than twenty years ago. If Bill was still alive, he'd have found some way to make contact with me by now."

"Why are you here in Vegas?" Carson asked. "You've been following me for weeks."

"I've been following you for your entire life," she corrected. "Looking out for you. Making sure you were okay. But I was usually able to stay on the sidelines. You've seen me before plenty of times. You just weren't paying enough attention to recognize or remember me. I just blended into the background.

"That night those security bastards decided to tune you up, I figured I had to jump in. My intervention gave you a reason to remember me. After that that you started noticing me in the crowd. But the truth is, I've always been there. Watching over you."

"Isn't that sweet?" Charlie cooed, his voice dripping with sarcasm. "Your own personal guardian angel."

"You weren't watching over me," Carson objected. "You were just watching me. Studying me. Waiting to see if this alien DNA inside me would make something interesting happen."

"That was part of it, yes," she admitted. "But I do care about you, Carson. You can't watch someone grow up and not feel something for them."

"Yeah, well, it's a one-way street."

"She did help save your life," Charlie reminded him. "You owe her for that at least."

"So now what?" Carson asked, refusing to acknowledge the debt. If she was hurt by his attitude, she didn't show it.

"We lay low for the next few days. Give me time to put some stuff together and figure a few things out.

"The three of us have been involved in a high-profile multiple murder," she continued. "The case is drawing tons of media attention. And I wouldn't be surprised if there were security cameras in the bar. The police may already have ID'd you. They could be trying to track you down even as we speak.

"Not to mention Dr. Singh will be looking for us. Maybe not yet, but sooner or later this case is going to pop up on his radar."

"You make it sound like he's some all-seeing god."

"That's not far off the mark. He has virtually unlimited resources and authority, including a team of brilliant scientists and engineers who answer directly to him. He's obsessed with the Dreamland project, and he'll go to any lengths to find you once he knows who you are."

"He already knows who you are," Carson reminded her. "You're the only one he'd recognize from the security footage. You've basically led him right to us."

"That's one of the reasons I stayed away from you for as long as I could," Dr. Schuller admitted. "But I figured it was better to risk getting involved than to let Mama Pearl put a bullet in your brain."

"Hey, I appreciate that," Charlie chimed in.

"We can't just hide out in this apartment forever," Carson said.

"No," Dr. Schuller agreed. "Eventually they'll track us down."

"You worry too much," Charlie said. "If these government spooks show up, Carson just does his thing and I clean house."

"That won't work if a sniper takes you down from a thousand yards away," Dr. Schuller warned. "Or if they drug your food. Or flood this apartment with nerve gas. You wake up shackled to a cell in the sub-basement of Dreamland and stopping time won't help."

"So they know what I can do?" Carson asked.

"What *we* can do," Charlie said. "It's a two-person operation. Without me, you can't do shit."

"I have no idea how much they've figured out," Dr. Schuller admitted. "I didn't have any clue what was going on until Charlie explained it to me. But after the massacre at the bar, they'll know you're dangerous. They won't take any chances."

"And we can't take chances either," she added. "No more stopping time. Not right now."

"Why not?"

"Dr. Singh's team has been studying this for decades. I have no idea what they discovered after I left the project. I don't know how much they know, or what they can do. Once they realize you're in Vegas, they might have some way to track you down if you stop time again. They might even be able to block you from doing it."

Carson had always taken his unique ability for granted. The idea that someone might be able to somehow track him – or even stop him from using his power – had never occurred to him. He found it strangely unsettling.

She's right, though. There's too much we don't know. Better safe than sorry.

"So you're saying we can't hide, and we can't fight," Charlie said. "That leaves only one option – we go on the run."

Dr. Schuller nodded. "I've done it before. We need to leave as soon is Carson is well enough to travel."

"I can't just disappear," Carson protested. "I have a daughter!"

"If you don't disappear," Dr. Schuller countered, "they will find you. What you went through with Mama Pearl will seem like child's play compared to what Dr. Singh might do to you."

"I have to warn them!" Carson insisted.

"Warn them about what?' Dr. Schuller asked. "Nobody's after them – you're the one they want. The only threat to them comes from you.

"I don't know how much Dr. Singh will have put together already," she continued, "but once they know who you are, they'll be watching

Sarah and Ella in the hopes you make contact. Every time you reach out to them, you'll be dragging them deeper into this mess. The less they know, the less involved they are, the safer they'll be."

Carson realized she was right. The best thing he could do for Ella was to go away. Cut himself out of her life completely.

"You have to give me a chance to say goodbye, at least," he mumbled, conceding the point.

Dr. Schuller considered his request, then nodded. "I'll pick up a burner phone so you can reach out to them without being traced. And we'll need to come up with some kind of cover story."

"Really?" Charlie chimed in. "You don't want to just tell her daddy is an alien-human hybrid being hunted by the government?"

Carson didn't bother to respond. With the excitement and intensity of Dr. Schuller's revelations fading – and the reassurance that Ella and Sarah weren't in any immediate danger – he suddenly felt absolutely exhausted.

"I'm going back to bed," he mumbled, leaning on the couch for support as he stood up. "Wake me up when I can call my family."

Dr. Schuller held out her hand, but he shook her off.

"I don't need your help."

"That's not true," she answered. "And the sooner you accept that I'm your only option going forward, the easier this will be."

CHAPTER 20

"This is bullshit!" Charlie shouted, stomping around the living room like a caged bull. "Total fucking bullshit!"

"The only reason any of this happened was because I wanted to help my daughter," Carson shot back from his seat on the couch. "I need that money to pay for her treatments!"

"So pay her out of your share!"

Dr. Schuller had managed to grab just over a hundred grand from Mama Pearl's backroom – a combination of the cash Carson had on him when he was abducted, plus a bankroll the bookie used to pay out her customers.

Enough to cover Ella's treatments, assuming I send it all to Sarah.

"My share alone won't cover it."

"You can have my share, too," Dr. Schuller interjected, trying to defuse the situation.

"It's still not enough," Carson protested. "Ella needs it all. If you're asking me to disappear from my daughter's life, the least I can do is make sure her medical bills are paid for."

"She's not the only one who needs money," Charlie snapped. "We're about to go on the run, remember? We'll need cash to pay for food, rooms, gas... it's not like we can put that shit on credit card!"

"We'll find a way to manage," Dr. Schuller said. "I've been doing this a long time. We'll figure something out."

"No," Charlie said, shaking his head. "It's about what's right. What's fair. I earned that money!"

"Really?" Carson snapped. "I didn't realize you were the one being tortured by Mama Pearl!"

"I earned it in the casinos," Charlie reminded him. "And by saving your god-damned life!"

"Ella's just a child! She needs this treatment!"

"She's not my kid," Charlie said with a shrug. "So she's not my problem."

Carson leapt up from the couch, his brother's callous words triggering a primal, protective parental fury. Several days had passed since Dr. Schuller had told him the truth about who and what he was, and Carson had recovered most of his strength. But his hands were still a mess of splints and bandages holding his mangled fingers in place while the bones slowly healed.

But Carson wasn't thinking of that as he launched himself at his twin in a blind rage. He lashed out with wild, flailing punches. Charlie blocked the blows, turning and twisting to absorb the impact with his shoulders and forearms before retaliating with a single, savage punch to the stomach.

All the rage – and all the breath – left Carson's body in a grunting gust of expelled air. He collapsed onto the floor, clutching his midsection and gasping for breath.

"Enough!" Dr. Schuller shouted, stepping between them.

Charlie tossed her aside, picking her up and flinging her through the air and onto the nearby couch as if she was a child. Then he kicked Carson in the ribs.

"You want to take a run at me, you skinny, crippled prick? Fuck you!"

Carson curled up into a ball as another kick landed.

"You fucking pussy!" Charlie snarled. "Get up and fight!"

"Stop."

Dr. Schuller didn't shout this time. Her voice was cold and unwavering. As was the pistol she was pointing at Charlie.

The big man slowly turned towards her.

"You really going to shoot me?"

"Not unless you make me."

He stared her down, but she didn't flinch.

"Fuck both of you," he said, finally turning away. "I don't need this shit!"

He stormed out the door without looking back. Dr. Schuler kept the gun trained on him the entire time.

Once he was gone, she set the pistol down and came over to check on Carson.

"Are you okay?"

"I'll live," Carson muttered. "Guess I owe you again."

"I'll add it to your tab," she said, helping him back to his feet.

"Stay here," she said. "I'm going after him. Hopefully I can catch up before he does something stupid."

Carson nodded, and she scurried out, leaving him alone in the apartment.

He took a few moments to collect himself. His ribs were sore where Charlie had kicked him, but he didn't think they were broken.

Guess I can take a lickin' and keep on tickin'.

He made his way into his bedroom and picked up the old flip-phone sitting beside the bed that Dr. Schuller had brought him.

Carson had thought a lot about what he would say to Ella, but so far he hadn't come up with anything that worked.

I'm basically abandoning my daughter. There's no good way to spin it.

He was running out of time; the plan was to leave tonight. Once they were on the run, Dr. Schuller had explained, they couldn't risk making contact again. This was his only chance.

Quit stalling, you coward!

He dialed quickly, hoping Sarah would pick up a call from an unknown number. To his relief she answered on the second ring.

"Hello?"

"It's Carson."

"Carson – oh my god! Where have you been? When you didn't call Ella this weekend I started freaking out!"

"I'm okay. Relatively speaking."

"Carson? What happened? Why aren't you calling on the iPad?"

"It's a long story."

There was a pause as Sarah waited for him to explain.

"I... I fucked up, Sarah. I have to go away for a while."

"Prison?"

"No. But I need to disappear."

"Disappear? For how long?"

"I don't know. A long time."

"I knew you were up to something," she said, her voice breaking slightly. "Carson – what the fuck did you do?"

"It doesn't matter. Not anymore. But I have to go. Tonight."

"You can't do this! What about Ella?"

"Don't worry. I'm still going to send you money for her treatments."

"That's not what I meant. You're her father. You can't just vanish from her life."

"I have to," he said.

"Carson – whatever's going on, we can figure this out. We'll get you a lawyer. Whatever you need."

"I don't need a fucking lawyer!" he snapped, his anger spilling over. "Jesus Christ, you think I'd be doing this if I had any other option?"

There was silence on the other end of the line.

"Sarah... I'm sorry," he said, feeling the tears welling up in his eyes. "I'm not mad at you. I'm just... this fucking sucks. But there's no other choice."

"No," she said, her voice sounding tired. "I guess there probably isn't."

"You'll be getting the money for Ella in the next couple days. A wire transfer. It won't say my name on it, but it's from me. A hundred grand. Enough to cover all her treatments."

"Okay," Sarah mumbled. All the anger and fight had gone out of her. Now she just sounded numb.

"I know this is a lot to dump on you," he said. "And I'm truly, truly sorry. I wish there was some other option. But there's not. Believe me."

"Okay," she mumbled again.

"Is Ella there? Can I talk to her? I want to say goodbye."

"Okay."

He heard Sarah calling for their daughter.

"Hello?"

"Hi, Ella," he said, struggling to hold back sobs. "It's daddy."

"Daddy! You didn't call me on Saturday."

"I know, honey. Daddy was busy."

"Busy with what?"

It was an innocent question, spurred by nothing more than childlike curiosity. But it cut him to the core.

"It doesn't matter. Stupid stuff. It's not important. Not as important as you."

"Are you crying, daddy?"

"A little bit," he admitted.

"Why?"

"I have to go away for a while. And that makes me very sad."

"Go away where?"

"I don't know yet."

"How can you go if you don't know where?"

Good question.

"I'll figure it out, Ella. But listen – before I leave, I want to tell you something."

"Okay."

She sounds like her mother when she says that.

Carson reached up and wiped away a tear that was rolling down his cheek.

"I love you, Ella. I love you more than anything. And I always will."

"I love you too, Daddy!"

"I know, sweetie. I know."

"When will you come back?"

"I don't know, Ella. It might not be for a long, long time."

There was a pause as she thought about what he said.

"Will you call me?"

"No," he said, choking back a sob. "I can't call you. Not for a while."

Ella began to sob.

"Don't cry, honey. Please, don't be sad."

"I don't want you to go!"

"I don't want to go, either. I wish I didn't have to. But sometimes grownups have to do things they don't like."

"Please, Daddy. Don't go." Her sobs were full blown crying now; her words a blubbery mess on the other end of the line.

"I'm sorry, Ella. I have to go. But I love you so much. Remember that. I love you more than anything."

Ella was crying too hard now to speak. Carson was barely holding it together himself.

"Goodbye, Ella. I love you."

The sobs continued for several seconds, then suddenly grew fainter.

"She can't speak anymore," Sarah said, struggling to keep the sobs from her own voice. "This is tearing her up."

"I know. I'm sorry. I'm so God-damned sorry."

There was a long silence. In the background he could still hear Ella crying. Carson took several deep breaths to regain his composure.

"Goodbye, Sarah."

There really wasn't anything more he could say.

"Goodbye, Carson. Good luck. I hope you figure this out, whatever it is."

"Me too. Go take care of Ella."

There was another long pause, then a click as Sarah hung up.

Fuck, I need a drink.

Carson tucked the phone in his pocket and wandered into the kitchen. He'd been beaten by security outside the Seigel Suites, kicked in the ribs by his own twin when he was down, and ruthlessly tortured by Mama Pearl's goons. But the pain he felt now was somehow much, much worse.

Come on… where's the fucking booze?

He rummaged around through the cupboards and the pantry but came up empty. There were two beers in the fridge – not even enough to get a buzz on, let alone drink himself into oblivion.

Guess I'm dealing with this sober.

He went into the living room and plopped himself down on the couch to wait for Dr. Schuller and Charlie to return. He flipped through the channels, trying to zone out. But he kept thinking about Ella and her pitiful sobs.

After an hour alone, he decided he needed to talk to someone – anyone. He was smart enough not to leave the apartment; Dr. Schuler was right about the risks of being seen. But he still had the flip phone in his pocket. And there was only one other number he knew by memory.

***

Maya glanced at her vibrating phone, saw UNKNOWN NUMBER, and rejected the call.

Fucking solicitors.

She continued getting ready for work. It was her final day at PH, and she couldn't help but feel a bit maudlin as she slipped on her black pantsuit one last time. She was moving on to bigger and better things – she was heading off to Quantico to begin her training in a few weeks – but she still felt a twinge of regret at what she was leaving behind. She'd dealt with her share of assholes over the years – both co-workers and customers – but she'd also made a lot of friends. They'd all promised to stay in touch, but Maya knew it was inevitable they'd drift apart once she moved away.

This chapter is over. Time to turn the page.

Her reminiscing was cut short as her phone vibrated again. UNKNOWN NUMBER. She rejected the call a second time. Not five seconds later, her phone buzzed again.

Jesus Christ, take a fucking hint!

"Who the hell is this?" she barked, finally answering the call.

"Maya? It's Carson."

"Holy shit. Carson? Are you okay?"

"Not really. No. Just needed a friend to talk to. Got a few minutes?"

"Yeah... I mean, I'm heading to work soon, but I've got time."

"It's good to hear your voice, Maya."

She hesitated, not sure if she should tell him about her interviews with the cops or the FBI.

He's a friend. He deserves to know.

"Carson? I know you were there. At the D Street Massacre."

Now it was Carson's turn to hesitate.

"Guess I'm famous now."

"Are you okay? Were you hurt?"

"I'm fine."

He's lying. She didn't know how she could tell, but she was certain he wasn't telling the truth. *How deep is he mixed up in this?*

"The police interviewed me," she said, deciding to come clean. "And the FBI. At least, I think they were FBI. They told me what happened."

"Yeah?" Carson said, trying to keep his voice nonchalant. "What did they say?"

"They told me they're looking for you. And Charlie."

"What did you tell them?"

"I didn't lie to them," she said. "This is serious. Six people are dead."

"Good," Carson said, to her surprise. "I don't want you to get in any trouble. You don't have to try and protect me."

"I know this wasn't you, Carson," she said. "It was Charlie, wasn't it?"

"He was trying to save me," Carson said. "He did what he had to do."

"I saw the photos," Maya insisted. "It was a bloodbath."

"Charlie does have a bit of a temper," Carson said, his tone light and teasing. "But we've all got flaws."

"This isn't a joke, Carson. Anyone who could do that is a psychopath. Charlie's dangerous."

"Yeah, I know." His tone was serious now.

"Is... is he there with you now?"

"No. I'm alone."

Maya breathed a silent sigh of relief.

"You need to go to the police, Carson. Charlie can't be allowed to just wander around. Not if he's capable of something like this."

"I can't do that."

"They can protect you from him. Put you in witness protection, if that's what it takes."

"It's not that."

"Then what is it?"

"It's complicated."

"Please, Carson. I'm worried about you. You need help."

"I've got someone on my side," he assured her.

"I'm on your side."

"I know that. Besides you, I mean. I'll get through this."

"Maybe. But I'm worried Charlie will bring you down with him. I know you watch out for him, but at some point you have to cut him loose."

Carson didn't answer right away. When he did, he didn't acknowledge her warning.

"I'm glad I met you, Maya," he said. "I don't have a lot of friends."

His words caught her off guard.

"I'm glad I met you, too," she echoed, uncertain of what else to say.

"I... I'm not sure why I'm saying all this," Carson continued. "Maybe it's because I know it doesn't matter anymore. But I always hoped we could be more than friends. I care about you, Maya. I care about you a lot."

"I care about you, too, Carson. That's why I want you to turn yourself in. So you don't get hurt."

There was a long pause.

"Carson? Are you still there?"

"I'll miss you, Maya."

He hung up before she could even say goodbye. For a few seconds Maya just stared at her phone.

I should call CJ. Maybe he can trace the call!

She went over to the file folder still sitting on her kitchen counter; it had been there ever since her interview at the FBI field office. Ignoring the bloody photos of the crime scene, she punched the number CJ had written on the inside flap into her phone. But she hung up before the call connected.

Carson doesn't want to be found.

She knew she didn't have the full story – not from CJ, and not from Carson. There were too many pieces missing, making it difficult to know who she should trust. But Carson was a friend. CJ was just some guy who'd promised he could help her career.

She tucked the phone back into her pocket and continued getting ready for work. She was running on autopilot, her mind replaying the phone call over and over. Even as she got into her car, she was still obsessing over it. There was something desperate in Carson's voice; something tragic. It wasn't just what he'd said, but how he said it.

I always hoped we might be more than friends one day.

She hadn't been shocked by his revelation; she'd felt a spark between them herself. But Carson had never asked her out; never acted on it. And neither had she.

If he'd asked me out on a date, would I have said yes?

She honestly didn't know the answer. She liked Carson; he was good looking, and funny. Friendly to all the dealers. Generous with his tips when he won, and easy-going when he lost. She always felt a tiny thrill when he came into the casino – of all the regulars, he was the one she enjoyed talking to the most. The one she always made a point to seek out whenever he came in. And he was the first person she told after getting accepted into the Academy.

Not that any of that matters now.

It was clear from the call that Carson didn't think he'd ever see her again.

He's probably right. Unless they catch him. And then what? How would it look for an FBI agent-in-training to be friends with a felon?

She was still thinking about Carson as she pulled into the top level of the garage, grabbing a spot right beside the sign that said EMPLOYEE PARKING ONLY. Normally there'd be a handful of other people arriving around the same time, but because of his phone call she was running a few minutes late. The garage was empty... or so she thought.

Slinging her purse over her shoulder, she locked her car and headed for the elevator. She pulled up short when she saw a large figure lurking in the shadow of one of the support pillars.

"Figured I'd find you here," a deep voice grumbled.

Instinctively, she took a step back as the man stepped out from the darkness.

"Remember me?" Charlie asked.

"You're Carson's friend," she said, trying to sound calm even though her heart was racing.

"Friend?" he snorted. "Not quite."

He was slurring his words and swaying slightly side to side; clear signs he'd had too much to drink.

"Me and Carson had a good thing going," he mumbled. "But it all got fucked up that night you had security drag me off."

Working in a casino, Maya had seen Charlie's type plenty of times: an angry, bitter drunk looking for someone to blame when his luck went bad.

And for some reason, they always want to pin it on a woman.

"Is Carson with you?" she asked, hoping she could talk him down.

"Nope. Just you and me, sweetheart."

He took a step forward, stumbling slightly as he did so. Maya took two steps back in response.

"What's the matter?" he asked. "You scared?"

"I don't have time for this," she said. "I'm late for work."

"Gotta go slap cuffs on some other poor son of a bitch?" he said.

"Only if they're asking for it."

He took another step forward. This time Maya held her ground. Sometimes a show of confidence was enough.

Pricks like him feed on fear. Makes them feel like a big man.

"Wait a minute," Charlie said, waggling a raised finger. "Now that I think about it, you didn't actually cuff me, did you? You had to call in backup." Charlie turned his head from side to side. "Funny, I don't see any backup here."

"What do you want, Charlie?"

"Payback."

The way he said it sent a chill down her spine.

"Payback for what?" she asked. She kept her eyes fixed on his, but with one hand she began to unzip her purse, hoping she could get the Taser she kept inside before he noticed.

"Payback for that silver-haired bitch pointing a gun in my face," he growled. "Payback for getting stabbed in the back by my own brother. Payback for getting cuffed and left to rot in a holding room by some uppity casino-cunt!"

He lunged towards her, charging hard. She backpedaled frantically, fumbling in the purse for the Taser as he tried to tackle her to the ground. Luckily, Charlie was drunk enough that his own momentum threw him off balance, and Maya was able to duck to the side, narrowly avoiding his clutching grasp. Instead of grabbing onto her, his shoulder slammed into her side.

Maya worked out almost every day, but Charlie was massive – he stood several inches taller, and outweighed her by at least a hundred pounds, most of which was muscle. The impact sent her flying backwards, the Taser slipping from her grasp and falling back into her purse as it went skidding across the floor.

She landed with a heavy thud on the cold hard pavement, rolling to take the brunt of the fall on her side and absorb some of the impact. She kicked off her high-heeled shoes and sprang back to her feet. Despite his inebriation, Charlie was already up again as well.

Shit!

He'd positioned himself to cut off her escape to the elevator, trapping her between a cement wall and a row of parked cars. She glanced over each shoulder, looking for a way out.

"Nowhere to run, sweetie," Charlie taunted as he came towards her.

This time he didn't charge ahead; instead, he moved in slow and careful, crouched low with his arms spread wide.

Stalking me. Corralling me.

He was panting heavily, though with excitement or exertion she couldn't tell. His eyes were wide and wild, and his lips were spread in a maniacal grin.

Maya dropped into a boxer's stance, turning sideways and keeping her left hand high while dropping her right foot behind her.

"Figured you had some fight in you," Charlie said with a chuckle.

She'd taken plenty of self-defense courses - enough to know that she was at a huge disadvantage. Charlie might be stumbling drunk, but he was still twice her size, and at least three times as strong. If he got his hands on her, it was all over.

"What are you waiting for, sweetie?" Charlie wheezed as he advanced on her. "Take your best shot!"

Maya stepped forward and delivered a sharp front kick to his midsection, driving her heel into his sternum. She moved fast, catching him off guard. The blow sent him stumbling back, but it didn't knock him off his feet.

"You wanna try that again, bitch?"

Maya took a small hop forward and crouched down as if loading up for another kick. Charlie fell for the feint, lunging forward to try and grab her extended leg, only to end up flailing at empty air and stumbling forward when she pulled her foot back before contact.

With her opponent off balance, Maya seized the opening by darting in and throwing a sharp elbow into the side of Charlie's head. There was a dull thud as she connected, and Charlie crumpled to the ground.

Maya leapt over he fallen opponent, hoping to make a break for the stairs. But Charlie's hand snaked out and seized her left ankle. She tried to pull free, but his fingers were like a vise. Charlie rolled onto his side, twisting her foot and dragging her down to the ground.

Fuck!

Landing on her back, she lashed out with her right leg, kicking at his face. Charlie ducked his head into his chest, and her foot bounced off the top of his skull. Keeping his head tucked, he reached out with his free hand and grabbed the knee of her captured leg, then used both hands to slowly drag her towards him as they both lay on the ground.

No, no, no!

Charlie was too big and strong for her to grapple with; all her training and technique couldn't overcome his inherent physical advantages.

Maya began to thrash, twist, and kick, savagely flailing her limbs and body in a desperate attempt to break free.

By some miracle, one of her desperate blows made contact as he dragged her in. Charlie grunted and let go as her knee slammed into his groin. Rolling onto her stomach, Maya scuttled across the floor towards her purse.

She grabbed the strap just as she felt Charlie's fingers clamp down on her ankle again. As he inexorably pulled her back in, her fingers wrapped around the handle of the Taser. She pulled it from the purse, twisted around enough to aim the weapon, and pulled the trigger.

Twin darts shot out, piercing the fabric of Charlie's shirt and burrowing themselves in the flesh of his chest. As 50,000 volts coursed through him, he began to convulse and writhe face down on the ground, releasing his grip on her ankle.

Knowing she only had a few seconds until he shook off the effects of the stun gun and came after her again, Maya leapt onto Charlie's back as he lay prone on the concrete. Wrapping a forearm under his chin, she locked her chokehold into place by grasping her wrist with the crook of her other elbow. As she applied pressure, Charlie clambered to his feet, twisting and bucking to try and shake her loose. Maya wrapped her legs around his waist and held on for all she was worth as he clutched and clawed at her, unable to find purchase. After a few seconds the big man went limp and slumped back down to the ground.

Breathing hard from the exertion, Maya released the hold and scrambled to her feet, ready to run if he came to. Fortunately, the combined impact of the choke-out, the blast from the Taser, and the alcohol coursing through his system were enough to put Charlie down for the count, and he lay there snoring in a drunken slumber.

Keeping a careful eye in case he woke up, Maya pulled out her phone. Her hands were trembling as she did so; an aftereffect of the adrenaline still racing through her. She started to call casino security but changed her mind before she finished dialing. Instead, she looked at her recent outgoing calls, then selected the number she'd punched in just before leaving for work. This time she didn't hang up, and someone answered on the second ring.

"Hello?"

"Is this CJ?"

"Yes."

"It's Maya Belfour. You gave me your number outside the FBI building."

"Maya. I remember. Did you think of something else to tell me about the case?"

"Even better," Maya said, staring down at the unconscious man at her feet. "Send a couple of your people to the Planet Hollywood parking garage. Level 5. I've got a present for you and your boss."

***

Carson almost didn't recognize himself in the mirror.

We need to change our appearance, Dr. Schuller had said. She hadn't found Charlie, but she'd returned from her fruitless search with several packets of hair dye. *This will make it harder for someone to recognize us if they start plastering our pictures all over the TV.*

Dr. Schuller's striking silver hair was now a dull brown, tied up in a stern looking bun atop her head. She'd ditched her long white coat and boots in favor of ill-fitting jeans and a bulky sweatshirt.

Carson's own hair had been buzzed short and bleached blonde, and he was wearing a pair of fake, thick-rimmed, hipster glasses.

"Quit admiring yourself," Dr. Schuller told him. "It's time to go."

"What about Charlie?" Carson asked, pulling his gaze away from the unfamiliar reflection.

"We can't wait any longer," she said. "Wherever he went, he's on his own."

"What if they catch him?"

"That's why we need to go," she said. "All he knows is this place. Once we're gone, he won't be able to give them anything useful."

Carson nodded. He knew he should be worried about Charlie – *he's your brother, after all* – but the truth was he was relieved not to have to deal with his antics anymore.

This is going to be hard enough as it is.

"Where are we going?"

She hesitated, as if reluctant to tell him. Then she finally relented.

"I've got a small place in Provo. Bought it years ago in case I needed somewhere to lay low."

"Provo? Huh. Never been to Utah."

"Yeah, well... maybe it'll grow on you."

CHAPTER 21

Part Four: Dreamland

August 11, 2019 - Utah
Four months after the D Street Massacre

Provo was a charming college town of just over 100,000 people. The site of the main Brigham Young University campus, the city was young and vibrant. It was a mecca for anyone who loved the outdoors, offering skiing in the winter and hiking, biking, boating, and golf in the summer. The economy was booming, but the traffic was light and the streets were clean. It boasted several of the nation's highest rated school districts, and the numerous parks and playgrounds made it the perfect place to raise a family. Even the restaurant scene was surprisingly diverse, considering virtually the entire population was whiter than a polar bear in a blizzard. All in all, it was one of America's hidden gems – an idyllic paradise tucked away in the natural splendor at the foot of the Wasatch Range mountains.

After living there for four months, Carson despised everything about it.

The first few weeks he'd barely left Dr. Schuler's modest bungalow; she wanted them to lay low in case their names and faces became plastered across every news feed in the country. But the national manhunt she feared never materialized. Officially, the D Street Massacre was unsolved – an ongoing case with few leads and no known suspects.

The lack of pursuit did little to quell her fears, however.

Dr. Singh killed the investigation, she'd insisted. *It's the only explanation.*

Despite her paranoia, after the first month even she'd grudgingly admitted they'd gotten away clean. The team from Dreamland might still be hunting them, but without any leads they'd be hard pressed to track them down here. Although at this point if they did find them Carson might actually be grateful.

He'd had grown up in LA, a sprawling mega-hub of urbanization. From there he'd moved to Vegas, living as a professional gambler. He craved excitement. Danger. Even a little bit of debauchery. All of which were in short supply in Provo.

If Charlie were here, he'd find some way to stir things up. Either that, or he'd get so bored he'd blow his brains out.

But Charlie wasn't there. They hadn't heard anything from him since the night he'd stormed out of the apartment. Dr. Schuller was easy to get along with, but it was hard to think of her as a friend. She insisted Carson start calling her Lisa, but it always felt odd to him.

Charlie and I had a connection. We were brothers. Even though we didn't know it at first, it meant something.

Carson still thought about Charlie often, wondering if he got away. Wondering if he was still out there somewhere, picking pockets and picking fights.

Other times he thought about Maya. *Give 'em hell down at Quantico.*

Mostly, though, he thought about Ella. He hadn't spoken with his daughter since they'd fled Vegas. He missed seeing her face. Hearing her voice. He missed her rambling stories and her laugh.

124 days and counting.

As he sat on the bungalow's porch, enjoying the warm summer evening and staring out at the sunset, he imagined what it would be like to share it with her.

Daddy! Look at all the pretty colors!

I see them, sweetie.

It's so pretty!

Not as pretty as you, Ella.

Daddy, where does the sun go at night?

She's sleeping, Ella. Just like you do.

The sun's a girl?

Sure. That's why she dresses up in all these beautiful colors.

Daddy – boys can dress pretty, too.

You're right, Ella. Boys can dress pretty too.

Carson reached up and wiped a tear from his eye, laughing ruefully at how a pretend conversation in his head could still make him cry.

Maybe if Ella was here with me, I wouldn't think this place was so bad.

He pushed all thoughts of his daughter away as he heard the familiar sound of a motorbike approaching. A few seconds later Dr. Schuller – *Lisa, call her Lisa!* - pulled into the driveway on her green Kawasaki Vulcan 900.

She pulled off her helmet and shook out her hair; it was long enough to reach well past her shoulders now, and she'd gone back to her previous silver sheen.

"Been sitting there all day?" she asked.

"Went for a run this morning," Carson answered. "And hit the gym this afternoon."

After his wounds from Mama Pearl's torture session had healed, Carson had embarked on an intensive physical fitness routine. He'd already added ten pounds of lean muscle to his frame.

Twenty more and maybe I'll give Charlie a fair fight if we ever tangle again.

"Good," she said as she tucked her helmet under her arm and walked up the porch. "It's important to stay active."

Carson nodded but didn't bother replying.

"Any thoughts about looking for a job?" Lisa pressed, realizing she'd have to be the one to keep the conversation going. "I haven't been pulling much in at the bar now that the college kids have gone home for summer, and money's starting to get a little tight."

"We could always sell your bike."

"I'm serious, Carson. We need to think long term. Figure out a plan that's sustainable."

"I'm not sure Provo figures into that plan for me," Carson said.

She sighed. "Okay. You just let me know when you come up with something better, then."

As she reached out to open the front door, the world suddenly stopped moving. Everything just sort of *flickered* – halting, then almost instantly starting up again, like an old projector hitching on a badly spliced frame of film. It happened so fast Carson almost missed it.

Did that just happen?

Carson hadn't used his power in months, but the sensation was something he'd never forget. Nothing else even came close: there was a hollow stillness – a *nothingness* – that was impossible to ignore.

But this wasn't me. I didn't freeze the world. Time just stopped on its own.

"Something wrong?" Lisa asked, her brow furrowed with concern. "You look like you just smelled the worst fart in the history of flatulence."

"What? Oh... no. I'm good."

She gave him a curious look, then disappeared inside the house.

Maybe I imagined it. A daydream. Or déjà vu... an echo of what used to be.

Mildly troubled, he managed to shake it off and follow her inside.

He thought about the strange incident over the next few days, slowly convincing himself that he must have imagined it. After a week, he'd almost forgotten about it. And then it happened again. As before, it came and went in the blink of an eye. But this time there was no doubt.

The world was frozen. And I didn't do it.

Over the next month it happened again a handful of times. Carson was on the verge of saying something to Dr. Schuller... but then the flickers stopped. A week went by without a single incident. Then a month.

But as the first hints of autumn's chill began to seep into the mountain air, the flickers suddenly returned. And it didn't take long for Carson to realize they'd gotten worse.

The stoppages became more frequent, from one or two a week until he was experiencing three or four each day. More troubling, as their frequency increased so did their duration. They went from sudden blips – tiny hiccups in the temporal stream – to long, drawn out pauses.

They'd hit without any warning. He'd be in the middle of watching a show, or making a meal, or in the middle of a conversation. And suddenly the world would freeze, cutting him off mid-sentence.

Whenever it happened, he was paralyzed, just like he'd always been in the past. He was completely aware while he was frozen, his conscious mind moving at full throttle. But his physical body – the entire physical world – was trapped in stasis. Unlike in the past, however, Carson didn't have the ability to make the world start up again.

Not that he didn't try. Each time he was swept up in one of the unexpected timeouts, he'd think *GO!* But the instinctive act of letting time slip loose – the inexplicable mental process he used to release his supernatural grip on the world – didn't work anymore. He'd remain trapped in place along with everyone and everything.

Eventually the timeout would end, and the world would plow forward again, but it was never because of anything Carson did. Like the stoppages, the restarts came without any warning, often catching Carson completely off guard and causing him to mess up whatever he was doing as the world unexpectedly snapped back into motion.

It even started happening at night; he'd wake from the deepest sleep, the sensation of being trapped in a timeout knifing through his subconscious awareness to viciously rouse his mind from darkest slumber. He'd lay in his bed, his eyes closed, helplessly waiting for the world to start up again. There was something deeply terrifying about the sensation, particularly when it hit him in the twilight hours: a combination of night terror and sleep paralysis to the nth degree. When it finally passed, his heart would start pounding and he'd break out in a cold sweat, shivering under the blankets for an hour before he finally fell back asleep.

After three mostly sleepless nights in a row, Carson stumbled into the kitchen, yawning and bleary eyed. Lisa was already sitting at the table, waiting for him.

"I made you some breakfast," she said.

"Thanks," he mumbled.

She got up as he sat down, then brough him over a steaming cup of coffee and a towering plate of pancakes.

"Chocolate chip," she said.

"My mom used to make me these when I was a kid," Carson said, smiling at the memory.

"I know."

He pushed the plate away without taking a bite.

"Christ. You even spied on me in my home?"

Lisa didn't say anything.

"What the fuck is going on?" Carson asked.

"I can tell something's wrong," she said, sitting down across from him. "I'm worried about you."

"Don't be."

"I promised your mother I'd watch out for you. Your real mother, I mean."

"My real mother was Evelynn Gaines," Carson declared through gritted teeth.

"Your birth mother, then. I made a vow to Beth."

"Yeah? Well it's going to take a lot more than a stack of fucking pancakes to fix my problems."

"So tell me what to do," she said. "I want to help."

Carson had spent his whole life with a secret power nobody else could understand. Growing up he learned not to talk about it. It was a huge part of who he was; it made him special and unique. But he never shared his secret with anyone.

That's one of the reasons my marriage fell apart. Sarah always sensed I was holding something back. She said I was emotionally guarded. Always shutting her out.

He'd spent his whole life treating it as something shameful. Something to keep hidden. When he tried to share it with Maya, she'd dismissed it as some kind of bad joke, reinforcing his urge to keep everything bottled up inside him. And even though Dr. Schuller already knew about his secret, for some reason it still felt wrong to talk to her about it.

It's personal. Private. She might believe me, but she won't really understand.

It was only when he found Charlie that he was able to have someone who truly understood what he was going through. Someone he could open up to about it.

And look how that ended.

"Carson – I'm on your side. Please, tell me what's going on."

She's right. Even if she can't really understand what I'm going through, it might help just to talk about it.

"I've been having... episodes," he admitted. "Freezing the world. Stopping time."

"I thought we agreed you weren't going to do that anymore," she said. She didn't sound upset; just concerned. "It's not safe, remember?"

"That's the problem," Carson explained. "I'm not doing it. Not intentionally. It's just happening."

"I'm not sure I follow."

"I used to freeze time by thinking about it. It was a deliberate act. I made it happen. But I haven't done it in months. Not since Charlie left."

He paused, wondering how much detail he should go into. How much he should admit. In the end, he decided to tell her everything.

"Over the past few weeks, though, I've felt the world freezing around me. It just happens, like some kind of accident. A glitch that appears out of nowhere.

"I never know when it's coming. And I can't make the timeouts end. I used to be able to start the world up again whenever I wanted. But now the timeouts just sort of end whenever they want. It's like I have no say in when it happens."

Lisa didn't say anything; but she nodded as if encouraging him to go on.

"It's getting worse," he added, the words coming out in a rush now. "At first the flickers were quick. The just came and went. But now they seem to go on and on. I'm trapped and I can't make them stop. I can't do anything!"

He realized he was choking up, and he felt a sudden flush of embarrassment.

Quit being such a fucking baby!

Lisa reached out across the table and grasped his hand. Carson found the gesture strangely comforting; it helped him get a handle on the emotions threatening to overwhelm him.

"I'm sorry," she said, speaking softly. "I don't know what to tell you. I suspect you know more about this than I ever will. But maybe if we talk this through, we can figure it out."

"Talk it through?"

She let go of his hand.

"Let's kick some theories around. Try to figure out why this might be happening now."

Standing up, she began to walk slowly back and forth across the kitchen.

"Before all this," she asked as she paced, "how often did you use your power?"

"I don't know," Carson said. "Sometimes I'd use it a few times a day. Other times I'd go a week or more."

"But nothing like what it's been?" she pressed. "You never went months without using it?"

"No."

"So it's possible the power is building up inside you and leaking out," she said. "Like a volcano beneath the earth. And these glitches you're talking about are gas and lava seeping out as the pressure builds."

"Are you saying I'm going to blow?"

"It's just a theory," she cautioned.

Carson shook his head. "If that was the case, why can't I start the world up again when the glitches happen?"

"Maybe something happened when Mama Pearl tortured you," she said. "You had a severe concussion. Maybe you suffered some sort of brain damage."

"That's not very reassuring," Carson told her.

"I'm sorry," she said. "But we need to consider all the possibilities. Your ability to control your power might be lost forever."

"No," Carson said. "I used it when you told me I was adopted. Everything seemed fine then."

"Hopefully, you're right. But we need to be sure."

"You want me to stop the world right now?" Carson said, incredulous. "After all your talk about how dangerous it could be?"

"It's a potential risk," she admitted. "But at this point, I think it's worth it to try and figure out what's going on."

Carson nodded, then took a deep breath. He was suddenly aware of his heart pumping at about a million beats a minute.

You're scared. What if it she's right? What if you try to stop time and nothing happens?

****FREEZE!****

The world stopped. Lisa was staring at him, unblinking. The second hand on the clock on the wall behind her stood motionless. But this felt different than the glitches. It felt more immediate. More personal.

Carson had made this happen. He was in control. And he could stop it whenever he wanted.

At least, I hope I can.

**** GO! ****

The world burst back into motion, much to Carson's relief.

"It worked," he declared.

"You stopped time?" Lisa confirmed. "And started it up again? Like you used to?"

Carson nodded.

"I noticed something when I did it," he added, realizing it actually was helpful to talk about it with someone. "The glitches – they feel less immediate. Distant, almost. Like they're coming from far away. When I stop time, it feels internal. Personal. Does that make any sense?"

"That's interesting," Lisa said. After a few seconds, she added, "Maybe you're not the one causing the stoppages. "Maybe Charlie finally figured out how to do this, too."

Carson knew that was possible, but something didn't quite track with her explanation.

"I doubt it. He could move when I stopped time, but he couldn't freeze the world. It's like he didn't get that gene."

"Oh my god, that's it!" Lisa declared. "Why didn't I see it sooner. *Your power is genetic!*"

It took a second for Carson to grasp the implication of what she was saying, but when he did it all suddenly made sense.

"Ella!"

"She's your daughter. It only makes sense she might inherit your power."

A terrifying thought entered Carson's mind.

"Ella has seizures. Bad ones."

"That might be unrelated," Lisa cautioned. "Though it's possible the second generation of hybrid-DNA offspring could manifest with adverse side effects."

That's just a fancy way of saying I gave my daughter fucked-up alien DNA.

"One thing I still don't understand," Lisa continued, "is why you didn't notice this before?"

"Maybe it takes time for the power to develop," Carson said. "I don't remember when I first started doing this. I was young, but maybe I grew into it. Maybe Ella's just starting to realize what she can do, too."

The more he thought about it, the more convinced he became he was right.

The first few times it happened she was just discovering what she could do by accident. That's why they didn't last. She was just learning what she was capable of. Now she's testing her limits. Getting more comfortable. Stronger. Freezing time for longer and longer spans.

"I need to call her," Carson said. "Explain to her what's going on!"

Lisa shook her head. "It's too risky."

"Please," Carson said. "I'm the only one who understands what's happening to her. What she's going through. Sarah can't help her with this. If Ella tells her what's happening, she won't even believe her."

Carson remembered what that was like. The uncertainty. The doubt. The frustration of trying to explain what was happening to his parents, and them having no clue what he was talking about. They acted like it was all in his imagination; something he made up. In the end, he just stopped trying to explain it. Locked his secret away. Cut that part of him off from the rest of the world.

I don't want that to happen to Ella. I don't want her to feel like she needs to hide what she is. I don't want her to think she's alone with her secret.

"Ella's probably scared," Carson pleaded. "Confused. I'm the only one who can help her understand what's going on."

"Dr. Singh probably has someone watching her," Lisa warned. "In case you ever try to make contact."

"All the more reason I need to reach out to her," Carson insisted. "What if she says or does something that tips them off? What if they realize she has this power, too? What happens then?"

"We don't know for sure that she's doing this," Lisa countered, walking back her own theory. "This is all wild speculation."

"But if we're right," Carson said, "she deserves to know the danger she's in."

"One call," Lisa finally conceded. "Five minutes. Just to find out if you're right."

"And if I am?"

"We'll burn that bridge when we come to it."

***

Carson's hands were trembling as he dialed the number.

It's been four months. What will I even say to her? Or to Sarah?

"Hello?"

"Sarah. It's me. Carson. I need to talk to Ella. It's important."

There was silence on the other end.

"Sarah? What's wrong?"

"Ella's gone, Carson," she said, her voice devoid of all emotion. "She passed away last month."

"What? No... that's not possible!"

"She'd started the new round of experimental treatments," Sarah explained, her voice hollow and empty. "She seemed to be responding well. But then she had a grand mal seizure. She's gone."

Carson was struck dumb as his mind wrestled with the horrifying news.

*** *FREEZE!* ***

Carson's grief was swallowed up by the familiar numbness of stasis. The chemical and hormonal reactions that drive human emotion were halted during the timeouts; the overwhelming sadness of his daughter's death was pushed away, leaving only cold logic.

Even so, his mind was flooded with memories of Sarah – the tiny bundle they brought home from the hospital. The nights he rocked her to sleep in his arms. Her first steps. Her first words.

But the more he thought about her, the more something didn't fit. In his hyper-rational state, without the clouding emotions of loss and sorrow, he realized that Sarah was wrong.

Ella can't be dead. Not if she's the one causing these glitches.

A crazy theory began to take shape – a wild, unbelievable conspiracy... but one that was far easier to accept than his daughter's supposed death.

Dr. Singh took her! He found out Ella was causing the glitches!

Lisa had warned Carson that Singh was a monster. From everything she'd told him, he was exactly the kind of man who would kidnap a young girl for his sinister experiments, then stage her death to keep her parents from ever knowing what had happened.

I'm going to fucking kill that bastard!

But even though Carson was convinced his daughter was still alive, he knew he couldn't tell Sarah. As much as he wanted to ease her suffering and give her hope, he had to keep her in the dark – for her safety and for Ella's.

If he was right, Singh was probably still watching her. Maybe even listening in on this phone call.

As horrible as it was, he had to let her live with this awful lie until he could figure out a way to get Ella back.

*** *GO!* ***

As the world started up, Carson felt his throat tightening and tears welling up in his eyes. Even though he had convinced himself Ella was still alive, now that the timeout was over his body was experiencing a natural, human reaction to the shocking news.

"I... I'm sorry I wasn't there," he mumbled into the phone.

"That was kind of your thing, wasn't it," she muttered. "Always off doing god knows what when your daughter needed you the most."

Her words stung, but Carson resisted the urge to hit back. *She thinks Ella's dead. She's lashing out at the world.*

Despite their problems, Carson still cared about Sarah. He understood the pain she was going through. He wanted to tell her not to worry. He wanted to tell her Ella was still alive. He wanted to promise her he'd get their daughter back. But of course, he couldn't tell her any of that.

"I... I don't know what to say," he mumbled.

"Nobody does," Sarah answered, her voice flat and empty. "And when they try, it usually just makes things worse."

"I have to go," he said, realizing the longer he stayed on the call the more likely he was to stay something he'd regret. "I'm sorry. I just... I have to go."

"Goodbye, Carson."

She didn't sound angry or upset. She just sounded tired. Defeated. Broken. Somehow, that was far worse.

As he hung up the phone, he saw Lisa staring at him.

"I heard," she said.

"I don't believe it," he replied, shaking his head. "Ella's not dead!"

"I agree," she said. "I think she's still alive."

Her agreement caught him off guard. He'd expected her to tell him he was concocting wild theories so he wouldn't have to cope with his grief.

"I think we were right about Ella," Dr. Schuller continued. "She's the one causing these timeouts. Dr. Singh found out somehow. And that's why he took her."

She slammed her fist on the counter.

"I fucked up, Carson. I was so focused on keeping you safe, I never considered your power could be passed on to your daughter. I'm sorry."

"All that matters is we get Ella back," Carson said, brushing aside her apology.

She shook her head. "I don't see how that's possible. Even if we weren't fugitives wanted for murder, we can't trust anyone. Not the government. Not the cops."

"Not the cops," Carson agreed. "But what about someone in the FBI?"

CHAPTER 22

Maya let the warm water of the shower wash over, soothing her aching muscles. She'd spent the afternoon running Quantico's endurance obstacle course – a brutal stretch of mud trenches, climbing ropes, razor wire, and twenty-foot-high walls, capped off by a 2.5 mile run through the rugged forests surrounding the base.

The obstacle course wasn't required for FBI recruits; it had actually been built for the marines that shared the base with the Academy. But as a resident of the base, she had access to all the facilities, and she liked the challenge.

"You almost finished?" Josie – her roommate – called out from the other side of the door. "I need to shower before we head down to the Shack."

The Academy pushed their trainees hard; it wasn't uncommon for recruits to head off-base Friday and Saturday nights to blow off steam at the local bars. Maya wasn't above joining them for a drink, though she could think of plenty of better places than the Shack.

"If we go to that dive again tonight," she called out to Josie, "you better finally ask that hot bartender out."

"Hey, I don't need dating advice from Mother Superior!" Josie called back with a laugh.

Maya rolled her eyes as she shut off the shower and grabbed her towel.

A few of the recruits had started calling her Mother Superior during the first month at the Academy because she was always the one reminding them to be back on base before curfew. Now that they were through the first four weeks of intensive training, Maya had lightened up and relaxed, but the nickname had stuck.

"All yours," she told Josie as she stepped out of the bathroom.

"About time," she replied. "You leave any hot water?"

"Cold showers build character," Maya told her.

"Of course, Mother Superior," Josie said, quickly shutting the bathroom door even as Maya grabbed a hairbrush off the dresser and threw it in her direction.

"Too slow!" Josie called out from inside the bathroom as the brush clattered off the closed door. "Gotta work on those reflexes!"

Maya sat down on the edge of her bed and grabbed her hair dryer. Her phone showed a waiting text. Curious, she picked it up.

Maya. It's Carson. I need to see you. It's important.

The message was coming from a number she didn't recognize, but that wasn't surprising – the last time Carson had reached out to her he'd used a burner.

There was a room number and an address below the text; she recognized it as a nearby hotel, just a couple miles off the base.

She stared at the message, her mind spinning. She hadn't heard from Carson in months. Why was he reaching out to her now? Did he know Charlie had attacked her? Did he know she'd turned his brother over to the authorities?

He's a fugitive on the run. You can't meet with him.

Over the past few months, she'd tried looking into his case. But even though she was an FBI agent-in-training, she didn't have access to any resources beyond simple internet searches. As far as she could tell, the D Street Massacre was still unsolved. There hadn't been any mention anywhere of Charlie being arrested, and there hadn't been any public manhunt for Carson.

But they know he's involved. They're still looking for him.

She still had CJ's number – no doubt he'd be interested in knowing Carson had reached out to her. But unlike Charlie, Carson was a friend. She wasn't going to rat him out.

The smart thing to do would be to just ignore the message and go out for drinks with Josie. She couldn't afford to get dragged into whatever trouble Carson was mixed up in. It could jeopardize her entire career, and maybe even result in criminal charges.

"What the hell are you doing?" Josie asked, emerging from the shower. "You're not even dressed yet!"

Maya looked up from her phone, realizing she'd been starting at it for almost ten minutes.

"Sorry. I can't make it tonight," she said. "Something came up."

"You okay?"

"Yeah. Just some shit I need to deal with."

Josie nodded, and turned her attention to getting ready for her night out.

Maya read Carson's text one more time, then typed out a quick reply. *I'll be there in an hour.*

***

The Ramada Triangle was a mid-rate hotel located on the I-95 just a few miles south of the Quantico base, right across the street from the US Marine Corps Museum.

As she pulled into the parking lot, Maya began to have second thoughts. Images of the bloody carnage of the crime scene photos flashed through her mind, but she pushed them away.

You've come this far. No sense turning back now.

She parked her car and went inside the building. Outside room 233, she paused again, steeling herself before she knocked on the door. She heard the sound of someone inside approaching, then a second later the door swung open.

"Thanks for coming," Carson said. He stood there awkwardly, as if waiting for her to make the next move.

Maya stepped forward and embraced him with a fierce hug. Carson responded by wrapping his arms around her.

"I'm glad you're okay," she whispered.

"I'm glad you came," he replied.

He's been working out, Maya couldn't help but notice.

"Shut the door, Carson," a voice noted.

Maya glanced over Carson's shoulder to see an older woman with silver hair sitting in a chair in the corner.

"Dr. Lisa Schuller," Carson said as he disentangled himself and closed the door. "She saved me from Mama Pearl."

Maya nodded by way of greeting.

"How's the Academy?" Carson asked.

"It's good. Challenging. Exhausting. But I love it."

"I figured. You were meant for this."

"Would you like something to drink?" Dr. Schuller asked.

"No, I'm okay," she answered. "Carson... why did you call me?"

"I need help," he said. "And I didn't know where else to turn."

"Help with what?"

"You haven't asked about Charlie," Dr. Schuller chimed in. It wasn't an accusation – not exactly – but it was clear she was suspicious.

Maya thought about lying; she didn't know how Carson would react if he found out she'd turned his brother in.

He deserves to know the truth.

"I know what happened to Charlie," she said. "He was arrested."

"How do you know that?" Dr. Schuller asked.

"Because I'm the one who turned him in," she said, turning to address Carson rather than the woman she'd only just met. "He attacked me in the parking garage back in Vegas. A few hours after you last called me."

"My god, Maya... I'm sorry."

"It wasn't your fault," Maya assured him. "He was drunk. Violent. But I managed to subdue him."

"And then you called the police?" Dr. Schuller asked.

"I called CJ," she said.

"CJ?"

"He works for the FBI. Well, with the FBI, I guess. I'm not really sure who he works for exactly. They interviewed me at the FBI field office, though."

"Was he alone?" Dr. Schuller demanded, her voice rising. "Was there an older Indian man with him?"

Maya nodded. "I think his name was Dr. Singh."

"I knew we shouldn't have come here," Dr. Schuller said, standing up suddenly. "We have to go!"

"No," Carson declared. "We're not leaving. Maya's my only chance to save Ella!"

"Ella?" Maya asked.

"My daughter," Carson explained. "She's five."

"I didn't know you had a kid."

Carson shrugged. "She lived in LA with her mother. We divorced years ago. I tried to keep that part of my life separate."

For some reason she couldn't explain, it bothered Maya that he'd never mentioned his daughter to her.

Quit being so petty.

"You said I was your only chance to save her," Maya said. "What does that mean?"

Carson looked over at Dr. Schuller, who sat back down and nodded, as if giving him permission to explain.

"The men who took Charlie – Dr. Singh and this CJ you mentioned – I think they took my daughter, too."

"What? That's crazy. Why would they do that?"

"You better sit down, Maya," Carson suggested. "This is going to take a while to explain."

She did as instructed, listening patiently as Carson spun a wild tale about secret government conspiracy projects and orphaned twins with impossible, super-human powers.

He told me about this once before, she recalled. *The stopping time thing, at least. That night he got drunk at the bar.*

She didn't say anything as he explained how he and Charlie had met at the bus station; how they had been scamming the casinos; how Mother Pearl had kidnapped and tortured him. She held her tongue as he described how Charlie and Dr. Schuller had rescued him; how they had gone on the run, and how he had learned about his daughter and her supposedly faked death. But even though she didn't voice her objections aloud, her expression must have revealed her doubts.

"You don't believe me," Carson said.

"I'm sorry, Carson," she said, reaching out to take his hand. "This story is insane. The conspiracies are hard enough to believe, but the things you're talking about – you and Charlie stopping time – it's impossible!"

Carson sat down on the hotel room's bed, his head and shoulders slumped forward in utter dejection.

"You think I'm crazy, don't you?"

"Carson, I'll never be able to understand what you went through," she said. "What Mama Pearl did to you... I can't even imagine how horrible it must have been. It's only natural you'd have some mental issues after going through something like that. And with your daughter passing away--"

"She's not dead!" Carson snapped.

"You need help, Carson," Maya said, her voice soft and soothing. "You're sick. But if you turn yourself in, maybe they can help you get better."

"I assure you," Dr. Schuller insisted. "Everything Carson told you is accurate. As unbelievable as it sounds, it's all true."

Maya didn't bother to respond. *She's the one feeding Carson all this nonsense. Fueling his insanity.*

"I'll go with you," Maya said to Carson. "If you turn yourself in, I promise I'll help you get through this."

"The way you helped Charlie after you turned him in?" Dr. Schuller interjected.

"That wasn't her fault!" Carson said, jumping to her defense. "Charlie brought that on himself!"

"I didn't know about Charlie before I called you," Carson said, turning back to Maya. "I never wanted you to get mixed up in my shit. Not over a piece of garbage like him, at least. You did what you had to do, and I don't blame you for that.

"But I'm talking about my daughter now. She's just a kid. They took her away because of me. Because of what I can do. I can't turn my back on her now. That's why I came to you.

"I was hoping you might be able to use your FBI contacts and help me track down Dr. Singh. I didn't know you'd already had direct contact with his people. But if they already know you, maybe you can reach out to them again. Please. For my daughter."

He's not listening to me. He's in denial. Still acting like this is all real, and his daughter has been abducted by some government shadow agency.

"If I reach out to them," she said, "I'll have to tell them about you. About the things you're saying. The things you believe."

"What if we can prove it to you?" Dr. Schuller asked. "What if we can prove all this is real?"

Carson's head snapped around. "How are we supposed to do that?"

Dr. Schuller hesitated, then shook her head. "I don't know," she admitted.

Carson stood up.

"I'm sorry, Maya. I shouldn't have called you. I think you should go."

"I don't want to leave you like this, Carson," she said.

"Goodbye, Maya."

There was a finality in his words she knew she couldn't argue with. She gathered up her things and left.

As she headed back to the base, she couldn't stop thinking about Carson.

You shouldn't have left him with that woman.

She thought about calling the police. Maybe if they took Carson into custody, they could treat him. But she quickly dismissed the idea; if he was arrested, it was more likely he'd get tossed in a jail cell and swallowed up by the system instead of getting the help he needed.

CJ.

When she'd turned Charlie over to the young man, he'd told her she should contact him if Carson ever reached out to her.

Why do you think CJ is a better option than turning him over to the police?

She couldn't explain it, but for some reason Maya trusted him. She prided herself on being a good judge of character, and she felt there was something fundamentally decent about him.

Maybe I don't need to tell him I met Carson in person. Maybe I can just reach out to him and see what he knows. Get a feel for whether he can help or not.

By the time she got back to the base, she'd made her decision. It was a longshot; even if CJ could help her, Carson and Dr. Schuller were probably already back on the run again. But at least she was doing something.

It was getting late, but she dialed the number CJ had given her anyway. He answered on the first ring.

"Hello?"

"CJ? This is Maya Belfour. From Las Vegas."

"Maya. I remember. You're at Quantico now, aren't you?"

She felt a brief flicker of fear. *How does he know that? Has he been keeping tabs on me?* But then she remembered it had come up during their interview in Vegas. They'd even offered to help her career.

Carson's conspiracy theories are making me paranoid.

"That's right. I've got another month of training before I go into the field."

"Congratulations."

"You told me to call you if I ever heard from Carson," she said, getting right to the point.

"He reached out to you?"

There was an eagerness to his voice that she found unsettling.

"He did."

"What happened? Tell me everything!"

Maya suddenly had reservations about sharing the details of her meeting.

"Can we talk about this in person?" she said. "It's a delicate matter. I'd rather do this face-to-face." *That'll give me a better read on whether I can really trust you or not.*

"I can be there tomorrow."

"Good. I'll text you a place to meet."

"Excellent, Maya. I'll see you then."

Hanging up, Maya couldn't shake the feeling that something was off about the phone call. *He seemed so excited. Like he just won the lottery or something.*

She crawled into bed, wondering if she'd just made a huge mistake.

***

"She's going to turn you in," Lisa said, hastily packing up her things. "Probably already made the call."

"Can you blame her?" Carson replied, jamming his toiletries into his travel bag. "Half the time I can't believe all this is real, and I've lived through it."

"I bet we have less than an hour before this place is crawling with Dr. Singh's people."

"I don't think that'll happen," Carson countered. "Maya's worried about me, but I don't think she's going to completely betray my trust."

"Really?"

"I could see it in her eyes. She doesn't believe me, but she knows something strange is going on."

"So?"

"Maya's not the kind of person to just let that go. She's going to dig a little. Try to find out more about what's really going on.

"You're probably right about her reaching out to this CJ person," Carson conceded. "But she's not going to just tell him we were here. If I know Maya, she's going to want to speak with him in person so she can judge him for herself."

"All the more reason we need to leave. Bug out before he shows up."

"No. He's my only lead to Ella."

"What?"

"They'll expect us to go back on the run," Carson explained. "I say we stick around. Go into hiding, but we keep an eye on Maya. If CJ shows up to meet her, maybe we have a chance to grab him up. Force him to tell us what he knows about Ella."

Lisa cocked her head to one side.

"You're talking about abducting and possibly torturing one of Dr. Singh's people. Do you know how dangerous that is?"

"They've got my daughter," Carson replied. "And I'll do whatever it fucking takes to get her back!"

CHAPTER 23

CJ was already waiting in the coffee shop when Maya arrived, even though she was fifteen minutes early. She'd wanted to get there before him; scope the place out and keep an eye on who came and went in case he wasn't alone.

He must have had the same idea.

As she made her way over to the table, she glanced around at the other patrons, looking for anything out of the ordinary. Nobody seemed to be watching her; everyone was focused on their coffee, their phones, or the other people at their tables.

Doesn't mean he's alone, though. Just means the people with him are good at their job.

"It's good to see you again, Maya," CJ said, standing up and offering his hand.

"You got here early," she said.

"I was dying for my morning cup o' joe," he replied, holding up his mug.

The waitress came over, and Maya ordered one for herself. When she was gone, CJ leaned forward in his seat, barely able to contain his eagerness.

"You said Carson reached out to you?" He wasn't whispering, but his voice was low enough to keep others from overhearing their conversation.

"He called me," Maya lied. "From a burner."

"What did he say?"

"He's... he's not doing well," Maya said. "He was spouting all these crazy conspiracy theories."

"About what?"

Maya hesitated, then decided she might as well come clean. There was no harm in telling him about the paranoid fantasies Carson had wrapped around himself.

"He thinks he can stop time. Claims that's how he and Charlie were scamming the casinos."

"Sounds like he's had a psychotic break," CJ said.

His response was normal enough. But Maya had spent several years as a cop, another two years working casino security, and the past few months learning FBI interrogation techniques. She'd learned to pick up on subtle cues that could tip her off when someone was lying or holding something back. A lot of the time these clues were so subtle they were almost imperceptible – a minute rise in the pitch of the voice; a slight change in the rate of breathing; an involuntary micro expression or facial tic. Her training had taught her to pick up on these tells subconsciously, giving her a remarkably accurate "gut feeling" of whether someone was telling the truth. And right now her gut was screaming *Liar!*

"It's not just that," she continued. "He knows who your partner is. Dr. Singh. Carson thinks you're part of some secret government program."

"Well, you already knew that about me," CJ admitted. "Or suspected it, at least."

He's still nervous. This is hitting too close to home for him.

"Did Carson say anything about where he was?" CJ continued. "Or how you could reach out to him?"

"No, he didn't. But he asked about Charlie."

"What did you tell him?"

"Nothing," Maya lied. "I said I hadn't seen him since the night Carson picked him up at my casino."

CJ nodded.

"What happened to Charlie, anyway?" Maya asked. "I didn't see any notice of his arrest."

CJ hesitated. "We worked out a deal with him."

"Witness protection?"

"Something like that."

He's still lying to me. Shit! Carson was right. Maybe not about stopping time, but they're up to something.

"Is there anything else you can tell me?" CJ asked. "Any little thing might help us track him down."

Maya realized that as careful as she thought she was being, there was still a chance she might give something away. Every second she spoke with CJ was putting Carson in danger.

"No, there was nothing else," she said, standing up. "I'm sorry, but I need to get going. I have an appointment."

"Maya, wait," CJ said, reaching across the table to grab her wrist. He didn't grab her hard, but she gave him a fierce glare anyway. Chastened, he let his hand fall away and leaned back.

"Sorry," he mumbled.

Maya's phone buzzed in her pocket, freezing her in place just as she was about to storm out.

***

"Maya's taking a seat at a table with a young black man," Lisa said, peering through her binoculars at the coffee shop.

She and Carson were sitting in a car parked across the street. They'd followed Maya when she left the base that morning, hoping Carson was right about her setting up an in-person meeting.

"That must be CJ," he said. "Any sign of Dr. Singh?"

"No," Lisa said. "He's sitting by himself. But I see at least one other table in the diner that could be undercover agents."

"We expected him to bring backup," Carson said.

"I really hate this," Lisa said, renewing her objection to the plan. "We're way too close. It's possible we've already been spotted."

Carson knew they were taking a risk. But what other choice did he have?

CJ's my only chance of finding Ella.

"What's happening now?" he asked.

"They're just talking," Lisa said.

"Any chance you read lips?"

"Sorry. Never picked that skill up."

They sat in silence as Lisa watched the conversation from a distance.

"Uh-oh. I think he said something that alarmed her. She's getting up to go."

Shit!

If Maya left, CJ wouldn't stick around long. And trying to snatch him up off the street outside the coffee shop wasn't an option as long as his backup was around.

"Shit – he just grabbed her wrist!" Lisa reported.

Carson whipped out his phone and sent Maya a text, hoping she'd check it before she left.

***

Maya pulled the phone out of her pocket.

GET HIM AWAY FROM HIS HANDLERS!

Carson's nearby! He's watching me right now!

Her heart began pounding as she realized what he was asking her to do.

What if he's right? What if they really did take his daughter?

She sat back down at the table.

"You're staying?" CJ said, somewhat surprised.

"If you really want me to tell you what I know," Maya replied in a barely audible whisper. "Then we need to talk alone. Just you and me."

To his credit, CJ didn't try to deny there were people watching them.

"Fair enough," he whispered back. "You got a plan?"

"How many of your people are here?"

"Just two. The table in the corner."

"Any watching outside?"

"No."

Her gut told her he was telling the truth.

"Okay, then – simple plan. We get up and make a break for it. On three I'm going to bolt for the door. All you have to do is keep up."

If Carson was watching her, hopefully he was ready to swoop in as soon as the coast was clear. It wasn't much of a plan, but it was the best she could do in the spur of the moment.

"Okay," CJ agreed. "On three."

"One," Maya whispered, wondering if she had lost her mind. "Two. Three!"

She jumped to her feet and sprinted across the diner and out the door. She didn't stop once she was outside – instead she began running down the street, only slowing down enough to glance back and confirm that CJ was following her.

***

"Shit!" Lisa shouted. "She's making a break for it!"

Carson looked up to see Maya bursting from the diner and out onto the street. She took off, heading away from them. CJ was following close behind.

Thank you, Maya, he thought as he started the engine and pulled a quick U-turn. As he did so, two men raced out of the diner in pursuit of the fugitives.

Carson floored the accelerator, leaving the agents in the dust as he sped down the block. He zoomed past Maya and CJ, then pulled over and screeched to a halt on the curb fifty feet ahead of them.

"Get in!" Maya shouted at CJ, solving the problem of how Carson would get the young man into the vehicle.

She yanked open the rear door and CJ stumbled into the back seat. Then she jumped in beside him and slammed the door shut as Carson peeled out.

"Carson," CJ gasped in surprise as he recognized the driver. "And Dr. Schuler."

"I guess my reputation precedes me," Lisa said, turning around in her seat. She was pointing a pistol right at CJ's chest.

"I don't think we need that," Maya said.

"Better safe than sorry," Carson replied as they sped away.

***

CJ did his best to remain calm, despite the woman in the front seat pointing a gun at him.

She killed Mama Pearl. She won't hesitate to kill me, too, if she thinks I'm lying to them.

"Turn off your phone and hand it over," Dr. Schuller ordered.

He did as instructed, moving slowly and carefully.

"Turn your phone off, too," she said to Maya. "Just in case they're tracking you."

Maya nodded as she complied.

"Where are we going?" CJ asked.

"Not far," Carson said. "We have some questions for you."

Five minutes later they pulled into the parking lot of a low-rent motel. Carson got out and checked to make sure nobody was around. He signaled once he'd confirmed the coast was clear.

"Don't try anything stupid," Dr. Schuller warned.

The four of them went into one of the first-floor rooms.

"Take a seat," Carson said, pointing to a chair in the middle of the room.

CJ sat down, then crossed his arms behind the back of the chair.

"What are you doing?" Carson asked.

"You're not going to tie me up?"

"Let's hope it doesn't come to that," Dr. Schuller said.

Carson pulled another chair over and took a seat facing CJ.

"I'm going to ask you some questions," he said. "Maya's going to tell me if you're lying or not. Trust me - you don't want to lie."

CJ glanced over at Maya, who was standing off in the corner. She looked nervous.

She's not sure who's side she's on, he realized.

"Dr. Singh told me about you," he said to Dr. Schuller, hoping Maya might be swayed if she knew who she was dealing with.

"Really?" the silver-haired woman replied. "What did he say?"

"That you're a traitor to your country. That you betrayed your friends and sabotaged the project."

Dr. Schuller smiled. "Technically that's true. But it doesn't even come close to capturing the real story. Do you even know what Dr. Singh had me working on?"

"He said you were studying the genetic remains of the alien pilots recovered from the crash site."

"Whoa!" Maya suddenly burst out. "Hold on a second… are you saying all that stuff Carson told me is real?"

"I don't know what he told you," CJ replied, evasive.

"That he can stop time? That you're part of a secret team at Area 51 studying the UFO from the Roswell crash?"

"He can't really stop time," CJ said. "Not completely. We've recently learned that time just slows down dramatically. Roughly $1/100,000^{th}$ of normal speed according to our measurements. But the rest of it is true."

"I think I need to sit down," Maya muttered, stumbling over to the bed.

"Stay with me, Maya," Carson said. "I'm counting on all that FBI training to let me know when this bastard lies to me."

Maya nodded, but all the blood had drained from her face.

"Where's my daughter?" Carson said.

"Your daughter?"

He reached out and casually slapped CJ upside the head, hard enough that his ear started ringing.

"Don't make this hard," Carson replied. "I know you took her."

"We've been watching her," CJ admitted, rubbing the side of his head. "Ever since you disappeared. But we haven't done anything to her."

Carson pulled his hand back, but stopped when Maya said, "Wait! I think he's telling the truth."

He lowered his hand, staring at CJ with narrowed eyes.

"We have agents watching her from a distance, but they don't interfere," CJ said. "She's living a normal life, except for the treatments she's taking for her epilepsy."

"It's not epilepsy," Carson said. "They ruled that out long ago. Something else is causing her seizures."

"Whatever the cause," CJ replied. "Her treatments seem to be working. But other than that, she's a completely normal child living a completely normal life."

"Bullshit," Carson said. "I spoke to her mother the other day. She told me Ella's dead."

CJ shook his head. "No. They send me a report on her activities every day. I just reviewed yesterday's before I flew out here."

"Looks like you've been getting bad information," Dr. Schuller said. "Dr. Singh must have wanted to keep you out of the loop. Told the field agents to file false reports with you."

"That doesn't make any sense," CJ said, legitimately confused. "I'm his right-hand man. Why would he give me fake reports?"

"This is a good thing, right?" Maya chimed in. "It means CJ wasn't responsible for taking Ella."

"It also means Dr. Singh doesn't trust him," Carson said. "I wonder what other secrets he's been keeping."

CJ didn't answer. His head was spinning. If what they said was true...

"Dr. Singh wouldn't do that," he protested. "Kidnap a child."

Carson laughed out loud. "Seriously? He was running lab experiments on unsuspecting young women. Impregnating them with embryos laced with alien DNA! You really think someone capable of that wouldn't kidnap my daughter?"

"What? Impregnating women with... no." CJ shook his head. "That's not possible."

"I was there," Dr. Schuller said. "I saw it with my own eyes."

"I don't believe you," CJ insisted. "You're lying!"

"Where the hell do you think me and Charlie came from?" Carson asked him.

Again, CJ had no answer. He wanted to reject everything they were saying as bold-faced lies, but part of him realized they were right.

What kind of monster am I working for?

"He must be keeping Ella in a secret lab on the base," Dr. Schuller said. "Isolating that part of their research to keep it hidden from the rest of the team. Minimal operations staff – probably only a couple scientists, a few guards, and the field agents filing the false reports know what's really going on.

"That's what he did with Beth and the other women when I was there," she added. "I bet he's keeping Charlie there, too."

"No," CJ mumbled, still struggling to cope with the new reality he'd been exposed to. "Charlie's working with us voluntarily."

"What?" Carson said.

"After we picked him up, Dr. Singh convinced him to join our team instead of going to jail. We're studying him to learn more about his link to the Core and why he can move while the rest of the world is frozen."

"But you couldn't do that unless time was still stopping," Dr. Schuller noted. "And Carson hasn't used his ability in months."

Of course. That's why they took the girl. She can trigger the Core, just like her father!

"I... I thought it was you," he said, finally realizing how blind he'd been.

I should have figured this out on my own. I was seeing what I wanted to see, instead of what was really going on.

He looked directly into Carson's eyes, recognizing the fear and desperation of a father terrified for his daughter.

"I'm sorry, Carson. I didn't know."

Carson glanced back over his shoulder at Maya.

"I believe him," she said.

"So do I," Dr. Schuller added.

"Does this mean you'll help me get Ella back?"

CJ nodded.

"We'll need a plan," Dr. Schuller said. "And that means telling us everything you know about what Dr. Singh is working on. I imagine a lot's changed since the last time I was there."

CJ nodded again.

"Good," Carson said. "Let's start with Charlie."

CHAPTER 24

Charlie's legs screamed in protest as he waded through the waist deep water. It was only a few degrees above freezing, but during the timeout he couldn't feel its frigid temperature. Still, the resistance as he sloshed along was amplified almost tenfold while time was stopped, making every step an excruciating ordeal.

He reached the other side of the 25-meter pool and pulled himself up onto the deck, the muscles in his shoulders, neck, and arms bulging with the strain. There were two mannequins standing at the edge of the pool, each equipped with multiple sensors at various locations: head, torso, elbows, knees, and groin. He pulled the knife from the sheath on his hip and slowly slid the blade into the mannequins at the targeted spots, knowing the force of the impact would be measured by the sensors once the timeout was over.

He continued his way through the rest of the obstacle course, wondering how far he'd manage to get before time started moving again. He reached the climbing rope and began to haul himself up towards the high, arching ceiling. Under normal circumstances he had the upper body strength to fly up a thirty-foot rope in seconds, but during stasis it felt like he was pulling at least twice his bodyweight.

His heart was ready to explode as he reached the platform at the top. Struggling to breath the thick, soupy air of the timeout, he glanced over at the men watching him through the chain link perimeter fence. Dr. Singh and two scientists Charlie just called Poindexter 1 and Poindexter 2 were completely still, frozen by the timeout. So was the armed guard –

one of the two men assigned to watch over Charlie at all times in rotating 12-hour shifts. Out of spite, Charlie flipped them off, even though he knew they'd never see it.

I'm the one doing all the fucking work. All they do is look at the numbers when I'm done.

The obstacle course had been built inside a massive airplane hangar: 500 feet long and a hundred feet wide. In addition to the course itself the hangar housed dozens of cameras, sensors, and other hi-tech equipment meant to record and analyze everything that happened during Charlie's runs.

He climbed down the ladder from the platform. Back on the ground, he pressed on to the next station: a series of freestanding locked doors. On the ground beside the doors was a large crowbar. Charlie scooped it up and set to work.

The first door was a simple lock; all he had to do was pry the crowbar into the small space between the door and the frame, then lean into it. After a brief moment of resistance, the lock gave way and the door silently popped open.

The next door was more secure; there was no chance of prying it open. Instead, Charlie raised the crowbar and brought it down on the door's handle with all the force he could muster. It took three swings before the handle snapped off. Instead of tumbling to the ground, it hung in the air – even gravity was halted during the timeouts.

With the handle broken free, Charlie was able to shove the second door open and move onto the third. But instead of trying to breach it, he simply stood in front of it, the crowbar hanging by his side. As tired as he was, he could have kept going. But he'd never managed to reach the doors before in any of his runs.

New personal best. Might as well stop here.

He always liked to hold something back during the tests.

No sense letting my handlers know the real limits of what I can do.

He stood there for a while, fidgeting impatiently. Every time he ran the course, he was getting better at it. But he also knew much of his improvement came from the fact that the timeouts were lasting longer now. The girl – Charlie didn't like to think of her by name, even though she was technically his niece – was getting stronger, too.

Not as strong as Carson, though. And she needs more time to recover than he did.

During their days in Vegas, Carson could seemingly stop time whenever he wanted. But the girl could only do it three or four times a day. Even on a short stoppage, she'd still need ten or fifteen minutes to recover.

Maybe someday she'll be up to Carson's level.

It took a long while for the timeout to finally end; today they were pushing the girl to her absolute limit. When the world started moving again, Charlie dropped the crowbar. It fell to the ground, clattering loudly. He doubled over, hands on his knees as he gulped in oxygen. The air whooshed in and out of his starving lungs in loud, satisfying gasps – a sharp contrast to the total silence of the timeout.

Gotta make it seem like I don't have anything left in the tank. Make them think I pushed myself to the absolute limit.

He took several more deep breaths, then stood up and slowly made his way back over to the chain link fence. Reaching the gate separating him from the observers on the other side, he unstrapped the knife from his thigh and hung it on a small hook. Then he waited while one of the Poindexter's came over and unlocked the gate, accompanied by the armed guard. The guard was watching him carefully, ready to draw his sidearm if Charlie tried anything.

You'd love it if I gave you an excuse to shoot me, wouldn't you?

Charlie waited until the Poindexter stepped clear, then pushed the gate open and stepped through. He followed the scientist towards the entrance at the opposite end of the hangar, the guard falling into step behind Charlie. Dr. Singh was waiting there, along with the other Poindexter. But they weren't alone.

Shit, they brought the girl today.

He hadn't noticed her with them during his run.

I fucking hate it when they bring her.

The little girl was strapped into a wheelchair, barely conscious. Her head was shaved, and there was a metal halo wrapped around it - a crown of wires and electrodes implanted in her bare skull. Her tiny arms and legs were secured to the chair to keep her from falling out in her semi-vegetative state.

She looks like a kid version of that X-men guy.

"Excellent work, Charlie," Dr. Singh said. "Your progress continues to be remarkable."

"Why'd you bring her?" he said in response.

"We need to evaluate whether her proximity to you has any effect on the limits of your abilities. Or hers."

"I fucking told you it doesn't work like that," Charlie said. "Carson used to freeze shit on me when he was on the other side of the country!"

"Even so," Dr. Singh countered, "we want to consider all the variables."

"And?"

"We haven't checked the data yet," Poindexter 1 said. He was holding a clipboard, and on his wrist was what looked like an oversized fitbit.

Charlie's gaze instinctively focused on the device; he knew it was what they used to trigger the timeouts.

Dr. Singh stepped forward, blocking his view as he placed a hand on Charlie's shoulder.

"I think we're done for the day. I'd like to schedule another session for tomorrow if you're up for it."

"Your call, man."

Charlie headed out of the hangar, escorted by his guard. There was a jeep waiting for him; the obstacle course had been built in a hangar on the farthest corner of Edwards Airforce Base. As part of his deal with Dr. Singh, he had access to all the amenities the base had to offer: the gym, the rec rooms, the commissary. But he would always have one of the two guards watching him, and he wasn't allowed to leave the grounds under any circumstances.

"Where to?" the driver asked.

"Just take me to my room," he muttered.

He hopped out of the jeep as they arrived at the destination. His guard followed suit, watching closely as Charlie opened the door and went inside. Mercifully, the guards never followed him into his room, though Charlie knew one of them would always be stationed outside his door.

His quarters were comfortable enough: a luxurious bed; a wide screen TV with all the streaming services; internet access (constantly monitored, of course); gaming consoles; even a hot tub.

It may be fancy as a four-star hotel, but you're still in fucking jail.

He picked up the phone and buzzed the commissary, putting in an order for his dinner. Then he stripped down and stepped into the shower. As the steam rose up to envelope him, he couldn't stop thinking about the girl in her wheelchair, and the bizarre metal halo surgically grafted to her skull.

Dr. Singh had explained why they needed to do it: she wasn't consciously capable of causing the timeouts yet. Either she was too young, or whatever gene Carson possessed hadn't been fully passed on to his daughter. The girl's timeouts were sporadic, unintentional, and unpredictable.

But by imaging her skull and studying her brain waves whenever a timeout happened, Dr. Singh's people had mapped the patterns that triggered them. Her metal halo was wirelessly connected to the device the Poindexter was wearing on his wrist. With a simple push of a button, they could light up her brain in all the right places to freeze the world.

Unfortunately, the timeouts also caused her to experience violent seizures. According to Dr. Singh, the only way to prevent the seizures was to keep her heavily sedated whenever they were testing her abilities.

Also makes her easier to handle.

Normally, Charlie didn't think about the girl – he had his own problems to focus on. But whenever they brought her to the testing grounds, it was hard not to feel at least a little sympathy for her.

Sometimes it feels like Singh trots her out just to fuck with me. Remind me of what they can do if I step out of line.

But right now they needed Charlie in a way they didn't need the girl. He was the only one who could actually move during the timeouts; they wanted him to be mentally and physically sharp during his runs. They needed his cooperation.

At least until they figure out a way to copy what I can do.

Charlie had no illusions about his fate if that should ever happen. Every week they took blood samples from him and ran a full battery of physical tests, poking and prodding him for nearly an hour. They'd figured out a way to trigger the timeouts in the girl, and could even control how long they lasted by adjusting the settings on the trigger. Eventually, they'd find a way to replicate whatever it was about Charlie that made him special, too. Once that happened, he'd be a liability. A loose end.

Something tells me Singh doesn't like loose ends.

Even though he'd agreed to work with Dr. Singh, Charlie had been plotting a way to escape the base ever since he arrived. At first, it had seemed hopeless. But once they tracked down his niece and strapped her into that chair, he saw a way out.

She's the key. All I need to go is get my hands on that trigger.

***

CJ was shaken from a fitful sleep as the plane touched down on the Dreamland runway with a gentle bump. He wasn't surprised to see Dr. Singh waiting for him as he disembarked.

"How was your trip?" he asked.

"Productive," CJ said. "Though we got off to a rocky start. Maya spotted my tails in the diner. She wouldn't talk to me until we lost them."

No doubt Dr. Singh had already been briefed on the mad dash escape from the diner. Hopefully, though, CJ could convince him that they were still on the same side.

"And once the two of you were alone?"

"She confirmed Carson reached out to her. He and Dr. Schuller have been hiding out in Provo the past few months."

"I'm surprised he told her that," Dr. Singh said.

"Actually, they've spoken several times," CJ lied. "He has a crush on Maya. She used that to build trust and get him to open up to her."

"I'm even more surprised she told you that," Dr. Singh added.

"It took a while. I had to make her certain promises."

"Like what?"

"That we wouldn't hurt Carson. That we wanted to work with him."

"And she believed you?"

"She did. After I told her Charlie was already working for us."

Dr. Singh's eyes narrowed. "That's classified intel."

"I had to give something to get something," CJ countered. "I figured it was my call."

"Of course," Dr. Singh said, his expression breaking into a smile. "I trust your judgement completely."

"She also refused to help us lure Carson in," CJ added. "And she didn't know exactly where in Provo they were hiding."

CJ had constructed his story very carefully, with a little help from Dr. Schuller and the others. It was a fine balancing act of giving Dr. Singh enough real information about Carson to entice him, but not offering so much that it seemed overly convenient.

I need him focused on how to track Carson down, not on whether he can still trust me or not.

"Provo isn't that large," Dr. Singh said. "I'll send a couple teams to start scouting it out. Hopefully they're still there."

They're not. They're on their way to Vegas. Driving all night so they can be here tomorrow.

"No reason to think they've left," CJ said out loud. "And Maya promised to call me if Carson reached out to her again."

Dr. Singh nodded.

"Good. You should get some sleep. You've earned it."

"I'd rather look over the latest reports on Charlie's progress," CJ said. It wasn't an unusual request – Dr. Singh was used to CJ pushing himself hard. "See if there's anything they missed while I was gone."

"I'll have Dr. Lantham send them your way."

CJ nodded, and Dr. Singh turned and climbed into his waiting jeep. CJ watched as he sped off. Once he was out of sight, he turned to the driver of his own vehicle.

"It's going to be a long night for me," he said. "Drop me off at Lab C and just leave me the keys. I'll drive myself back to the barracks when I'm done."

The driver nodded; as Dr. Singh's right hand, the personnel at Dreamland were used to following his orders.

At the lab, CJ spent the next six hours reviewing all the reports on Charlie's progress. He'd seen them before, but now he was examining them with the knowledge that Carson's daughter was the one causing the timeouts, not Carson.

How are they getting her to cooperate? Fear? Manipulation?

More importantly, where were they keeping her? Dr. Schuller had told him about a section of the base she used to call "the nursery" – a small series of underground bunkers used to house the young women she and her partner experimented on back in the 80's. It was located on the far northwest corner, beyond the airstrips. Officially, that area of Dreamland was decommissioned, meaning nobody ever had any reason to go there.

They must be keeping her in the bunkers.

He had no idea how many people were involved in the plot to kidnap Carson's daughter. The agents who filed the false field reports were in on it; probably Dr. Lantham and Dr. Perron as well. Maybe two or three guards to keep an eye on Ella.

I hope they're treating her well, at least.

At most, CJ guessed a half-dozen people were involved. The more people who really knew what was going on, the more likely someone would either let the secret slip or realize what they were doing was unconscionable.

Keeping Charlie here on the base as a virtual prisoner so they could study him was one thing: he was an adult, and a legitimate danger to society. It was definitely illegal, but CJ had no problem justifying the morality of it. But knowing he was part of a project that had abducted an innocent child made him feel physically ill.

We'll get her back, Carson. I promise.

But as much as he wanted to do something, he had to be careful. If he came forward with the truth, he had no way to know who would support him and who would back Dr. Singh.

At the very least, I'm going to need some proof of what's going on.

He glanced at his watch and realized he'd been working all night. He wanted to go check out the nursery, but he wasn't going to risk it with the sun about to come up.

Tonight. After the sun goes down and most of the base has turned in for the night.

His chances of actually getting into the nursery were slim. If Ella really was being held there, she'd be under guard 24/7. But the first step was verifying her location.

Exhausted, he went back to his quarters and fell into bed, setting his alarm to wake him just as the sun was going down.

CHAPTER 25

"You didn't bring the girl this time," Charlie noted as his guard escorted him into the hangar with the obstacle course.

"This is a control run," Poindexter 1 said. "We'll compare today's progress to yesterday's and see if her proximity affected the results."

He was carrying what appeared to be the same clipboard as yesterday, but this time it was his partner who was wearing the trigger strapped to his wrist. He'd noticed the Poindexters alternated who was in charge of the trigger, but he didn't know if that was part of the experiment or just a way to make them feel equally important.

"Where's Dr. Singh?" Charlie asked. "Is he with the girl?"

"Dr. Singh will review the results later," Poindexter 2 replied, ignoring his question.

Charlie didn't know where they were keeping the girl – just one of many things they kept him in the dark about.

"Head on down to the course," Poindexter 1 instructed.

The guard nodded his head in the direction of the access gate, his hand resting on the hilt of the pistol holstered on his hip. Charlie dutifully made his way along the entire length of the hangar, following the perimeter fence until he reached the gate. The guard followed about ten feet behind him the entire way. Charlie stepped through the gate, and he heard the guard snap the padlock into place with a sharp *click*.

Today's the day, he thought as he grabbed the knife from its hook by the gate and strapped it to his thigh.

Making his way over to the obstacle course starting line, he turned and flashed a thumbs up towards the Poindexter wearing the trigger.

As the world froze around him, Charlie sprang into action. But instead of heading for the pool, he ran along the edge of the obstacle course. Ignoring the climbing rope, he headed straight for the free-standing doors. The smashed locks and frames had been replaced in anticipation of his next run, but Charlie ignored them. He scooped the crowbar up off the floor, then turned and raced back towards the starting line... and the locked gate.

The guard was still standing on the other side of the fence, motionless and completely unaware Charlie was bearing down on him while time was frozen. Charlie jammed the crowbar in between the gate and the fence, then wrenched it hard to the side. The chain links buckled, but the padlock held.

Fuck!

He tried again, leveraging his entire body against the end of the crowbar until he felt the metal lock finally give way. He flipped the latch up and pulled the gate open. The crowbar was heavy enough that it would just slow him down, so he tossed it aside. It hung comically in the air the instant it left his hand.

Grinning, he approached the frozen guard as he drew his knife. He shoved the blade deep into the man's throat. The guard didn't react, of course – it was like stabbing the dummies on the obstacle course; mannequins made of flesh-colored plastic. But once the timeout ended, he knew blood would gush from the fatal wound in a crimson waterfall.

He yanked the pistol from the guard's holster. With the gun in one hand and his knife in the other, he charged in what felt like slow motion towards the Poindexters. Like the guard, they were motionless as statues; completely unaware of what Charlie was doing while the world was stopped.

In the back of his mind, Charlie was trying to get a sense of how long the world had been frozen so far, and when the timeout might end. But there was a surreal quality to everything during stasis that made tracking time almost impossible.

No turning back now. Go, go, go!

Churning his arms and legs, he fought against the oppressive inertia of an entire reality in stasis. Each step brought him closer to his prey, and his eyes widened with anticipation.

The world was still frozen when he finally reached Poindexter 1's side. Charlie dragged the knife across the scientist's throat, pressing firmly to ensure the blade sliced deep enough to carve through skin, muscle and trachea. As he reached Poindexter 2's side, though, the world started moving again.

The scientist had just enough time to register Charlie bearing down on him and let out a yelp of surprise before Charlie's fist caught him across the jaw. He crumpled from the blow, and Charlie fell on top of him. He threw a flurry of punches, quickly beating the scientist into unconsciousness. Then he unsnapped the trigger from the Poindexter's wrist and strapped it onto his own.

He knew it would be a while before he could use it again – after the extended timeout he'd just been through, she'd need time to recover. That was okay; Charlie had to wait for the scientist to regain consciousness anyway. He still needed the Poindexter to tell him where they were keeping the girl, and what kind of security she had watching her.

Let's see if this so-called genius is smart enough to answer my questions the first time I ask, Charlie thought, idly sliding his thumb along the edge of his knife's blade.

***

Dr. Singh set aside the report on CJ's meeting with Maya. Everything CJ had told him matched up with the account from the agents who'd been tailing him. Still, something didn't feel right.

Did CJ find out about the girl?

Only a handful of people knew about her; Dr. Singh had kept the team as small as possible. Everyone inside the circle had been carefully chosen; it was doubtful any of them would say anything about her to CJ.

Charlie knew about her, as well. But Dr. Singh was careful to keep CJ away from Charlie. CJ wasn't ever present at any of Charlie's runs, though he was still given copies of all the data and reports. Dr. Singh suspected CJ might have some ethical reservations about what they were doing, but his data analysis was still valuable enough to keep him in the loop on their progress.

If he did learn about the girl, what would he do?

Reporting Dr. Singh for abducting a child wasn't really an option; for years their experiments at Dreamland had operated without any real oversight or accountability. CJ had been here long enough to understand that.

Would he go public? Expose everything we've been working on?

That wasn't really an option either. There were already plenty of rumors about Area 51, many of which contained bits and pieces of the truth. That wasn't by accident – over the decades the military had carefully cultivated an aura of crazy conspiracy about the project. If anyone ever did go public, they would be dismissed as a crackpot or kook.

If CJ had found out about the girl somehow, there was only one real play.

Grab her and run. Go into hiding. Like Dr. Schuller did with Beth.

Keeping the girl on the base was convenient, but it was starting to seem less and less necessary. The evidence supported the theory that her connection to Charlie during the timeouts wasn't related to the distance between them. That fit with the quantum entanglement theory CJ had proposed; the distance between two twinned particles was irrelevant to the behavior.

Maybe it's time to move her to a more secure location. Somewhere off base.

That would likely involve bringing a few more people in on the secret. But he couldn't risk losing the girl. She was the key to everything.

A sudden sense of dread swept over him; an inexplicable fear that something had happened to his most valuable resource.

I should go check on her.

He knew he was probably being paranoid, but there was no harm in paying the girl a visit.

Leaving his office, he grabbed a black SUV from the motor pool and drove across the base to the nursery. As he approached the small concrete shed that housed the entrance to the underground bunker, the sense of dread continued to build.

He pulled to a stop outside the shed. The door should have been shut tight, but it was sitting just slightly ajar. Heart pounding, Dr. Singh slowly pushed the door open. Behind it was a long staircase descending into the earth. At the bottom of the steps was a second door. Normally it was locked, with a guard stationed on the other side. But to Dr. Singh's horror, it was wide open.

Moving cautiously, he crept down the stairs until he could peek through the open door. Just beyond it he could see the guard. He was lying on his back on the concrete floor of the bunker's small entrance chamber, bleeding from a gunshot wound to the chest. His eyes were wide and unblinking, his face a frozen mask of confusion and surprise.

Where's the girl?

Dr. Singh continued down the staircase, careful not to make any sound. The guard still had his sidearm, so he crouched down and pulled it from his holster. Then he crept down the hall towards the living quarters, pressing himself against the wall. There were half a dozen private rooms inside the bunker, each built off a single access hall. But only one was being used currently.

The girl's room was the first one on the left. The door was closed, and Dr. Singh pressed his ear up against it. He could hear someone inside, rummaging around. Tightening his grip on the pistol, he kicked open the door. But to his surprise, it wasn't CJ on the other side.

***

Charlie had just picked the girl up to move her from her bed into her wheelchair when Dr. Singh burst into the room. Seeing the gun pointed at him, Charlie clutched her tiny body tight against his chest, using her as a human shield.

"Put her down!" Dr. Singh ordered.

"Put your gun down, first," Charlie said.

Neither of the men moved.

"What's your plan, Charlie?" Dr. Singh asked. "Where do you think you're going with her? You'll never get off base. The guards will shoot you on sight!"

Not if I stop time.

Charlie had killed the guard at the door without using the trigger. He'd just knocked, then shot him point blank when he opened the door.

Dumb bastard got careless. Probably thought I was Dr. Singh coming to check up on the girl.

More than an hour had passed since he'd tortured and killed Poindexter 2; the girl might have recovered enough to use her power again. But even if she had, he couldn't activate the trigger on his wrist while he was holding her in his arms. And if he set her down...

"Drop the gun or I snap her neck," he declared.

"You'd be signing your own death warrant," Dr. Singh warned.

"I don't think so," Charlie snarled. "You need me."

"Not if the girl is dead," Dr. Singh countered. "She's the only one who can stop time. She's the catalyst. You're just a reactionary element in this equation. If she's out of the picture, you are of no use to us."

Charlie didn't say anything, but he got the sense the other man wasn't bluffing..

"However," Dr. Singh continued, "if the girl remains unharmed, then you still have value to this project. As long as we have her, we still need you."

But for how long? Charlie wondered, thinking back on all the blood and tissue samples they'd taken from him.

"I'm not going back to that prison," Charlie told him.

"Of course not," Dr. Singh conceded. "But maybe we can work out another arrangement. Instead of being a prisoner here on the base, you'd be a partner on this project. I can arrange for you to have a lucrative salary. I can even authorize occasional furloughs from the base, within reason."

"You're offering me a fucking job?" Charlie asked, carefully keeping the girl's limp body between him and the pistol's muzzle.

"You've proven yourself far more resourceful than I expected, Charlie. The project is always looking to add capable people."

"What about the guard I killed? And the Poindexters?"

"Sacrifices to the greater cause," Dr. Singh said with a shrug. "What's more, they're proof you have the stomach to do whatever it takes. Sometimes our work requires us to do unsavory things."

"Like kidnap little girls."

Dr. Singh smiled. "Precisely."

"How do I know this offer is real?" Charlie asked.

"Think about it from my perspective," Dr. Singh explained. "Nothing means more to me than this project. Having you as a willing ally moving forward will make thinks so much easier for me. You won't have to keep holding back on all your runs, for example. I won't have to adjust for compromised data."

Figures he'd know about that.

"I understand you're reluctant to trust me, Charlie. But you don't have any other viable options. I won't let you leave with the girl. You don't have any other way out."

He's right. I can't stand her using her like a human shield forever.

"This partnership will benefit both of us," Dr. Singh insisted. "All you have to do is set the girl down."

As Charlie thought about it, he realized Singh was actually making sense. He wouldn't care about the dead guards or the Poindexters. The only thing that mattered to him was the project.

And he needs me for the project.

"Okay," Charlie said. "I'm going to set her down on the bed."

"Good," Dr. Singh said, lowering the pistol. "Nice and slow, and let's both stay calm."

As Charlie turned and bent down towards the bed, a thought flashed through his head.

The blood and tissue samples. They have my DNA. What if I'm already expendable?

He tossed the girl onto the bed, throwing himself backwards as he did so. The deafening roar of the pistol firing echoed through the room, bouncing off the walls of the bunker. The bullet clipped his bicep, sending a flash of pain up through his arm.

Landing on the ground, Charlie rolled onto his back, fumbling for the trigger on his wrist. He hit the button just as Dr. Singh fired another round.

The sound of the second gunshot never came; snuffed out as time screeched to a halt. Dr. Singh had been frozen in the millisecond after he'd pulled the trigger, arm extended and braced for the anticipated recoil that hadn't happened yet.

The bullet itself had already launched; it hovered in the air a few inches from the barrel, creeping along its trajectory so slowly that the motion was almost imperceptible.

That's right. Time isn't actually stopped. It's just really fucking slow.

Charlie picked himself up off the floor and examined his wounded arm. During the timeout he still felt the pain, but it was a distant echo of what it would be once the world started moving again.

His shirt was torn and there was blood welling up along a wound that ran across his upper arm. But the bullet had just grazed him; it hadn't actually penetrated the flesh.

Going to sting like a bitch, but nothing serious.

He marched over to Dr. Singh and wrapped his arms around his paralyzed assailant. Even though he was a small man, it took all of Charlie's prodigious strength to pick him up. Straining and sweating, he carried him a half dozen steps before setting him down in the path of the bullet from his own gun. He turned the doctor so he was facing the bullet, checked that everything was lined up properly, then stepped back to wait.

When time inevitably started up again the bullet struck Singh right between the eyes, blowing his brains out the back of the skull.

CHAPTER 26

Carson squinted into the setting sun, his hands clutching tighter on the steering wheel as they roared down the I-40 at eighty miles an hour. They'd left Quantico almost thirty hours ago, sharing the driving as they traveled non-stop across the country towards Las Vegas.

"Watch your speed," Lisa warned from the passenger seat. "Flagstaff PD are always set up on this stretch."

Carson backed off the accelerator, dropping the vehicle to 70. As desperate as he was to get his daughter back, they couldn't afford to get pulled over.

A cell phone rang from the backseat. In the rearview mirror Carson saw Maya sit up and bring her phone to her ear.

"Hello?" she said, her voice still groggy.

Carson knew she felt guilty about turning Charlie in, even though he'd assured her over and over that he didn't blame her for what happened. But she'd insisted on coming, even though it meant she was going AWOL from the Academy.

She's throwing away her career to help you. To help Ella.

Part of him felt bad about what she was giving up, but another part of him was glad she was here.

"It's CJ," Maya announced, the phone still pressed up against her ear.

Instinctively, Carson turned his head around, eager to hear the news.

"Eyes on the road!" Lisa barked as the car began to drift out of the lane.

Carson snapped forward again, the car swerving slightly as he brought them back on course.

Keeping his attention focused on the endless ribbon of blacktop rolling out in front of them, he strained to listen in on what Maya was saying.

"What? He's really... yes. Are you sure... okay, I understand. Yes. I'll tell them, but I can't promise anything."

She hung up the phone. From her expression in the rearview mirror, Carson could see she was troubled.

"What did he say?"

"Dr. Singh's dead."

Carson was too stunned to reply, but Lisa asked, "What happened?"

"He said he couldn't get into the details over the phone. The line wasn't secure."

"Did he say anything about Ella?" Carson asked.

"Not really. I think he was worried about who might be listening in." After a brief hesitation, she added, "He said we have to meet him at Edwards Airforce Base."

"That wasn't what we agreed on," Carson said.

In the original plan, once they reached Vegas they'd call CJ to find out what he'd been able to uncover. But Carson had no intention of meeting him in person again or telling him where they'd be holed up; he still didn't fully trust him.

"He said with Dr. Singh gone, he's in charge of the project now. He promised we'd be safe. But he said we have to hurry – every second counts."

"It could be a trap," Lisa warned. "He might be luring us in."

"I don't think he'd do that," Maya said.

"Maybe he didn't have a choice," Lisa countered. "What if Dr. Singh isn't dead? What if he found out CJ was trying to help us? They could have caught him snooping around. Tortured him for information. Forced him to make the call."

Maya didn't bother to argue against her. Instead, she focused on Carson.

"It's your call, Carson. Whatever you decide, I'm with you."

"So am I," Lisa added. "Just as long as you understand what we might be walking into."

Carson's first impulse was to freeze the world so he could consider all the angles. But he fought against his instincts; if he felt trapped and powerless whenever Ella stopped time, then she probably felt the same when he did it.

I'm not going to do that to her.

Instead, he focused on the road stretching out before him, driving in silence as he mulled his options over. He'd lived his entire life through the prism of careful analysis; calculating the odds and choosing whatever course of action would minimize risk.

This isn't just about me anymore.

If CJ was telling the truth, they didn't have time to stop in Vegas now. *If* he was telling the truth.

You know what the smart play is. Stick to the original plan. Find somewhere safe to hide out first, then make contact.

Going to the base meant exposing himself – not to mention Maya and Lisa – to unnecessary danger. It was reckless. Foolish. Desperate. It went against everything Carson believed in.

But it might be Ella's only chance.

"Fuck it," he declared. "Next stop, Dreamland."

***

CJ's phone buzzed with an incoming text: 15 MIN AWAY.

He headed down to the main entrance; he'd already given the order for Carson to be allowed onto the base, but he wanted to be there in person to make sure everything went smoothly.

Allowing civilians access to a restricted military facility was highly unusual. Fortunately, the soldiers at Dreamland were used to obeying Dr. Singh's orders without question. With his death, that authority had now been transferred to CJ. Or so he hoped.

The sun had set hours ago, but the floodlights at the checkpoint lit the area up as bright as day. In the darkness beyond the glaring lights, he saw a pair of headlights approaching. He nodded to the guards on duty, and they opened the gate.

CJ positioned himself so he'd be immediately visible as they pulled up; he didn't want there to be any confusion. The car rolled to a stop beside him, and the rear door opened. Glancing back at the guards, he climbed into the vehicle.

Maya and Carson were sitting in the front. Dr. Schuller was in the back, turned to face him. She had her pistol sitting on the seat beside her, her hand resting on the handle.

"If the guards see that gun," CJ warned, "there could be trouble."

"Just a precaution," she assured him. "In case anyone here recognizes me."

"I think everyone who worked with you has retired," CJ said. "Dr. Singh was the only one left from that time."

"So he's really dead?"

"He is."

"What about Ella?" Carson asked.

"You were right," CJ admitted. "Dr. Singh kidnapped her. They were keeping her in an underground bunker on the edge of the base."

"I want to see her."

"She's not here anymore. Charlie took her and fled the base. Last night."

"Charlie took her? Where? Why?"

In the dim light of the car's interior, CJ couldn't read the expression on Carson's face. But he could only imagine the emotional hell he must be going through.

"I think I know a way to get your daughter back," he offered, hoping to soften the blow of his shocking news. He glanced out at the gate guards, who were clearly getting curious about what was going on in the idling vehicle. "Let's go somewhere private and I'll explain everything."

"I want to see where they were holding her." Carson's voice was cracked and strained.

"I'm not sure that's a good idea," CJ cautioned.

"I want to see it!"

Realizing he wouldn't be dissuaded, CJ pointed in the direction of the nursery. "Head that way."

They drove in silence until they pulled up beside the concrete shed. CJ stepped out of the car, then waited for the others to join him.

"We found Dr. Singh's body here," CJ said, before leading the way down the steps.

"This is where they were keeping your daughter," he said as they entered Ella's room. "Don't' worry – we analyzed the blood and it isn't hers."

Carson turned his head slowly from side to side, taking in the spartan surroundings.

"It's like a prison," he whispered.

"They kept her sedated most of the time," CJ said, then realized that probably didn't make him feel any better.

Carson walked over to the bed, his steps halting and unsure. He bent forward and plucked a single eyelash off the pillow, clutching it tightly between his thumb and forefinger. He stared at it for several seconds before letting it fall from away his grasp. Then he sat down on the edge of the mattress, put his head in his hands, and began to silently sob.

Maya came over and sat down beside him, wrapping her arms around his shoulders and gently rocking him back and forth.

"This is Dr. Singh's blood?" Dr. Schuler asked.

"Mostly. A few small drops were traced back to Charlie."

"Was Charlie kept here, too?" Carson asked, looking up. His face was streaked with grimy tears.

CJ shook his head. "He was being held in a different part of the base. Away from your daughter. Dr. Singh wanted to study what he could do during stasis. They ran him through a battery of tests. He was under constant supervision, but something must have gone wrong. He killed a guard and the two scientists observing him.

"Our best guess is Dr. Singh confronted him here, and Charlie shot him. Then he took Ella and fled the base in an SUV Dr. Singh had checked out from the motor pool."

"He could have taken her anywhere." Carson's voice wasn't angry or upset. He just sounded numb.

It's a lot for a parent to take in.

"I've been studying the notes from the scientists Charlie killed," CJ explaind. "They reference a subdermal locater Dr. Singh had implanted on your daughter. Once we finish decrypting his personal laptop, we'll be able to track the signal."

"How long will that take?" Maya asked.

"I've got a team on it now. A few hours if we're lucky. A couple days if not."

"Then you'll send someone to get her? And Charlie?"

"Unfortunately, it's not that simple."

"What do you mean?" Dr. Schuller demanded.

"Dr. Singh found a way to force Ella to stop time using neural implants and a remote trigger. They used it whenever they wanted to run a test on Charlie. That trigger is missing. We think Charlie took it with him."

"So Charlie can use Ella to stop time whenever he wants?" Dr. Schuller said, putting the pieces together.

"Yes. There are some limitations – data from the Core shows Ella's timeouts don't last nearly as long as Carson's used to. And it doesn't seem like she can trigger them in rapid succession; she needs some time to recover between them. But Charlie can still freeze time long enough to take out anyone who comes after him if he sees them coming."

"That's what long-range snipers are for," Dr. Schuler said.

"No!" Carson snapped. "I'm not going to risk anything happening to Ella!"

"I'd advise against calling a team in anyway," CJ said. "It's going to take a while to sort out everyone on base who was involved in this cover-up. Until then, I don't know which personnel we can trust."

"Then we do this ourselves," Maya said. "Maybe we could use a tactical takedown to incapacitate Charlie before he can activate the trigger."

"The timing would have to be perfect," Dr. Schuler objected.

"Not necessarily," CJ chimed in. "There may be a way to take away Charlie's advantage. Theoretically."

"How theoretically?" Dr. Schuler wanted to know.

"I've been studying the Core for a decade," CJ explained. "For years we couldn't understand how the technology actually worked. There were too many unknown variables. But once we learned about you and Charlie, everything changed. In the past few months I've learned more about how the Core operates than in the entire last decade. Understanding the catalyst behind the bursts was the missing key."

"Bursts?" Maya asked.

"For years, we've been tracking massive surges of energy emanating from the core. Each time it happened, the entire world – the entire universe, for all we know – would slow down to 1/100,000 normal speed. But inside the Core, time kept moving normally, allowing us to record the event and measure all the data for later analysis.

"We used to think the bursts were random, but now we know Carson was causing them. Well, you and Ella."

"You told me you didn't know what they were doing to her," Carson said darkly.

"I didn't. I swear. I thought you were still the one causing all the bursts. I had no idea about what they'd done to your daughter. To be perfectly honest, it messed up all my calculations – even though you both can trigger the bursts, you each create a unique probability wave on the readouts. I couldn't understand why all my previous data was suddenly out of sync."

"How does this help us with Charlie?" Dr. Schuler asked, getting them back on topic.

"Like I said, learning about Carson helped us fill in a lot of missing pieces. But while my team was focused on the data from the bursts, the team studying Ella and Charlie were unravelling how their alien DNA connected them to the Core. Being able to study them in person every time she triggered a burst brought them to the brink of finally understanding how the technology actually works."

"You're talking about the scientists Charlie killed?" Maya clarified.

"I have access to all their notes now," CJ reminded her. "And once we crack Dr. Singh's laptop, we'll be able to see how he was combining their results with my team's analysis on the Core. The genetics stuff is a little over my head, but with Dr. Schuller's help I think we'll be able to piece everything together."

"It's been almost thirty years since I've done anything like that," she cautioned.

"Dr. Singh said you were the most brilliant geneticist he ever worked with," CJ countered. "Based on what I've seen so far, I think there might be enough there for the two of us to reconfigure the Core and sever Charlie's connection to it."

"Why not just destroy it?" Maya asked.

"It's too risky. For all we know, that could kill Ella. You and Charlie, too."

"So if you sever Charlie's connection to the Core," Carson clarified, "then he won't be able to move when the world is frozen? He'll be trapped in stasis like the rest of us?"

"That's the theory."

"But he'll still have my daughter as a hostage."

"We'll find a way to get her back safely," Maya said, squeezing Carson's hand. "I promise."

CJ's phone buzzed in his pocket. He pulled it out and quickly read the message.

"They've cracked Dr. Singh's laptop," he announced. "We've got a lock on the subdermal tracker."

"Where are they?" Carson wanted to know.

"Vegas."

CHAPTER 27

"Uncle Charlie? I'm hungry."

"I called room service. The food will get here soon."

Ella didn't answer – her eyes were fixed on the cartoon playing on the hotel room's TV. Charlie couldn't tell if she was actually watching the show or was just transfixed by the sounds and colors emanating from the screen. He suspected it was the latter.

It had been almost twelve hours since he'd shot her up with a dose of the sedatives he'd stolen from the base. In her current state, the girl was able to talk and even walk around with awkward, halting steps. But she still seemed groggy, and her eyes were unfocused.

Poindexter told me it would take at least a couple days to clear her system completely.

That wasn't going to be an option anytime soon. In a couple hours, Charlie was going to hit the casino again. At some point in the evening, he was going to need to stop time, and the trigger wouldn't work unless she was sedated.

"Uncle Charlie?" she said again. "I'm hungry."

"I said the food is coming," he growled.

Repeating herself was a side effect of the drugs; the Poindexter warned they blocked short term memory. Even though it wasn't her fault, Charlie still found it fucking annoying.

Five more minutes passed as she stared at the screen with her jaw hanging open. She didn't move; she barely even blinked. Charlie found himself staring at her, hypnotized by her unnatural stillness. With the metal crown of electrodes and wires perched atop her shaved head, she looked like some surreal artist's image of the postmodern child monarch, her kingdom confined to a tiny hotel room and the flickering images on the TV.

A knock on the hotel room door snapped him out of his trance. He got up and opened it, blocking the way when the bellman tried to push the food laden cart into the room.

"I got it from here," Charlie said, taking the cart from him.

The bellman nodded and stepped back, standing patiently in expectation of a tip. Charlie turned away and shut the door in his face.

"Uncle Charlie? I'm hungry."

"Jesus Christ, kid. I know already. The food's here."

Ella turned away from the TV and stared at him.

"Come on over. I don't want you eating on the bed and getting crumbs and shit everywhere."

It took several seconds before she reacted, almost as if her chemical-addled brain was struggling to process what was happening. Eventually something clicked and she crawled down from the bed and padded her way over to the room service cart.

Charlie lifted the metal cover off the tray to reveal a sorry looking PBJ and a juice-box. Ella picked up the sandwich and took a bite, chewing it with a mechanical, joyless determination.

Christ – what kind of kid doesn't like peanut butter and jelly?

She didn't touch the juice box until the last bite of the sandwich was gone. Then she picked it up and held it out towards him.

Sighing, Charlie detached the plastic straw and punctured the opening on top, then handed it back. Ella sucked down the contents in one slow, steady, continuous act, her eyes fixed on Charlie the entire time. He knew her odd mannerisms were caused by the drugs he was giving her. Still, part of him imagined a cold defiance in the way she acted, as if she understood what was going on and disapproved.

I had a shitty childhood too. You get over it.

She finished her drink, slurping loudly to get the last few drops. Then she set the juice-box down on the cart and turned away without saying a word. She walked back over to the bed and climbed atop the covers, her attention once more transfixed by the insipid cartoon. Charlie briefly thought about changing the channel to something less irritating, then decided against it. Letting her watch her stupid show was the least he could do for her.

After two hours, he finally decided she'd had enough.

"Okay, Ella. Time for your medicine."

She dutifully pulled her attention away from the screen, clambered off the bed, then climbed into her wheelchair. Charlie strapped her in, making sure the safety harnesses around her waist was secure so she wouldn't slip out once she lost consciousness.

He pulled out a fresh syringe and filled it from one of the vials in the medium-sized, black leather bag he'd found in her room.

Twenty bottles left. Only 40 more doses.

He wasn't sure what he'd do when the sedatives ran out and the trigger stopped working. But he knew one thing for certain – he was going to use Ella while he still could and earn enough money to set himself up for life.

He slid the tip of the needle into her flesh just below the crook of her elbow. The skin was purple and bruised from the repeated injections, as was her other arm. She didn't flinch or pull back – she never showed any reactions to the needles.

Either she's gotten used to them, or the sedative lingering in her system from the last shot has her too drugged up to notice.

Whatever the explanation, Charlie was glad she didn't seem to be suffering. He needed Ella, but he didn't want to cause her unnecessary pain; he wasn't a complete fucking monster.

It took less than five minutes before her eyes closed and her head drooped down against her chest. Knowing she wouldn't wake up for hours, Charlie changed his clothes and slipped out the hotel room's door, flicking off the light behind him.

He took the elevator down to the casino, his mood lightening now that Ella was out of sight and out of mind. The trigger was strapped to his wrist, tucked under the sleeve of his button-up shirt.

The Wynn casino was always packed on a Friday, and tonight was no exception. He wandered past the craps tables, eyeing the stacks of chips tucked into the racks in front of each player.

The first night here he'd noticed a pair of high rollers, each with more than fifty grand in chips. He used the trigger to stop time and swipe a couple grand from each of them, confident they'd never even realize they were missing. Even if they did, by the time the world started moving again Charlie was already long gone.

He used the trigger a couple more times the first night, setting himself up for big wins on the roulette table each time. But he was careful not to overdo it. He'd adjusted the settings to make the timeouts as short as possible, but even so he was worried about how much Ella could handle.

Don't want to kill the golden goose.

By the time he went back up to the room the first night, he had over ten grand. Tonight, he was determined to walk away with at least fifty.

Don't get greedy. It had been months since he and Carson had worked together, but he couldn't help but imagine what his brother would say about all this. *Win too much and you'll attract attention!*

You don't call the shots anymore, he silently replied to his imaginary sibling, even as he decided he might be better off stopping at twenty instead.

"Welcome back, sir," the host in the high limit room greeted him.

"Vodka soda," he replied as he brushed past, heading for the roulette table. "And tell the drink girl to keep them coming. Got a feeling I'm going to be here for a while."

***

Maya let her eyes wander across the crowd, scanning the casino floor. Ella's subdermal tracker had led them to the Wynn, but she didn't see any sign of the girl or Charlie yet.

"I got him," Carson's voice whispered in Maya's earpiece, tense and urgent. "Playing roulette. Ella's not with him. He must have left her up in one of the rooms."

"Fall back so he doesn't see you," Maya replied into her mic. "Meet me by the elevators."

She crossed the casino floor, passing through the Wynn's ostentatious lobby. By the time she reached the elevators, Carson was already there.

"Did he see you?" she asked.

"I don't think so."

"Any word from CJ and Dr. Schuler yet?"

Carson shook his head. "I can't wait for them any longer. Can we use the tracker to figure out which room Ella's in?"

"Maybe. It'll take some time – we won't pick up much of a signal in the elevator. We'll have to search floor by floor until we get a hit."

"Then let's get moving."

"I think we should wait to hear from CJ," Maya cautioned. "If Charlie catches us before they figure out how to disable that trigger, we're dead."

"He'll be in the casino for hours," Carson countered. "He hasn't even triggered a timeout yet tonight. This is our chance to get Ella before he knows we're here."

Maya hesitated, weighing all the options. If they could find Ella quickly, they could be miles away before Charlie noticed she was gone. But if he caught them in the act and CJ hadn't figured out how to stop the timeouts yet...

"I can't just sit here and wait," Carson said. "She's my daughter. I have to do something."

"Okay," Maya said. "Let's go find her."

***

CJ was used to working long hours; sometimes he'd go an entire day without sleep while he analyzed the results from a particularly interesting experiment. But he'd never worked under the pressure of a literal deadline before. The added stress was simultaneously energizing and draining. He was completely wired, but he also felt utterly exhausted.

He and Dr. Schuller were huddled together in his office, frantically working their way through all the data Dr. Singh had compiled on Ella and Charlie, then cross-referencing it with ten years of CJ's own work on the Core itself.

The pieces are all here. I know it! We just have to figure out how to put them together.

Despite her long sabbatical from the project, Dr. Schuller's brilliance was on full display as they worked. Within hours she had absorbed every detail of the reports from Dr. Singh's geneticists, surpassing their understanding and moving on to bold new hypotheses in her efforts to connect their work to CJ's.

They were so close... but something still wasn't adding up. CJ scowled as he looked at his most recent calculation, as if his grimace could force the two sides of the unbalanced equation to match up.

And then he saw it.

"Holy shit!" he shouted, the solution exploding in his brain like a mushroom cloud. "Lisa – come here."

As Dr. Schuller scurried over, he made a few quick alterations to his math.

"Does this make sense to you?" he asked her.

"I mean, you're the expert on the Core," she said, wavering. "But it fits in with my side of things."

This is it! It has to be!

"We need to call Carson."

***

The world froze around Carson as he was stepping off the elevator onto the 33rd floor, trapping him in mid-stride. It was the second time-out since he and Maya had started their floor-by-floor search. Despite his urgency to find Ella, there was nothing he could do but wait for it to end.

How many more times will Charlie do this before he's done for the night? How long before he comes back to the room?

Fortunately, he wasn't trapped in stasis long.

"Another one?" Maya asked after time had started up again.

"Yeah. How'd you know."

"You get this strange expression on your face whenever it happens. Does it hurt?"

"Not really," he muttered.

Recognizing she should let it drop, Maya turned her focus to the screen on her phone.

"We're getting closer," she said, though not for the first time.

The Wynn hotel was enormous: 2,716 rooms spread across 45 floors, plus another 2,000 rooms in the adjacent Encore tower. The tracker could give them a rough idea of Ella's location; that's how they'd arrived at the hotel. But the signal wasn't precise enough to pinpoint her exact room from a distance. The only way to find her was to wander up and down the halls, looking to see whether the signal was getting stronger or not.

With Maya leading the way, the duo began to traverse the maze of crisscrossing hotel corridors. They weren't even halfway done with their current floor when Carson's phone rang.

"CJ, please tell me you have some good news."

"Maybe. There doesn't seem to be any way to break Charlie's connection to the Core – not without destroying it. And we don't know what that would to you or Ella... it might kill you both.

"But we've isolated two distinct energy waves emanating from the Core whenever there's a burst: one for you and one for Ella. If we collapse them into a single function, it should synchronize you."

"What does that even mean?"

"We can't stop Charlie from using Ella to trigger a timeout, but maybe we can make it so that you'll be able to take control during stasis."

"So I'd be able to make the world start moving again?"

"Theoretically."

It wasn't ideal, but if Carson could end the timeouts as soon as they started, it would take away Charlie's biggest advantage.

"But Carson... there's a catch."

Carson sighed. "Of course there is."

"Time doesn't stop inside the Core, so we'll be able to collapse the fields even while the rest of the world is frozen. But we can't actually do anything until after Charlie triggers a burst."

"So we have to wait until he freezes time before you can even try this."

"It looks that way."

"Are you sure this will even work?" Carson asked.

"Yeah. I think so."

He was hoping for a more definitive answer, but at this point he'd take whatever he could get.

"What's your status right now?" CJ wanted to know.

"Charlie's down in the casino. Maya and I are searching for Ella's room. If we can get her out of here before we run into Charlie, none of this will even matter."

"Good luck," CJ said. "Dr. Schuler and I are headed to the Core now just in case."

Carson hung up the phone.

"What's the story?" Maya asked.

"It's complicated," Carson said. "But finding Ella is still the first step."

CHAPTER 28

"I think this is it," Maya said, holding her phone up beside the door. Carson glanced at the room number: 3913.

Shit. Lucky 13. Good thing I'm not superstitious.

"Are you sure?" he asked.

"It has to be," Maya assured him. "The signal's stronger here than anywhere else."

Despite her confidence, Carson still hesitated. The door was locked; they'd have to force it open. Doing so would set off a security call on the room's electronic lock, meaning they'd only have a few minutes to get in and out before security came looking for them. They'd only get one chance at this. If it turned out to be the wrong room...

No! That's the old Carson talking. The one who always wanted to play it safe. The one who never took a chance.

Sometimes trying to avoid risks at all costs did more harm than good.

I'm coming for you, Ella!

Carson took three steps back, lowered his shoulder, and charged into the door. He hit it hard, the extra muscle he'd added over the past few months super-charging the impact. A sharp pain shot up from his deltoid and through his neck, but the door buckled and gave way.

He stumbled through the breach, momentarily blinded by the darkness of the room as he struggled to keep his footing. Maya followed in behind him, flicking on the lights as she entered.

Ella!

His daughter was there; strapped into a tiny wheelchair. Her eyes were closed, and her head was slumped forward against her chest. Her long, blonde hair had been shaved off, leaving her completely bald. A metal halo jutting with wires and screws was wrapped around her naked skull.

Dear God!

He ran over to his daughter and crouched down beside her, gently tilting her head back.

"Ella? Can you hear me, Ella? It's Daddy."

She didn't respond. For a horrific instant he thought she was dead, then he noticed her chest faintly rising and falling with each frail breath.

Oh, Ella... what have they done to you?

Instinctively, he wrapped his arms around his little girl, as if trying to shield her from all the horrors she had experienced.

"Carson," Maya called out from the door in a soft but insistent whisper. "We have to get out of here!"

Her words didn't even register in his mind; all his attention was focused on his daughter.

She's here because of me. Because of my power. Because of my fucked up DNA.

"I'm sorry, baby," he whispered as he embraced her, gently rocking her side-to-side. "I'm so, so sorry."

He didn't look up until he felt a hand on his shoulder.

"Carson – we have to go. Now!"

"Too late, sweetheart," a familiar voice said from across the room.

Both Carson and Maya wheeled around to see Charlie standing in the door. At first Carson thought he had his arms crossed in front of his chest. Then he realized he was holding up his arm with the wrist mounted device that controlled Ella's timeouts, while his opposite hand was poised to press the trigger.

"If I knew you were coming, I would have ordered room service," he said, grinning.

Carson had no way to know if CJ and Lisa figured out how to give him control of the timeouts yet.

I'd rather not have to find out.

From the corner of his eye, he saw Maya's hand inching towards the gun holstered on her hip.

Gotta distract him. Keep the bastard talking.

"You sick fuck," Carson hissed at him. "She's just a little girl!"

"Singh did this to her, not me," Charlie protested. "And I took his ass out. Maybe you should be fucking thanking me."

Maya's hand flickered as she drew her gun. But as quick as she was, she couldn't bring the barrel up and fire before Charlie pressed the trigger on his wrist.

Time stopped, freezing them in place. Carson tried to make the world start moving again, but nothing happened.

Charlie – unaffected by the timeout – stepped into the room, then turned and closed the door behind him. He moved with the easy pace of a man who knew he literally had all the time in the world. Then he turned back towards Carson and shook his head in an exaggerated display of disappointment.

Shit! Come on, CJ. You said you could do this. Sync me up with Ella!

***

Inside the Core, CJ felt the overwhelming wave of euphoria as the burst washed over him. His mouth flopped open, and his eyes rolled back into his head as he bathed in its glory.

No! You have to fight it!

He whipped his head from side to side, shaking off the effect. Beside him, Dr. Schuller was standing motionless, her arms hanging limp and her eyes closed as she swayed ever so slightly from one foot to the other.

"Snap out of it!" he shouted, grabbing her by the shoulders and giving her a good, hard shake.

Her eyes popped open, wide and dazed. But a second later her gaze refocused.

"We have to collapse the wave patterns," CJ said.

She nodded and rushed over to the Core's control panel. CJ turned his attention to the screen that monitored the Core's energy signature.

The image on the readout screen was a seemingly random mess of flickering lines and colors. But CJ knew the pattern wasn't actually random. He was looking at the chaotic visualization of the quantum fields emanating from the reactor – a picture of time and space being twisted and stretched in unfathomable ways.

Inside the Core time was still behaving normally, but CJ knew the world outside had slowed down to the tiniest fraction of normal speed. With Ella as a catalyst, the incredible alien technology had effectively frozen time for everyone outside the Core except Charlie. But if CJ's calculations were correct, there was a way to shift control of the burst from Ella over to Carson.

He'd spent the last decade studying the reconstructed alien technology of the Core. He'd memorized every dial, switch, button, and lever on the control panel until he could recreate the entire layout from memory. By subtly adjusting the various controls, he'd learned how to alter the complex patterns of a burst's energy signature; shifting and manipulating the images displayed on the monitor. But without any context or relevant feedback there had been no way to observe the results of his actions - it was like turning the dials on a radio where every station was nothing but static.

It was only after Charlie had fallen into their hands that he'd been able to start unravelling the relationship between the Core, the catalyst, and Charlie himself. But everything he thought he understood was still theoretical. An untested hypothesis based on assumptions and expectations. And if he was wrong...

He looked up from the screen at Dr. Schuller, poised by the control panel and awaiting his instructions.

"Ready?"

"Ready!"

Christ, I hope this works.

***

Completely paralyzed, Carson watched helplessly as Charlie slowly crossed the room over to where Maya was standing, caught in the motion of drawing her weapon. He rubbed a finger slowly down her cheek, then gave Carson a sinister wink.

Leave her alone, you son of a bitch!

As if responding to Carson's unspoken command, Charlie turned away from Maya and approached a room service cart just on the edge of Carson's peripheral vision. He picked something up off the cart, then held up his prize for Carson to see – a serrated steak knife.

No, no, no, no!

Turning back towards Maya, he began to advance on her with the blade held out in front of him.

CJ, Carson silently screamed, *what the fuck is taking so long?*

***

"We need to isolate the catalysts!" CJ called out. "Shift your signature two degrees down."

CJ's fingers flickered across the control panel, hitting buttons, flipping switches, and adjusting the dials with confidence and precision born from years of study. Beside him, Dr. Schuller mirrored his actions, adjusting her own section of the control panel with a proficiency that rivaled his own, despite having only one day of training.

It's incredible how fast she picked this up. No wonder Dr. Singh brought her onto the project – she's brilliant!

The image on the monitor flickered and changed. Now, amidst the chaos, CJ could see two distinct probability waves highlighted on the screen, running parallel to each other.

"Increase the resonance."

In response to the two scientists' efforts, the parallel lines representing the probability waves began to pulse.

"Let's sync them up."

The two lines slowly converged... then suddenly crossed, inverting their relative positions.

"Too far – pull back!" CJ shouted, frantically trying to reverse the flow.

The lines began to jump and twitch, the regular rise and fall of their sine wave patterns becoming a twisted, jumbled mess. Their bright glow began to fade as they were swallowed up by the chaotic interference that now filled the screen.

"No – we're losing them! Increase the energy output!"

The Core's generator began to hum, and the green glow intensified as they forced more power through the system. Slowly the two lines came back into focus, stabilizing into their previous oscillating forms.

"Okay – let's sync them up again. Slowly this time!"

Once again, the lines converged until the two waves were perfectly atop one another.

"Locking in on 3... 2... 1... now!"

Moving in perfect unison, CJ and Dr. Schuller clicked the final buttons into place to complete the process. To CJ's horror, the screen before him suddenly went blank.

He looked up to see the Core had also gone dark, the tall cylinder of luminous green liquid at its heart suddenly going inert, its glow extinguished. Then a high-pitched whine filled the room, causing the two scientists to cover their ears in a desperate attempt to block it out. The sound stopped abruptly, and the Core flared back to life as a blinding white flash erupted from the cylinder.

A wave of heat rippled through the air, followed by an invisible force that lifted CJ and Lisa and hurled them against the far wall. Dazed, CJ managed to get onto his hands and knees. He crawled across the floor as the high-pitched whine rose up again, even louder than before.

Reaching the observation monitor, he hauled himself up to check the patterns on the screen.

No! That's... that's not right!

As the implications of the new pattern dancing across the screen dawned on him, he realized there had been a critical flaw in his calculations.

***

Carson was still frozen, watching helplessly as Charlie slowly stalked towards Maya, knife raised in anticipation. And then the world *rippled* around him.

The sensation was unlike anything he had ever experienced. Normally when time was stopped, he didn't feel anything at all. But suddenly his stomach lurched up into his throat, as if the ground had dropped out from under him. At the same time, the air around him grew heavy and thick, like he was walking along the floor of the ocean with a thousand tons of water pressing down on him.

His knees collapsed under the unexpected pressure and he stumbled forward, barely getting his hands up in time to keep his face from slamming into the floor.

Holy shit – I can move!

The rest of the world around him was still frozen. Maya was still caught in the act of drawing her gun, and even sound itself had stopped, enveloping him in an oppressive silence.

But Charlie was still moving. His back was to Carson as he marched towards Maya with measured, deliberate steps, savoring the impending slaughter.

Carson clambered up onto his feet, feeling like there was a sack of concrete tied to his back trying to keep him down. Then he charged at Charlie... or tried to.

Each step was an effort – he wasn't frozen, but it was like the universe was resisting his efforts. He fought against the inertia, knowing what would happen if he didn't stop Charlie.

Fortunately, in stasis there was no sound to warn his brother he was coming. He closed the space between them just as Charlie raised the knife above his head for the first blow.

Carson wrapped his fingers around Charlie's wrist, pulling the blade back and away from Maya as his brother slashed down.

Charlie turned to face him, moving as if in slow motion. His eyes were wide with disbelief. Seizing on his confusion, Carson threw a punch at his brother's face. His fist felt like it was moving through water. He made contact, but there was no force behind the blow, and Charlie didn't even flinch from the impact.

The sensation of something pressing against his side caused Carson to look down. To his horror, he saw the tip of the knife plunging deep into his abdomen. There was a brief flicker of pain, but it felt muted and far away – like a memory... or a premonition.

As Charlie pulled the knife out, Carson grabbed his brother's wrist with both hands. He tried to twist the blade free, but he lacked the leverage or the strength. As they struggled for control of the weapon, Carson felt blood slowly welling up from his wound.

Charlie wrapped his free arm around the back of Carson's neck, then wrestled him to the ground. They landed with Charlie on top. Carson felt the force of the impact, but like the stab wound it was merely an echo of the true sensation. Even so, it caused him to lose his grip on Charlie's wrist, and a moment later he felt the blade pierce his side again.

Charlie pulled the blade out, then placed his free hand on Carson's sternum and leaned forward. His weight felt like an anvil on Carson's chest, pressing down so hard he could barely breathe.

The blade came at him again, this time aiming for Carson's heart. Wrapping both hands around Charlie's wrist, Carson fought to keep the knife at bay. For a brief moment he succeeded. But he felt his strength ebbing, draining away like the viscous blood crawling out from the wounds he'd already suffered.

Sensing his brother's weakness, Charlie wrapped his free hand around the knife's handle. Using both arms, he began to overpower Carson, pushing the blade inexorably closer and closer. The tip slowly slid between his ribs, and Carson wondered how long it would take him to bleed to death in slow motion.

Charlie pulled the blade free once more and stood up. Carson tried to rise, but his body wouldn't respond. The best he could do was clutch feebly at Charlie's leg as he turned back towards Maya.

Charlie looked down at him, his face twisted into a mask of hatred and contempt. And then something *SNAPPED* as time started up again.

The cocoon of silence was obliterated by waves of sound crashing down on them from all sides. It was immediately followed by flashes of searing pain, and Carson grunted as he clutched his hands over his gaping wounds in a vain effort to staunch the river of blood suddenly gushing out.

There was a roar of gunshots – *bang, bang, bang* – and Charlie crumpled to the ground beside him.

Gasping, Carson tried to sit up, only to have Maya appear at his side and push him back down to the floor.

"Stay still," she said. "Don't move."

He lay motionless as she scooped up the knife and hacked off a piece of Charlie's shirt. Wadding it up, she jammed the makeshift poultice into one of his wounds, causing him to grimace and flinch.

"Sorry," she said. "But I have to stop the bleeding."

Her words were calm, but Carson saw the look of terror in her eyes.

She can't save me, and she knows it.

Before she could cut off another strip, he reached out and grabbed her arm with a bloody hand.

"Promise me you'll take care of Ella."

"That's your job," she shot back.

"Not anymore."

"Shut up! Don't say that!"

"Just... promise."

There were tears in her eyes as she nodded and said, "I promise."

Carson smiled and let his hand fall away as he surrendered to the darkness.

Epilogue

Carson floated in the darkness, drifting alone through an empty universe devoid of light or sound. It wasn't good; it wasn't bad. It just was.

"Daddy?"

The voice was faint – it came from another place. Another world. It didn't matter.

"Daddy?"

Louder this time. More insistent. Still, he ignored it.

He felt a jab in his arm. Then another. And another - a finger poking him over and over.

"Daddy? Time to wake up, Daddy!"

"Honey, don't do that." Another voice this time. Older. Familiar. "Let him sleep."

"He's waking up," the child responded. "His eyes are moving under his skin."

Carson's eyelids fluttered open, then snapped shut as he was assaulted by the harsh, white brightness of his surroundings.

"Oh my God – he opened his eyes!"

"See, Mommy? I told you!"

"Stay here, Ella – I have to get the others."

Carson let his eyes open again, squinting so that only the narrowest slit of light came through. As he adjusted to the brightness, he opened them wide enough to take in his surroundings.

He was in a hospital. Several chairs were lined up beside his bed, but only one was occupied right now. Ella gave him a wide smile. Her metal halo was gone, replaced by a pink bandana covered with purple unicorns and rainbows.

"Time to wake up, Daddy!" she said, poking him in the arm again and laughing.

"I'm up, honey," he muttered. The words crawled their way up from his throat; he suddenly realized he was absolutely parched.

He tried to sit up but abandoned the effort almost instantly – it hurt too much to move.

There was a small table beside his bed, with a plastic cup and pitcher on it.

"Can you pour Daddy a glass of water, sweetheart?" he croaked.

Ella nodded, jumping up for the task with the unbridled enthusiasm only a child could muster.

She poured it carefully, not spilling a drop. Then she grabbed a straw and dropped it in the cup.

Clever girl.

Carrying it with two hands, she brought it over to his bed. Carson tried to reach out and take it from her, but even lifting his arm was beyond his meager strength.

"Here, Daddy."

She leaned in and gently guided the straw towards his lips. Carson drank deep, finishing the entire cup in seconds.

"Thank you, honey," he said.

As Ella was putting the cup back on the table, there was a flurry of movement by the door. Sarah, Maya, CJ, and Lisa all piled into the room.

"Thank God," Maya gasped. "The doctors didn't think you were going to make it."

"That alien DNA must make me hard to kill."

"What?" Sarah said, her brow furrowing in confusion.

"He's probably still a little delirious," Lisa offered.

Sarah nodded, accepting the explanation.

"Can we have a minute alone with him?" Maya asked her.

"Of course. Ella, come on – let's go get an ice cream."

"Wait," Carson said. "I don't want her to go."

"We just need a minute," Maya said.

"We'll be back before you know it," Sarah promised.

She held out her hand for Ella, who rushed over to her mother's side. *She loves her ice cream.*

"Are you hungry, Daddy?" Ella asked, turning back towards him just as they were about to leave. "They have chocolate!"

"I'm good, honey," he replied.

The trio remaining waited a few seconds until Sarah and Ella had disappeared. Then CJ shut the door, while Maya sat down in the chair beside his bed.

She reached out and began to stroke his forehead, her fingers soft and soothing.

"I can't believe you're still with us," she said. "I wasn't kidding about what the doctors said."

"How's Ella doing?" he asked.

"She's going to be fine," Lisa assured him. "Better than you, I'd wager."

"She barely remembers anything that happened," CJ added. "It's a side effect of the drugs they were giving her. Probably a good thing in this case."

Carson nodded, though he couldn't help but wonder if the trauma she'd suffered was still there, lingering beneath the surface in her subconscious.

I still have nightmares where I'm strapped to that chair in Mama Pearl's storeroom.

"What about you?" Lisa asked, interrupting his thoughts. "How much do you remember about what happened?"

Images of his fight with Charlie flickered through his mind, making him wince and shudder.

"All of it."

"We told Sarah you had to go into hiding because you were working with the FBI," Maya said. "We didn't go into any details. Figured it was better this way."

"What about Ella? What did you tell her about that?"

"Only that she was taken as a way to get leverage over you. She doesn't know anything about the timeouts."

"Maybe she should," Carson said. "It'll be better for Ella if her mother understands what she's going through as she grows up."

"That might not be necessary," CJ chimed in. "Something happened to the Core. It's like it burned itself out when I tried to sync you up with Ella. We don't know if the damage can be repaired."

"You were a bit off base on that, by the way," Carson told him. "You ended up linking me with Charlie."

"Yeah, sorry about that. But I'd like to study what happened in more detail. Assuming you're willing to work with me and Dr. Schuller, of course."

"You're back on the project?" Carson asked.

Lisa nodded. "But we're going in a different direction. Less kidnappings and murder, for one thing."

"Wait a minute," Carson said. "If the Core is damaged, does that mean I can't stop time anymore?"

"Probably not," CJ said. "Do you... do you want to give it a try?"

"No," Carson said after a brief deliberation. "Not right now."

CJ nodded, though Carson thought he could see a twinge of disappointment in his face.

"Fair enough. But I hope you'll think about my offer to join us. I promise everything will be safe and legal. And you'll be well compensated for your time."

"I'll think about it," Carson said.

"If you take a job on the base," Maya added, "then we'll be able to stay in touch. I've been offered a posting at the Bureau's Las Vegas branch when I finish my time at the Academy."

"You didn't get in trouble for going AWOL?"

"CJ pulled a few strings," Maya said with a smile. "It's good to have friends in high places."

There was a knock on the door, and Sarah opened it a crack and poked her head through.

"We're back. Okay if we come in again?"

"I think we're done here," CJ said.

He and Dr. Schuler exited the room as Sarah and Ella entered. Ella was clutching an ice cream cone in her tiny fist; it was already melting and running down over her fingers.

Maya stood up but lingered a moment before following the other two out.

"I hope you think about CJ's offer," she said. "You still owe me that goodbye dinner you promised."

She bent down and gave Carson a quick peck on the cheek, then quickly stood up and turned towards Sarah. She almost seemed embarrassed.

"Sorry," she muttered.

"Hey, we're not married anymore," Sarah said, shrugging her shoulders.

Maya nodded and smiled.

"I'll come back and check on you in a bit," she told Carson as she headed out the door.

Ella came over and sat beside Carson, her face covered in sticky chocolate.

"You got more on your face than in your mouth," Carson teased her. "Maybe you should slow down."

"It's melty, Daddy. I gotta eat it fast."

Can't argue with that logic.

Sarah was still standing near the door, watching silently.

"I'm sorry Ella was dragged into this," Carson said. "I never meant for her to get hurt."

"Your FBI girlfriend told me you were working with them so you could get the money for Ella's treatments," Sarah said. "It wasn't your fault the bastards came after her."

"Mommy said a bad word!" Ella squealed, laughing with mischievous delight.

"Were the treatments working?" Carson asked.

"They seemed to be. She'll start up on them again when we get home."

Carson nodded. Despite Sarah's absolution, however, he still felt guilty.

They said she won't remember what happened. But she still went through hell. Not to mention the suffering I put Sarah through. She thought Ella was dead!

"Hey," Sarah said, "I know that face. Stop beating yourself up over this!"

"Easier said than done. I can't believe you don't hate me."

"Hate you? Everything you did was to help our daughter, Carson. You're a good father."

"Yeah," Ella agreed. "You're my favorite Daddy!"

Take that, Other Daddy!

"I need to go call Greg," Sarah said. "He'll be glad to know you're doing better."

"He's a good guy," Carson told her. "I'm glad you found him."

"Yeah," she said with a slight smile. "Me, too. Can you watch Ella for a bit?"

"Of course."

She stepped out, leaving the two of them alone. Ella didn't say anything – she was too busy chowing down on her ice cream to speak. She looked so perfect and precious Carson wanted to hold onto the moment forever.

For a split second, he thought about freezing time.

Will my power still work? And what about Ella? If I stop time, will she know?

But at the last instant, he pulled back. In that moment, Carson realized he didn't actually care if he still had his power or not. It didn't define him, and he wasn't about to let it define his daughter.

"Daddy? Why are you smiling?"

"I'm just happy to be here with you, honey. Right now, that's all that matters."

ABOUT THE AUTHOR

Drew Karpyshyn is a NY Times Best Selling novelist and award-winning video game writer. Born in Edmonton, Alberta, Canada in 1971, he decided to escape the frozen winters of the Great White North in 2009 by moving to Texas.

He now lives in the Austin area with his wife, Jennifer, and an assortment of furry, four-footed companions.

Twitter: @DrewKarpyshyn
www.drewkarpyshyn.com